YOU'RE MY HOME

KATIE MOORE

Edited by

KAREN MEEUS EDITING

Winter
FairyTale
Publishing

You're My Home

Copyright © 2021 by Katie Moore

Winter FairyTale Publishing LLC

Cover Design:
Sleepy Fox Studio

Editing:
Karen Meeus Editing

ISBN 978-1-955730-00-6 (e-book)
ISBN 978-1-955730-01-3 (paperback)

Zach and Brady's story is dedicated to Nathan. May you always know how much I love you. You are beautiful as you are and will be beautiful if you change, too. I'm so proud of you.

You're My Home is also dedicated to all the individuals that have struggled with their sexuality or had to stay in the closet to be safe. To the ones that have felt judged, afraid, or ashamed. To everyone who has been bullied or hurt because of who they are. This story is for all of you.

I wish that I could change the world, and maybe this book will make an impact, even if it's a small one.

Kindness is a beautiful gift to give someone, and love is everything.

TRIGGER WARNINGS

This story contains domestic violence, trauma, PTSD, and religious homophobia.

ONE

ZACH

Christian music fills the house, and I hear my mom singing while she bakes cinnamon rolls for tomorrow morning. My dad always likes to have them before church and eats most of them without sharing. I tuck my book under my shirt and walk quietly to the back door.

"Where are you going?"

I pause, swallowing hard and turning to face my dad. "I was going outside for a walk…" *Please, don't see the book. Please, God.*

He gives me a stern look, crossing his arms. "Did you get all your chores done?"

"Yes, sir." *When have I ever not done my chores?*

"What is that under your shirt?" He steps closer, holding out his hand.

Trembles of fear flow through me as I slip the book out and hand it over to him. I'm not allowed to read any books that aren't from the Christian section at the library. I pray he doesn't open it up and read any of it.

"Totally Joe?" He raises his eyes to stare at me. "Did your mom approve this book?"

"No, sir." There's no use in lying. He'll know, and my punishment will be worse.

"You know that's not allowed. What's so special about it?" He flips through it and reads a little; his face gets redder as he goes. I know what he's reading—Joe has a boyfriend. When he looks at me again, I wish I could become invisible and hide away. "Go get my belt."

"No," I plead, "please, not the belt. I'm sorry that I got the book."

"Now, Isaac!" he shouts.

My mom comes around the corner of the kitchen to look at us. "Tom? What's going on?"

He shakes the book at her. "This is what is going on. He's reading a demonic book where they promote homosexuality."

She gasps, pressing her hand to her chest. "I didn't know he had such a book. I'm sorry."

My mom doesn't stand up for me, and it hurts my heart. All she cares about is being a good wife and not upsetting my dad.

"You should watch him better, Joy." Dad turns back to me. "I gave you the order to go get my belt. Now go!"

My legs follow his command, but inside, all I can feel is fear. It makes me sick to have to get the leather strap from his closet and carry it back to him. After that, I try to hide inside myself while he strikes me with the leather belt. I can't keep from crying out, no matter how much I want to. It's not like Dad will stop until he hears me in pain, anyway.

When he's done, I pull my jeans up as quickly as I can, trying not to sob in front of him.

"Now, you need to repent and ask God to forgive you."

Without looking at him, I close my eyes and say the prayer I know he wants to hear. "God, please forgive me for reading this book and hiding it from my parents. I ask you to wash away my sins and cover them with the blood of Jesus. In Jesus's name, amen."

Don't ask me why I have to put the blood of Jesus in there because I don't understand it. I just know that my dad gets angry if I don't use that exact line.

"You can be excused now, and I never want to see a book like this again. I'll discuss it with the library. They shouldn't have this on the shelf. My son is not gay and doesn't need this influence from Satan to turn him that way. If you start to have thoughts, we will take you to see Pastor Dan and get these demons out of you."

I don't argue. I just walk away until I'm out the back door and then start to run into the woods. Tears stream down my face as branches scratch me, and I trip over the sticks littering the ground. When I break into a small clearing by the creek, I drop to my knees and sob into my hands.

"Hey…are you okay?"

My head whips up and I see a boy standing off to the side. His black hair is tousled and styled in a way that makes him look like he's older, but I think he has to be close to my age. He walks over to me, and I notice his deep blue eyes are sparkling with his own tears. He squats down, repeating his question, "Are you okay?"

When I can't talk through my crying, he takes my black-rimmed glasses off and then tugs his shirt off over his head. He uses his shirt to wipe away my tears, his tender care only making me cry harder.

He sits down, pulling me into his lap and hugging me tightly while I sob against his bare chest. Maybe I should find out who he is before letting him hold me, but no one ever holds me like this, and I need it. I need it so much it hurts.

The boy is bigger than me, and in this moment, that makes me feel safe. I'm tinier than everyone my age and wish I would grow bigger.

When I finally go silent, he loosens his arms up enough to hand his shirt over so I can blow my nose in it and wipe my tears away again. "I'm sorry," I whisper but don't make a move to get away.

"Nah, don't worry about it. We all need someone, sometimes. Do you want to tell me what you were crying over?" He shifts so he can see my face better, but his leg rubs against my butt, bringing out a small whimper that I can't hold back.

"What's wrong? Did someone hurt you?" His voice gets higher at the end. When I don't answer, he leans over to raise my shirt enough to see the welts that stripe up my lower back. "Jesus… Who did this to you?"

"My dad…" My back isn't nearly as bad as my butt. Dad isn't the best at aiming and sometimes gets too high.

"We should tell someone," he murmurs, lowering my shirt and moving so he can see my face.

"No…if they take me away from my parents, I'll be in foster care. I just need to be better," I reason, more for myself than him.

"What's your name?"

"Isaac Matthews." I inwardly cringe at hearing my own name.

I think he heard the dislike in my tone because he raises his eyebrows and asks, "You don't like your name?"

"It's a *biblical* name. You know…the story where God asks the father to kill his son, Isaac, to prove his loyalty or whatever."

He wrinkles his nose. "That's the dumbest thing I've ever heard.

Why would God ask that? I thought he was supposed to be loving and all that shit."

I pick at the seam on my jeans, wishing I had all the answers. "I don't know. My dad reminds me of it all the time. As if he would kill me if God asked him to. I hate my name."

"I'm not going to call you Isaac then. How about Zach? It's kind of like the sound of the last part of your name."

"Zach...okay. What's your name?"

"Brady Wellman. How old are you?"

"Almost thirteen. You?"

"Just turned thirteen. You're really tiny." He wraps his arm around me protectively.

"The doctor said it's because I was so premature... I was born at twenty-six weeks. They said I might grow later than most." I shrug, trying not to show how much it bothers me. I'm almost a teenager, and I'm not even four feet tall yet. "You're really tall."

Brady sighs. "Yeah, my dad is tall, too."

I remember he was crying when I first saw him. "Why were you crying?"

He's quiet for a minute before answering. "My little brother died a few weeks ago..."

It's my turn to hug him tightly. "I'm sorry. Why did he die?"

"He came down with cancer when he was little...and was always weak and sick. My parents did everything to save him, but he died," Brady whispers, tears falling down his cheeks. I reach up and wipe them away like he did for me.

"Then Mom and Dad decided we needed to move, and I had to leave all my friends and everything that reminded me of my brother." He stares off in the distance, like he's remembering things. "I miss my brother. Even if he was sick all the time, he still talked to me, and I was never alone."

The sadness in his voice makes my chest feel tight. "I know that I'm nothing special, but you can talk to me...if you want. You won't be alone."

Brady hugs me to his chest, kissing the top of my head. "You can be my little brother. We can be there for each other."

I'm not sure I want to be his brother but definitely his friend. There's this connection I feel with him that I've never felt before. Like we were meant to be together. "I'm not sure my dad will approve, but I can meet you here. Where do you live?"

He points in the opposite direction of my house, where all the rich people live. The trees separate the small ranch-style homes from the mansions. "That way."

"I live on the other side…where the poor people live."

Brady gently tilts my chin up so I'm staring into his blue eyes. "I don't care about that. We can build a little shelter here and meet up as much as possible. Maybe you can sneak over to my house sometimes. We have a pool and can go swimming. Do you think your dad will let you do that?"

My dad will probably want to talk to his dad and go on and on about religion. "I don't know if he would. He doesn't let me do much unless it's going to church."

"We will work it out. Maybe my dad can talk to him," Brady offers, giving me a smile.

Hope blossoms in my chest. Maybe Brady will be the best friend I've always wanted. "How are we going to build something out here?"

"I'll get my dad to help." He looks around the area we are sitting in. "We need something with a roof to keep us dry if it rains."

"Can we have snacks?" My stomach growls as if to echo the need for food.

Brady grins, nodding. "Yep, my mom will give me snacks."

I lean into his chest again, feeling a little cold even though it's hot outside. "I wish my parents were like yours."

"What did your dad beat you for?"

"I brought home a book from the library that wasn't Christian," I murmur against him.

His shoulders tense and he makes this huffing noise. "I will bring books here for you to read. It can be our secret."

An uncontrollable grin spreads across my face, which makes him smile, too. I have found my person, and I can handle anything as long as I don't lose him.

We sit here forever with me in his lap and him telling me about all the funny things his brother used to do. We laugh and he cries a few more times.

It's hard to go back home when all I want to do is hold on to him and beg him to take me to his house.

He slides my glasses back on before we part ways. "Tomorrow, can you meet me here?"

"I can, but not until after church. My dad usually takes a nap at about two, and I can make my escape then."

Brady leans over to kiss my forehead. "I'll see you then, buddy."

THE NEXT DAY I manage to sneak out after Dad falls asleep in his recliner. Running as fast as I can, I pray to God that Brady will be there and not have been a figment of my imagination. When I spot him sitting in the clearing with a backpack, my legs almost give out with relief. I don't stop running until I am next to him, and he pulls me onto his lap to keep me from falling.

"Whoa there, Zach, you about face-planted."

My face breaks out in the biggest grin over him calling me Zach. "Thanks for saving me. I was worried you wouldn't be here."

"I'll always be here." He gives me a hug before letting me sit between his legs while he digs out a book from the pack beside us. "I thought we could take turns reading this book together." He hands it to me. "I've brought snacks, too."

I've died and gone to heaven. Opening the book, I lean back against him and start reading the story aloud. I didn't think I would be confident enough to read to anyone, but with his arms around me, I feel like I can fly and do anything.

After I finish a chapter, he gives me Cheezits and a bag of m&ms to eat while he reads the next chapter. He pauses long enough to hand me a juice box, the little straw stabbed into it for me already. My parents would never buy juice boxes or snacks, and it makes me feel warm inside.

When he finishes, we take off our shoes and socks to wade around in the shallow creek before we have to go home.

"My dad and mom would like to meet you. Do you think you could come over tomorrow? My dad doesn't start his job for another week and can help us build something out here."

I bite my lip, worrying over whether or not to tell my parents. "I'll figure something out. How will I let you know?"

He bends over to pick up an unusual-looking stone. "Don't you have a cell phone?"

"No." I've never even held a cell phone before.

His eyebrows furrow. "I'll show you which house is mine, and you can walk over whenever you want."

We wade a little longer before stepping out to get our socks and shoes on. Brady leans over to tie my shoelaces, even though I can do it myself. I think he likes to take care of me, and I like it so much that it makes me want to cry.

He slings the backpack over his shoulder and takes my hand, guiding me over some large rocks in the creek to get to the other side. It only takes about twenty steps before we leave the woods on this side, and I can see the backside of some huge houses. Brady stops and points to the one that is the closest to us.

"That darker brick one is ours. See the pool behind it?"

The woods sits slightly up on a hill, and I can see the pool with a small waterfall behind the house. There's another smaller house next to it. "Do you live in the smaller house or the big house?"

"Smaller house?" He looks down toward his home again. "Oh, you mean the pool house. That is just for parties or as a guesthouse."

The pool house is almost as big as the little house I live in; he must be really rich. I see a woman step out the patio door and wave toward us.

"That's my mom," he explains, waving with his free hand. "I'll walk you back across the creek before I go home."

He holds my hand until we are both standing on my side of the creek. I can't help but step forward and give him a hug, smiling when he kisses the top of my head.

"You be safe and run home quickly, okay, buddy?"

Nodding, I walk away, staring over my shoulder until I can't see him anymore, and then I run as fast as I can to my house.

When I walk in, my dad is reading his bible aloud to my mom. They both look up at me. "Where have you been?"

Please, God, don't send me to hell, I pray silently before telling them a lie. "I was exploring the woods and talking to God. I decided to pray more."

Dad gives me a rare smile. "It's about time you take your faith more seriously. Next time, take your bible with you."

"Yes, sir, I will do that tomorrow."

"Good. Now, why don't you go read and memorize some scripture until your mother serves supper."

I hurry to my tiny room and collapse on my twin-size bed. My bible is on the side table, and I pull it over to lay on my chest, just in case Dad walks in here.

All I can think about is Brady and the way he held my hand and hugged me. I wish I could be at his house with him instead of alone here.

I can't wait until tomorrow.

TWO

BRADY

"If you're going to stare out the window for hours, you might as well go outside to wait for him."

I'd woken up early because I didn't know what time Zach would come over and have been sitting here ever since. "I know, Mom. Maybe I will. He's just so little that I worry about him."

He is so very tiny, just like my brother always was. I can't stop thinking about the way he'd looked crying in the woods or the welts I'd seen on his back. I want to protect him, keep him safe.

Movement by the woods catches my attention, and I spot Zach coming out of the trees at a run. He trips and falls down, and I find myself hurrying to the back door to jog out there. By the time I reach the edge of the pool, he's resumed his way toward my house, shoving his glasses back on his face as he goes. I swear he looks like he's barely seven, and I'm not sure how he can be only a few weeks younger than me. He stumbles but catches himself this time, giving me a small wave when he notices me. I'm pretty sure part of the reason he keeps falling down is that his jeans are baggy and overly long on him. His shoes also look like they are too big and should be thrown away.

We reach each other, and he doesn't slow down fast enough, slamming into me to stop himself. I wrap my arms around Zach, keeping him upright until he gets his feet under himself again. "Hey buddy... you okay?"

He's out of breath and leans back from me long enough to dig an inhaler from his pocket. Worry fills me. What if he gets sick like my brother? I rub his back until his breathing is better.

"Sorry, I have asthma."

"It's okay." I wait for him to put his inhaler away and then turn around to lower myself a little, patting my shoulder. "Climb on my back."

He breathes out this little sigh of relief before hooking his arms around my neck and letting me carry him the rest of the way to the house. Once we are inside, I carefully let him down and take his hand.

Mom is waiting for us in the kitchen and stares down at Zach, her eyes softening when she takes him in. I'm sure she sees how small and fragile he is, just like I did. "Mom, this is Zach. Zach, this is my mom, Emily."

She gives him a big smile. "It's so nice to meet you, Zach. I'm glad you became friends with Brady. May I get you something to drink? A juice box?"

Zach's eyes move over to me as if to ask for permission, and I give him a nod. He turns back to my mom, whose eyes have been moving from him to me and back to him. "Yes, ma'am, I would like that, please."

She gets this smile at how polite he is and moves to the fridge for a juice box. "Why don't you boys sit at the island?"

I have to lift Zach up onto the barstool before taking the one next to him. Mom slides a juice box over, and I poke the straw through for him, gaining a smile from my buddy.

"Hey boys," Dad says as he walks into the kitchen to stand next to Mom. His eyes take in Zach, and pain flashes over his face. I think he's missing my brother. "You must be Zach," Dad finally adds, reaching his hand over the counter to offer it to him.

Zach tentatively gives his hand to my dad for a small shake. "Y-yes, s-sir."

"This is my dad, Michael. He's a judge." I'm really proud of my dad being a judge. He's explained how important it is to be fair and follow the law. I think he's smarter than anyone.

Dad smiles. "It's nice to meet you, Zach. So Brady tells me you both want some type of shelter in the woods?"

"Y-yes s-si-ir, o-only if it's n-not too m-much tr-trouble," he answers, his voice trembling like he's scared of my dad. I put my arm around his back, and he relaxes a little.

"I think it's doable. My dad built a tree house with me once, and it was my favorite place to be when I was growing up."

My new friend is staring at my dad like he doesn't know what to make of him. I wonder what his dad is like.

Mom leans over, resting her arms on the island counter. "Do you have any siblings?"

Zach finishes sucking on the straw. "No, ma'am, it's just me."

"Brady has two sisters, who you'll get to meet soon. Right now, they are at ballet class."

Mom had enrolled them the second we'd moved here, saying that it would help them make friends in this new community. Meg used to take ballet classes all the time, but this last year with Owen being sick, she had stopped going. Anna is finally old enough to try ballet, too. My sisters are annoying, but I love them. Now it seems like life is going back to normal, and I'm not sure how I feel about it. I don't want us to forget my brother. Even Mom is going to be opening her own law office when we go back to school.

My parents ask Zach a few basic questions, and he answers but looks super uncomfortable. "I'm going to take Zach up to see my room." I hop down off the barstool and lift Zach down, grabbing his hand to drag him up the stairs to my room.

He stands inside the door, looking around in awe. I follow his eyes, seeing my TV and gaming systems, my posters, and shelves of books. I'd never really thought about how much stuff I have until seeing his expression right now. His whole face lights up as he takes in all the books. "Wow…you have your own library."

It's not that big, but I smile at him. "How about I read you the next chapter in our book?"

Zach nods emphatically.

We sit side by side in the bean bag chair, with my arm around his frail, little back and his legs draped over mine. He turns the pages for me as I read and keeps pressing his thumb to his lips like he wants to suck on it but doesn't. He seems so innocent and sheltered in a way that is hard for me to understand.

Just as we get done with the chapter, Dad's voice comes through my room's intercom, telling us to come downstairs.

My mom is baking cookies while she watches a cooking show on our kitchen TV. Zach stops short, his wide eyes fixated on the television screen. Mom gives me a raised eyebrow, and I shrug, not knowing why he seems so enthralled.

"Do you watch this show at home?" Mom asks.

Zach shakes his head but doesn't take his eyes off the television. "No, we don't have a TV."

Mom and Dad exchange looks, and I can't help but think his parents are weird.

"Have you seen movies at school?"

"No, my mom homeschools me." He looks uncomfortable telling us.

Taking his hand, I squeeze it gently.

"How about you boys show me where this tree house needs to be built? I'd like to get started on it tomorrow."

I'm grateful my dad changed the subject, and soon we are walking up to the woods together. We show him our spot, and he searches out the perfect tree to build our house into. I help him take measurements, with Zach standing quietly close by. Anytime Dad doesn't need me to hold the tape, I offer my hand to Zach, and he grips it tightly. Maybe it's weird for boys to hold hands like this, but I can tell it helps Zach feel safer, and I kind of like feeling his hand in mine.

When we get done, Zach has to go back home for lunch, even though I can tell he doesn't want to. He hugs me tightly before waving at my dad and leaving us.

Dad puts his hand on my shoulder after Zach disappears from our sight. "Come on, Son. Let's get home so I can make phone calls and figure out what I want to do out here."

THAT NIGHT, Mom and Dad ask me about Zach. "Do you know anything about him?"

"No. He seems so sad to me, Mom. I wish he could stay here."

"I'm sure his parents wouldn't go for that. For now, I'm not going to push the issue that he lets his parents know, but eventually, they'll have to know what he's doing."

"Okay. Maybe you could talk to them, Dad? I think he's scared to."

"Sure, Son, you know I will help in any way I can."

Mom starts crying and Dad is instantly holding her. "He's so small —like Owen was. I miss him so much."

"I know. Maybe Owen sent us Zach because he knew he needed us," Dad murmurs against Mom's head, his voice sounding shaky to me.

I knee-crawl over to my parents, and they envelop me into their hug as we all cry. My sisters pile on, and I feel the strength of my dad holding us all together.

It isn't long before Anna starts to tickle me, her giggles pushing back the sadness. She's only five and the youngest of our family. I tickle her back, and then Meg tackles me. At seven years old, she's usually the calm one of the two. Dad and Mom don't try to save me, and in trying to be gentle with them, I finally admit defeat and call uncle.

Lying in bed that night, I think about what Dad said. Maybe Owen did send us Zach because he needs us. Part of me feels bad that it's like I'm replacing my brother, but if Owen were here, he would want me to be Zach's friend. He always had the biggest heart and would cry over the kids he met during treatment. He tried to be this light and comfort to everyone he encountered. If he'd met Zach, he would have worried about him just like I do.

"I'll take care of him," I whisper into the dark, hoping my brother hears my promise.

THREE

ZACH

Mr. Wellman spends every day this week building us a tree house. Brady says it is some pre-cut kit that he bought at a lumber yard. I was picturing this little, tiny makeshift overhang that we could sit under to keep out of the rain, but Brady's dad is building a tree house that is big enough that even he can lie down in it if he wants. He has some guys come out and help a few times, but I stay back and try not to get in the way when they are here.

Sometimes, Brady and I will help with things on the ground, but his dad doesn't want us in the tree house until it is safe. So instead, we explore the little woods and wade in the creek. We read to each other and sometimes just lie on the ground, staring up at the sky without saying a word.

My mom doesn't seem to care that I am off in the woods. She used to leave me alone for a couple of hours a few days a week, but this week it's been every day and for much longer. I feel like something is changing in the house, but I don't know what yet. I am afraid to question it because I don't want to lose being able to see Brady.

Now it's Friday, and the tree house is finished. His dad is letting us go up the ladder for the first time. Brady makes me go up in front of him in case I fall, and I climb carefully. Mr. Wellman built it partially in a tree but not so high that it's scary. There's a railing in the front for if we sit outside and two plastic chairs for us to use. I open the door and walk inside, my mouth dropping open at how perfect it is. Brady follows me in, his mouth dropping open, too.

"Wow, Dad, this is awesome!"

Mr. Wellman is behind us, a smile on his face. "I wanted it to be a place you could come to for years, even as you get older."

I'm not sure when he snuck this stuff in here, but on one side, there's a small table with two chairs, and on the other side, there's a cushioned mat on the floor, right next to where you can open a hatch into a window. It's open now, and the breeze feels good in this heat.

"In that tub, there are sleeping bags for when you're out here or if you want to camp out overnight. There are flashlights and a lantern in there, too."

Brady turns to hug his dad, and I get pulled in for one with them. I swallow down the sobs that want to come out. Why can't my dad be like this and love me? I wish that I could be adopted into the Wellman family and never have to go home again. My mom's face flashes before me, and I feel guilty for thinking that. "Thank you, Mr. Wellman," I say when the hug breaks.

"You're welcome. I'll leave you boys to have fun now."

Brady stands in the doorway as his dad climbs down. "Thanks, Dad, you're the best."

After his dad is gone, we both grin at each other and hurry to get out the sleeping bags to put on the thick camping mat. Brady has brought his backpack with the current book we are reading and some snacks. We spend the day lying here reading and talking.

When it's time for me to go home, we put the sleeping bags away.

"My dad is home tomorrow… I'm not sure when I'll be able to come out here."

Brady frowns. "He's not going to hurt you again, is he?"

I hope not, but you never know with my dad. "No, I won't give him a reason to."

"I've brought something, but I wasn't sure if you would get into trouble for it." He takes out two things that look like clunky cell phones. "They are two-way radios that go really far. My dad said they will work all the way to your house. Do you think your dad would let you keep one there?"

I haven't even told my parents about Brady yet. "I don't know if he would…"

"I'll leave it in this tub, and if you need me, at least you can come here and radio me. Maybe you can take it home once you ask your dad?"

"Okay, I'll ask him." Dread fills my stomach at the thought.

"When you get out here tomorrow, you can radio me, and I can come to meet you." He shows me what buttons to push on the little device.

Brady goes down the ladder in front of me and then waits at the bottom until I'm down safely. I hug him a little longer this time, worried that my dad will keep me from seeing him again.

"Bye, Brady."

"Bye, buddy."

SATURDAY MORNING, Dad and I work outside. I get lectured for not memorizing five scriptures this week. He makes me skip lunch and spend time in my room learning them by heart. I try to pick short scriptures to make it easier. I have a photographic memory, but scriptures seem to blur in my mind because I hate having to do this. Most of the time, they don't make any sense, and I end up questioning them more than anything.

It isn't until I recite the scriptures back to my dad that he lets me go off into the woods. I run as fast as I can to the tree house and radio Brady that I'm here.

We spend the afternoon with him teaching me how to play Settlers of Catan at our little table, eating snacks and laughing. I make sure to leave before suppertime so that I don't give Dad a reason to be mad at me.

I'm setting the table for Mom when Dad walks in. "What were you doing all afternoon?"

"Exploring in the woods."

Dad gives me this stare that makes me tremble. "Your mom said that you've been spending all your time out there. Are you playing alone?"

He already knows and is seeing if I will lie to him. I've seen this expression before. "I've been hanging out with a boy I met. He's my friend."

"Is he a Christian?"

"I…I d-d-don't kn-know," I stutter out, backing up slightly to put more space between us. Not that it'll help me in any way.

"Go to your room and stay there. I'll be in later to punish you." He pulls out his chair to sit down as if he didn't just destroy all my happiness.

Mom nods at me to go, offering no hope at help from her. I rush to my room and curl up in the corner, waiting for my dad. I'm not even sure why I'm getting punished this time. I didn't lie, and I haven't done anything bad or sinned against God. Why can't I have a friend to play with? Brady and his parents seem like the best people in the whole world, too.

My father doesn't come into my room until it's dark outside. Waiting to be beaten is torture, and I think that's why he does it. He doesn't even tell me why I'm getting beaten with the belt over this. He just does it and walks away, leaving me on the bed crying until I fall asleep. I hate him. I hate him so much.

Sitting in church on Sunday is another form of torture. The wooden pew is harsh after being punished last night. My dad has this knowing look and smile, like this is just extended punishment.

I spend the rest of my day grounded to my room. My stomach protests because I haven't eaten anything since yesterday's snacks with Brady, but I don't even care. I'm too upset over losing my new best friend.

As soon as Dad leaves for work on Monday, Mom comes into my room.

"May I go outside to play?"

She shakes her head. "Your dad doesn't want you running around with a degenerate boy. Go get your chores done, and then you can read a book quietly in your room."

I hurry with my chores and then hide away in my room, lying on the bed and staring up at the ceiling for hours. They don't even come to get me when they eat supper, and that's fine with me.

It's about seven o'clock when the doorbell rings. No one ever comes to our house, and I sneak down the hallway to peek into the living room to see who is at the front door. My mouth drops open because Mr. Wellman is standing on our porch with Brady next to him.

"Mr. Matthews, I'm Judge Wellman, and this is my son, Brady. May we come in?"

Dad opens the door, letting them enter. His face has that fake smile he gets when he's around people he wants to impress. "Please have a seat. This is my wife, Joy."

As soon as they are all sitting, my dad asks, "So what brings you here?"

"My son made friends with your son, and when he didn't come out to play, he was worried about him. We met Isaac earlier this week and were very impressed. You've raised a polite and respectful boy and should be quite proud."

Surprise flickers briefly across my dad's face before he fixes his smile again. "Yes, Isaac is a special boy. He had a stomach bug over the weekend, but I'm sure he can play tomorrow."

"That would be wonderful. With us being new to town, Brady needs a friend, and he really hit it off with your son. We wanted to know if Isaac could stay for a sleepover tomorrow night?"

"We have very strict rules that we expect Isaac to follow. No television or technology are allowed. He can't be around foul language, and we expect him to behave according to our faith."

Judge Wellman nods, although I notice the stiffness in his shoulders. "I will make sure that your rules are followed under my watch. We, too, expect good behavior from our own children. A father has to be strict, or a child gets spoiled."

Brady gives his dad an odd look, but then I see him scan his gaze around the room. His eyes find me in the shadows, and worry crosses his face. I shrink back more, not wanting him to see how messed up I am right now.

"It's good to know that, Judge Wellman. A man has to follow Proverbs thirteen twenty-four and guide his family in righteousness."

Mr. Wellman gives a short nod. "Would you mind if Brady said hi to Isaac while we're here?"

"I suppose I can allow that," Dad says. "Joy, show Brady to Isaac's room for a brief visit."

I rush back to my room and sit on my bed, cringing over the pain from putting pressure on the welts. The door opens, and my mom shows Brady in. As soon as she leaves us alone, he rushes over to sit next to me, and I can't keep from sobbing into his chest.

"Are you okay, Zach?" he asks several times as I cry. I shake my head no, and his arms tighten around me. "Take a deep breath for me so you can talk."

I do and force my cries under control. "I thought I had lost you," I half sob into his shirt.

"Nah, I won't let that happen. I was so worried when you didn't show up all weekend. I was afraid your dad had done something to you." He leans back and tilts my chin up to look at him. A gesture I think he's done a few times. "Do you really have the flu?"

"No, Dad found out I was hanging out with you."

"Did he beat you again?"

Fear over telling him the truth makes me ignore the question. "I really get to come for a sleepover tomorrow?"

His eyes narrow like he knows I'm not telling him on purpose, but he doesn't push. "Yes, and we can stay up talking as late as we want."

"With food?" My stomach growls loudly as if it was summoned.

"Have you not eaten anything?"

I shake my head.

"For how long?"

"Not since the snacks we had," I whisper, lowering my eyes so I can't see the pity in his, or I'll start to cry again.

"I will bring food for you," he promises, using his thumbs to wipe my tears away.

His tenderness is undoing me. "I don't want you to leave."

That earns me another hug and a kiss to the forehead. "Just think about how the sooner I leave and you go to sleep, the faster it'll be tomorrow."

Mom shows up right then, and I can tell she doesn't approve of our hug. We separate quickly, Brady giving me one last look before following her out.

Collapsing back onto the bed, I let hope seep back into my body and pray for tomorrow to come.

FOUR

BRADY

Dad is quiet on the short drive back home. I can tell he's pissed about what Zach's dad said, and I feel the same way. Twice now, I've opened my mouth to tell him about Zach getting beaten by his dad but then stopped myself. Zach asked me not to tell anyone, and I don't want him to end up in foster care because of me.

"I'm not going to police you both constantly while he's here. Whatever you do, it stays here and doesn't leave here. Do you understand what I'm trying to say, Son?"

"If we don't follow his dad's rules, you don't want to know about it?" I shift in my seat so I can see him better.

"I'm not sure what you're talking about," he says, opening his door. His tone is saying yes that's exactly what he means.

I get out and follow him into the house. Mom steps into view before we get into the kitchen. "How did it go?"

"His dad is a piece of work. He claimed Isaac had the flu."

"He didn't have the flu," I mutter, earning full-on looks from my parents. "His dad found out he was hanging out with me and grounded him. And he hates to be called Isaac, so call him Zach when he's here."

"So what was the verdict?" My mom sounds like an attorney right now.

"He's allowing him to come over. I used being a judge to make an impression and help persuade them. I hate doing that, but I don't think Zach's dad would have agreed if I hadn't." He sets his keys on the counter. "Oh, and I basically said I am a strict father who doesn't spoil his kids."

Mom laughs at that one. "You spoil our kids more than I do."

He spoils us in all the good ways. Like always being there for us and giving more love than I see most parents do, stopping for ice cream even when he's in a hurry to get somewhere, and showing up for every school event. My dad is the best.

ZACH SHOWS up on my back porch while I'm still eating breakfast. He's pale and shaky, yet smiling as widely as I am.

I give him a hug and then take his hand. "Come on, I'll make you some breakfast."

He's carrying this little plastic grocery bag and drops it on the floor next to the bar. "My parents said I don't have to come back until tomorrow."

Today is going to be better than I'd thought, and I grin as I lift him up onto the bar stool. He winces and it reminds me that his dad must have beaten him. I hurry to get one of Mom's living room pillows and bring it back to slide underneath him. His eyes well up with tears, but he tries to blink them away. My heart physically hurts that he's about to cry over me being kind to him. I end up hugging him for another minute before getting us bowls out.

"Do you like Cap'n Crunch Berries?"

"I don't know, but I've always wanted to try it."

I pour us both bowls and add milk, then take a seat next to him. "The best way to eat them is to eat the crunchy yellow things first, and then at the end, eat all the berries."

He mimics me but in a rush, trying to shovel it into his mouth quickly. If his parents not giving him food is a regular thing, I'm going to make sure I bring him something to eat every day. I can't even imagine my parents taking away food; it would hurt me so much if they did.

"Do you want another bowl?"

He starts to nod but then shakes his head. "I'd better not. I don't want to throw up."

My mom comes in with my sisters, and they are immediately drawn to Zach. *Who* wouldn't be? He's so fragile and sweet-looking.

After they've bugged him enough, I make excuses for us and get my backpack so we can head out to the tree house. Mom packs us up some sandwiches while I put in a million drinks and snacks. We wave good-bye, and then I hold his hand as we walk out to the woods.

We put our sleeping bags over the mat and lie here, reading chapter after chapter to each other.

"Let's eat lunch," I say after hours of reading. My stomach is growling almost as loudly as his is.

We share the food and then lie back on the sleeping bags side by side. Zach breaks the silence between us with, "Do you think we'll be friends forever?"

There's a tremble in his voice that makes me roll onto my side so I can see his face. "Yes, friends forever. You're going to be my best friend for life, I promise."

He turns his head so that I can see the tears filling up his green eyes. "What if I do something that makes you mad?"

"So what if you do? Friends always forgive and love each other no matter what." I want to reassure him somehow that I'm not going to hurt him that way. "How about we make a pact?"

"A pact?"

"Yeah, like we swear to each other that no matter what, we will always be there and will always love each other." Maybe boys don't normally say "love" to each other, but I don't care about that right now. Zach needs some love, and maybe so do I.

He nods slowly and then reaches over to take my hand. "I solemnly swear to be your best friend forever. I'll always be here for you and love you, no matter what happens."

Squeezing his hand, I let his words settle into my heart and take away the pain I've been feeling since Owen died. "I solemnly swear to be your best friend and to never leave you. I'll never hurt you and will always love you. No matter what happens."

A tear escapes down his cheek, and I have to blink back a few of my own. This moment feels special, and I know deep in my heart that we will be best friends forever.

Lying back again, I am not surprised when Zach falls asleep next to me. He looks so tired today, and I worry his dad has hurt him more than I know. When he rolls over to cuddle into me, I carefully move my arm to wrap around his back and let myself go to sleep, too. All while vowing that I'll protect him and make him happy.

THE DAY GOES by far too quickly, and it's truly the best day I've ever had. My parents love Zach as much as I do. It's odd how easily we get along, considering how different we are. I'm big and he's small. I love sports and he loves books. The list goes on and on.

That night he's in a sleeping bag on the floor, and I'm in bed, but he looks so alone down there, and it feels wrong.

"Come share my bed," I offer, leaning over the side to give him my hand. It's a twin bed but about the same size as the mat in the tree house, so we make it work. We talk forever, both of us staring up at the ceiling and laughing over silly things. Zach falls asleep first and I follow.

His cries wake me later, and I realize he's having a nightmare. I pull him into my arms and croon to him like I used to with my brother when he was in pain. It only takes a minute, and he's buried into me, quiet and peaceful. Having Zach close like this feels perfect and heals even more of the pain I've been feeling lately. Like he's a special gift given to me.

FIVE

ZACH

That summer is the best time of my life. Brady and I are inseparable. At least when my dad doesn't interfere. He surprisingly ignores me most of the summer as long as I do my chores and can recite new scriptures each week. Brady helps me study them, even if we both think the verses are weird and don't make any sense.

I really think my dad is letting me be simply because Brady's dad is a judge. He's brought it up so many times it makes my stomach hurt when he starts in. My friendship with Brady isn't about his dad being a judge or money; it's about how much I love my best friend.

Brady's parents are unreal, and I'm not sure he realizes how lucky he is. They don't enforce my dad's rules either but instead pretend not to notice if we are watching TV or playing video games. I get to do all the things I've always wanted to, including swimming in the pool almost every day.

But none of it means anything next to Brady and his friendship. He doesn't act like it's weird that we hug a lot or that I always sleep in bed with him. I live for our sleepovers because those are the only times I feel completely safe and can sleep soundly.

When Brady goes back to school, it's harder than I even imagined. Every day is depressing and lonely. Mom is leaving a lot more without any explanation, and I end up doing most of my schoolwork alone. It's not hard for me; I learn easily and have been studying books I get from the library that are way above my grade level. Studying is all I have to keep me busy while I'm stuck at home.

Brady always meets me at the tree house when he gets off school. I help him with his homework, and we eat snacks together. Weekends are usually spent at his house, but his parents never seem to get tired of me coming over.

The following summer is when I start to realize I'm different. Brady has a birthday party and invites kids from school to come. He's turning fourteen and will be a freshman this fall. I am, too, but not for another couple of weeks. His body is changing, and he's even bigger than before. Our size comparison is ridiculous. Half the time, it makes me feel safe, and the other half of the time, I feel like people must see me as his much younger brother. I just want my body to grow up some more.

His friends are smaller than him but still much taller than me. I get a lot of looks like they think I'm weird, and they don't include me in any of their conversations. Brady doesn't seem to notice, but he does stay next to me, our legs and arms touching. He knows that when he's close, it helps me through the panicky feelings I get frequently.

Brady keeps looking at a girl, and she's smiling at him. It makes my stomach hurt a little, and I don't even know why. He leans over to whisper in my ear, "Brittany is cute."

Cute? I study her again and don't see it. She's not ugly or anything, but otherwise, she just looks like any other girl to me.

Shrugging, I stick my finger into a hole in my shirt and wonder why Brady is even friends with me. All his other friends are rich like him, with nice clothes and perfect everything. I'm just sitting here looking like a dork with braces still on my teeth. My parents only let me get braces last summer, right after Brady and I started spending so much time together.

I'm grateful when the party is over and everyone leaves. Brady and I go to his room, taking turns showering before crawling into bed together. His parents bought him a queen-size bed a few months ago and stopped putting an air mattress on the floor for me when I stay over. Not that I ever used the air mattress anyway.

He's lying in bed facing me when he asks, "So why were you so quiet today?"

I roll over to my side to look at him. "I don't get around people or kids much… I don't know what to say to them."

He brushes some hair back from my face. "It's more fun when it's just the two of us."

Butterflies start up in my stomach as his fingers lightly move down my cheek. "Happy birthday, Brady," I whisper. "I'm sorry I didn't have money to get you anything."

He smiles and then pulls me closer so I can snuggle into him, kissing my forehead. "Having you for my best friend is the best gift you can give me."

My face is pressed against his chest, and I relax into him as his arm tightens around my back.

"Go to sleep, buddy. I won't let anyone hurt you," he whispers above my head.

It isn't long until I can tell that he's asleep. I try, but thoughts keep running through my head. Why didn't I think that girl was cute? Is it wrong to love sleeping next to Brady? Is it normal to love a boy as much as I love him? My dad has said many times how homosexual people go to hell and how sick they are. Even these thoughts of how much I love Brady make me feel like I should be ashamed.

Stuffing down these weird feelings and trying to quiet the butterflies that appear when Brady holds me, I force myself to think of girls and pray that I find one that I can say is cute.

SIX

BRADY

Turning my head, I double-check that Zach is still under the tree near the edge of our practice field. He looks up almost like he knows I'm staring at him and gives me a small smile before going back to reading. Football practice started last week, and he's been getting up early with me every day, biking down to the field so we have more time together. I feel bad that he sits out here for hours in the heat, but I can't bring myself to tell him not to come. It bothers me when I don't know where he is or can't watch over him. Going to school during the winter without him is hard enough, but I'm not leaving him alone in the summer, too. He looks up again, and I point toward the small cooler I've brought along. It earns me a nod and a little bigger smile as he moves to dig out a bottle of water.

"Wellman! Get your head into practice!" coach shouts my way.

A few of the guys snicker, but when I turn my gaze on them, they shut up. I'm the biggest guy here, and they aren't stupid. Even as a freshman, I'm as tall as the seniors out on this field.

Connor, who is my second-best friend, runs next to me as we do laps around the perimeter. "So what's the deal with you and the nerd?"

Maybe I should tell him not to call Zach a nerd, but I like that he's a nerd. "His name is Zach. You met him at my birthday party, remember?"

"Yeah, I know. It's just weird that you have this little kid tagging along with you to practice."

I like Connor, but he's going to piss me off if he's not careful. "He's not a little kid, dumbass. He's our age and my best friend."

"Whoa, sorry if I said the wrong thing. It would suck to be that little at our age."

"Just be nice to him, okay?"

"Yeah, I will."

For the rest of practice, I keep an eye on Zach to make sure he's okay. He's still under the tree when I come out after taking a shower in the locker room.

"How was practice?" he asks, stuffing his book into my backpack.

"Hot," I mutter, taking the pack from him and shoving the little cooler in, too. "Some of the guys seem like pricks."

He gets on his bike and grins over at me. "In all the books I've read, most jocks are pricks."

I flick the bill of his hat but grin back. "Let's go get ice cream."

We bike over to the ice cream shop at the very edge of town. Zach and I sit at the picnic table outside, eating our favorite chocolate ice cream cones.

Zach pauses, staring over my shoulder, his ice cream slowly melting down one side of his cone.

"What's wrong?"

"My mom is over there with some guy..."

Looking over my shoulder, I spot Mrs. Matthews leaning against a car in the parking lot of our community park. The guy with her is standing close and laughing at whatever Zach's mom is saying. I turn back to Zach and have to lean over to lick up the side of his cone that is about to drip ice cream on the table.

His eyes are drawn back to me, and he gets this odd look on his face. I point to his cone, which is about to drip down the other side. "Do you know who that guy is?"

Zach licks up the melting ice cream before staring back over my shoulder. "No. She's been leaving a lot but never says where she's going. I don't think dad knows she leaves the house every day."

"Are you going to tell him?"

He shakes his head. "No way. If he loses his temper, I'll somehow end up on the other end of it. Maybe it's just some guy asking Mom questions, and she's being nice."

I don't think he believes that any more than I do, but all I can focus on is his worry over his dad's temper. "Is your dad still hurting you?"

Zach concentrates on his cone but shakes his head. "I'm fine... I'm barely home anymore."

That part is true. He is at our house more than he's at home, but somehow I get the feeling that he's not telling me the truth. "You'd tell me if he was hurting you, right?"

His eyes move away and then widen. "She's kissing him."

Sure enough, his mom is kissing the man she's with, and it's not a friendly peck, either. "Oh, shit..."

"I don't understand," he says in such a low voice I can barely hear him. "They preach at me about the bible and act so holy, but then she goes and cheats on my dad?"

I reach across the table to take his hand. "What are you going to do?"

"Nothing. I'm going to pretend I don't know." His eyes fill with tears. "If she leaves me... I'll be stuck with Dad alone."

Shit. I take both our cones and chuck them into the nearby trash before pulling him around the table to sit on my lap, rubbing his back until he stops shaking. "You're going to be okay. I'm going to be with you."

A few people are looking at us weirdly, but I couldn't care less. Zach is the most important person to me, and nothing else matters right now.

When he calms down, I sling the backpack on, and we bike to the tree house together. Lying on the sleeping bags with him under my arm and resting his head on my chest, I read to him until he falls asleep. He looks so tired all the time; it worries me. I know he has nightmares when he sleeps over, but as soon as I hold him, he sleeps peacefully. What are his nights like at home, though?

I let Zach sleep for a couple of hours before waking him to come home with me. There's no way I'm letting him sleep at home tonight. Not after what he saw today.

THINGS GO on as normal after that. Zach pretends he never saw his mother, and I don't push him to talk about it. I hate it when the

summer ends because it means I can't watch over him. What's worse is
now that I'm on the football team, we have less time together.

Zach comes to every game with my parents and watches me play,
even though I know he hates sports. They sit in the same spot every
time, and I find comfort in seeing him right there whenever I look over
during the game. He even rides along for away games and then stays
overnight with us.

Summer arriving is sweet relief because I can have more time with
Zach. We both turn fifteen, and Zach finally grows a few inches. Everything should be going great, but I notice that he's increasingly
depressed. Always staring off in space like he's in his own little world.
He looks lonely all the time, even when he's with me. I get more and
more worried as the summer goes on, but when I ask him if anything is
wrong, he just says no.

Finally, I break down and decide to talk to my parents about him. I
choose a Sunday morning since Zach is at church with his parents. All
it takes to get my parents' attention is to sit down on the couch and
look at them.

Dad turns off the show they were watching. "What's wrong?"

Shrugging, I bring up Zach. "I'm worried about Zach. He's not
been himself lately, and I don't know what's wrong with him."

"I've noticed, too," Mom says, worry clear on her face. "Something
is troubling him."

"Yeah, but what is it?"

Dad leans forward, giving me a serious expression. "Sometimes a
person has to work things out for themselves. Maybe he's going through
something personal that he's not ready to share yet. All you can do is be
there for him, and when he's ready to talk about it, do everything in
your power to let him know it's okay."

I feel like he is trying to tell me something without actually telling
me. "I will always be there for him, Dad. You know how much he
means to me."

He nods. "I do, Son. You two have a special friendship that anyone
around you can see. We love Zach like he's our own, and if you find out
something is wrong, I want you to come to us so that we can help."

It's on the tip of my tongue to tell them that I worry his dad might
still be hurting him, but I swallow down the urge. Zach hasn't acted like
he hurts or has been hit. God, if I find out his dad is hitting him again,
I'm going to come unglued.

"Do you think we could get Zach a cell phone on our family plan? I'll pay for it out of my allowance or do extra chores…please?"

They both are immediately nodding. "I think that's a good idea," Dad answers, "but you don't need to pay for it. I'll take care of it tomorrow."

Later that night, when Zach crawls into bed with me, I try to talk to him. "Buddy, you know that you can tell me anything, right?"

He rolls to face away from me, but I refuse to let him out of my arms.

"I'm fine, Brady…just been tired. Nothing to worry about." There's a catch in his voice that says I should absolutely be worried about it.

"Okay," I murmur, kissing the back of his head. What else am I supposed to say? He's my best friend, and I feel like I'm losing him somehow.

Football practice so early in the mornings has been kicking my ass, and I fall asleep as soon as I shut my eyes.

Later, a noise wakes me, and my arms are empty. Sitting up quickly, I scan the bedroom and don't see Zach anywhere. Another faint noise comes from my bathroom that sounds like Zach is crying, and I hurry from bed to rush in there.

Zach is in the corner, huddled up with his face buried into his hands. Muffled sobs escape from him, tearing at my heart.

Sinking down next to him, I go to move him into my lap, but he jerks away.

"Nooo," he sobs. "I don't want you to see me like this."

"Zach, what is wrong? You're scaring me." I try to hold him again, but he flies off the floor. And that's when I see he has a wet spot on the front of his boxers. "Is that what you're upset over? It's a wet dream… not a big deal. It happens to me, too, sometimes."

"It hasn't happened while you're in bed with me! I don't want you to hate me for it," he half sobs, half exclaims.

Getting off the floor, I take his hand and squeeze it. "It has, but I wake up earlier than you and take care of it. Dad said morning wood and wet dreams are normal for boys our age. It's bound to happen. We are best friends, and it's not something we should freak out over."

He stares down at the wet spot on his boxers. "I didn't even know this could happen."

His words remind me of how sheltered he's been. He's not in

public school, and when we watch movies, they aren't the kind that talk or show this sort of thing. God knows his parents would never talk to him about it, I'm sure. No wonder he freaked out. "It happens to every teenage boy. It's not something you can control or should be embarrassed about. Hell, I have one friend at school that brags about how he jacks off seven times a day."

"Jacks off?"

Shit. "Errr…you know where you use your hand to get off until you come." My dad would be so much better at this conversation.

"I…I didn't know guys did that," he says, squinting his eyes at me.

I realize he doesn't have his glasses on and probably can't see me very well. "Yeah, they do. It'll happen when you're ready." He's so delayed with everything that it's hard to remember he's fifteen, too. I've been getting off since I was thirteen and thought every boy my age was doing the same. "Let's get you some clean clothes so we can go back to bed."

He nods, and I leave the bathroom to get him one of my longer shirts, taking it back to him to change into. I sit on the bed until he comes out and smile when he finally appears. My shirt goes almost to his knees, and he looks adorable.

Adorable?

Are guys allowed to think other guys are adorable?

I notice he's clutching his wadded-up clothes close to his chest. "Let's take your clothes down to wash. We can sneak some ice cream and watch a movie." I'm going to be dead for football practice tomorrow.

I grab my hamper of dirty clothes, and we quietly tiptoe down to the laundry room. He throws his clothes in the washer, and I add the dirty ones from my hamper.

Thankfully, my parents don't wake up, and we are soon sitting side by side in my bed eating ice cream and watching Tangled.

Zach never says he loves Disney films, but I know they are his favorite. I'm pretty sure I've seen Tangled at least a dozen times.

By the end of the movie, he's passed out with his glasses askew on his face. I carefully remove them to set on the side table and then carry our ice cream bowls down to the kitchen. I transfer the load of laundry into the dryer before I climb the stairs to my room. Zach has edged his way onto my half of the bed, his hand splayed out as if he's trying to find me.

I don't even try to scoot him over; I just crawl into the little space left and cover us both up. He's instantly glued to me, his fingers digging into my back like he's afraid I'm going to disappear.

I'm so tired, but my mind replays Zach crying in the bathroom, and I try to make sense of all these feelings. I'm fifteen, and I'm cuddled up with my best friend. We sleep together more than we sleep apart, at least in the summertime. Deep down, I know we don't have the typical relationship, but I love him too much to push him away, nor do I want to. Zach has been my lifeline since Owen died, and I'm ashamed to say that losing Zach would kill me even more so than losing my own brother.

Kissing the top of Zach's head, I force my eyes shut. I just hope this episode tonight will take away the tension and sadness that he's been carrying around for a while.

My alarm goes off shortly after I get to sleep. Groaning, I drag my ass from bed and turn to tuck the blankets up to Zach's chin. He usually wakes with my alarm and the fact that he didn't shows how tired he must be. I throw on some clothes and hurry downstairs to eat breakfast.

Mom has a plate ready for me, and I stab some scrambled eggs to fork into my mouth.

"What were you two doing up in the middle of the night?"

My next forkful gets paused. "Zach was upset... He needed ice cream and a movie."

"Upset? Did you finally figure out what is wrong?"

"I'm not really sure, but don't ask him about it, okay?" The last thing he needs is for my mom to bring up what happened.

She gives me an assessing look. "Is it something I need to know about?"

"No! God no, Mom! Some things are private, and this is one of them."

She holds her hands up. "Okay, okay, I get it. I'm glad you were there to help him through it."

"Jesus, can we not even talk about this at all?" The thought of my mom anywhere near Zach's wet dream makes me want to throw up.

As soon as I finish breakfast, I get the clothes out of the dryer. Mom notices me carrying the basket and gets a funny look on her face but doesn't say anything. I run it upstairs and fold his clothes to leave on the bed for him.

He's still sleeping but hugging my pillow to his chest. Leaning over, I kiss his forehead and brush his hair back from his face. "I love you, buddy," I whisper.

HALFWAY THROUGH FOOTBALL PRACTICE, I look over to see Zach sitting under the tree with his book. Any tension I was feeling eases away at having him close by. We skip ice cream after practice and just go straight to the tree house. At fifteen, a tree house should be lame, but we still love it. It's like a little hideaway where no one bothers us and the rest of the world fades away.

It doesn't take me long to figure out that Zach is still hiding something from me. He's still moody and withdrawn. Something is going on with him, but what?

SEVEN

ZACH

I stare out the window at the pool where Brady is swimming with a few of his school friends. He keeps looking toward the house with a worried look on his face. I know he's waiting for me, but I don't want to go out there.

His friends from school are so outgoing and confident, the exact opposite of me. Why would he want to have me as a best friend when he could have Connor or Derek?

Brittany hangs her arms around his neck, squealing when he unhooks them and tosses her away. The girls all like him, but that's no surprise. Brady is hot and only gets more so as he grows older.

There's a smaller girl in the group, Ivy. She's the only one that's almost as short as I am. She's wearing a pink bikini and is what most guys would call pretty. *I think.*

My stomach hurts as unwelcome thoughts pop into my mind.

Find her attractive. Do it!

I will my body to listen to me, but I feel nothing toward her.

As if I'm cursed, Brady climbs out of the pool to get a drink and shakes his hair out. Water drips down his chest to his red swimming trunks, and I feel my cheeks grow hot. He laughs at something Brittany says, and suddenly my throat feels tight. Tingles burn through my skin until I'm digging my fingernails into the palms of my hands.

This is wrong, so wrong.

Not only is it wrong to be attracted to someone who trusts that I'm just his best friend, but it's a sin against God. Dad always said it's a choice, but I'm constantly choosing no and praying, yet it's not working. Nothing is working. Keeping these thoughts away is exhausting me, and it's tearing up my insides until I don't even know what is me anymore.

How can loving someone send you to hell?

"Are you going out to swim?"

Mrs. Wellman's voice makes me jump, and I look over to see her studying me. "I don't know... I don't fit in with his friends."

She gives me a smile. "Ah, I see. You know that you're the most important friend that Brady has, and he loves having you here."

"Maybe, but the rest of his friends don't. I'm just a tiny, little geek to them."

"They just need to get to know you, Zach. You're *so* special, and they will see that if you give them a chance."

They won't see the real me. All they'll see is someone less than them. Someone who is messed up and poor and has crappy clothes. Someone who can hardly talk around them. They won't see that I'm dying inside. A tear slides down my cheek at the thought, and I swipe it away.

"Zach," Mrs. Wellman says in a low voice, "we love you. I hope you know that."

They won't love me once they find out that I love their son the way I do. I stuff those feelings inside and make myself not see Brady that way. I can't betray him like that. I just can't.

"Why don't you help me bake cookies with the girls for a while?"

I want to run away and leave, be by myself. But being at home is torture. Knowing that Mom is having an affair and then trying to avoid getting beaten all the time. I can't go home. I don't even consider it my home.

My home is Brady.

"Zach?"

Pay attention... You're zoning out again.

"Sure, Mrs. Wellman, I'd like that."

She gives me a hug. "You can call me Emily or even Mom. You're a part of this family, and Mrs. Wellman is too formal."

Don't cry. Don't cry.

I give her a hug back and then follow her into the kitchen. Meg and

Anna are like my own little sisters. They've grown so much since I first met them, to the point that Meg is as tall as I am now. It's a bit embarrassing being the same height as a nine-year-old.

While I'm helping Anna put dough on the cookie sheets, Brady comes in from the patio door looking for me.

"Hey bud, are you coming out to swim?" He puts his arm around my shoulder, his touch sending shivers over my skin.

Stop it. I shrug off his arm and then inwardly wince at the hurt look on his face. "You're getting me wet." I offer as an explanation, even though that's not why I shrugged his arm off.

He grins and gives me a hug, swinging me around in a circle.

"Brady, leave the poor kid alone. You're soaking wet and dripping water on the floor."

Brady does set me down like his mom said, but he smirks at my wet shirt. "Come out and go swimming with us."

"Ehh...I don't feel like swimming right now."

He frowns. "Are you feeling okay?" His hand comes up to rest on my forehead to check for a fever.

I lean into his touch and then silently berate myself for craving to be close to him. "I'm just tired, and swimming takes a lot out of me."

His hand slides down to cup my cheek as his eyes soften. "Do you want me to come inside? I can sit with you while you take a nap?"

How could anyone not fall in love with him? He's the sweetest person I've ever met. "No, I don't want you to leave your friends. I'll hang out with your mom for a while."

"Alright," he says, reluctance in his voice. "I'll check on you a little later."

I get a kiss to my forehead, and he leaves to go back to his friends. Instant emptiness hits me once he's gone.

His mom gives me this understanding look and puts her arm around my shoulders. "How about a spoonful of cookie dough?"

The last thing in the world I want to do lately is eat. "I'm not really hungry, but thanks."

"Can I have his?" Meg is already getting a spoon out of the drawer and helping herself.

"No fair," Anna whines, rushing over to get her own spoon.

Baking cookies takes about an hour, and then Brady's friends descend upon the kitchen for snacks. I hear Derek make some comment under his breath about Brady's stalker being here, and panic fills me. Brady is changing in his room and thankfully didn't hear him, but it's so embarrassing that his friends think I'm some kind of stalker that won't leave Brady alone. I can't deal with them right now. It's hard enough to feel like I'm not even me inside my own skin, this constant reminder that I'm not normal.

I don't go to get my phone or backpack from Brady's room, slipping out the patio door to walk the path to the tree house instead. It's the only place that feels like it's mine, and I need that right now. I curl up in a sleeping bag and cry myself to sleep.

"ZACH, ARE YOU IN THERE?"

Brady's voice brings my eyes open seconds before he's rushing through the doorway and over to me. "Are you okay? Have you been crying?"

I shrug and whisper, "I'm fine."

"You had me worried when I came down to find out you'd left without a word and didn't even take your cell phone with you. Why did you leave?"

My shoulders lift in another shrug. Brady's eyes narrow, and I find myself being dragged from the sleeping bag until I'm in his lap. "Talk to me, Zach. Why were you crying? Did something happen?"

"Do you think I'm a stalker...like you can't get rid of me and I'm following you everywhere?" A tear slips down my cheek at hearing my own words.

Brady tenses and leans back so he can see my face. "Why in the world would you ever think that? You're the most important person in my life, and I want you everywhere I am, *all the time.* It's not the same when you're not with me."

He's so serious that it's easy to believe him.

"Other people think I'm your stalker..."

"What other people? Who said this to you?"

"Don't worry about it," I mumble, wishing I hadn't said anything in the first place.

"I *am* going to worry about it. Who told you that you were my stalk-er?" He forces my chin up when I try to look away. "Tell me, Zach."

"It's nothing. It's just...I overheard Derek telling your other friends that your stalker was there."

Brady's jaw clenches, anger spreading across his face. He's gentle, though, when he hugs me to him tightly. We stay like that for a few minutes before he pats my leg to get up and then follows, taking my hand to leave the tree house. As soon as we are both down the ladder, he lowers himself and pats his back. I know what he wants and climb onto his back for him to carry me back to the house.

"You know I'm too old for you to do this still," I murmur close to his ear.

"You'll never be too old for this. Besides, you barely weigh anything."

I have to admit that he does carry me like it's nothing.

"The next time someone says one mean word about you, I want you to come to me. Don't run away from me. Because none of them mean to me what you do. Do you understand, buddy?"

Buddy is so little kiddish, and it's a reminder that he still sees me as his little brother. Maybe that reminder is good for me. He's so sweet, though, that I lean forward just enough to kiss his cheek.

Neither of us says anything the rest of the way back. It isn't until we get to the patio door that he lets me slide down his body to stand on my own. Gripping my hand tightly, he forces me to follow him into the living room, where I'm unhappy to learn his friends are still sitting along with his parents. He doesn't stop until he's standing in front of Derek, who is lounging on the couch next to Ivy.

"Get up," Brady bites out to his friend.

"Whoa, dude, what's wrong?" Derek gets up, his eyes moving over to me.

"You're leaving. My dad can take you home."

Brady's dad stands, waiting to see how this plays out.

"Dude, what's your problem? You pissed or something?"

"Yeah, I'm pissed. I invite you over, and you talk about my best friend like that?" Brady takes a step closer to Derek. "He's not my stalker, and if I ever hear you say a mean word about him, I'll punch you so hard you'll wish you hadn't. Do I make myself clear?"

Please, God, let me sink into the floor and disappear. Brady's dad now looks as upset as my best friend. His other friends' eyes go wide at the whole exchange.

"Let's go," his dad orders, stepping closer and waiting for Derek to come with him. "You're not welcome in our home anymore."

Wow, I'd never thought that Derek saying something mean about me would cause them to respond this way. It makes my chest burn with emotion that they would defend me like this. Brady's mom comes over to put her arm around me, even though Brady still has a death grip on my hand.

Derek's eyes darken with anger, but he follows Mr. Wellman to the door.

Brady turns to the rest of his friends. "Sorry for the drama, but I won't put up with one unkind word toward Zach. He's as much a part of this family as I am and if you can't be friends with him, then feel free to take your leave."

Connor looks straight at me, and I sidle a little closer to Brady. "I'm sorry, Zach. I didn't join in with Derek, but I should have defended you when I heard him. I hope that we can become friends and you can feel comfortable in our group."

His brown eyes are saying he means it, and I relax, giving him a small nod.

"Thanks, man," Brady says, nudging his friend's foot with his own.

I've never really paid much attention to his friends, but then I always felt like an outsider. Connor is on the football team with Brady and is a fairly tall guy. He's leaner than Brady, with blonde hair that hangs down over his ears. Alex, one of his other friends, gives me a smile that looks genuine. He's shorter than both of them, stockier, and has deep brown skin that matches his warm amber eyes.

It's not lost on me that I've noticed how attractive both his male friends look but not the girls. I wish my brain would stop focusing on guys. It's not normal. *It's because you're...* I push the thought as far back into my mind as I can before it has a chance to form.

Brady takes a seat on the couch and pulls me down next to him, keeping an arm around my back. It's closer than two guys should sit, or at least, I think it is. I don't know what kids do at school. His friends don't say anything, though, and they talk like nothing happened. I notice that Connor tries to include me in the conversation as often as he can, which means a lot to me.

Later that night, Brady's dad comes into his bedroom to sit on the edge of the bed, where we are both watching a movie.

Brady pauses it. "Hey, Dad."

"Son." His dad gives me a smile before looking back at Brady. "I wanted to tell you that I'm proud of you for what you did today."

"I didn't do anything special, Dad."

"I think you did. I should tell you that threatening to punch him might not have been necessary, but I get why you said it. Just remember to keep your cool and find ways to make a stand without using your fists, if at all possible. Although, you know if anyone ever tries to physically hurt you, I expect you to defend yourself."

"I know, Dad."

My dad pops into my mind, and I wish that I could defend myself. What fifteen-year-old still gets beaten by his dad and doesn't do anything about it? Not that it would matter if I fought back because my dad outweighs me by at least a hundred and fifty pounds. He's a big, beefy guy, and I'm this scrawny thing with no strength. I'm not sure where I got my looks from because I don't resemble my dad at all.

That thought rolls around in my head long after his dad leaves us alone. Finally, I can't take it anymore and turn to Brady. "I look nothing like my dad."

He pauses the movie again, turning those deep blue eyes of his toward me. "Isn't that a good thing? Your dad is an ass and ugly as hell."

"I'm glad I don't, but isn't it odd that I have none of his traits? I don't look like my mom either."

His brow furrows in thought. "You think maybe he's not your biological dad?"

I shift in the bed so I'm facing him more. "I've never thought about it before, but if my mom is having an affair now… Couldn't she have had one back then, too?"

"It's possible. You really don't look like either of them." He reaches out to rub my brown strands together between his fingers. "We can pretend he's not your dad and you have a nice one somewhere out there that you don't know about."

That makes me smile. "I'd like that. He can be some geeky science professor that is super cool and nice."

"You could ask your mom?"

"No, then she would know that I know about her affair. Maybe someday when I move out of the house."

Brady sits up, propping himself on his hands and leaning back slightly. "Zach, what are you going to do after high school?"

I've thought about it, but I am terrified to go off on my own. "I don't know. College seems so scary. I know there's this big world out there, but what if I can't survive on my own?"

"You're not going to be on your own. We will do whatever it is, together."

He sounds so determined that I almost believe him. "You can't know that for sure. What if you get a football scholarship or want to go to a different college? What if I don't go to college, but you do?"

"I don't want to play football in college."

"You don't? But you love football?"

"I do love it, but I do it for fun. College football will mean practices and training…and away games. Since I don't want a career in football, I think that my time would be better spent studying."

"What do you want to go to college for?"

Brady tilts his head to the side. "I haven't a clue. Mom and Dad would love it if I become an attorney, but I don't think I can stomach sitting behind a desk and wearing a suit for the rest of my life."

"So basically, neither of us knows what we want to do."

"I'm sure we will know by the time we graduate. We have three more years of school."

I flop back onto my pillow. "I doubt that I'll have the money to go to college even if I wanted to. My parents won't help, and I'll be working just to pay rent so I can leave home."

"I thought we'd get a place together, and as smart as you are, I'm sure that you could get grants and scholarships for college."

Will he still want to live with me once he knows I'm gay? My stomach rolls, and I feel like throwing up over the fact I'd actually let the words form in my head.

You're not gay. You're not gay.

Deep down, I just know that Brady will look at me differently if I tell him that I'm having these thoughts. I could lose him forever over this.

Stop thinking about it!

Rubbing my forehead, I get back to our conversation. "Will your parents help you with college?"

"They don't need to. I have a trust fund that my grandfather left me when he died. It'll be mine when I turn eighteen, and it's enough that I don't have to worry about money."

Our social status is so far apart that I don't think there's a bridge that could span it. I'm happy for my friend, though. "I'm glad you have that, Brady."

"That's why I don't want you to worry about where you're going to live after high school. I can afford a place for us, and if you want to go to college, I'll help you apply for every scholarship out there…or even pay your way."

"What if you get a girlfriend and she wants to live with you?" It'll kill me to watch him with the girl he loves all the time.

"A girlfriend? Hmm…then I guess she'll stay in my room, but I can't see me asking some girl to move in with me right after high school." He flops back on the bed next to me. "Although, neither of us knows how to cook, so maybe she could cook for us so we don't starve."

"I'll learn how to cook…so you don't starve." The thought of cooking for him makes me feel warm inside. I never feel like I can do anything for him like he does for me, but maybe this is something I can manage.

"Aww, buddy, you are sweet," Brady teases, poking me in the side.

"Hey! You know I hate to be poked!" I poke him back, and a wrestling match ensues, which I have no way of winning. Brady pins me down, and I'm mortified to realize that I'm starting to get hard. "Get off me," I beg, suddenly feeling like the world is crashing down around me.

Brady does, and I bolt from the bed and run into the bathroom.

The mirror above the sink shows this pale, scared boy that I don't recognize. Who have I become?

More fears pour through me. *What if people can tell I like boys?* I stare at my high cheekbones and full lips. *Do I look feminine? Do I sound feminine?*

There's a knock on the door, and Brady's voice comes through. "Zach, are you okay?"

No, I'm not okay. I'm hyperventilating and need some air. Leaning over, I try to catch my breath, but the room is spinning, and I end up knocking his cologne bottle off the counter as I try to catch myself from falling.

"Zach?"

Brady's next to me in a flash, putting his arm around my chest to support me. "Take a deep breath and let it out slowly." He repeats that until I have control over my breathing. It reminds me of the first time I ever met him and how he helped me to breathe.

Easing out of his hold, I slide down to the floor and lean against the vanity, hiding my face in my hands. I feel Brady sit down next to me, our arms and legs touching.

"Did I hurt you on the bed?"

His voice sounds so torn that I move my hands away from my face. "No, of course not. You've never hurt me."

"Why did you freak out then?"

Maybe I was lucky, and he didn't feel what happened. "I just panicked," I whisper. I should tell him now. Tell him what a freak I am. *You'll lose him forever.* My stomach lurches, and I move quickly to the toilet to hurl my guts out.

"Fuck," Brady says from behind me, and I feel his hand rubbing my back while I die puking.

When I'm finally able to sit back, he gets me a wet washcloth to wipe my face with. "Just stay here; I'm going to get you some Sprite. It always helps me when I've thrown up."

As soon as he's gone, the tears come, and I fight them with everything in me. I can't fall apart and give in, not if it means that I lose the only person in this world that I love. Forcing myself off the floor, I flush the toilet and wash my hands. I've just managed to brush my teeth when Brady comes back in.

"I told you to stay there until I got back," he chastises me. He doesn't let me walk back to the bed but insists on carrying me.

"I could have walked," I mutter as he pulls the blankets up to my waist and hands me a glass of soda.

"After watching you about fall down and then get sick, I don't think it'll kill you to be carried this one time," he smarts back. "Now, take some sips."

I do and then ask, "Don't you get tired of taking care of me?"

That earns me an *are you stupid* look. "I like taking care of you. If one of us is going to be the superhero, it's going to be me." He raises his arm to show off his muscle, which I'll admit is bigger than most fifteen-year-olds.

A small laugh escapes from my mouth. "You're a dork."

He ruffles my hair with a grin. "Yeah, but I'm *your* dork."

My heart skips a beat, and I rub my chest to ease this feeling. "Yeah, you are," I reply softly.

We finish watching the movie with me curled up against his side and his arm around my back. When he turns off the light for us to sleep, I feel his lips brush against my forehead. "I love you, buddy."

How I get out "I love you, too" without crying is beyond me. As soon as Brady's asleep, I roll over to the edge and press my hand to my mouth to cry quietly.

You're just his buddy. He's straight and you're…gay.
Gay.

How can I deny it after tonight? I got hard when he was on top of me. What type of sick friend does that without their friend's permission? I'm so messed up and dirty. Shame fills me up and comes pouring out in more sobs.

Easing from the bed, I creep out of his room and down the stairs to the living room. Using a pillow, I muffle my sobs until I can get them under control.

I sit here in the dark for hours, trying not to let the truth suffocate me. Some of it is spent praying that God won't hate me and send me to hell.

When the morning light starts to filter in through the blinds, Brady's mom comes out to make breakfast. She stops short when she notices me sitting on the couch. Maybe she sees how I'm about to break apart because she gives me a soft smile but doesn't ask what's wrong with me. I'm sure I look like hell, with puffy red eyes and exhaustion lining my face.

"Do you want to help me make breakfast?"

Nodding, I follow her over to the kitchen, and she gives me a side hug before starting in. I suddenly remember how Brady was worried we would starve after high school. "Mrs. Well…I mean Emily, can you show me how to cook? Please?"

"I would love to, Zach. I can also make copies of all the recipes that have been passed down from my grandma and mom to me. We have some secret ones that we never share outside of our family."

I take the apron she's gotten out of a drawer for me. "Are you sure you want me to have them then?"

Emily smiles as she slips on her own apron. "Zach, you are a part of this family. I'd be honored if you'd learn how to make them."

She teaches me how to make pancakes and scrambled eggs, promising to teach me bacon next time. She's so kind about it and never impatient, giving me side hugs often. I love every minute of it but would love it more if I didn't feel like a five-hundred-pound weight was sitting on my shoulders. The very act of breathing feels difficult right now.

Mr. Wellman comes in to eat before work, and his eyes keep

studying me. I can only imagine what he's thinking about my appearance right now. He exchanges a few looks with Emily but doesn't say anything.

Brady and the girls show up at the same time. I duck my head and avoid looking at Brady, hoping that he won't see what a mess I am. It is a pointless endeavor because the first thing he does is stop on his way to the fridge and hug me.

He leans back to look at me and then scowls. "What the fuck, Zach? Did you sleep at all last night? And why do you look like you've been crying?"

"Brady, language," Mr. Wellman says from behind us.

Brady doesn't even look at his dad; his focus is solely on me. "Zach?"

"I made you pancakes," is all I manage to get out.

His mom comes up to put her arm around my back. "Zach made breakfast. Why don't you sit down and eat before it gets cold?"

My best friend's eyes pin me to the spot. "Fine, but you're going to bed after this, and we *are* talking later."

That's what *he* thinks. I'm going to disappear for the day and avoid the conversation. We sit down to eat, and I watch Brady take a bite of my pancakes.

"They taste just like Mom's. You did good, buddy."

Any pleasure I felt from him liking them is gone with the word *buddy*. I push my food around my plate, but can't find the appetite to eat the breakfast I made. It doesn't go unnoticed by Brady, and he rubs the back of his neck like he's stressed. It's a habit he has when something is bothering him.

"Maybe I should stay home from practice today and make sure you rest."

"No, I'm fine. Go to practice. I need to go home and get some chores done anyway."

He hesitates but finally nods in agreement. I get a long hug before he bikes off to practice. After he's gone, I help Emily with the dishes before walking home.

Mom is in the kitchen when I walk in. "Isaac, can you sweep the garage today while I'm gone? Your dad brought it up last night, and I don't want him upset."

Hi Son, so glad you're home.

Instead, she hardly looks at me.

Why doesn't my mom love me like Emily loves Brady? Does she secretly know I'm gay?

"Sure, Mom, I'll sweep it."

"I'm going to be running some errands and stopping by the church to help with things. It could be later this afternoon before I'm home."

Church things is code for her affair, but I don't say anything. When she doesn't acknowledge me anymore, I carry my backpack down to my bedroom and lie on my hard bed. I miss Brady's bed already. I miss the warmth I feel when I'm at his house or close to him.

As soon as Mom leaves, I force my weary body up to get things done. I throw in a load of my laundry and work on the list of house chores that are my responsibility. Mowing the lawn and weeding the flower bed are next. Exhaustion helps me not to think about the bad stuff because it's all I can do to keep my eyes open while I work. Lastly, I switch my laundry around before sweeping out the garage.

When everything is finished, including my shower, I work on memorizing my five scriptures for the week. It takes longer than usual because I'm so tired. Writing them over and over sometimes helps me, and I do that until my hand hurts.

After folding my laundry and putting it away, I stuff some clean clothes into my backpack for when I go to Brady's next. Like always, I do a once-over through the whole house to make sure I don't forget anything or leave any lights on. Any little thing can set my dad off, and I can't handle it tonight. Not that I can handle it on any other night, but I'm seriously so stressed that I need some peace.

My phone is lit up when I get back to my bedroom, and there are missed texts from Brady on it.

Brady: Hey buddy, where are you?
Brady: Want to come over for supper?
Brady: Buddy?
Brady: Zach?
Brady: Are you okay?
Me: I'm fine. Not coming over. Don't feel good.

I want to go over so badly. The thought of being here with Dad makes me feel sick all over again.

Brady: I'm worried about you. Would you at least come over to sleep?
Me: I'll see how I feel
Brady: I'd rather you be sick here than at home

Why does he have to be so sweet all the time?

Me: I'll be over after supper
Brady: (smiley face emoji)

Why do I always give in when I should be keeping my distance? Not telling Brady this secret is wearing on me. He's my best friend, and I don't like hiding anything from him.

Before Mom gets home, I stuff my cell in the bottom of my backpack and go out to set the table.

She shows up half an hour before Dad is supposed to come home. "Isaac, put these hamburgers on the grill, quickly."

I take the plate she's shoving in my direction and go out to grill them. Would it kill her to hug me just once and maybe say that she loves me?

By the time Dad gets home, the food is on the table and waiting for him. He takes his seat like he's the king and we are his lowly subjects. My parents have this rule that you should eat whatever is on your plate, and I'm smart enough to only take a small scoop of veggies. Dad won't care if I skip the rest, but he's asinine when it comes to vegetables. We eat in silence until Dad is done, and while they retire to the living room, I do the dishes.

Dad's in his recliner when I'm finished, and he calls me in. They are both holding bibles and were probably doing their nightly devotional. Mom has this docile, beloved wife look that drives me crazy now that I know it's a lie.

Dad asks, "Do you have your scriptures memorized?"

His tone and expression are practically screaming he hopes that I don't. They aren't even due for two more days, but he's good about switching it up and claiming that they were due on a different day.

"Yes, sir."

Disappointment flashes across his face for a second before he nods at me to quote them. I carefully recite all five and answer Dad's questions about the scriptures. He seems mollified by my answers and excuses me to go. It only takes me a minute to grab my bag and head out the back door at a run.

Brady is waiting on the patio for me by the time I get there. "Jesus, Zach… You look like you're going to fall over from exhaustion."

"I'm okay."

He takes my backpack from me and grabs my hand to drag me through the house up to his bedroom. "Get ready for bed because you're going to rest all evening."

I want to protest, but he has his arms crossed over his chest and is wearing a scowl. Knowing it's pointless to argue with him when he gets like this, I strip down to my boxers and crawl into his comfortable bed.

Brady follows with a book and raises his arm so I'll scoot over to snuggle against him. He ends up reading until the soothing tone of his voice lulls me to sleep.

IF ONLY THE peaceful sleep had lasted all night, but I wake an hour later to find Brady texting on his cell phone. I can see the name at the top is Brittany, and it breaks my heart a little. I'm going to have to watch him date and kiss and go out with girls. He'll probably ask me to be his best man at his wedding, and I will do it, all the while knowing that he'll never be mine. Or he could ditch me when he finds out the truth, and I won't get to see any of it. Not having him at all would be more than I could bear.

My stomach cramps and I rush off the bed to the bathroom to throw up. The only thing I've eaten today is the small scoop of corn, so mainly it's just dry heaving.

I didn't even know Brady had followed me until he hands me a washcloth for my face. He crosses his arms, giving me another one of his classic scowls that he loves to use, meaning he's pissed and worried at the same time. I can't handle his piercing blue eyes seeing inside me right now and lower my gaze to the floor.

"What the fuck, Zach? You're not sleeping or eating. You're puking but don't have the flu? What is going on with you?"

How do I tell him when I've barely accepted the truth for myself? If I say those two words out loud, it'll be real and definite, with no recourse to choose from. He deserves to know, and it's tearing me up inside.

Sobs pour from me at the sheer agony of hiding something from him.

Brady lowers to the floor, pulling me into his lap and holding me gently. "What is it, Zach? Please tell me."

"I can't," I sob into his chest. "I just want to be normal... I can't lose you."

"Whatever this is...it's not going make you lose me. I promise." He presses his lips to the tears running down my cheek, and it breaks me into pieces.

"I...I'm...I think that I'm...gay," I gasp out between sobs. "I'm sorry, I'm sorry," keeps coming out of my mouth over and over.

It's like every second takes an hour in my mind, this slow motion of torture just waiting for him to reject me.

Brady tightens his arms around me, pressing his head against mine. "Oh buddy, is that what you're tearing yourself apart over? Did you really think you would lose me because you're gay?" He continues without me answering, "You're my best friend, and I love you. Gay or straight, it doesn't change anything. You are who you are, and I love the person you are. If you're gay, you've been gay this whole time, and I loved you then, so I'll love you now."

His words sink into me, and this time the crying is out of sheer relief. Some of the weight that's been suffocating me is gone, so I can breathe again.

"You're not going to leave me?" I hiccup out when my crying is under control.

"We made a pact, didn't we?" He tilts my chin up, so I'm staring into his eyes that are wet with his own tears. "There's nothing you could ever tell me that would make me abandon you."

I wrap my arms around him and hold him as tightly as he's holding me. "I love you, Brady."

"I love you, buddy," he whispers back.

Not even him calling me buddy ruins this moment. I won't be his partner or lover someday, but I can handle that if I don't lose him altogether. He's not going to leave me, and that's all that matters right now.

We sit on the floor like this for a long time until I can't keep my eyes open any longer.

EIGHT

BRADY

Zach's frail body is clinging to me, his fingers digging into my back with a death grip. My shirt is soaked from his tears, but I still don't move from the floor. I can't believe I didn't see this before now. My best friend has been dealing with this on his own and half killing himself over it.

How could he ever think that I would leave him for being gay? The scriptures his dad made him memorize come back to me. Jesus, he's probably dealing with all the religious crap going on in his head, too. I don't think it's safe for him to tell his dad that he's gay. My own stomach feels like throwing up at the thought.

Zach's breathing becomes more even and his grip relaxes, telling me that he's fallen asleep. I maneuver off the floor while holding him and carry him back to my bed. He barely weighs anything, and I have to keep reminding myself that he's my age.

Tucking the blankets up to his chin, I go around to sit on my side of the bed with my laptop, pulling my wet shirt off before getting comfortable. It only takes a minute before he gravitates to lie against me, his head resting on my arm. I put my earbuds in so I won't wake him and start googling one-handed on how to support a friend who comes out as gay. A lot of it is stuff we learned in sex ed. I try to think if there are any gay kids at school, but I don't know any personally. I've heard rumors about a few in the musical program but didn't pay attention to what people were saying. I know in this small conservative town, the LGBTQ+ community is not exactly something people here talk about much. Whereas I was brought up in a big city and seeing lesbian or gay couples walking around was the norm. Plus, my parents have always been very open with us about inclusion and loving people for who they are. But there are a lot of Mr. Matthews's type in this town.

Determination to support Zach every step of the way spreads through me. No one is going to make fun of him or hurt him over this, not as long as I have a breath in me. The articles talk about how each person needs to decide when they want to tell people, and not to out them because it's a deeply personal journey and it's their choice how they do it.

I rack my brain to think of signs he gave that he was gay, but I can't think of any. Maybe his complete lack of interest in Ivy, who has tried to talk to him numerous times. Come to think of it, he always moved away and stuck to me. Knowing his heart, I would imagine he was scared to lead her on when he knew that he wasn't interested.

I know that you're not supposed to stereotype gays, and Zach drives that home. He doesn't have a feminine voice or act different than any other guy. He's just a quiet bookworm that carries this open vulnerability—which he so desperately tries to hide but fails.

Mom peeks in the door, and I close my laptop before she can see what I'm looking at. She comes over and stares down at Zach snuggled up next to me.

"I'm glad to see him sleeping," she whispers. She has to see that he's cried himself to sleep. With his red, swollen eyes, it's totally obvious. All she asks, though, is, "Is he okay?"

"Yeah, he's going to be okay." I refuse to out him, even though I know my parents would support him.

She gives me this nod like she understands I can't tell her anything. "You can come to me if you need help for you or him. Always."

"Thanks, Mom."

She tiptoes out of my room, and I go back to researching anything that might help him. There are a million coming-out videos on YouTube, and after watching several, I'm angry over what they have to go through. Swiping a few tears away, I hear my phone buzz and pick it up to see that Brittany has texted. Shit, I'd forgotten we were texting before.

She's sent one of those duck kissy face pics, and I roll my eyes. I don't know why girls think that we like that shit. They look ridiculous and fake, and after everything that happened with Zach, texting dumb stuff back and forth seems meaningless. I send her a text that I have to go and goodnight. The guys all think that I should ask her out, but I'm not sure I'm ready for that. I can't even drive yet, and I don't think my parents would go for it anyway. Nothing like saying, *Hey, will you go out with me? My mom and dad will pick you up.* Yeah, totally lame.

Zach stirs beside me, and I close my laptop, laying it behind him on the bed so it's out of the way. His glassy green eyes flicker open and look up at me. I can see the second he remembers what he told me because his cheeks pinken and he looks away.

"Hey, don't get upset. Everything is fine," I tell him, laying my hand over his that is still gripping my arm.

"Are you sure you aren't mad at me?" His voice is hoarse from crying so much. "I kept it from you...and you're the person I tell everything."

"Zach, you should never feel like you owe anyone an explanation about your sexuality. Not even me." I squeeze his hand gently. "I'm glad you told me, though, because I want to be there for you every step of the way."

"Thanks, Brady." He gives my arm a loving kiss that threatens to make me tear up all over again.

"Can we talk about it all?"

Zach lets go of my arm and moves into a sitting position, crossing his legs in front of me. I do the same, facing him and taking both of his hands in mine.

"What do you want to know?" he asks hesitantly.

"How long has this been tearing you apart?"

"Do you remember when we first met and Dad had beaten me for reading a non-Christian book?"

"Yeah, I remember."

He shrugs. "It was a book about two boys. I don't think I really knew why I got the book. I just wanted to read that one so badly. It felt right to me." He stares off behind me. "After that, I didn't really think about it for a while, but then slowly, I noticed that I was attracted to boys and not girls. I think it was your 14th birthday party that I started fighting with myself over the truth. You were talking about Brittany and how she was cute, and I didn't find her cute at all. And it's been downhill from there..."

"You were so quiet that day, and I didn't have a clue what was wrong." Maybe I should have tried harder to find out what was going on with him.

"I wouldn't have told you… I hadn't admitted it to myself yet." His green eyes pool liquid, but he blinks the tears away. "I didn't admit it to myself until last night."

"You panicked over me wrestling with you… Do you need me to stop being this close to you? I don't want to make you uncomfortable, being close to a guy." The question forms a lump in my throat. I'll be devastated if he doesn't want to be close anymore.

He thinks for a minute before answering. "I'm going to be honest about it. When we wrestled…my…errr body…responded without me wanting it to."

My eyes widen with understanding. "Oh, I see."

"I panicked because I felt so guilty, even though I have no control over it."

"So you're attracted to me?" For some reason, that makes me grin.

He rubs his thumb over my hand in light circles. "Let's say Ivy and you were best friends. You knew that she liked girls, and you'll never be together, but you hang out and are super close. You love each other. She's sweet and pretty, but you respect her and would never willingly do anything to disrespect the friendship. But then one night, you're wrestling and she's lying on top of you. Even though your brain knows not to react, do you think your body would?"

I've never really experienced anything with a girl before, so I have no clue what my body's response would be. But I'm not telling him that right now. "I would probably have the same reaction you did."

"Doesn't mean you want to have sex with her, though."

"True. I would be scared she would be offended or take it the wrong way and end the friendship."

He looks down. "That's why I panicked. You're my world, Brady. I don't ever want to do anything to ruin that."

"You're not going to ruin it. If something like that happens again, we'll just laugh it off because we are best friends and should be able to be comfortable around each other."

"I would never do anything to hurt our friendship," he says earnestly, tears in his eyes all over again.

"I know you wouldn't. Nothing has to change simply because I'm hot and you like boys," I tease.

He grins and relaxes a little. "Whatever, you're not that hot." The blush spreading across his face tells me he's lying, but it makes me feel good.

"Not to get serious or anything, but you haven't told your parents, have you?"

A shudder wracks his body for a second, sheer panic in his eyes. "No, my dad will kill me if he finds out!"

I can tell he's about to flip out and pull my hands free so I can move him to my lap. His body stops trembling once I wrap my arms around him tightly. "You can't tell him, Zach. It's not safe for you to be honest about it at home, and as much as I want you to be yourself, I don't trust your dad either. Promise me you'll be careful, and if he so much as threatens to hurt you, you tell me. Promise me, please?"

"I promise if he tries to hurt me for being gay, I'll tell you."

He seems sincere, so I relax a little. "Are you going to tell anyone but me?"

"I don't think that's a good idea. If someone finds out and tells my dad... It's best if I just stay in the closet until I leave home."

"You could tell my parents, and they wouldn't tell anyone."

"No. What if they make me stop staying with you? They might think a guy like me shouldn't sleep in your bed."

My parents are pretty cool, but I don't want to take chances about that either. Zach needs me too much, and he would feel rejected. I won't do that to him. "Okay, whatever you want."

"Brady? Do you think God hates me now and that I'll go to hell?"

Religion is pissing me off. "No, Zach. You have to stop believing everything your dad has told you and start finding your own beliefs. You are the gentlest and kindest person I've ever met, and if there is a God, he definitely doesn't hate you."

"I spent so much time this last year trying to pray this away, but it didn't work."

"Because it's who you are and who you are meant to be."

He sighs, reaching his hand up behind him to rub my cheek. "I think Dad suspected after the book. He's threatened conversion therapy a few times in passing when talking about *if I'd ever have gay thoughts.*"

I've heard horror stories about conversion therapy, and real fear pulses through me. I turn my head to kiss his hand. "Your dad can never find out, and if he does and threatens to take you, I want you to get out of there as fast as you can."

Zach trembles in my arms. "I'll try, but he's so much bigger than me."

"Call me. Whatever you do, don't go with him. Those places are hell from what I've heard about them. I'll get my dad involved, and we'll figure out a way to stop him." There's a movie about conversion therapy, but I haven't watched it yet. I will, but not with Zach around. I don't want to scare him more than he already is. "Are you feeling better about telling me now?"

"It's a huge relief. I really needed you," he admits quietly.

"You have me." I pat his leg. "Now you're going to eat something if I have to feed it to you myself, bite by bite."

"I am kind of hungry now that I am not worried about losing you."

I hate that he's been so worried about losing me that he hasn't been able to eat. Even as he gets off the bed, I can see how weak and exhausted he is. "Get on my back, and I'll carry you downstairs."

He does and I carry him down to the kitchen, leaning back by the barstool to let him off. "What sounds good?"

That only earns me a half-shrug. I doubt he would eat if I weren't forcing the issue. The fridge has all sorts of leftovers, but I don't think tacos or spaghetti are a good idea on his unsettled stomach. "What about toast? Might be easier on your stomach after throwing up?" At least that's what my mom always tells me when I'm sick.

"Whatever is fine."

Mom and Dad join us, both of them looking over at Zach with worry.

"What are you two up to?" Mom asks.

"I'm making him some toast."

She walks over to run her hand over Zach's head. "Would you like scrambled eggs, sweetie?"

"You don't have to do that but thank you for offering."

"It's no problem. A little protein might do you good."

Mom makes scrambled eggs quickly, and soon Zach is forking some into his mouth. Dad still hasn't said much, but I can tell he's worried about my best friend, too.

Zach manages to eat almost all his food, and I carry him back upstairs the same way as coming down.

After we both shower, we lie in bed with him half splayed over my chest. I strum my fingers over his forehead and cheek until he's asleep before following him into dreamworld.

NINE

ZACH

Brady has been glued to my side ever since I told him that I am gay. If he's not trying to force food down my throat, he's bossing me to take a nap. I know that losing his brother has made him super protective, and honestly, I love that he's like this.

My best friend insists that we learn about the LGBTQ+ community together. I can tell he wants me to feel comfortable sharing things with him and is putting in the effort. We watch coming out videos first but then start to watch vlogs made about single gay guys or couples on YouTube. It's weird to see other people like me who seem completely comfortable with their sexuality.

We read up on the nicknames for gay body types because when couples mentioned twinks and bears, neither of us knew what they were talking about.

Brady looks over at me. "So I guess you're a twink?"

"I guess so. I am tiny. But who knows, maybe I'll grow a ton in the next few years."

That earns me a dubious smile. "I have a feeling you're going to stay a twink."

"Probably, I can't picture me big and hairy with tons of muscles."

He laughs, shaking his head. "God no, you are definitely not a bear."

"Brady?"

"Hmm?"

"Thanks for doing this with me," I murmur, moving to kiss his arm.

"You're welcome, buddy."

THINGS ARE GOING PRETTY WELL until Brady goes back to school at the end of August. Being at home all day brings a sense of sadness that I have a hard time shaking off.

My mom is home less and less. When she is home, she's distracted, and it's almost like she's trying to forget that I exist. I've heard my dad and her having arguments at least a few nights every week. I'm constantly worried he'll take it out on me and end up sleeping at Brady's most nights.

The first week in December, my life gets turned upside down. Mom's been home all morning, gathering up various things and disappearing into her bedroom. I'm sitting at the table doing my homework when she hauls out some suitcases.

"Isaac, take these out to the porch for me," she says, her eyes not meeting mine.

They are heavy and definitely full of stuff, but I obey and lug them out to the porch, shivering at the chilly wind we are having today. Shielding my eyes, I see a car idling in the driveway; the man she's been having an affair with is sitting in the driver's seat. When he notices me, he gets out and comes over to get the suitcases, avoiding looking my way the entire time.

Fear starts in the pit of my stomach, and I rush back in to see Mom holding a box with her purse on top.

"Mom? Where are you going?"

She finally looks at me. "I'm leaving your dad and moving to Texas."

"What about me?" I move closer to stand in her path. "You can't leave me here with him, please, Mom."

"Get a hold of yourself, Isaac. I can't take you with me."

"He'll hurt me, Mom! You know he will!"

"Move aside, Isaac. Trey is waiting on me."

When I don't move, she walks around me and hurries toward the door. I follow her out to the porch, but she doesn't even turn around to look at me or say she loves me. She just gets in the car, and they drive away.

I'm not sure how long I stand here waiting for her to change her mind and come back, but it feels like hours. Finally, I go inside and sit in the living room in her chair, waiting for the inevitable hell that is about to happen with my dad.

The garage door opens, and I flinch at the sound. I hear him come in and wash his hands before calling out my mother's name. He stops still when he sees me sitting here and then scowls. "What's going on? Where's your mother, and why isn't there any food on the table?"

I clear my throat. "She left."

He comes closer. "Left? Left for where?"

"Texas," I whisper.

"Texas? What are you talking about?"

"She packed up her stuff and said she was leaving you and moving to Texas. Now she's gone."

Dad's face turns red, and he storms off toward their bedroom. Drawers slam and I hear him yelling. He comes back to the living room, shaking with rage. "Why didn't you stop her?"

"I tried, Dad, but she wouldn't listen to me." I sob out the words.

"It has to be your fault! She would never have left me! What did you do?" He's screaming now, and I know this is going to be bad.

"I didn't do anything, I promise."

"Go to your room! I don't even want to look at you!"

I hurry to my room, praying that he'll leave me alone. I think about texting Brady, but I'm scared to even get my cell out of its hiding spot right now. I pace my room while reminding myself that I've lived through this before and I can again.

My bedroom door opens, and Dad's standing there with a belt. "You're going to pay for her leaving. This is your doing; I know it."

"Dad…please, don't do this," I beg, hating myself for it at the same time.

He comes in and grabs my arm. I'm fifteen, and I'm so sick of this. I try to fight him this time, but he's so much stronger than me that all it does is piss him off more.

By the time he's done, I can feel sticky blood run down the side of my hip. Something inside of me dies in that moment, and I don't think that I'll ever get it back.

. . .

Hours after lying on my bed, I stumble to the bathroom and try to clean myself up. Dad has shut himself in his room, and I quietly get my cell out from its hiding place.

> Me: Won't be over tonight
> Brady: Why? You okay?
> Me: I'm okay. Dad wants me to stay home
> Brady: You sure you're okay?
> Me: I'm okay
> Brady: Text me if you need me
> Me: Love you
> Brady: Love you

God, I want nothing more than to beg him to come here and protect me. I can't risk it, though. What if Dad bans me from seeing Brady ever again? Worse yet, what if he makes us move? I'll suffer through anything to stay close to Brady.

All night I lie on my stomach and pray that my dad will leave me alone. I faintly hear him leave in the morning and edge out of bed to see if I can find any pain meds in the house. Four Advils later, I crawl back into bed because it hurts too much to sit down.

The day passes with me in a numb haze of hiding away in my mind. When the clock shows Brady should be finished with school for the day and on his way home, I get up and retrieve my cell from my backpack to carry into the bathroom with me. I know he'll text soon, wondering why I'm not over there yet.

Pulling my shirt off, I step into the shower and lean against the tiled wall as the water runs over my back. The cuts burn like fire, a painful reminder of what I let my dad do to me. I try to think back over the years to a single time my dad beat me for something I actually did wrong. Maybe this is God's way of punishing me for being gay. The videos of gay couples that Brady and I watched flit through my mind. There was so much love between them. I can't believe that it's wrong.

Turning the water off, I carefully pat my body dry and turn so I can see my back in the mirror. Blackish blue bruises cover my lower back and down to my thighs. Welts and open slices mix in to add red across my skin. It's the worst that Dad has ever beaten me, and I don't know how to hide this from Brady. I know he'll tell his parents if he sees me like this, and I can't risk being taken away from my best friend.

It hurts to wrap a towel around my waist, and I finally just hold it to my front, picking up my cell to carry back to the bedroom with me. It buzzes, signaling the text from Brady that I was expecting. I have two hours until Dad gets home, and I need to figure out a way to go to Brady's without him noticing how much pain I'm in.

I'm almost to my bedroom door when my dad comes around the corner from the kitchen.

He's supposed to be at work.

It takes him about two seconds to see I'm carrying a cell phone. I back into my room as he walks toward me.

"Give it to me," he orders, holding his big, beefy hand out for the phone.

"It's not mine; it's Brady's," I say quietly as I hand it over.

He doesn't say anything as he looks through the messages, reading everything Brady and I have texted each other. His face is mottled red by the time he's done, and I watch as he throws the phone across the room. "Love you! Love you!" Spit flies out of his mouth as he yells, "Boys don't tell boys that they love them unless they are fucking faggots!"

Dad hits me across the face so hard that it sends me to the floor, my glasses flying off to somewhere behind me.

He looks down at me, lying at his feet. "Painted toenails? You really are a fag! I won't have a demon possessing my son!"

I'd forgotten about the painted nails. It has nothing to do with me being gay. Meg and Anna are obsessed with painting nails right now, and they painted everyone's toes during movie night with Brady's family. Even his dad let them paint his toes because it makes the girls happy.

Before I can explain, my dad screams, "I'm calling Pastor Dan and sending you to conversion therapy!"

Brady…

I scramble up from the floor and back away until my legs hit the bed, shaking my head. "No! I won't go! You can't make me!"

Dad snaps. I can see it in his face as he goes into a full-on rage. His fist connects with my face, and the room spins. Pain sears through my stomach, and somehow, it registers that he's punched me there, too. I don't realize I'm on the floor until I see his shoe coming at me. I try to cover my face and curl up into a ball to protect myself as he kicks me.

"Pack your bags; you're going to therapy," I faintly hear him yell before he walks out of my room. It's weird how sounds can be magnified yet muffled.

"Brady," I moan, consumed by the thought of leaving him. Without my glasses, everything is blurry, but I can just make out the shape of my cell on the floor across the room. A small glimmer of hope drives me to scoot my body over to it, ignoring the excruciating pain and trying to keep the black from edging in on my vision.

By some miracle, the cell isn't broken, and I hit Brady's number, praying he answers before Dad comes back in.

Brady, all I need is Brady.

TEN

BRADY

Z ach isn't at my house when I get home, and the unease I've felt all day grows into full-blown worry. I dig my cell out of my pocket and send Zach a text before getting the orange juice out of the fridge.

After a few minutes with no response, I text him again. If his mom is home, I don't want to get him in trouble by calling.

I'm just plopping down on my bed to do homework when he calls.

"Hey, you coming over?"

"Brady..." It's barely even a whisper.

"Zach? Are you okay?"

"Help me...hurt bad..." His weak voice fades in and out. "...sending me away...don't let him take me."

I'm already running for the stairs when I hear a faint sob and then nothing. My heartbeat is pounding in my ears as I run out the back door, calling nine-one-one as I go.

"Nine-one-one, state your emergency."

"I need police at seven twelve East Arbor Street. My friend is hurt."

"How do you know he is hurt? Who is hurting him?"

"He called me and it's his dad. Just send someone now!"

There's a brief pause while she says something in the background.

"They are on their way. Are you there?"

"Almost." My lungs feel like they are going to burst out of my chest from running so fast through the woods. "Call my dad, Judge Wellman, and tell him I need him at Zach's house."

"Judge Wellman is your dad?"

"Yes, call him!"

"We are contacting him now. Wait to go into the house until the police get there and stay on the phone."

Never going to happen. I reach Zach's backyard and shove my cell into my pocket as I plow through the backdoor that I'm grateful is unlocked.

"Brady," I hear Zach moan out and then his dad yelling. I've barely been to his house a handful of times, but it's small, and it only takes me a few seconds to run to his bedroom. Zach is on the floor, naked and moaning, with his dad standing over him, screaming and holding a belt. A mixture of agony and rage pours through me, and I see red, moving faster to ram my body into his dad's to knock him away from Zach. We both crash into the wall, but whereas I think he's stunned over the impact, I immediately scramble back to Zach to stand in front of him.

His dad gathers his wits and realizes it's me. "I should have never let you two spend time together. You've turned my son into a Satan-worshiping queer! Get out of my house, or I'm going to teach you a lesson, too."

"I'm not letting you hurt him," I grit out, watching him advance and ignoring how badly my body is trembling.

"It's my right as his father to discipline him!"

"This isn't discipline!" He's getting too close, and I want him away from Zach, who hasn't moved at all.

His dad swings the belt out, and I lunge forward to throw my body into him again, sending us both backward to the floor. I've never punched anyone before, and it hurts my hand way more than I'd imagined. My satisfaction that his nose spurts blood is short-lived when he rolls us over. I'm as tall as him and in better shape, but Zach's dad is overweight and heavy. His fist raises back, and I jerk my head to the side just enough that it doesn't connect fully but still makes it feel like my head is exploding. One minute he's raising his fist again, and the next, he's flying off to the side. A police officer is on top of him, pinning him down as another one rushes in to help.

Zach!

I crawl over to him in a rush, terrified that he's dead. His body is a mess, and I can't tell which part is bleeding.

"Zach...Zach." I sob, smoothing back the hair from his face. A face that I can barely recognize with the swelling and blood.

"Brady?" It's only the faintest of sounds.

"I'm here..." My own tears drip down his cheek. "You're okay. I'm here."

Mr. Matthews is yelling behind me as they drag him out of the room. I wish Dad were here because I don't know what to do now.

A police officer kneels down next to me and leans over to pick up a towel on the carpet nearby, draping it over Zach's lower half. "You need to move so I can see him."

I scoot up a little but refuse to move any further. The officer feels for a pulse and then looks up at me. "You Judge Wellman's son?"

I nod.

"And this is?"

"Zach...Isaac Matthews," I answer, running my fingers over Zach's hair gently.

"I'm Officer Andrews. You both are safe now. The squad will be here any second to help Zach."

He stays kneeling by me, his hand on my back. "You were really brave, but everything's going to be okay now."

The paramedics come rushing in, and the officer moves a little behind me.

"Let us work," one of them says to me, but I still refuse to move.

"He can stay," Officer Andrew orders, "and he needs his face looked at."

My head is pounding, but I'm too focused on Zach to care.

When they roll him onto his back, he cries out this painful sound that breaks my heart. I cry right along with him but keep my hand on his hair so he knows I'm still here.

They put in an IV and give him some oxygen. Zach's shaking so much that his teeth are chattering when he moans.

"It's the shock," Officer Andrews explains to me.

A paramedic looks at my face and then presses an ice pack against the upper part of my cheek and by my eye.

It's at that moment that my dad comes in the room. The look on his face when he sees me is one I've never seen on him before. He's pissed, beyond pissed. His eyes move to Zach and he visibly pales.

Officer Andrews gets up to move so my dad can squat down next to me, putting his arm around my back.

"Are you all right?"

I nod, leaning into him a little for the support I know he'll give. We both watch as the paramedics check Zach's vitals again.

The paramedic must recognize my dad because she pauses to tell him, "We are taking him to Rockville Health if you want to ride along."

"My wife is outside and will ride with him," he informs her.

There is no way I'm leaving Zach. "I'm going with him, too."

She shakes her head and starts to tell me no, but Dad intervenes. "He is going along. He needs his head looked at as well." Dad brushes my hair back so he can see the side of my face better. "Did that bastard hit you?"

"Yeah, I was trying to keep him away from Zach until the police could get here."

"You did real good, Brady. I'm proud of you," Dad says, side-hugging me tightly.

We follow the paramedics out of the house, and Mom starts crying when she sees us. She hugs me, but I pull away to follow Zach to the ambulance. Mom and Dad are right behind me, and I hear him say, "You go with Zach and Brady to the hospital. I want to talk to the police, and then I'll join you. I want to make sure this is done right so he doesn't get away with it."

The ride to the hospital is short since this is a small town. The nurses run out along with a doctor, and I'm forced to stand aside while they rush him into the hospital.

Mom has to drag me away from his room and into the one they have for me. I spend the entire time pacing and worrying Zach will need me.

The doctor comes in to look at my face, but it's not Zach's doctor, and he says he doesn't know anything about his condition.

Dad joins us, along with Officer Andrews and another man that introduces himself as Chief Kuhn. They ask me to give my account, and I tell them everything I can.

Officer Andrews writes it all down. "We've discovered that his mother left them yesterday and is on her way to Texas. She's not answering her cell, and we've yet to locate her."

His mom left him? I can't believe he didn't tell me last night when he texted.

His doctor comes in to update everyone, and Dad keeps his hand on my shoulder while we listen to the news. "Isaac's condition is stable for now. We've sedated him because he was in so much pain and upset. He kept asking for Brady." The doctor gives me a slight nod and then continues. "He has a lot of edema and bruising, but it's his spleen I'm most worried about right now. There's considerable swelling. Most likely from being hit or kicked there. We are going to watch it, but there's a chance it could rupture and require immediate surgery."

I've never wished anyone dead before, but in this moment, I want his dad to die a slow and painful death.

"I don't think this is the first time he's been abused. There are lacerations that look older than a few hours. Some of the bruising and open wounds are probably a day old. There are some scars that I would say are from the last year or two, maybe longer."

Guilt spreads through me that I didn't know and didn't protect him. I should have told my dad the second I saw the welts the first time. "It's not the first time his dad has beaten him," I interject, gaining all of their attention. "When I first met Zach in the woods, he was crying and had welts on his back. He asked me not to tell anyone and said if it happened again, he would tell me." I swallow back the lump in my throat. "He never mentioned it again. I didn't know it was still happening. I didn't know."

The doctor puts his hand on my arm. "Most abuse victims hide it and no one knows. This isn't your fault, and from what I've heard, you saved your friend's life today."

Dad squeezes my shoulder, but none of it makes me feel any better. Zach is so small and couldn't defend himself. I should have been the one to defend him.

They finally let me go in to see him, and I barely recognize my best friend. His face is swollen and his lip busted open. There's a cut next to his eye where the skin split, and they've stitched it. I sit next to his bed, holding his hand until they make me leave so the nurses can work on him.

In the waiting room, I sit in silence next to my dad as he calls the mayor, the district attorney, and some private investigator to help find Zach's mom. He talks to Social Services, and I hear him asking about getting guardianship over Zach.

"I am going down to the jail to see if I can get guardianship papers signed by his dad," I hear him tell Mom. "I expect Social Services to show up in the morning to take over."

They exchange a look that I don't like.

"You won't let them take him away?" I ask Dad before he leaves.

He squeezes my shoulder with his hand and shakes his head. "I'm doing everything in my power to keep him with us, okay, Son?"

I nod. "Okay, thanks, Dad."

"Is there anything you can tell me about his family or his mom that might help us locate her?"

"She's been having an affair for a while. We saw her with the guy at the park over a year ago. He's shorter than me...more Mom's height, with brown hair. I think his car was blue. I don't know much." I rack my brain to think of anything else. "Zach has been wondering if his dad is really his dad."

"Thank you, Brady. That might help."

Dad leaves and they let us back in Zach's room. I know that we aren't family and aren't supposed to be in here, but this is a small enough town that they are turning a blind eye. I've never really cared about money or social status before, but I'm grateful right now that my dad has the power and influence to help Zach.

Zach cries in his sleep off and on, which makes me cry, too. Mom tries to get me to go home to rest, but I refuse to leave Zach for anything other than using the bathroom. The nurses bring in pillows and some blankets for Mom and me to use during the night.

It's four in the morning when Zach's monitor starts to alarm. I watch in horror as the nurses run in and check his blood pressure again. We are shoved to the side as the doctor comes in and checks him over, too. They wheel his bed out of the room, and the doctor pauses long enough to explain to us what's happening. "They are taking him to prep for surgery. We think his spleen has ruptured, and he's bleeding internally. That causes the blood pressure to drop, and his is going down rapidly. We've called in our best surgeon for him; he's on his way."

He doesn't wait around for us to ask questions. I leave Mom, walking out to the waiting room because I have to move. She follows and I hear her on the phone with Dad, telling him what's happening.

Pacing the room, I go from wanting to punch something to praying to a God I'm not sure I believe in or even want to believe in.

Dad and my sisters show up half an hour later. I'm not ashamed to admit that I cry when Dad hugs me. We end up sitting as a family, holding hands for the next two and a half hours until a doctor comes in to talk to us.

"I'm Dr. Hollis, the surgeon who performed Isaac's splenectomy. The surgery went well, but we did have to remove his spleen. He's lost a lot of blood and has needed two blood transfusions so far. We've moved him to ICU to monitor him more closely. Isaac's underweight, and with all the trauma to his body, I think he needs the extra care. We will be watching him for infection, but this next week is vital."

Dad asks, "How long do you think he'll be staying here?"

"At least a week so we can monitor him, and four to six weeks total recovery. He will be more susceptible to infection and will need to take precautions, but we can discuss that before he's released."

"Thank you, Dr. Hollis. When can we see him?"

"It'll be a couple of hours. I'll have a nurse show you to the ICU waiting room." He eyes my sisters. "They won't be able to see him, and if anyone is sick, they need to stay away from him."

A nurse shows up to guide us up a floor and into the ICU waiting room. Dad googles the procedure and reads the precautions and complications of not having a spleen aloud to us. It sounds scary what could happen if he gets sick while healing and even later on in life.

"Did you get guardianship?"

Dad looks at me. "His dad signed guardianship over to me, but I either have to get his mom's signature, too, or Zach has to wake up and sign the paper. It has to be two out of three. The firm I hired to find her is good, and I pulled some strings to track her cell to a general location. We should know more this morning."

"How did you get his dad to sign over guardianship? He must hate us right now."

Dad lowers his voice. "The DA cut a deal for a guilty plea and for him to sign over guardianship. He will serve less time, but it's better this way. Zach won't have to go through a trial and his dad signed the paperwork."

I'm guessing not everything Dad did was normal protocol, and he called in favors. "Thank you for helping him, Dad."

"We love him, too. He belongs with us, and I don't want to ever see either of you hurt like this again."

Mom ends up taking the girls home and says she'll be back as soon as Grandpa and Grandma fly in. I'm amazed at how my family is pulling together for Zach. My grandparents see him at Christmas and love him as much as we do.

Zach is deathly pale when I am finally allowed into his room. I'm glad he's asleep and not feeling the pain he must be in. I scoot my chair as close as I can and hold his hand, resting my head on the bed next to him to close my eyes for a few minutes.

The nurses wake me up later, and I feel like my body has been run over. The side of my face hurts worse today than it did yesterday, but I ignore it.

Mom shows up to take over for Dad, who leaves to deal with guardianship issues. She gives me some painkillers and gets a soft ice pack for my face. I can tell she's upset over me being hurt, but she refrains from saying anything.

A social worker comes into the room close to noon and asks to speak to my mother in the hallway. The door opening again catches my attention, and I look up to see Mom motioning for me to come out of the room. She looks really upset.

"Brady, they aren't going to let us in with him since we aren't family. We have to stay in the waiting room."

"No! You can't do that to him! He will freak out if he wakes up and I'm not there!"

The social worker gives me a condescending look. "He will be fine. Kids are resilient."

"You don't know him," I bite back.

As soon as we are in the waiting room, I ask, "Where is Dad?"

"He's trying to get Judge Harris to fit in the guardianship hearing today. Your dad can't sign off on the case since it's personal. He was able to get Zach's mom to sign guardianship papers, but there are a few other hoops to jump through to get this done legally." She hugs me, but it doesn't help. I need to be with Zach, and all I can think about is him waking up without me there.

Mom suggests I go home to shower, but I refuse. I do change into the clean clothes she brought and stuff down a sandwich that I don't even taste. Time passes slowly until I feel like I'm going to go out of my mind.

Around three, a nurse comes into the little waiting room looking for us. "Isaac is awake and won't calm down. He keeps asking for Brady. The social worker is gone, and the doctor said that we won't notice if you happen to be in his room. We would rather not have to continuously sedate him."

I'm already off the chair and walking as fast as I can to his room. He's on his side, dry heaving into a little pink tray the nurse is holding for him. His heart monitor is beeping rapidly. The nurse moves out of my way, and he sees me. "Brady…"

"I'm right here," I say, my voice catching with emotion as I take his hand.

Zach inches back, even though I can tell it hurts like hell. I know what he wants and lie down facing him, letting him bury his face in my chest to cry. "I'm sorry," he sobs.

"You have nothing to be sorry for." I can't hold back my own tears. "You're okay. I'm here." I gently put my arm around his upper back, trying to avoid putting any weight on him.

"Don't leave me," he sobs, clinging to me.

"I'm not leaving you," I promise. They will have to drag me out of here to get me to leave.

Mom is standing on the other side of the bed, crying too. How anyone could listen to Zach cry and not cry themselves is beyond me.

Zach falls asleep and I stay with him, regardless of what nurses come in and out. They don't ask me to move either.

When Zach wakes again, he calms as soon as he sees me still here.

"Hey…you look like hell," I quip, giving him a half-grin.

He manages a small grin back.

The room door opens and Dad comes in along with another man, a woman following them. They take in Zach and me lying here with him clinging to me, and I see the horror on their faces over what Zach looks like.

The man steps closer. "Isaac, I'm Judge Harris. I'm sorry to have to do this now. I know you've been through a lot, but we need to get this taken care of quickly, and since you couldn't come to court, we brought it to you."

Zach tenses next to me, his heart monitor beeping a little faster. "Don't take me away from Brady," he says slowly, obviously hurting.

Dad moves to stand next to Zach's side. "Don't worry, Zach. Just answer his questions."

"Your parents have signed legal guardianship over to the Wellmans. Are you okay with them being your guardians and living with them?"

He gives a slight nod and then winces from doing it.

"You have to say it out loud for the recorder," Judge Harris says.

I notice the lady is sitting and typing away on something.

"Yes, I want to live with them."

"I've heard you're a big part of their family already. Do you have any questions or concerns about staying with them?"

"No."

Judge Harris gives my dad a nod and then smiles at Zach. "Thank you, young man, for speaking to me. I'm sorry for all you've gone through."

By the time they leave, Zach looks like all his energy is gone. The nurse comes in to give him some pain meds through his IV, and soon he's fighting to keep his eyes open. "Do I really get to stay with you?" he whispers.

"Yes, you get to live with us."

A tear slides down his cheek, and then his eyes close. I don't think I can ever thank my dad enough for all he's done to make this happen.

THE NEXT WEEK is spent at the hospital with Zach. The nurses let me shower in Zach's bathroom, even though they aren't supposed to. I refuse to leave him to go home for anything. Anytime Zach wakes and doesn't see me, he panics, and it takes a bit for him to calm down.

He hasn't said much about what happened yet, and I don't push him to talk about it.

By the time they release him from the hospital, the swelling has gone down around his eye, but the bruising is still vivid with colors.

My parents completely redid what used to be the girl's toy room into a bedroom for Zach. I told them he could share my room, but they insisted that he should have his own room, in case he wants privacy.

They show him his new bedroom when we get home, and he stands there like he doesn't know what to do or say. They know what Zach likes, and there are tons of books everywhere. He has his own TV with Disney movies stacked on a shelf for him. There are little touches everywhere that show how much thought they've put into it. They painted the walls a bluish green, but there are touches of every color in the rainbow in here.

He walks over to the desk and runs his finger over the laptop they put there. "This is mine?"

Mom gives him a smile. "Yes, it's all yours. Your clothes from home are here, but I thought as soon as you feel up to it, we can go shopping to get new ones."

"You don't have to do that. I'll be happy with what I have."

I get the feeling he's uncomfortable with them buying him things.

"We'll leave you to get some rest. I know Grandma and Grandpa would like to see you before they fly home, and Connor has stopped by several times to see if you were back."

Zach does look exhausted, but he's eyeing his bed with worry. I take his hand and walk with him down to my room, where I carefully help him get his shoes and pants off before he crawls into bed. It still makes me sick every time I see the bruises all over his skin, but I pretend it's all fine.

He moves into his usual spot in the middle of the bed and closes his eyes. "Will you stay with me until I fall asleep?"

"I'm going to pass out with you. I barely slept at the hospital, with the nurses always coming in and out of your room." I take off my own jeans and slide into bed, too.

It still hurts him to have any pressure near his incision, so I let him curl up against me, instead of me holding him. I'm pretty sure we are both asleep in seconds.

ELEVEN

ZACH

I think that my dad actually killed me, and I went to heaven. Living with the Wellmans can't really be true. I keep waiting for the bad news that my dad is back home, and I have to live there again.

The first week home—can't believe it's my home—is spent resting. They let Brady stay home with me, but he spends a lot of the time sitting on the bed next to me doing homework. I've yet to sleep in my room and don't want to be alone. This whole incident has made me clingy and scared to be without Brady. I know it's not rational, but the fear is there, nonetheless.

The school sends a teacher over to test me to see where I am in my classes, and since I've been so tired, they break it up into two hours for three days. Brady always makes sure to sit at the opposite end of the table, doing his own homework while the teacher is here.

Football season is over, and I discover Brady backed out of playing basketball after what happened. He seems sincere when he says it doesn't matter to him, and I'm too tired to fight him over it.

Slowly my body has been healing, and it looks like I'll be starting public school next week. I'm not allowed to do any sports or physical activities for the next month, but that's okay with me. The testing shows I'm ahead of most kids in my grade and qualify for AP classes.

My anxiety over going to school grows the closer to the weekend I get. To the point that Brady's parents talk to the school about putting me in all of his classes and making sure my locker is close to his.

Brady finally lets Connor come over on Saturday after he's repeatedly asked to visit. We are sitting on Brady's bed when his friend comes bursting into the room.

Connor's face reflects how bad I still look from what happened. "Jesus, Zach, I've been so worried about you."

"Not worried about me?" Brady throws a pillow at his friend.

Connor throws it back. "Jealous?"

"Yeah, totally." Brady smirks.

Connor sits down on the bed and hands me a stuffed puppy. "Thought you might need a buddy."

I hug it to my chest. "Thanks, Connor, that was sweet of you."

He grins and shrugs his shoulders. "So I hear you're going to be coming to school next week?"

"Yes, but I'm a bit terrified," I murmur, lifting an ear on the puppy and watching it flop down.

"No reason to be scared, Brady and I've got your back."

I look up to see the sincerity in Connor's brown eyes. "Thank you. I'm not sure I'll fit in there."

Brady rubs my arm. "Quit worrying; I'm going to be with you the whole time."

"So what happened, anyway? The paper said your dad was arrested for assault and took a plea deal of eighteen months. There are all sorts of rumors flying around about your mom running off with some guy. No one really knows what happened exactly."

"You don't have to talk about it, Zach," Brady says, giving his friend a look. "It's no one's business but ours."

"It's okay," I whisper. "The rumors are true."

Brady immediately changes the subject to all the high school gossip of girls and guys. I sit here quietly, trying to get a grip on the emotions that are threatening to surface. Brady keeps giving me worried glances and finally tugs me over to sit between his legs, wrapping his arms around me. If Connor thinks it's weird, he doesn't say anything. Instead, he works at cracking jokes to make me smile.

That evening after supper and a shower, Brady sits on the bed facing me and brings it up again. "You haven't talked about what happened. Do you want to talk about it with me?"

"I don't know… Sometimes I wish that I could block it from my mind forever."

"What happened, Zach? How did your dad find out you're gay? Actually, start from the beginning when your mom left."

Even thinking about her leaving me without a second thought brings sharp pains to my chest. "She packed up her stuff and asked me to take it out to the porch. Her boyfriend was there and loaded it up without a word. I begged her not to go, but it didn't matter." I meet his compassionate gaze and let out my sorrow. "She didn't even hug me or say she loved me. It was like I was nothing to her."

Brady leans forward to hook his hands on my hips, tugging me forward until I'm sitting close between his legs, facing him. "I'm sorry, Zach. I can't believe she did that to you."

"I keep going over in my mind what I did wrong to make her not love me."

He brushes hair back from my eyes. "You didn't do anything wrong. Some people are just bad people."

His words soothe a little bit of the hurt. "Dad came home and blamed me for her leaving…" My voice trails off into a whisper. "…and he used his belt on me. He's never gone quite that far. I couldn't hardly move afterward."

"Why didn't you tell me when you texted? I would have brought Dad and got you out of there. Why didn't you tell me this was going on all this time?"

"Because I didn't want to be taken away from you. I could have ended up in a place where they wouldn't let me see you. You're my family, Brady."

He leans forward to press his forehead to mine. "I couldn't have handled that either, but if you ever keep something like this from me again, it'll really hurt me. Promise me you won't hide getting hurt from me again, ever. Promise, Zach."

"I promise," I whisper, hating that I've hurt him by keeping it from him.

"So then what happened?"

"I stayed in bed until I knew you'd be off from school. Dad normally isn't home until a few hours later, so I took a shower. I was trying to figure out how to come to your place and not have you see how much pain I was in. I couldn't even sit down."

Brady's eyes fill with tears, which makes my own tear up. "Dad was home when I was walking back to my room, and he saw the cell phone. He went through our texts and read the *love yous*…and he went off the deep end about me being gay. Then he saw my painted toenails, and that made me gay in his eyes—"

Brady interrupts with, "But they were just from my sisters? They paint my toes all the time."

"I know, but he flipped out. Said he was sending me to conversion therapy, and when I said no, he started punching and kicking me." I pause to take a deep breath, my body trembling at the memory. "I don't even know how I managed to crawl to the phone and call you. If I couldn't have reached you—" I choke on a sob, and Brady pulls me into his arms to hug me close.

We cry together, the pain of what happened shared between us. "I'm sorry I got you hurt," I sob into his neck.

"I'm sorry I didn't protect you all that time," he sobs back.

When we are both done crying, I feel lighter after sharing my pain with him. He kisses my cheek and wipes away some of my tears.

"Are boys supposed to cry this much?" I murmur against him.

I feel the rumble of laughter in his chest under my ear.

"Who cares," he replies. "My mom always says that if you feel like crying, you should cry because keeping it inside only saves the hurt for later."

"Do you think they know I'm gay? Your dad talked to my dad, and I can't see him not bringing it up."

Brady is quiet for a minute. "I think they might, but I don't know for sure. Do you want to tell them?"

"I am scared to tell anyone after how Dad was…"

"I think you should tell them then. You shouldn't have to be scared to be who you are in your own house. I know they will be fine with it."

"I want to, but what about us? Do you think they will be scared for me to be close to you if I'm gay?"

Brady moves back and takes my hand to have me follow him off the bed. "I think they know, and they haven't separated us so far. I'll be with you when you tell them."

I feel like throwing up the whole way down to the living room, where his parents are sitting together. When Brady tugs me to the couch and puts his arm around me, they sit up and give us their attention.

Brady's dad leans forward a little. "What's up, boys?"

"Zach has something he wants to tell you," Brady says, rubbing my arm.

Swallowing hard, I try to fight back the fear at telling someone other than Brady. "Umm…please don't be mad or think badly of me." I take a deep, shaky breath. "But I think that I…that I'm gay."

His mom smiles and neither of them looks shocked or surprised like I thought they would. She comes over to sit on my other side, brushing some hair back from my face. "Honey, we are proud of you for being brave enough to tell us. Of course we aren't mad or think badly of you. We are here to support you in any way we can and want you to feel free to be who you are."

"You're okay with it?" I think that I'm in shock.

"We have thought you were for a while but felt that you needed to tell us when you were ready."

"You knew? How?"

"Just little things we saw and how hard you tried to hide them. You didn't need to hide them. We accept and love you, whether you are gay, bi, or straight."

"I was afraid you wouldn't want me around Brady," I whisper, picking at my pajama pants.

Brady's dad speaks up from the opposite couch. "We aren't worried about you being around Brady. We trust you both and know that Brady wouldn't do anything to hurt you."

Hurt me? They seem more concerned about me than if I would do something to Brady. "Thank you. I'd never do anything to hurt him either."

"Do you want us to keep this between us, or are you going to tell people?"

I consider his mom's words and don't know what the right answer is. "I don't know. It's not easy to tell others something that on some levels, still feels wrong, and yet it's not easy to hide something that feels so right, too."

"We won't say anything to anyone. You decide when and who you want to tell," Mr. Wellman says. "But if you do choose to be open about it, you have our full support."

"Thanks, Mr. Wellman."

He smiles. "We'd be honored if you would call us Mom and Dad or Emily and Michael. You're as much our kid as our other children, no matter what your last name is."

I'd thought that I'd make it through this without crying, but that brings the tears I didn't know I had left.

Emily embraces me gently, and then Michael gets up to pull me into a hug. He hugs like Brady and has this strength that makes you feel safe. My dad has never hugged me, and I hold onto him longer than I probably should, crying a bit too much.

By the time we are back up in Brady's room, I feel like I've run a marathon. I still haven't recovered completely from my surgery, and doing things takes the life out of me. Brady waits for me to snuggle in close to him before tucking the blankets around us. We talk for a few minutes, and then I can't keep from giving into sleep.

The next morning, the whole family goes to the mall. Brady holds my hand even though we are in public. I think he's worried I'm going to fall over or maybe freak out; I don't know.

Despite my protests, Emily buys me clothes and shoes. Once she knows my size and that I'll say no to everything, she stops asking and just buys whatever she wants. I don't have my stamina back yet and end up sitting in the food court with Brady while she finishes shopping.

Michael has taken the girls to Build a Bear Workshop and has been stuck in there forever.

Brady gets a text from his mom that she's about done, and we head off to meet her. I really have zero interest in shopping until we walk by the Disney store. I stop short, staring at everything inside. Brady grins and tugs me into the store to look around.

I can't help but love all of it. There is something about being around anything Disney that makes me smile. I pick up a plush, cuddly Eeyore and hug him to my chest for a few minutes. It's hard to put him back, but I do, moving on to look at the holiday ornaments that I can only dream of having.

Brady has picked up a few things and leaves me at the ornaments while he goes to check out. When we leave the store, he pulls the same Eeyore out of the bag and hands him to me.

"You bought him for me?"

"I think he wanted to come home with you as much as you wanted to take him home," Brady answers, smiling.

We are on our way home when his dad brings up Christmas. "We usually have the tree up by now, but with everything going on, it's been delayed. What do you say we pick up a tree on the way home and put one up tonight?"

It dawns on me that this year I truly get to celebrate Christmas with them and not just bits and pieces when my parents let me visit. I lean over to rest my head against Brady's arm, grateful that he's sharing his family with me.

We do stop to get a tree, and by the time we are home, I don't feel the best. Brady notices like he always does and carries me on his back upstairs, insisting the tree can wait until I've taken a nap.

That evening is magical to me, and I'll never forget it. We listen to Christmas music while hanging lights and ornaments and then watch The Santa Clause movie as a family. I end up lying down with my head on Brady's leg. He absently runs his fingers over my forehead and through my hair while watching the show. I want to believe that he feels more than friendship but remind myself that he doesn't. He's just being sweet like he always has been.

Anna comes over to lie in front of me, resting her head on her brother's leg, too. I grin and hug her to my chest. She reaches back to pat my cheek a few times, and it drives home that this family really does love me.

Monday morning, I throw up twice before we even leave for school. Brady keeps trying to reassure me, but going to public school with tons of kids is beyond scary.

He picks out one of my new pairs of jeans and a long sleeve shirt for me. Wearing shoes that are new and fit me feels weird, too.

My new glasses are supposed to come in this week, but for now, I'm using a previous pair that they found in my old house when they collected my things.

Brady's parents drive us to school, walking inside with us to the office and making sure that everything I need is taken care of. The principal talks with his dad for a few minutes and then meets me. Brady stays by my side the entire time, holding my backpack, which he refuses to let me carry.

Far too quickly, I'm walking with him down hallways with tons of teenagers—all of who seem bigger than me. They part ways for Brady, and it's obvious that everyone knows him. I get a lot of stares, and it makes my nerves worse. It's all I can do not to hide behind Brady and beg for him to take me home.

My locker is a few down from Brady's, and he shows me how to unlock it with the combination they gave me.

"Zaaaaach."

I turn to see Connor walking up with a big grin on his face. Alex and a bunch of other guys are following, all of them staring at me. I feel like a bunny surrounded by a pack of wolves eyeing me like I'm their prey.

Brady is completely at ease, of course. "Hey guys. This is Zach."

Most of them give me a nod or a smile, their eyes glued to the bruises that still linger around my right eye. I'm sure they all know that I'm the kid that was assaulted and whose dad is in jail.

"You look terrified," Connor says, tousling my hair like I'm a little kid.

"I am terrified."

Brady rubs his hand over my shoulder. "It's going to be fine."

I'm not so sure about that, especially when I see Derek walking in front of us to his locker across the hallway.

He gives me the look of death, clearly not over being asked to leave Brady's house. "I think you've got the wrong school, Matthews. Fourth graders are in the other building."

Ouch. I've been here five minutes and already I feel like I'm going to be a target because of my size.

"Shut your mouth, Sanders," Brady smarts back. "No one thinks you're funny."

Connor flips Derek off as we walk away to our first class.

We have three classes before lunch, and Brady stays with me. He refuses to let me carry my own books, and I don't argue. My energy is draining, and I'm not even past lunch yet.

Brady and I walk into the cafeteria, which is loud and packed with kids. All the football players and cheerleaders sit together, and I find myself between Connor and Brady. Brittany is on his other side and all over him about being gone for two weeks, going on and on about the whole ordeal. It's making me feel a little sick when everyone starts asking Brady about it.

My stomach lurches when they ask about my dad, and I stuff the uneaten food back into my lunch pack.

"Guys...not cool," Brady says, shaking his head.

Derek says something at the end of the table that I don't hear, but whatever it was, it makes a few of his friends laugh. One of them coughs and says, "Hobbit," and they all laugh again. When one of them snarks off something about Brady's queer boyfriend, it's more than I can handle.

My face feels like it's on fire as I get up from the table, walking to the doors because I don't have the energy to go any faster. I don't fit in here, and I feel bad for bringing embarrassment to Brady, too.

"Zach…"

Brady catches up with me as I push through the door. "You don't need to leave. The guys won't ask about it again, and Derek is just an asshole that nobody cares about."

"I want to go home." My voice sounds shaky even to me, and I have to fight the tears from coming. "I want to go home."

"Okay." He walks with me to the office while calling his mom. He signs me out and stands with me by the doors until his mom pulls up. He's so quiet that it's making me feel worse than I already do. My coat is back in my locker, but I barely feel the cold when I walk out to his mom's SUV. She gets out and talks with Brady beside the vehicle before coming back to drive me home.

"Are you okay?"

I nod, leaning my head against the cold glass window. "I'm sorry you had to leave work for me," I murmur, feeling guilty for that as well.

"You're more important than work. Let's get you home; you're really pale." She reaches over to rub my arm.

As soon as we get home, I go upstairs and shut myself in my bedroom. Crawling into the bed I've never once used, I pull the comforter over my head and try to pretend that I'm not different, that my dad never hurt me. That I fit in with Brady's friends instead of being this sheltered geek who doesn't understand the world.

TWELVE

BRADY

I'm so pissed that I don't trust myself to talk in front of Zach. Seeing his face, all pale and exhausted, is hard enough, but there's also this hurt and shame there that I never want to see again. I walk back into the cafeteria and go straight to Derek and his friends, leaning my hands on the table in front of him.

"If I hear you make fun of Zach one more time, I'll turn you into the office. You think it's funny, but have you read the posters that say this school has zero bully tolerance? If they don't do anything, I'll have my dad get involved, and trust me when I say that he will make a *huge* deal out of it. Do you not have any fucking compassion? He's been through enough and doesn't need crap from spineless assholes that feel so shitty about themselves, they need to put someone else down to feel better."

Derek pushes back his chair, standing up like he's going to fight me.

Connor and Alex move to stand next to me, one on each side.

"Dude, you look like an ass," Connor says to Derek.

Derek's eyes flicker from me to Connor. "Fuck off, Connor. You have nothing to do with this."

Connor crosses his arms. "You take issue with Zach or Brady, then you take issue with me."

"And me," Alex chimes in.

I love my friends. I think Derek finally realizes that the entire cafeteria has gone quiet and is looking at him because he knocks down his chair and storms out of the lunchroom. I eye his friends and they all duck their heads. "Coach finds out about your comments, you'll be off the team. Remember that," I say as I walk back to my seat to get my lunch pack. So much for eating lunch today; the bell is about to ring.

Back at my locker, my friends who were asking questions in front of Zach stop by to say it won't happen again. I know they meant well, but Zach has been so fragile since he woke up at the hospital and doesn't need a constant reminder of what happened thrown in his face.

As soon as school is over, I catch a ride with Connor and his older brother to drop me off at home.

Mom steps out of the kitchen before I can head upstairs. "He hasn't come down since he got home."

"I'll check on him." I take the stairs two at a time and hurry to my bedroom. He's not lying in my bed like I thought he would be, and fear hits me more than it should. I check the bathroom, but he's not there either, and then head down to the bedroom that he never uses. The room is dark, but I can see the covers are messed up and an arm is poking out from one side.

He's never slept in this bed before, and if he came in here to sleep, he must be upset with me. I hear a whimper coming from under the blankets and something that sounds like no.

Nightmare.

He's been having them every night since the incident. I kick off my shoes as I take my coat off and crawl into bed with him, uncovering his head and pulling him close to me.

"Brady," he mumbles so faintly that I barely hear it.

Kissing the top of his head, I run my fingers over his hair and stare down at his pale face. He always looks so peaceful when he's close to me. It's noticeable how his expression changes from when he's across the room to when he's up against me.

I don't sleep, just lie here watching him until his eyes flicker open. He sees me and immediately buries his face between us, hiding from me. "Zach...don't hide. I'm sorry about what happened today. I should have talked to the guys first."

He turns his head to look at me. "You're sorry? I'm the one who is sorry. I never wanted to be the reason that people say mean things about you."

"What mean things about me?"

"That I was your queer boyfriend," he whispers, shame covering his features again.

"That's what you're upset about?"

"Part of it…"

"First of all, who says queer boyfriend? That's just dumb. If I had a boyfriend, of course he would be queer…like duh."

Zach gets this half smile over that comment.

"Secondly, Derek is a douche, and nothing that comes out of his mouth matters to me." I run my fingers down his cheek. "If he wants to think we are boyfriends, let him. Who cares."

His eyes have moved to a spot on my shirt, and I tilt his chin so those green eyes of his are meeting mine. "You have nothing to be ashamed of, Zach."

"I thought you were mad at me," he whispers, his voice breaking.

"What? I have never been mad at you. Why would you think that?"

A tear trickles down his cheek. "You wouldn't look at me and didn't say anything."

God, I'm such an idiot. "I wasn't mad at you. I was furious with Derek and his friends for hurting your feelings. I was contemplating if I should go back and punch him or not."

"Oh," he whispers.

"I can promise you, Zach, that there will never be a time when I'm angry with you. We may not always agree and may argue about something, but I won't be angry with you." I use my thumb to wipe the tear that is making its way down the same path. "Got it?"

He nods, hugging me tightly. All the tightness that I've been feeling since he left school eases from my chest. I can't handle Zach being hurt or scared.

"The guys won't ask about what happened again; they felt bad over today. And if Derek says anything to you, I want you to tell me. Okay?"

"Okay, but I don't think I'll fit in there. It's all so big, and there are so many people. It makes me feel…stressed."

I don't know what to say to make him feel better because I can't imagine being homeschooled and then being shoved into public school. "How about we get a snack, and I read some Harry Potter to you?"

That makes him sit up and smile. He loves it when I read Harry Potter to him. I read the first two when I was eleven, but after what happened with my brother, I never finished them. I started over for Zach and read to him when he's down or before we go to sleep.

We both change into pajama pants and T-shirts before going down to the kitchen. Mom's eyes immediately go to Zach and then me, as if to ask if he's okay. I nod and open the fridge door to get out Zach's favorite juice boxes and an apple.

We have an apple slicer that cuts it into wedges easily, and I pile them into a bowl for us to carry upstairs.

"Supper will be ready in an hour," Mom calls out after us as we leave.

Zach and I sit side by side in bed as I read. He's leaning against me, munching on an apple slice and sucking down his juice. Every so often, he holds up an apple slice for me to take a bite or gives me a sip of my own juice box. The stress of the day fades away with Zach next to me. He has this gentleness about him that I've honestly never seen in anyone else. Even my mom isn't as gentle as Zach. Every touch seems measured so he doesn't hurt anyone. Every single word from him means more than an entire conversation with someone else.

As soon as he's done with the apples, I put my arm around him, and he lays his head against my chest, turning the page for me whenever needed. I read to him until Mom's voice comes through the intercom in my room and says it's time to eat.

When we get downstairs, my dad is home, and he gives me the usual hug that I love. He moves to hug Zach, kissing the top of his head like I always do. Zach smiles shyly, but I can tell it makes him feel good. Anna and Meg run over to hug Zach, too. Clearly, my family loves him.

My parents avoid asking about school while we eat. It's probably a good thing because when Zach gets stressed, he can't seem to eat at all. It isn't until supper is over and we've helped clear the table that Dad brings it up.

"So, what happened today?"

Zach sidles closer to me until our arms are touching. He doesn't say anything, so I go first. "Zach wasn't feeling too great by noon, and then lunchtime didn't go well."

He raises his eyebrow. "Didn't go well?"

"My friends asked a bunch of questions about what happened... and a few guys said some mean things."

Dad doesn't look happy, and Zach squashes himself against me. Dad notices and immediately relaxes his body. My chest hurts thinking about how afraid Zach gets every time someone is upset. I put my arm around him and can feel him trembling.

"Sorry that happened today," Mom says. "We talked about it, and we think that a half a day might be best for this week. The last thing we want is for you to get run down and open yourself up to getting sick."

We all know that without his spleen, it's harder for him to fight off infections. I don't think I could survive if Zach died. It hurts too much to even think about.

"I don't want to be here alone…"

"We wouldn't let you be alone, not until you're ready. Tomorrow and Thursday, I'll pick you up and be here, and Wednesday, Michael will pick you up. Friday, we are going to have Brady come home with you since we both have court appointments we can't miss. Is that okay?"

Zach nods against me.

Mom continues, "And then there are two and a half weeks of Christmas vacation. Grandma and Grandpa will be flying back in to stay for part of that. Hopefully, by the time you go back, you will be recovered more from the surgery."

"If you two study for your permit test, I'll take you both in to get them next week," Dad offers.

"Really?" I can't wait to drive.

"Me?" Zach presses his hand to his chest like he doesn't understand.

Dad nods. "You, too. You'll both be old enough. Then we'll get you signed up for driver's education in January."

"Do I have to be alone with the teacher?" Zach digs his fingers into my back. "Maybe I should wait to drive."

Sympathy crosses Dad's face. "How about I call and find out? If you can be together and take turns driving, we'll sign you up. That way, whenever you decide you want to drive, you can have it done."

Zach nods in agreement, loosening his grip a little.

"I know it's a lot of changes and experiences that you aren't used to. You need to tell us if things get to be too much, and we will reevaluate how we are doing things."

"Okay, thank you, sir."

Dad tilts his head toward the living room. "Zach, why don't you go find out what kind of ice cream the girls want and help Mom dish it out."

It's the first time that Dad's called my mom, Mom, to Zach. My best friend freezes for a second before blinking back some tears. Mom takes his hand, and they go into the living room together.

"I want to talk to you." Dad walks down the hallway to his office, knowing I'll follow him. I lean against the doorframe, staying just far enough out that Zach will know where I am if he comes back into the kitchen.

Dad sits on the edge of his desk, facing me. "Who were the kids that were being mean?"

"Derek Sanders, the one I asked to leave here when he called Zach a stalker. Along with a few of JV freshman players that I don't know well."

"Not surprising, he seemed like a dick."

My dad doesn't usually call someone a dick, and it catches me so off guard that an abrupt laugh escapes from my chest.

"What were they making fun of him about?"

"His size...being a fourth-grader...a hobbit. Then they called him queer, and he got up and left."

"No wonder he was so upset." Dad rubs the back of his neck, and I realize that I have that same habit when I'm stressed.

"He was upset because he thought it would embarrass me. He never wants to hurt anyone, and when he thinks he's the cause of it, he can't handle it."

"That's why it makes me livid that someone would hurt him, even with words. God knows the kid has been through enough already."

I catch movement out of the corner of my eye and turn to see Zach in the kitchen, looking lost. I wave my arm so he sees me, and he smiles. I watch him walk over to help Mom with the ice cream before looking back at Dad.

"He trusts you, Brady. The kind of trust that most people will never give. Be sure to treasure that and not do anything to break it. I'm not sure you could get it back if you did."

Dad's words feel heavy, like I need to memorize them and keep them close. "I wouldn't do anything to break his trust."

"I know you never would intentionally, but you're young, and teenagers do stupid things. I think you're mature beyond your years, and I am so proud of the young man you're becoming. I'm only cautioning you because I see the bond you have with Zach, and I'm not sure you truly understand what it would mean to lose that. It's a once-in-a-lifetime kind of friendship…love…and so many go through life searching for what you've found so young. Many never find it."

He walks over to put his hand on my shoulder, squeezing gently. "All I'm saying, Son, is that when it comes to Zach, think before you react and don't take all the love and trust he gives you for granted. Someday you'll truly understand the depth and beauty of what he gives you. And what you give him." His hand moves down over my heart. "You've given him a lot of space in here. Take care of your heart, Son, because that boy in the kitchen is most of it."

I nod, speechless at my dad's words.

"We should get back for the ice cream, but when it comes to school, I want you to come to me if these kids continue to say such things. I won't put up with it, and it *will* stop." He walks by me and back down the hallway.

I stay here feeling like there's something in what he's saying that I'm not quite getting. Like I'm missing something important. I try to sear his words in my memory so I can revisit them later and make my way back to the kitchen, where Zach has my favorite peanut butter and chocolate ice cream waiting for me. I ruffle his hair before sitting down to eat with my family.

THAT NIGHT we are lying in bed when Zach breaks the silence in the room. "Do you think Derek said that because he knows I'm gay?"

"I don't know. I doubt he knows anything. It's just him being an ass."

"Do I look or act gay?"

I roll over so I can see his face and he can see mine. "You act like *you.* I don't think there's one way that gay people act like. If being sweet and gentle and reading tons of books screams gay, then yeah, you look and act gay."

He gives me a slow smile. "How do you always know what to say to make me feel better?"

"Ehh…I just tell you the truth. Really though, you need to stop worrying about how you look or act. If you want to wear makeup and talk in a higher-pitched voice, then do it. I'll be there for you every step of the way. Just be you."

I can tell if I don't make him laugh, he's going to cry. "Except for one thing…I don't do glitter. Glitter is banned from this room and your body because it would get all over me, too, and sparkles do not go well with my complexion."

That makes him grin, and he rolls his eyes at my dramatic tone. "Glitter is at the top of my list now." He smirks.

If he really wanted glitter, I'd buy it for him and wear it wherever it landed if it would make him happy, but I don't tell him that. "How about we skip glitter and start with some painting or cooking together. It seems like all the gay couples do that on their vlogs." The words are out of my mouth before I realize that I basically compared us to a gay couple.

Zach is laughing and pointing at my face. "Oh my God, your face! That was priceless!"

"Shush it; you know what I meant." It's the first time I've heard Zach laugh like this in ages, and I don't want him to stop. I hook my arm around his back to pull him closer—until he's where he usually sleeps—and kiss him on the top of his head.

I stand behind Zach as he pukes for the third time this morning. His nerves are worse today than they were yesterday.

"Is it the ice cream from last night that's making you sick?" I know he has to watch his diet now that he doesn't have a spleen.

He leans back to rest against the wall. "I had frozen yogurt that your mom bought for me instead of the good stuff."

I hand him a cool washcloth to wipe his mouth with and then offer him the Sprite that I went to get the last time he threw up. He sips it slowly, his hands shaking so much it's noticeable.

"Do you want me to tell Mom that you need to stay home today?"

I can tell he wants to say yes, but he shakes his head. "I don't want to be away from you for a whole day."

My stomach feels a little funny over how sweet he is. "Okay, then we need to get you up and brushing your teeth, or we're going to be late." I give him a hand up, and he brushes his teeth before following me out to get our coats.

"Did you bring my backpack home with you yesterday?"

"Yes, but you don't need it today. You're only there for three classes. I'll just put your things in with mine."

Instead of sitting in the front with my dad when he drives us to school, I sit with Zach in the back and hold his hand in hopes it'll help calm him.

Dad turns to look at Zach when he parks in front of the school. "If you need to go home or have any problems, you call and we will come to get you right away. Okay?"

Zach looks like he's about to beg to go home, but when I squeeze his hand, he gets out of the vehicle. Dad gives me a *call me if you need me* look, and I nod my understanding before following Zach out the door.

I'm not sure Zach will want me to hold his hand, so I put my arm around his shoulder instead and guide him through the kids lining the halls.

Connor is waiting by our lockers and gives Zach a smile. "About time you two got here. I've been waiting forever."

I scoff and open my locker, taking out the books Zach needs for this class from my backpack. Connor helps Zach to open his own locker and watches as he puts his coat inside. I can tell my friend is worried about him and is trying to help.

Zach rubs his forehead as the noise from kids slamming their lockers shut magnifies. I can't imagine how this must feel for him after always being at home with only his mom for company—if she even was company. I have to give my friends credit because they all pause by us when they walk by and make a point to say hi to Zach or give him a fist bump. Except for Derek and his friends, of course, who give me a sneer on their way to their lockers. I don't care if they act like that toward me, as long as they leave Zach alone.

I think the morning goes okay. Zach sticks to my side between classes, but I can tell he's trying not to look like he is. Connor is a huge help by staying close to Zach and trying to make him laugh all the time. My best friend smiles a little, but he's not made it to laughter yet.

When the lunch bell rings, we take him to get his coat, and I promise to bring home the books he needs. We are in the same classes, so I don't need to haul home two copies of everything. When Mom pulls up, I walk him out to her SUV and give him a hug, promising to be home later.

Connor is waiting for me when I come back inside, and we walk to the cafeteria together.

"How is he doing?"

I shrug. "He doesn't have much energy, and he's scared to death of school."

"I wanted to punch Derek for yesterday. He's such an asshole," Connor says.

"Yeah, me too."

"Do you guys want to go to the movies this weekend? I thought maybe Zach would like to go."

"I can ask him. He's never been to the theater; his dad would never let him."

"I heard his dad is going to give an interview to share his side of the story."

My steps falter. "Are you kidding me?"

"Nope."

I take out my cell and call Dad, not caring if I get in trouble for using my phone in school. He answers right away, and I tell him what Connor said. Dad says he'll take care of it and hangs up quickly. There has to be a law against bringing the trauma of a minor out into the public. I hope Dad can stop him.

"The last thing Zach needs is to see his dad on TV saying all sorts of untrue things about him."

Connor pushes open the cafeteria door, and we both go to sit with our team. Even though football season is over, we still work out most days after school. Coach doesn't want us falling behind on things. I've missed the last two weeks and should stay after school today.

Brittany squeezes in next to me and tries to get my attention constantly. It's annoying, and I roll my eyes at Connor halfway through. He grins and pulls me into their conversation so that she has to shut up.

We are walking back to the lockers when he asks, "So what's up with you and Brittany?"

"Nothing. She's pretty and all, but she messages all the time and talks so much it gives me a headache."

"Girls take up a lot of time," he admits.

"My parents won't let me date until I get my driver's license anyway. And when I do, I'm not sure I want to date Brittany. Ivy is nice, but I think Alex has his heart set on her."

"Yeah, he does. He's been crushing on her since kindergarten."

"Why don't you ask Brittany out?" I give him a pleading look.

He laughs, opening his locker and taking out his books. "Oh no, you're on your own with that one. If I ask a girl out, it would be Tessa."

Tessa is sweet, but she's Brittany's friend and stays clear of showing interest in me. Zach pops into my mind, and the thought of leaving him at home to go out with some girl doesn't appeal to me right now. Maybe when he's recovered from all that's happened, *then* I'll go out on dates. We walk into class, and our conversation ends as we take our seats.

THE REST of the week goes fairly well. Connor and I stay close when Zach's at school, and then when I get home, he's always asleep on my bed. It really bothered me when he went to his own bed, and it's a relief that he hasn't done it again. I don't like feeling as if he's pushing me away and don't want to experience it again.

His color has improved, but he still looks worn out by the time he leaves school every day. Mom has taken him to pick up his new glasses, and he claims the world looks much clearer now.

Friday, Dad picks us up before lunch and drops us off at home. Zach ends up passing out on my bed while I do homework. It's hard to do when he gravitates to my side, Eeyore smashed between us. I grin at the sight of him sleeping with the stuffed animal. Eeyore's become a permanent fixture in my bed, and even though Zach doesn't usually cuddle with him when we go to sleep at night, he always has the stuffed donkey in his arms when I come home from school and he's napping.

I go back to reading The Frontiersman, a required book for American History. Zach has already read it, or I'd be reading it aloud to him. Mom told me he scored so high in his testing that they considered his level of education to be post-graduate. I guess that's why they don't seem to care that he's missing the afternoons this week. I always knew he was smart and that he would read anything he could get his hands on while he was here. He told me once that he studied so much when he was home because there was nothing else to do. I guess without a TV or radio or internet, there wouldn't be much to do besides study, especially when his parents were so strict about what he could get from the library. Most of what he brought home from there were non-fiction history and science books that would bore most people to death.

"Brady...I don't have any money to get you all Christmas presents."

Zach's quiet voice draws my attention to him, and he's looking up at me with these sad eyes that always make my heart hurt. I lower the book and run my fingers through his hair in the way that I know relaxes him.

"You don't need to get us anything. It's your first real Christmas. We just want you to enjoy it."

"I feel like a charity case," he whispers, kissing my arm like he always does.

"You're part of the family, not a charity case."

He doesn't look convinced at all.

"If you want to get presents, I can give you some money to buy them."

"That would make them from you, not me." He rolls onto his back, absently rubbing Eeyore's ears through his fingertips.

"If I was spending Christmas with you and didn't have any money to buy you anything—would you care, or would you just be happy I was with you?"

He sighs this long, drawn-out sigh of acceptance that sounds a lot like a groan.

THAT NIGHT we are sitting in the living room with my parents and sisters, watching our usual Friday night family movie. The girls are doing their favorite activity—painting nails—and mine are now some shade of purple that I'm sure the guys will tease me over. Meg starts on Zach, who's slouched against me with my arm around him. I feel his body tremble in almost a shudder and whip my head over to see him trying to suck air in like he's suffocating.

"Zach… Zach!"

Mom and Dad are both up in seconds, and Meg scoots back so Dad can kneel in front of Zach.

"Where's his inhaler?" Mom asks me in a rush.

"My bedroom. Side table," I say, rubbing Zach's back and feeling helpless as he tries to suck in air.

Dad's eyes move to mine. "I think he's having a panic attack."

It's in that second that I realize that Meg painting his nails probably did this. I move him into my arms and hold him close. "Breathe, Zach. I've got you. No one is going to hurt you."

"Try to take slow breaths," Dad adds, removing Zach's glasses that are crooked from him pressing into my chest.

He's shaking so badly in my arms that it's scaring me. "I'm right here," I whisper, pressing my face as close to his as I can.

Mom comes rushing back in with his inhaler, and I hold it for him, hoping he sucks some of it in with these gasps so it can help. A few seconds later, he drags in a little deeper breath, shuddering with it.

"That's it," I murmur against his ear. "Slowly take another deep breath."

When he can finally breathe, deep, wracking sobs rip from his chest. I know he'll calm down more if we are alone and scoot to the edge of the couch holding him. Mom has tears in her eyes, and Dad just gives me a nod like he knows what I'm doing. Both my sisters are huddled together crying, too.

I carry him out of the living room and up the stairs to my bedroom, scooting back to lean against the headboard so I can support both of us. Eeyore is within reaching distance, and I let one arm go from Zach so I can grab the soft animal, tucking him close to Zach's chest and then hugging them both to me.

Zach cries for so long that I'm worried he will make himself sick, but finally, he falls into an exhausted sleep and relaxes against me. My heart feels raw watching him go through this, knowing it was all triggered by something as simple as painted nails. I want to kill his dad for doing this to him.

Mom peeks in a little while later, and I motion her over. "Mom, can you get nail polish remover and take the paint off his toenails before he wakes up."

She whispers, "Do you think that's what caused this?"

"A major part of why his dad almost killed him was because the girls had painted his nails," I explain as quietly as I can. "His dad thought that made him gay."

"Oh God… I know he hasn't talked to us about what happened exactly, but I had no idea that was why it happened. I'll go get the remover."

She comes back a few minutes later and gently removes the paint from his toenails. He must have worn himself out and then some because he doesn't stir at all.

"Maybe we should remove yours just to be on the safe side," she whispers.

I nod and watch her take the purple paint off mine, too.

"Do you need anything else?"

"No, thanks, Mom."

Once she's gone, I carefully ease Zach onto the bed so I can take off my soaked shirt and lie down beside him. Staring at his face, I take in his long lashes resting on his pale cheeks. He has these delicate yet sharp cheekbones and a clear complexion that most guys would kill for. And the thing is, I don't think he has a clue how attractive he is. Right now, he looks so young and small, but when he gets a little older, he's going to draw eyes to him, just by being him.

A worried expression crosses his face even in his sleep, and I wrap my arm around his back to hug him closer. It's so unfair that he's gone through so much. He's kind and gentle, and everything so many people should inspire to be.

THIRTEEN

ZACH

My throat hurting forces me from the darkness and into the reality of what happened. I inwardly cringe at how I freaked out over Meg painting my toenails. When my eyes flutter open, they are met with deep blue ones, filled with worry and love. An intense yearning fills me, but I squash it down. Brady loves me, but he's not *in* love with me.

"I'm sorry," I whisper, my voice scratchy and low.

He runs his fingers over my forehead and through my hair. "There's nothing to be sorry about."

"I don't know why that happened. I saw the paint and couldn't breathe."

His touch soothes me as he continues to softly move his fingertips over my skin. "You went through a trauma, and that's not going to magically disappear, Zach. Give yourself time to heal from it all."

Does someone ever heal from having their dad almost kill them? Even seeing him in my mind makes me bury into Brady more.

"Do you want to go back to sleep, or are you not tired anymore?" Brady's lips press to my cheek lovingly.

"I don't think I can sleep now," I murmur against his bare chest.

"Let's watch a movie then…maybe Tangled?"

God, my best friend is so sweet. "Don't you ever get sick of watching that movie with me?"

"Nah, as long as we fast-forward the 'Mother Knows Best' song, I enjoy it."

"I really hate that song."

"I know you do."

We end up raiding the kitchen for snacks and then watch Tangled on his bed together. Brady keeps looking at me as if I'm about to fall apart, always keeping a hand on me in some way. His touch grounds me, and I wonder how I will ever cope when he moves on.

WE SLEEP until noon on Saturday and find his family eating lunch when we stumble downstairs. Meg is obviously still upset over last night, and I make a point to give her a hug. "I love you, Meggy. You didn't do anything wrong."

"I love you, too." She gives me a teary smile before sitting back down at the table.

I ruffle Anna's hair as I walk by to my own chair. "Love you too, princess."

She grins, blowing me a kiss. Brady messes up her hair as he walks by, too, and she squeals, smacking his hand.

Brady slumps down in his chair with a fake hurt look. "Why does he get all the love and I just get hit?"

"Because he is sweeter than you," Anna pipes back.

"I'm so hurt." Brady smirks, sticking his tongue out at her.

"See! Zach would never stick his tongue out at me!"

I smile and shrug when Brady nudges me with his arm. "She's right."

Michael clears his throat, "What are you boys up to today?"

"Connor invited us to go to the movies tonight," Brady answers.

This is the first I'm hearing about it.

"What movie?" Emily asks, her eyes moving to me.

I get the feeling she's worried about it being too scary for me. I'm a wimp when it comes to anything even remotely scary.

"I don't know. I think the newest Star Wars movie is on right now. It'll be something…good." Brady's eyes give me a side look, and I know he's telling her he understands.

"Should be fine. Your dad can take you and pick you up." She passes the platter of grilled chicken breasts over to me. "I made you a doctor's appointment for Monday to get your asthma checked. All we have is the inhaler we picked up from your old house, and it's outdated. When was the last time you saw your asthma doctor?"

"Asthma doctor?"

"Where did your parents take you to get your inhaler?"

"I went to a clinic once when I was younger and couldn't breathe. They gave me a couple of sample packs. My par...they didn't believe in doctors." I don't want to call them my parents anymore. When I was a baby, they still went to doctors, but as time went on, my dad became even more religious and said God would heal us.

Emily's eyes fly to Michael's, and he rubs his hand over his face. "No worries. We'll take care of it."

Brady leans over to press his forehead to the side of my face briefly before taking the platter from my hand. I forgot I was even holding it since they brought up stuff about *them*. He stabs a chicken breast to put on my plate before forking two on his own.

When he does things like that, it calms me in a way that nothing else does. Everything is divided in my mind like a river running between the desert and a flowery meadow. Everything before Brady and everything after. Nothing matters before him and everything matters after him. He's the river that brings life to me. He's the butter-flies and flowers, the sun and the warmth it shines down.

"You okay, Zach?"

Brady's concerned voice brings me out of my sappy thoughts, and I realize that I've been staring off into space like a dork. "I'm okay."

AFTER LUNCH, we watch YouTube videos and game for a while. He starts playing Rainbow Six Siege, and I curl up next to him to read a book.

We take showers and get ready before supper. Connor and Alex end up coming over for pizza before the movie, then Brady's dad drops us off at the theater. I'm excited about seeing a movie with Brady, right up until I see Brittany is there. Brady groans when he spots her, giving me the idea he's not so happy with her being there, either. She and some other girls invite themselves to watch with us whether we want them to or not. Brady buys my ticket and then pays for us to get snacks and drinks from the concession stand. I'm surprised he's letting me have this much sugar since normally he's concerned about my diet. My spleen being removed means I have to be careful with sweets and sugary drinks.

I'm in awe at actually being at a theater and at how big the screen is.

Connor leads the way to seats a little closer up, and Brady walks all the way down the row to take the end seat with me following him. Right before I sit down, Brittany knocks into me to get past and sits next to him.

Brady scowls. "Get up. Zach is sitting there."

She huffs, giving me the look of death before knocking into me again to stomp back in the direction we came. Brady rolls his eyes and takes my drink from me until I can get my coat off and sit down.

Connor takes the seat next to me and grins over at Brady. "Finally had enough, huh?"

"Yeah, and you know she's going to talk the whole damn movie."

Alex sits on the other side of Connor, with Ivy next to him. It's obvious that he likes her, and I hope she likes him back. It sucks to have a crush on someone and not have them return those same feelings.

After the movie starts, Connor offers to share his popcorn with me, and I end up eating way too much. I've never tasted popcorn as good as this buttery stuff. Brady keeps looking over at me, and when I'm done eating, he puts his arm around my back so I can lean against him for the rest of the movie.

It's a perfect first movie, but I'm exhausted by the time it's over. All my energy is gone, and I'm not feeling so good. Seems like I can't go six hours without needing sleep, and I'm way past that now.

The lights come on and Connor looks over at me. "Fuck...you okay, Zach?"

Brady moves so he can see my face and is immediately helping me get my coat on. "Hang on, Zach. We'll get you home shortly."

I don't want to ruin their time. "I'm okay...just tired."

"You're not fine," Brady says, zipping up my coat.

The girls are waiting at the end of the row when we walk out, and Brittany flips her hair over her shoulder, glaring at me still. Brady picks me up, and I'm too tired to care that everyone sees. I sag against him, closing my eyes.

"What's wrong with him?"

Her snotty tone makes me flinch.

Brady doesn't answer as he carries me out of the theater, but I hear Connor telling her to shut up.

The cold air hits my face when we make it outside, and the next thing I know, I'm in the back of the SUV—still on Brady's lap with my legs on Connor's.

"Is he okay?" I hear Michael ask.

"Yeah, I think he's just wiped out."

I vaguely remember Brady carrying me upstairs and taking off my coat so I can sink into the bed. Someone pulls my shoes off and draws the blankets up to my chin. Connor says something, but I'm too tired to make it out.

FOURTEEN

BRADY

I sit on the edge of the bed, staring at Zach to make sure he's okay. When he gets that pale, it freaks me out.

"Is he going to be okay?"

"I think so…" I turn to see Connor's worried expression. "His body has been through a lot, and it will take about six weeks to recover from his surgery."

"I hate his dad for doing this to him," he mutters.

"Me, too." I move Eeyore closer in case Zach wants him.

"Is it true that you fought his dad off to protect him?"

Motioning to where I have two gaming chairs, I move over to them so we won't disturb Zach. "I did my best until the police came. Zach was a bloody mess on the floor, not moving at all, and all I wanted was to keep his dad away from him."

Connor swears under his breath. "You're a hero, you know."

"Nah, Zach's the hero for living through that hell and still smiling."

"Not many people would have put themselves between Zach and his dad. I've seen pictures of him, and he's pretty big."

"I would die protecting Zach. He needs someone that never hurts him." I hand Connor a controller and turn on my gaming system. "Your parents picking you up, or are you staying the night?"

"You're okay if I stay the night?" He looks surprised.

I realize that I haven't invited anyone to stay the night besides

Zach, not even once. "You can stay. You can sleep on the floor in here or in Zach's bedroom."

He's probably wondering why Zach sleeps in my bed, but I refuse to move Zach to his own room. I didn't like it when he napped in his room; I know I wouldn't like it if he was away all night.

"A sleeping bag in here is fine."

We game for a couple of hours, keeping the sound down low so we don't disturb Zach. We are in the middle of a match when I hear Zach crying *no* over and over. I toss the controller down and hurry over to the bed to lie down next to him, holding him to me. "Shhh, you're okay. I won't let anyone hurt you." I murmur the words that always calm him down. He does this half sob of my name in his sleep but slowly relaxes against me.

I notice Connor is standing to the side with a torn expression on his face. Running my fingers through Zach's hair, I wait until I know he's sleeping peacefully again before gently moving out from beside him. I stuff my pillow where I was lying so he thinks I'm still there.

Connor and I sit back down, but my friend doesn't pick up his controller. "Does he have nightmares a lot?"

"Every single night. This one wasn't as bad as they can be." I feel uncomfortable sharing even a tiny bit of Zach's personal life.

"He's lucky to have you," Connor says, his brown eyes showing he genuinely means it and cares.

"You want to play one more match and then head to bed?"

"Sure, bro."

We play the last game, and then I get a sleeping bag and pillow for Connor. While he's in the bathroom, I work to get Zach's jeans off without waking him up. He must be beyond exhausted because he sleeps through the whole thing.

I take my turn in the bathroom, and then we turn out the lights to sleep. I debate keeping the pillow between us for Connor's benefit for all of fifteen seconds before I move it and wrap my arm around Zach. He scoots closer until his head is resting against me and his leg is in between mine. I kiss his forehead and doze off to sleep.

Zach pulling away brings me awake enough to see him slip from the bed and head toward the bathroom. He sidesteps Connor and looks back at me in surprise. I point to his legs, and he detours to my drawers to get one of his pajama pants out before shutting himself in the bathroom.

He comes back out and crawls into bed but stays on his side, facing away from me. I'm going to guess he's worried about embarrassing me with Connor in here. I scoot over and spoon him, knowing he won't relax otherwise. He takes my hand and holds it to his chest in this sweet way that makes me smile.

We fall back to sleep until Connor wakes us both up by hitting us with a pillow and complaining that he's hungry. He doesn't seem bothered that I'm cuddling my best friend, and it takes away the worry I've been feeling. I'm not sure most would understand our relationship, but Connor doesn't seem to care.

"You're looking better today," he tells Zach as we crawl out of bed.

"Sorry about last night. I just lose my energy all of a sudden, and then my body is done."

"Don't worry; you'll get back to normal soon."

Zach helps my mom finish making breakfast, or maybe I should say brunch. He's learning more and more how to cook and seems to love doing it.

Connor ends up staying most of the day, hanging out in the basement where we have a pool table and a big screen tv. Zach mainly curls up in a blanket on the couch, reading a book while we play pool, and then lies with his head on my leg for the movie until he falls asleep. I carry him upstairs to bed to sleep so we don't have a repeat of last night. Then Connor and I game together for a couple of hours before his parents pick him up.

He takes one last look at Zach passed out on the bed. "Tell him I said goodbye for me, will you?"

"I will."

Mom and Dad ask me to come into the kitchen after Connor leaves.

Mom leans against the island, holding her coffee cup and studying me. "Did you have a good time?"

"Yeah, Connor's cool."

"Brady, I scheduled Zach an appointment with a therapist for tomorrow afternoon," Mom says. "We haven't told him yet because we didn't want to stress him out this weekend, but we think it's best for him to be in therapy after what happened. He needs to talk to someone."

I'm torn between not wanting to make him go through it and wondering if it'll help. "He talks to me about it."

Dad nods. "We know that, Son, but we want to make sure he's

okay. Panic attacks aren't something we want to mess around with. The doctor we spoke to said he could have post-traumatic stress disorder. Certain triggers could cause panic attacks."

"Don't blindside him with this. He needs to know ahead of time."

Mom nods. "That's why we are talking to you. It might be best if you tell him, and if you're okay with it, go along with him until he's comfortable."

"Like I'd let him go alone," I bite out, upset he has to go through something else.

"We also want to check in with you and see if you need to talk to someone? You went through an ordeal too, Son."

I stare at my dad and see he's serious. "I am fine, but thank you for asking."

"Alright, but if we see any indications that you're not fine, you'll be going whether you like it or not."

I don't talk to Zach until we are in bed, and I'm getting ready to read him more of Harry Potter.

"Zach, I need to talk to you about something that my parents asked me to tell you."

His eyes get big and glassy. "Your parents aren't going to make me leave, are they?"

Shit, I didn't even know he was worried about that happening. "No, of course not. You're with me and not going anywhere I don't go."

"Oo…okay. Then what is wrong?" He scoots closer to me, and I kiss his forehead.

"Nothing is wrong. Mom and Dad want you to see a therapist tomorrow. They are worried about you and want you to have someone to talk to."

"But I talk to you."

"I know. I told them that, but they insist you need to go. I've heard that therapists can give you methods to help when you have panic attacks, so maybe go and at least learn those."

"You're not going to leave me alone there?" There's panic in his voice.

"No, I'll be with you the entire time. I can learn the methods with you, and then if it happens again, I'll know how to help you better."

"Okay, but I don't want to keep talking about what happened."

I don't want him feeling forced to talk about it again, either. "I'm sorry you have to go through this, too, but maybe it'll help more than we think."

He doesn't answer, and I end up reading Harry Potter until he falls asleep. He has three bad nightmares throughout the night, and I know it's because of the appointment. The dark circles under his eyes the next morning show how much the nightmares take a toll on him.

After breakfast, we go to his new asthma doctor. It takes forever for them to do a breathing test with Zach, and he looks exhausted by the time they are done. He's on a daily inhaler now and has a new rescue inhaler.

Thankfully, his therapist appointment is later in the afternoon, and he's able to sleep a couple of hours before we leave.

ZACH KEEPS a death grip on my hand when we are shown into the therapist's office to sit on the couch together. My mom has already talked to her for about ten minutes and is now in the waiting room.

Dr. Dietz smiles at both of us, her eyes zeroing in on Zach glued to my side and my arm around his back.

"Isaac, I'm Dr. Dietz; it's nice to meet you both."

"He hates to be called Isaac. His name is Zach," I offer when Zach doesn't say anything.

"Zach, that's a good name." She goes on with small talk before addressing the real reason we are here. "Mrs. Wellman told me you had a panic attack the other day. Would you like to talk about it?"

Zach shakes his head no, keeping his eyes down on his hands.

"Alright, do you think you can write about it for your next appointment and maybe read it to me?"

Another headshake.

"Is there anything you want to talk about while you're here? I'm willing to listen."

Zach is quiet and doesn't even shake his head this time.

I decide to ask for help, for him. "We would like to learn any methods or whatever they are that help you cope with panic."

Her eyes move to me. "I think that's an excellent idea. Coping mechanisms can really help." She continues. "He doesn't have to talk about anything he doesn't want to. This is a safe place with no pressure."

Some of the tension eases from Zach's body. Dr. Dietz does teach us ways for Zach to ground himself or do breathing exercises. I type everything in my cell so I can remember for later.

Zach is quiet on the way home, and Mom keeps looking back at him with worry. He seems depressed from the visit and doesn't say a word when we get home, climbing the stairs slowly and turning toward his own room. *Shit.*

Mom stops me before I can follow. "Did he talk to her about it at all?"

"No, Mom, he's not ready to revisit it right now. Since the panic attack, anything to do with his dad makes him anxious. He told me about it, and I can't see him telling anyone else."

She nods, and I hurry up the steps to his room. He's changed into a T-shirt and pajama pants, ones he never wears because he only keeps a few in my room, and they get used constantly. I watch him move from one place to another in his room, straightening everything to perfection until he sees me.

I walk in and sit on the edge of his bed. "What are you doing?"

"Cleaning… I don't want your mom to think I'm messy," he says quietly, smoothing out the other side of the bed's comforter to look untouched.

"Mom doesn't care if your room is messy. Besides, you're hardly ever in here." I catch his hand and tug him around the bed to stand between my legs. "What's really going on with you?"

"I don't know. I feel like I messed up with the panic attack, and now your parents must think I'm a mental case. Who wants to keep a mental case? And what happens the next time I have a panic attack?"

He tries to step back, but I grip his hips so he can't.

"And you're stuck with me all the time, and it's unfair to you… Why can't I just be normal?" A few tears escape his green eyes that are so earnestly staring into mine.

"My parents love you, Zach, and they want to keep you forever. They don't think you're a mental case at all. They just want to make sure they don't fail you in any way. And the next time you have a panic attack—if you have one—we will breathe through it." I wrap my arms around his back and hug him closer. "I want you close to me, and I know for a fact that if something happened and I needed your support, you would be right there with me."

"I would," he whispers.

"As for normal, I don't think anyone is normal. We all have our own issues and personalities. Normal is overrated anyway."

"What issues do you have?"

"Hmm… I attract girls that are annoying and talk too much." Tapping my finger to my lips, I try to think of another one. "I drool when I sleep…and I get stage fright when I have to speak in front of people."

"Those aren't really issues, and you don't drool when you sleep." There's a hint of a smile in his voice.

"Zach, please stop worrying. I'm your family, and nothing else matters. It's you and me, forever."

He gets this deep sadness in his expression, one that makes my heart hurt. "I love you, Brady."

His words feel heavy but also ease the worry all this created. "I love you, too."

I kiss his cheek and then tug him down to my room. We sprawl out on the bed with his head lying on my arm, and I read more Harry Potter to him. He flips the pages until he falls asleep.

FIFTEEN

ZACH

Grandma and Grandpa fly in the next day to spend the holidays with us. I don't even know their real names because they insist that everyone calls them Grandma and Grandpa. They are Michael's parents and treat me just like they do the other kids in the family.

Emily's parents have both passed away already, leaving a trust for each of the kids. Brady never flaunts it or talks about it much, except for when he's reassuring me that he can afford a place for us after high school.

I spend a lot of the time in the kitchen helping with desserts and learning how to cook Grandma's dressing—a secret family recipe. Cooking feels good, like I'm a part of the family and can actually take care of them all in my own way. My happiness is made even bigger when every time I bring Brady sweets to sample, he tells me he loves me in this teasing, exaggerated tone.

He usually sits in the living room where he can see me, reading a book or typing away on his laptop, or sometimes he joins us in the kitchen and talks to me while I help.

As soon as lunch is over, he drags me upstairs for a nap. I like to protest that I don't need one, but my body screams that it does.

. . .

ON CHRISTMAS EVE, we watch Christmas movies and eat way too much food. Brady is lying on the couch with me in between him and the back cushions, my head resting on his shoulder. His fingers brush up and down my arm in a comforting way that makes my eyes close.

"Brady! Zach!"

Anna's loud voice wakes me, and I realize that I'm in bed now. Brady must have carried me up here last night after I fell asleep watching movies.

"Go away!" Brady's chest rumbles under my ear, and he pops his head up to look at the clock. "Go back to bed. It's only just six o'clock."

"Santa came," Meg whines, tugging on the blankets. "Mom said we can't open gifts until everybody is up."

"Fine. Go downstairs and we'll be down shortly."

The sound of feet running from the room tells me they left. Brady's breathing evens out again, and whenever his chest rises under my cheek, it always relaxes me and puts me to sleep. I'm almost there when he shifts against me. It's just enough to give me morning wood, and my eyes fly open. I try to untangle myself from Brady, but he only holds me tighter.

"Brady," I hiss, feeling my face heat up.

He shifts again, and I groan. I'm going to die of embarrassment. "Brady!"

"What?" He opens his eyes and finally realizes why I'm trying to get away. "Go back to sleep; it's too early for this."

"Brady!"

He lets me up, and I scoot off the bed, running to the bathroom to take a shower and give myself some relief. When I come back out with a towel wrapped around my waist, Brady is sitting up in bed and gives me a smirk, like he knows exactly what I was doing in there.

"Don't say a word!"

He holds his hands up. "I wouldn't dare." He grins, and I roll my eyes at him.

"Close your eyes so I can get dressed," I order.

He rolls his eyes at me this time. "You're being ridiculous."

I wait for him to close them before turning to get dressed. They are still closed when I turn back around. "Okay, you can open them."

"You realize I've seen you naked before. It's not a big deal."

My skin flushes hot. "Wait? When did you see me naked?"

"Let's not talk about it. We have Christmas presents to open." He climbs out of bed and puts his pajama pants back on, sliding a T-shirt over his head.

It dawns on me that I was naked when he saved me from my dad. Shame fills me that he had to see me so broken and battered.

"Hey, no sad faces." He walks over to kiss my forehead, ruffling my hair. "Today is Christmas, and I know for a fact that you're going to love your Christmas present."

"What is it?"

He taps my nose. "Not telling you."

We race downstairs and find everyone is already up. Presents get passed around until everyone has a pile. I look at my stack of gifts and swallow hard so I don't cry. The girls go first, opening their presents and squealing over everything. They tell Brady to go next, and he smiles, giving thank yous to his parents and grandparents. Most of what he gets is gaming stuff, clothes, and an iPad.

Then it's my turn. Brady holds some of the presents back, saying they need to go last. I get books from his grandparents. Then I open some presents from Brady, and one is a purple Eeyore pj shirt that says *has anyone seen my bright side?*—along with tight purple pj bottoms to go with it. It's obviously a girl's outfit, but the fact he doesn't care makes it all the more special. There's a Disney sweatshirt and some Disney socks. No one says anything about the outfit, thankfully. It's not that I want to dress up like a girl; it's that Brady didn't care that it was different and bought it anyway because he knows how much I love Eeyore. He also bought me a snow globe with Disney World inside.

I lean sideways to hug him tightly. "Thank you. I love all of it. It's perfect."

He hands me a pretty big box to unwrap next, and everyone seems to be holding their breath. I open it up, pulling out a collar, a leash, and what looks like dog toys. "I don't understand," I say, staring at all of it.

His mom hands me a card, and I open it to find a letter written inside.

Dear Zach,

We want to thank you for giving Honey a home. She needs to be spoiled and loved after everything she's been through. To give you some history on Honey, let us tell you all about her.

Honey's family bought another puppy and decided they didn't want to keep Honey anymore. They dumped her out in the country, where Honey almost starved to death. When she was found in the middle of the road, she had been shot, and some type of chemical burn was down her side.

Honey was brought to our rescue and given all the medical treatment she needed. We had fundraisers for her, and through social media, we found her previous owners and discovered what happened.

When your mom and dad contacted us looking for a dog to adopt for you, we knew you were the right match. You see, Honey gives so much love and yet is still sad. She needs an owner who will understand and give her all the love she needs to heal. Maybe you both can help each other because she needs you and we think you need her, too.

Honey hasn't had any accidents with us, but you might need to show her where the door is to go outside. She is three years old but looks older because of the trauma she went through. She has all her vet work done for this year, but remember to give her flea and heartworm prevention on the first of every month. Her microchip is already registered in your name.

We would love to see pictures and get updates over the years if you have time. The volunteers and vet staff took really good care of her and would love to see her happy.

Congratulations and best wishes on your adoption of Honey. Please contact us if you need any help at all.

Merry Christmas,

Hannah Parker

Second Chances Rescue & Adoption Center

Tears stream down my face and onto the words. How could anyone hurt a dog like that? I look up to see Emily with tears in her eyes, too. "You got me a dog?"

That's when I see Grandpa walk around the corner with a dog on a leash. She's a Golden Retriever, I think. But right now, she's still thin, and her hair looks unhealthy. I slide off the couch to kneel in front of her, and her soulful brown eyes have the same hurt reflecting in them that I feel often. Her fur is shaved where she must have been shot, but the wound looks freshly healed over. There are areas where her skin looks scarred from the chemical burns, and whereas some people might think it's ugly, I only see how precious she is. I can't help but cry, though. Cry for what someone did to a helpless dog that never hurt anyone.

"You're okay," I whisper, hugging her as gently as I can. "You're safe now. Brady won't let anything happen to you either." I figure if Brady's words always help me, they will probably help her, too.

Brady sinks down on the floor beside me, putting his arm around my back and running his hand softly over her head. "He's right. I won't let anything happen to either of you."

I raise my head to look at his parents. "She's really mine?"

Emily wipes some tears away and nods. "She's all yours, sweetie."

"I've always wanted a dog, but I never thought it would happen." I leave Honey with Brady for a second so I can hug both his parents. "Thank you for giving us both a home."

"Always," Emily says, her eyes reflecting how much she means it.

While the adults open up their presents, I sit next to Brady with Honey lying against me, her head on my lap. She seems to love the soft, gentle pets over her fur, and I make sure to say plenty of sweet things to her.

Brady and I put the dog dishes they bought on a mat in the kitchen. She drinks a little but ignores the food. We take her outside, and she goes right away. Brady's dad says he's going to have a privacy fence put in come spring so we can let her out the back door to run around without worrying about her.

After eating breakfast, we carry up all our gifts to Brady's bedroom, leading Honey with us. A big dog bed is now on his floor, and we put some water and food in his bathroom in case she wants to eat or drink when up here.

Every time I see her scars, I want to cry. Brady lifts her up on the bed, and I lie with my arm around her, kissing the back of her head.

Brady curls around me, reaching his arm over so he's holding both of us. We lie here quietly for a while before Brady turns on the TV. Home Alone 2 is on, and even though I've seen it with Brady before, I can't help but laugh.

Brady leans over to kiss my cheek and whispers, "Merry Christmas, Zach."

I lean back to kiss his. "I'm so grateful I get to spend it with you."

ALL OF CHRISTMAS Day is perfect. Honey seems to know she's my dog and sticks close to me wherever I go. She loves Brady, too, and watches him when he's away from us. Maybe she's seen that I watch him wherever he goes and is just copying me.

The rest of the week is spent loving all over Honey and spending time with Brady. We take her on walks and hand-feed her when she doesn't want to eat. Brady reads to both of us whenever I ask him to. At night, I start out comforting her but always end up snuggled into Brady with Honey lying against my back.

Brady and I study for our permit test and pass it with flying colors. I'm not sure I want to drive, but I figure I'll get over the learning part while Brady can do it with me. Honey stays with the girls while we are gone, but when I get home, she's waiting by the door for me.

Slowly, I start to take shorter naps, and I don't get exhausted quite as quickly. Honey seems to be improving with me. Her appetite is better, and she can jump up on the bed by herself now.

Connor comes over for New Year's Eve and falls in love with Honey, too. I'm glad he's here because I know that I'll never make it to midnight without falling asleep, and he'll be able to keep Brady company. Honey and I end up passing out in bed while they game.

Throughout this holiday time, Emily teaches me how to cook supper dishes and Grandma teaches me how to bake desserts. I'm determined that when Brady and I move out in two and a half years, I'll be the best cook there is and know all his favorite dishes.

The day before we go back to school, Emily takes me in to get my braces off. I was supposed to get them off a few weeks ago when they had my retainer made, but it got pushed back because of the incident.

We are standing at the checkout window, and Emily asks if every-thing is taken care of for the retainer or if she needs to pay for it now.

The receptionist looks it up on the computer to double-check. "No, Ma'am, it says here that Mr. Wellman paid the full amount before the braces were put on and that included the retainer. But now, if he loses it, it'll be a hundred and sixty to replace."

My brain is working overtime, and as soon as I'm in the backseat, I ask, "Why did she say Mr. Wellman paid for my braces back when I was thirteen? Did you guys pay for them?"

Brady bites his lip and looks out the window. His mom is quiet for a minute and then answers. "Yes, we paid for them back then. Your teeth were so bad, and we knew your parents weren't going to get them for you. Michael went over to talk to your parents while you were at our house with Brady and asked them if they would let you get braces if he paid for them."

I don't understand. "But why would you do that for me? You barely knew me."

Brady reaches over to take my hand, his face serious when he answers, "Because we loved you then, too."

His mom does this humming sound. "He's right. You walked into our lives, and we knew you were ours even then."

I blink the tears away, trying to process it all.

She continues. "You know, we never planned on moving after Owen died. But a long-time friend that Michael hadn't seen since high school ran into us at a restaurant. In fact, he's the mayor of this town. He told Michael about the position here, and it just seemed like something was pushing us in this direction. It was a leap of faith moving our family here, but we both agreed when Brady brought you home that Owen had sent us here for you. We needed you as much as you needed us. You filled up this hole and healed a lot of the hurt we were all going through. We truly believe that Owen sent you to us."

It sinks in that they truly want me. I'm not a charity case or bothering them. *They want me.*

Brady presses his forehead to the side of my face like he does sometimes, giving me the strength and comfort that I need. "She's right. I thought that Owen sent me you to love."

So much for not crying. I keep brushing the tears from my cheeks and let their words settle deep inside, healing some hurt parts of my heart.

Honey is waiting for me when we get home, *my home,* and she licks all over my face, like she missed me, wagging her tail until it's thumping on the floor. "I love you, Honey."

That earns me another kiss and her running up the stairs with me. I think Honey is starting to realize she's home, too.

SIXTEEN

ZACH

Life gets into a routine after that. School is stressful at first but gets better. Mainly because I'm never alone there. Either Connor or Brady is at my side all the time. If they work out after school, I sit to the side and do my homework. Derek still hates me, but he never gets close enough to bother me now.

Dad teaches both Brady and me how to drive. Yes, I'm calling them Dad and Mom now. After accepting that they really want me as a part of their family, it came easy. I know it's weird, but I think of them as my in-laws, and I get to call them Mom and Dad because I'm with Brady.

I know that I'm not really with Brady, but it feels like it with how much time we spend together.

Brittany finally gets the hint and leaves him alone. It's usually Connor, Brady, and me doing things together, but sometimes Alex and Ivy join in or other guys from his team.

Honey has blossomed as time goes on. Her hair has grown back, and she's a healthy weight now. There are some scars still, but I don't even see them anymore. She's beautiful and sweet and loves all of us. She follows me everywhere when I'm home, but when I'm gone, she'll cuddle up to whomever is there—mainly Grandma and Grandpa. They bought the house next door right after Christmas and insisted the fenced-in yard be one big one with theirs included. Honey goes over to their house if no one is home and lies at Grandpa's feet all day.

I still have panic attacks sometimes. One was when our driving instructor looked like my dad and seemed angry. Brady held me and talked me through the grounding and breathing methods we had learned together. Then Dad got us a new instructor, a woman, and it went easier after that.

We continue therapy, but I bring Honey along every time. Dr. Dietz now has me on a *call if you need me* basis.

I haven't heard from either of my biological parents, and I'm happy about it. If Matthews even is my biological father. Knowing he will get out of jail before I turn seventeen is a constant buzz in my ear that I try to ignore.

As for my health, it's better. Well, besides the occasional panic attack or asthma attack, it is. We also found out that I am anemic if I don't take iron supplements. The doctor explained the anemia was behind the fatigue and me feeling sick all the time. I've not really gained much weight if I look in the mirror, but I don't look sickly anymore. I've also grown a couple of inches and have made it to a whopping four foot ten.

Brady is now six foot two and is filling out even more. He's hot as hell, and pretty much every girl in a hundred-mile radius of him knows it. I feel like this bubble of him and me being close is about to burst, changing things forever.

I stare out the window waiting for him to get back from taking his driver's test. I have to wait until my birthday in a few weeks to take mine. Not that I'm crazy looking forward to driving. Driving means I will be separate from Brady and that life is moving on.

Connor leans his head over my shoulder to see what I'm looking at. "He'll be back soon."

I'm grateful that Connor never judges or makes me feel stupid for being so attached to Brady. He never looks at us weirdly, and if Brady has to go do something, Connor usually sits with me until he gets back.

Mom's SUV comes into sight, and before long, Brady is walking in through the door from the garage with a grin. "It's official; I can drive on my own now." He walks straight to me and gives me a hug, kissing my forehead like he always does. "I can drive us places now."

Connor and him fist-bump. "Happy birthday, bro. I guess you can finally start dating, too."

Dating. He's going to be taking out girls now, and I'll be the one left at home. My stomach cramps and I pull away from Brady, leaving them to talk.

Mom gives me a hug when I walk into the kitchen, and I busy myself helping her make some trays for the party later. She cuts up fruit while I make a meat and cheese tray, arranging it all fancy.

"I'm going to get a job," I tell her, placing a triangle of Colby cheese in line with the previous slice. Knowing that Brady is going to be dating soon makes me realize I will be alone a lot.

She pauses slicing the kiwi. "A job?"

"Yeah. I need to be saving money for a car and the future." I shrug. "Just seems like the thing to do."

"You know that we will take care of you, Zach. You don't have to rush out to get a job right now."

"I know, but I want to be able to pay for things." They've tried to give me an allowance, but I've refused to take it. I don't need to waste money, and they pay for my clothes. Brady pays for the movies or food or whatever we do when we go out.

"Are you going to be okay being out around people without Brady?"

No.

"Without me? Where are you going, Zach?" Brady leans on the island; Connor's standing next to him. I hadn't realized they'd come close enough to overhear the conversation.

"Umm…I'm going to try and get a job."

Brady frowns, his blue eyes studying me. "No."

Connor raises his eyebrows at the firm no from Brady, and he steps over a little.

I'm a little shocked he said no like that, too. "No?"

"You heard me. *No.*"

"Brady!" Mom says from beside me.

His eyes flash to hers and then back to mine. "He's not getting a job."

I've never seen him so adamant about anything. "Why not?"

"Because I don't want you to." His eyes dare me to argue with him.

I know my best friend better than myself, and if he's upset over me getting a job, I shouldn't take that lightly. "Okay, but I want to talk about it later."

He nods and the tension eases a little. Brady and I always talk about things that are bothering us, but we do it late at night when we are lying in bed, just the two of us. Everything between us feels so private, as if no one else has any right to be a part of it.

Connor flashes me a sympathetic glance before persuading Brady to go for a swim. Brady gives me one last, intense look before leaving to change into his swimming trunks.

Mom and I quietly finish the trays together. Before I leave the kitchen, she gives me a side hug. "If you want to get a job, don't let Brady stop you."

I mutter an okay, but I think we both know that if Brady tells me not to do something, I'm not going to do it. There is no one in this world I trust more than him.

Grandma and Grandpa walk over for the party, giving me hugs the same as they do Meg and Anna. Dad comes home and gives me a hug, too. They are a huggy type of family, and I love that about them.

Soon a lot of Brady's friends start to show up. Alex and Ivy, who are dating exclusively now. Josh, Elliot, Jace, Mike, and Hammer show up next. Tessa shows up with a few girls that hang around her at school, but I don't know their names.

They all head out back to swim, and I could join them but don't. Whenever they are all in their bathing suits and swimming trunks, I just look like a twelve-year-old with pale skin and no muscles. It doesn't bother me when it's just Connor and Alex over, but when all his friends show up, I get too overwhelmed still.

Honey and I go up to Brady's room, but then I decide to go to my own room. I'm never in there, but today it feels like I should be. Flopping down on the bed, I cover my eyes with my arm and then smile when I feel Honey lay down half on my chest. "I love you, pretty girl. At least I know you're never going to start dating and leave me alone." She gives me a lick as if she totally understands.

I can't believe how much my life has changed in less than a year. My past seems like a distant memory, and yet it's so close to the surface at the same time. Before that monster can consume my thoughts, I picture Brady holding my hand and relax into the bed more.

My friends are all laughing and having a blast while swimming. I glance toward the patio door again, but Zach still doesn't appear. It's hard to have fun when I don't know where he's at.

"I'll go check on him," Connor offers, his gaze following mine to the door.

"Nah, I'm going to go." I climb from the pool and dry off as best I can before wrapping a towel around my waist and going inside.

Dad passes me with hamburgers he's taking out to grill. "Where's Zach?"

"I don't know. I'll find him."

Mom tilts her head toward the stairs when I walk by. "He headed up there about an hour ago."

My room is empty.

Shit.

Big clue that something is wrong with my best friend. I walk down to his room, and he's asleep on the bed, cuddled up with Honey.

Leaning against the door frame, I watch his slow, even breaths, and some of my tension eases. He's grown a couple of inches but is still small and slender. There's almost a feminine quality to his shape at times. Especially when he wears his girly Eeyore pajama outfit, and he wears it a lot. Or maybe it's his softness and gentleness that give him a feminine edge. Tenderhearted would be the perfect word to describe Zach.

He's doing so much better, but there are times where he panics over things that trigger his PTSD. He still has nightmares several times a week, especially if I'm gaming and not in bed with him. If he's not close, I want him close.

We are so comfortable with each other; I can just be me with him. Doesn't matter if what I say sounds stupid; he won't judge me and will listen. Doesn't matter if I do something wrong because he will hug me and forgive me without question.

Honey lifts her head to look at me and does a little whine to say hi, thumping her tail on the bed with happiness. The noise and movement bring Zach's eyes open, but it takes a second for him to wake up fully and focus on me.

"Hey, are you feeling okay?" I ask, moving forward to sit on the edge of the bed.

"Yeah, I'm fine." He reaches out to lay his hand over mine.

Entwining our fingers, I use my other hand to brush the hair from his eyes. "Why are you up here and not outside with everyone else?"

"There are a lot of people here...and I don't know if you've noticed, but I look like a little kid next to all you footballers." He looks away from me. "I'm scrawny."

"Who cares what anyone thinks? I like you the way you are, and my opinion is the only one that counts."

He rolls his eyes, but I see the hint of a grin play across his mouth.

"Seriously, it's not the same without you. I don't have anyone to throw around in the water."

"You can throw the girls," he says, pulling his fingers away from mine.

"I suppose there is that, but the girls don't want to get their hair wet." It's my turn to roll my eyes. I'll never understand girls. Why go swimming if you don't actually want to swim?

"I bet the guys wouldn't want me swimming with them if they knew I was gay," Zach whispers.

He hasn't come out to anyone at school, not even to Connor. I hear comments about how close Zach and I are, but I ignore them. I have zero interest in homophobes and their opinions. I never say anything because if people are going to think something, I'd rather they direct it at me than center all their attention on Zach.

"If any of the guys have an issue with it, I'll show them the door," I counter. "What's this really about? You've been around the guys plenty and never had an issue."

"It's nothing." He sits up on the bed, avoiding looking at me.

"It's not nothing. Now tell me."

He gives me a forced smile. "It's your birthday. I'll come downstairs. Everything is fine."

"Not until you tell me what's bothering you." I won't be able to enjoy myself if I know he's upset.

He sighs, running his hand through his hair in exasperation. "It's nothing, *really*. I guess that I feel like with turning sixteen, things will change and we'll grow apart."

That's not going to happen. "Why would you think that?"

"Because things will change." He looks like he's going to say more but then closes his mouth.

The sad look on his face makes my stomach hurt. I catch his hand and drag him over to my lap, hugging him.

"I'm too big for your lap," he argues but leans into me.

"Pfft, you're smaller than Meg."

"Ugh, you're not helping me any."

"Stop worrying so much about things. Nothing is going to change just because we are getting older."

"You're getting my clothes all wet."

"Great, then you can change into swimming trunks and come outside with me." I kiss his forehead and then push him off my lap. "Do it now because people are going to wonder where the birthday boy is."

He grins, rolling his eyes again. "Who says *birthday boy* anymore?"

I grin back. "Grandma."

His swimming trunks are in my room, and I wait for him to change before dragging him downstairs with me. Mom smiles when we walk through, and Dad gives me a nod when he sees Zach with me. No matter how much time passes, we all still worry about him. Zach carries this fragility about him that we can all see. Even my friends go out of their way to watch out for him.

As soon as we get to the pool, I pick up Zach and toss him in the water. I've done it so many times; he doesn't even try to fight it. Connor yanks Zach up to the surface, holding onto him until he catches his breath and wipes the water from his face.

I dive in and swim over to them. We splash around, and Zach gets tossed a few times by both of us. He tries to push us under the water, but he can't do anything and only makes us laugh.

Some of the girls swim over to talk, and Zach ends up on a lounge with sunglasses on, looking relaxed with the sun beating down on him. "Zach!" I yell, trying to get his attention.

He pops his head up, raising his glasses.

"Sunscreen!" He burns really easy, and then he is miserable for days.

He sighs but gets up to get the sunscreen. I resume chatting with my friends but keep an eye on him to make sure he actually puts it on.

"You're really protective of your brother," one of the new girls, Mia, says from beside me.

"He's not my brother," I mutter, bothered by her assumption for some reason.

"Oh, I thought I heard him call your parents, Mom and Dad."

"He lives with us and is part of our family."

She gives me an odd look but doesn't say anything more. Tessa throws a ball at me, and I throw it back, glancing over at Zach again to check on him. Connor is on the lounge next to him, coating Zach's back with sunscreen. He tosses the bottle down, lying back and chatting with Zach about something that is making Zach laugh. It irks me a little that he's getting Zach's time instead of me. Zach has a million times more depth than any of my friends in the pool with me.

My dad calls out that the food is ready, and we all get out of the water to sit on the patio or around the pool to have a bite to eat.

"My God, where did you get these Reese cup cookies?" Alex moans, popping another one in his mouth.

Connor nods to Zach. "Zach made them. He makes desserts that I have dreams about later."

Zach turns red, ducking his head. "Thanks, Connor."

"You bake a lot, do you?" Mia asks with a snide tone to her voice.

Her bitchy attitude, along with the judgmental gaze she's giving Zach, is grating is on my last nerve. She might as well just blurt out that she thinks a guy baking is gay because she's clearly giving off that impression.

Connor answers her before I can. "Lots of guys bake. I can make some monster cookies to die for."

Dad sits forward and gives Mia a pointed look, successfully stopping her from spewing out another hurtful response.

The damage is done, though. Zach is super sensitive when someone implies he's gay. Even if he is, why should the things he does have to be measured by his sexuality? It pisses me off how people look at things. Straight guys bake and cook, too, for fuck's sake. Baking doesn't make a person gay.

He's quiet and stops eating. My friends are oblivious, all except for Connor, who keeps glancing over at him.

Zach escapes inside the house with his plate and I follow, trying to figure out a way to make him feel better. He's dumping the plate into the trash when I reach him. "Zach, don't let her make you feel bad."

"I'm fine, Brady. I just wish there wasn't this stigma that if you bake or do something girls do, it means you're gay. And if you do those things and *are* gay, people will judge you for it because somehow being gay makes you a sissy. Why can't they take it as I like to bake because I'm just me?"

I rub his back, wishing I had the answers. "People are stupid."

"This is why I don't come out. It's bad enough being judged when they don't know, but if they do know, it'll be a million times worse."

A throat clears and Zach whips around, his face paling. Connor is standing there, obviously having heard our conversation.

"Don't freak out," Connor says, walking closer. "I kind of knew already or thought I knew. I'm not going to tell anyone."

Zach clutches my hand for support. "You don't care?"

Connor shakes his head, setting his plate on the counter. "Why would I?"

"How did you know?"

Connor is quiet for a few seconds and then shrugs. "Just did, but then I'm around you more than everyone else."

"Oh...I thought I was hiding it well," Zach murmurs, staring down at his feet.

"You don't need to hide it from me anymore."

"Thanks, Connor."

I give Connor a grateful nod, appreciative that he's been so good with Zach throughout our friendship.

Zach leans against me, and I slide my arm around him to rub his arm. "You ready to go back out? I think we're going to play some volleyball." Dad set a net up yesterday.

"You're joking, right? Me, play volleyball with guys twice my size? No, thank you," he huffs.

"Twice your size might be an exaggeration, but okay. Just come out and watch then."

"I'm going to change first and get a book to read, then I'll be out." He pulls away from me and heads for the stairs, Honey following him.

As soon as he disappears, Connor finishes throwing his plate away. "Sorry I walked in on your conversation. I know how important it is to come out in your own time."

"He handled it well, and it's probably for the best. He can be open about it around you now. Although, I don't think even Grandma and Grandpa know."

We walk to the door together, Connor opening it to let me through. "Eventually, he'll tell everyone. He's going to want to date and meet guys, have relationships."

The implied *he'll want to have sex* is in there. I feel a little nauseous thinking about it. Zach is too fragile, and what if he gets hurt? "I'm not going to let him get hurt. Guys can just stay away until he's older. For now, they are going to have to come through me to get to him." I sound like an ass but can't take the words back.

Connor doesn't say anything, but I get the sense that my words bother him. I can't explain this intense protectiveness I have for Zach, but I'm not willing to give it up.

We form teams for volleyball. Zach does come out and lies on a blanket my mom has spread on the grass for whoever wants to watch the game and not play. Honey lies with him, letting Zach use her body as a pillow while he reads.

I relax, enjoying the game now that he's out here and I can keep an eye on him. We play several games until everyone is hot and needs to cool off in the pool. Zach moves to a lounge chair nearby but doesn't say a word to anyone. We swim for an hour, and when I look over to check on him, Zach is gone.

He comes out of the house carrying a cake to set on the patio table. Mom and Grandma are talking to him, and he smiles at something they are saying. I smile, too, because nothing is better than him being happy.

"Time for cake," Mom calls out to everyone.

We all dry off and crowd around the table. It's a big sheet cake, and there are sections decorated on it. There's a tree house that looks like ours, and then little football players on what looks like a field, and then there's a section with books and a Harry Potter wand. All of it means something to me, or me and Zach. I look up to catch his eyes on me. "Did you do this?"

He nods, his green eyes telling me he cares and hopes I love it. "It's perfect, Zach, thank you."

I blow out the candles, my wish being that I never lose Zach. Mom dishes out the chocolate cake to everyone. It's unreal how good it is, but I'm almost sad that we cut into it. At least Mom took plenty of pictures beforehand.

"When did you decorate the cake without me knowing?"

"Last night, when you and Connor were busy gaming, and Meg and Anna came in begging me to watch a movie."

Meg giggles, and I try to give her a fake stern look. "You girls lied to me?"

"Mhmm. We were helping Zach with the cake," Anna admits with a smile.

"It was my job to keep you occupied," Connor adds, "which is why I kicked your ass royally."

Mia keeps staring at Zach, and it's pissing me off. I can tell she wants to make a comment about him baking a cake, and so help me God if she does, I'll tell her to leave. Her eyes catch my look, and I think she gets the hint. I'm going to tell Tessa not to bring her over anymore. This is Zach's home, too, and he shouldn't have to take crap from anyone here.

Everyone starts to leave after that, including Connor. He gives Zach a hug before he leaves, saying something in his ear that makes Zach smile. That familiar twinge of protectiveness hits me, and I try to push it away. It's Connor; he would never hurt Zach.

EIGHTEEN

BRADY

Now that everyone is gone, I go up to my room to take a shower and put clean clothes on. Zach hasn't come up yet, and I meander back downstairs to see him helping Mom clean up from the party. He stops to braid Anna's hair when she stands next to him with a brush. Then he goes back to stacking the dishwasher.

Dad comes up behind me and puts his hand on my shoulder, which makes me realize I've been standing here for ten minutes, just staring at Zach.

Dad's eyes follow mine to where Zach is taking the washcloth from Mom and shooing her away while he finishes. "There is something so special about him, isn't there."

He says it more as a statement than a question, but I answer anyway. "He really is, Dad. I am grateful every day that I found him in the woods and became his friend."

Zach finally sees us standing here and gives me a questioning look. I smile and he smiles back. He's truly beautiful when he smiles.

"Alright, Son. Time for your birthday present." He squeezes my shoulder before calling for my mom. "Everyone outside!"

Zach reaches me and I take his hand. "Do you know what it is?"

"No, but maybe you should close your eyes and let me guide you out."

I do, but only because he sounds so excited for this to be a surprise. He stops somewhere in the driveway, I think.

"Okay, open your eyes," Mom says.

My eyes open and in front of me is a pickup truck. It's sharp, with shiny red paint and chrome trim. My mouth drops open as I stare at it. Glancing over at my Dad, I find him smiling widely.

"It's yours. Happy birthday!"

"You bought me a truck?"

"We wanted you to have something reliable, and it's four-wheel drive for snow. It should get you through the rest of high school and college without any issues."

I know my parents have money and that I'm going to have a big trust fund, but I still didn't expect them to buy me a vehicle. I figured I'd have to drive Mom's SUV when she wasn't using it. This moment feels huge, and I realize that Zach is right. Things do feel like they are changing.

"Thanks, Mom, Dad. It's perfect. Exactly what I would have picked out."

"We know. You look at car magazines enough and bring up trucks often," Mom says, smiling. "We chose a bench seat, in case you need to fit three people in."

Dad hands me the keys, and I open the door to see inside. It's so sharp and new that I can't help but grin. I have a truck, which means more independence and freedom. I can date or go out after games without having to ask my parents to drive me.

"You want to go for a drive with me?" I ask Zach, who is standing next to me, looking shocked at my parents' extravagant birthday gift.

He nods and I motion for him to crawl up from the driver's side. He tries and it's too high for him to do easily. Picking him up by the waist, I deposit him in the truck, and he crawls over to the other side. "Might need to add some running boards so Zach can ride with me easier."

Dad nods in agreement with a chuckle. "Might be a good idea."

Zach grins as I pull out of the driveway, and soon we have music on and are cruising down Main Street. Not that Main Street is any big deal, but it's cool just to be out driving with only the two of us.

By the time we get home, Mom and Dad have gone inside. We spend a little time talking to them, teasing my sisters, and putting Honey outside to potty quickly before going up to my room.

Zach disappears into the bathroom to shower, and I strip down to my boxers, crawling into bed with Honey. I text Connor a picture of my truck, and he has to know all the details. When I hear the shower turn off, I message him goodnight and toss my cell onto the side table.

Zach comes out of the bathroom in his favorite Eeyore pj's and tries to crawl into bed. "Scoot over, Honey." He pushes her a little, really gently, but she doesn't budge.

"Honey, move," I order, and she gets up and moves to her normal spot.

Zach huffs. "Why does she obey you right away?"

"Because I'm the alpha between the three of us."

"The alpha, huh… What does that make me?"

"I don't know…the beta? Whatever is second in a wolf pack."

"What if I don't want to be a wolf?"

"It is just a figure of speech!"

He grins like he's been teasing me this whole time and couldn't care less. I growl, ruffling his hair and smacking him in the face with a pillow.

"Stoooooop," he whines, grabbing the pillow and tossing it on the floor. "Hope you don't need that to sleep."

"Get up and get that." I grab his pillow and lay my head on it, keeping a firm grip so he can't take it back.

He tries and fails. "Brady! No fair! You're a hundred times stronger than me."

"Just a hundred?" I pretend to sound offended.

"Ugh!" He flops back on the bed, lying there without a pillow at all.

"Hope you're comfortable all night without a pillow."

He rolls on his side to face me. "I always use your arm for a pillow, so I'm not getting up to get it only for Honey to use like usual."

He has a point. He uses my arm every night or my chest. We've gotten so used to sleeping together that I feel an instant loss if he gets out of bed during the night. I offer him my arm, and he lies with his head against it.

"You ready to talk?"

I know what he's referring to and have been hoping he would forget. "I don't want you to get a job."

"Why?"

"Because I can't protect you if you're somewhere without me."

The worry in his eyes tells me he's not as keen on the idea as he's pretending to be.

"Why do you want a job?"

He runs his finger over my chest in patterns. "I need to make money."

"Is there something you want to buy?" His soft touch trailing over my skin is sending tingles over my body. I lay my hand over his to keep it still.

"I want to save for a car, and I want to be able to buy you a Christmas present or a birthday gift. I can't buy you anything." It's obviously upsetting him.

"You know I don't want anything," I murmur, turning on my side so I can see him without cricking my neck. His green eyes are only inches away, staring into mine. They always show everything he's feeling; it's one of the things I love most about him.

"I know you don't, but I want to have a little money of my own."

I rub the back of my neck and try to think of a way to do this. "Let me think about it, okay?"

"Okay, it's not that I want to get a job around people. Honestly, it's a little scary to me. At school, I knew you were right there. What if I have a panic attack while at work? I worry about all those things."

Hearing him echo my own thoughts, my every instinct is to say no.

"I just want to be able to pay my way," he whispers.

The fact that he has to worry about panic attacks and how to cope with them isn't fair. He should be able to live a normal life. Maybe if it's something gradual, where he can ease into working. "I'll figure out a way, but let's not rush into anything."

"Alright, thanks, Brady." The way he says it makes me feel like I've hung the moon for him just by taking him seriously.

"Don't thank me yet, because if I don't find a solution I like… you're not getting a job."

He doesn't argue with me, just buries himself closer. I lean back long enough to turn off the light and then wrap him up in my arms like usual. Honey crawls up to lie against his back, and I smile at how Zach manages to glue himself to me.

OUR SUMMER CONTINUES and we do a lot of swimming, the heat so oppressive for June. We still go out to the tree house sometimes, but not as much as we used to. He always looks down the trail to his old house and ends up practically in my lap the rest of the time out there.

Instead of going to the theater, we hang out at the drive-in now that I have a truck. I back it into our favorite spot, and we lounge on the bed of the truck with our cooler and snacks. Girls often flock over to sit on the tailgate, quietly chatting with Connor or me. I've yet to ask a girl out, and I don't even know why. None of them have really caught my attention.

I've been looking at jobs for Zach, but most of the places hiring are loud and high traffic. I don't think Zach could handle working in fast food with all the noise and stress. Gas stations are definitely out. I mention it to Dad, and he says he'll see what he can find that would fit Zach. Part of me wants to tell Zach that he can't do it at all.

Zach doesn't say a word about the job idea, and I know he's trusting me to work it out. I should find a job, too, but since I know what I want to do for a career, I'd like to concentrate on that. No one in the family knows what I want to do, not even Zach.

Today is Zach's birthday, and he got his driver's license this morning. He had a hard time with the fact I couldn't ride along but made it through. I stood outside, knowing it would help if he knew I was close by and waiting.

For his birthday, he didn't want a party with tons of people around. No surprise there. Instead, Connor comes over for supper. Mom makes Zach's favorite meal of chicken parmesan. Zach makes it better, but I'll never tell my mother that. He cooks everything better, and everyone benefits from it. Connor is constantly coming over for meals or begging for sweets that Zach makes. He says he upped his time in the gym but that it's worth it.

After supper, the dishes are cleared, and we eat the cake that Zach made himself. He doesn't like box cake or even bakery cake. He likes homemade from scratch cake from my great-grandmother's recipe. I honestly think it's just ingrained in him, this need to care for others. The only person he lets do things for him is me. Even then, he tries so hard in return to do things for me back. He cleans my room, changes the sheets on the bed, bakes, and cooks for me. He still comes to football practice and sits under the tree; only now he brings Honey with him.

"Okay, time for the gifts," Mom says, clearing the cake plates.

Meg and Anna give him a chef's apron. It's red with a little Mickey Mouse on the front pocket. My grandparents give him a Mickey waffle maker and some more Disney socks. Connor surprisingly brings out a gift and watches intently as Zach unwraps the box. It's a throw blanket with Rapunzel and Eugene on the front, along with Maximus the horse. Zach hugs it to his chest, giving Connor a big smile. "Thank you, Connor. I love it."

"I thought you could use it when you're reading or watching a movie," Connor replies, staring at Zach like he truly hopes he loves it.

"Okay, my present is next." I hand over the box and hope that I picked the right thing. Most people would think it's a stupid gift, but I think it'll mean something to him.

He unwraps it carefully and pulls out a football jersey. It's identical to mine, only smaller, and has my number and name on it. Below it is a hoodie to match, for when it's cold at games. I know the guys get them for their girlfriends, but Zach is my constant supporter and there for every practice, every game, and deserves to be wearing my number.

He's quiet for a minute, staring at the jersey and running his fingers over my name on the back. I start to worry he doesn't like it when he looks at me with tears in his eyes. "You did this for me?"

"Of course. No one else I'd rather have wearing my number."

He's struggling to get control over his tears before he straight out cries. I've seen him do it a million times. I move from my chair to sit next to him, my mother scooting down to give me room. I shift him over to my lap and hug him close, kissing his cheek. "Don't cry; it's your birthday."

Zach hugs me back until he gets control over himself, and then I help him get the jersey on over his shirt. "Thank you, Brady," he whispers, giving me those liquid green eyes of his.

"You're welcome, buddy."

The light in his eyes dim, and he picks up his things to put in a pile, leaving my lap to carry them upstairs. Connor shakes his head, staring at me for a second before following Zach.

Mom and Dad exchange looks and I throw up my hands. "What?"

"Nothing, Son, but please remember that Zach is sixteen and when you call him buddy, it makes him think you see him as a little kid."

Shit. I haven't called him buddy in a long time, and I don't know why it slipped out now. "I didn't realize it bothered him."

Mom gets up to take the Mickey waffle maker into the kitchen and pats my head on the way by.

Meg rolls her eyes as she follows. "You're really dense sometimes."

"Hey," I say, but she's already out of the room.

Everyone is mad at me, and all I did was call him buddy.

NINETEEN

ZACH

I pull the jersey up over my head and fold it to put away. It was a perfect gift from Brady, right up until he called me buddy. I'm just a little kid to him, always have been and always will be.

Connor walks in the room and sits on the bed, giving me a sympathetic look. "Don't take it to heart. He doesn't see you as his buddy. You're his best friend and mean everything to him."

Shrugging, I put the jersey and hoodie in a drawer, along with the socks. Connor's blanket gets placed on the bed with Eeyore. "Thank you for the gift. I really love the blanket. Tangled is my favorite movie."

He smiles. "I know. You've watched it while we were gaming—numerous times."

"Oh, I didn't even know you noticed. You two are always so into your games." I sit down on the bed next to Connor. "I wish that I would grow some."

"I think you're pretty perfect the size you are. You realize that twinks are the most wanted gay guys." His lopsided grin is saying he doesn't really know for sure who is most wanted but would tell me anything to cheer me up.

It dawns on me that Connor is talking about twinks and my mouth drops open. "How do you know about twinks?"

He gets this sheepish expression. "I might have looked up the terminology and things I should know. I didn't want to say something that might offend you or mess up something that has everything to do with you."

"Aww, Connor… You're pretty sweet, thank you."

He puts his arm around me. "You're welcome."

"If you call me buddy, I'm going to wrestle you down on the floor and have a smackdown."

Laughter bursts from his mouth. "Smackdown? I'd like to see you try."

"Shush it." I nudge his arm with my shoulder. "Thanks for being a friend."

Brady comes in and frowns at the two of us sitting here. "Connor, can I talk to Zach alone for a minute?"

"Okay." He tousles my hair as he gets up from the bed. "I'll be waiting downstairs for that smackdown."

"Don't worry; I won't hurt you too badly," I say, smirking at him.

He laughs on his way out the door.

"Smackdown?" Brady doesn't look happy.

"It was a joke."

He folds his body down next to me, the blatant size difference reminding me yet again that I'm his buddy. *His sidekick.*

"I'm sorry I called you buddy. I don't think of you as a little kid… and I haven't called you that in a while. It just kind of slipped out."

Slipped out because that's how he really feels. "It's okay," I say, focusing on Honey, who is at my feet wagging her tail. I pat the bed, and she jumps up next to me.

"Zach, look at me," Brady orders, cupping my chin and turning my face until I have no choice but to meet his gaze. There is an apology in his intense blue eyes, and I know it's because he hurt me, not because he truly doesn't think I'm his buddy. "I'm sorry. You know I would never do anything to hurt you. I'd never forgive myself if I did. You are the most important person in this world to me."

Just like that, my heart holds onto the hope that someday he'll see me as more. I'm an idiot and a sucker for torture, apparently, because I lean over to press my lips to his arm briefly. "I know you wouldn't."

"Don't be mad at me, please," he pleads. "I can't handle it if you are upset."

"I'm not upset." *Anymore.*

Brady gives me a tight hug, kissing my forehead. "Okay. You forgot Dad and Mom's gift. They are waiting on you."

I can't believe that I forgot their gift. They must think I'm totally ungrateful.

We hurry downstairs and Brady steers me outside. Oh no, my stomach starts to hurt at the reality of what they've done. Everyone is standing next to a silver SUV, smiling like I should be jumping up and down.

"Happy birthday," Dad says, holding out my keys.

That's when it hits me, a full-blown panic attack. One minute I'm standing here, and the next, I'm on the ground gasping for air.

"Zach!" Brady's voice sounds far away as a waterfall rushes through my ears.

I need to breathe, but it's like my chest doesn't want to expand. Brady's arms are around me, and I can finally hear him say slowly, "Breathe in, one-two-three-four. Breathe out, one-two-three-four. Breathe in, one-two-three-four, Breath out, one-two-three-four."

Somehow I manage to breathe in and out with him, although it's ragged and forced.

He moves on to the grounding method of senses. "Hear my voice, Zach. See my eyes."

His deep blue eyes are completely focused on me.

"Feel my arms around you. You're safe."

I bury my face in his chest, clinging to him.

"Smell my cologne. You're right here with me."

I inhale and the familiar smell of Brady's favorite cologne mixed with his scent grounds me a little more. As with every panic attack, as soon as I come down from it, intense painful sobs hit me. I hate this part, but I can't seem to control it.

"You're okay. I'm not going to let anything happen to you," he murmurs near my ear, saying the words that always help.

It isn't until I've cried myself out and can lie against him in total quiet that I open my eyes to see we are in his bedroom. He's leaning against his headboard, still holding me tightly, with Honey lying against our legs.

"I'm sorry," I whisper, wishing I wasn't so messed up.

"You did nothing wrong."

"I messed up Mom and Dad's present." I feel terrible for it, too.

"It's not like you have control over when this happens, but can you tell me why you freaked out?"

How do I explain to him when it sounds stupid even to me? I shrug, choosing to stay quiet.

Brady shifts me so I'm forced to see his face, and he can see mine. "Talk to me. We don't hide things from each other."

Well, except for the fact that I'm in love with you. I look away. "It's dumb."

He moves my chin so I'm back to looking at him. "Nothing that makes you this upset is dumb, so just tell me."

"It's just that…if I have my own car…then I won't need to ride with you anymore." I feel ashamed to have to admit it. "I don't know if I can drive without you. What if I have a panic attack? I'll be separated from you…"

Understanding is there in his eyes. "I'm not ready for you to drive off on your own either. We can take turns driving, and then when you're ready, you have a car of your own."

Some of the tension leaves me with those words, and I relax a little. "They shouldn't have bought me a car. It's too much money. I was going to save for one when I got a job."

He clears his throat and looks like he wants to say something.

"What?"

"I'm going to say no on the job for now. After this panic attack, I don't think you're ready."

The relief that flows through me says he's right; I'm not ready. "Okay."

"If you really want to get a job, I'll get one with you. I don't want to keep you from doing something, but not alone, Zach."

It's really sweet that he would get a job just for me. "No, it's okay. I'm not ready."

We sit here quietly for a while with him holding me and me still clinging to him. It reminds me how special Brady is and how much he gives to me all the time. He always seems older than kids our age and talks like his dad does. It draws people to him, this calm, confident way that he has—like he's wiser than the rest of us. Maybe it's from losing his brother, or maybe it's all he's gone through with me, or maybe it's having his dad's positive influence. Dad shows so much love to us, but he always has a way of giving advice or saying things that make you know he's far wiser than everyone else. Brady has that same quality, and it only gets stronger as he gets older.

"You ready to go downstairs? Mom and Dad are probably worrying about you."

"I ruined their gift," I say sadly.

"No, you didn't. They love you and that is all that matters. The car isn't important."

He sounds so much like his dad with what he just said. It's hard for me to wrap my mind around an expensive vehicle not being important.

Brady holds my hand as we go to find his parents, Honey trailing behind us.

They are in the kitchen cleaning up supper dishes. Connor is sitting at the bar and gives me a sad smile. This is the first bad panic attack he's witnessed, and I'm sure it wasn't pretty.

Mom and Dad notice us and come over to give me a hug. Brady wraps his arm around my waist when they step back, giving me some support.

"I'm sorry about earlier. I'm grateful for the car...even though you spent too much money on me and I never expected you to give me anything. I hope you both know that."

"We do," Mom says, "but your Dad and I want to know that you're safe if you're out driving. We don't want you on the side of the road with a broken-down vehicle or worry that you're stranded somewhere. We wanted to do this."

Brady takes over for me to tell them the hard part. "Zach isn't ready to drive on his own yet, but we'll take turns driving, and hopefully, he'll be ready soon."

I stare at my feet, wishing that I was a normal teenager.

Dad puts his hand on my shoulder, drawing my attention to him. "There's no pressure, Son. It's there for when you need it. Whenever you're ready."

Son. That means more to me than the vehicle. I take the step to hug him, and he envelops me in his arms. Blinking back tears, I know that I'll remember this moment forever. "Thanks, Dad."

"Always. We are here for you."

How in the world did I get so lucky as to have this family? It's a miracle that I met Brady that day and that we became best friends. Especially considering we both come from such different backgrounds.

I step back to stand with Brady, and he uses his arm to pull me closer, kissing my forehead like he does so often. "Okay, how about you take Connor and me for a drive, and then we'll watch movies or swim. Whatever you want."

Mom and Dad walk out with us, showing me the Audi SUV. It has leather interior and gadgets that I'll have to read the manual on. It's nicer than anything I ever thought I would have.

"We didn't think a truck would be what you wanted, especially since you have a hard time climbing up into Brady's, but we wanted you to also have something good for driving in snow."

"It's perfect. I never dreamed I would have anything like this."

It's a dream to drive, too. Brady messes around with everything on the dash and soon has Maroon Five blaring through the speakers.

He reaches over to run the back of his fingers down my cheek. "Are you getting tired?"

Panic attacks suck the life out of me. "Yeah, you want to drive back?"

"Pull over in this parking lot up here," he says, pointing to the drive I need.

We switch out and I sink into the seat, trying not to fall asleep yet.

When we get back home, Connor heads out since there's practice early in the morning. Brady and I lie in bed with him reading to me in the voice that offers me so much comfort. I'd give anything to freeze time and stay here with him forever.

TWENTY

ZACH

The rest of the summer is pretty perfect. I quit worrying about a job, and it eases some of the pressure I've been feeling. Mom and Dad sit me down and explain that I do so much around the house, more than anyone else, that I'm accepting the allowance every week, whether I like it or not. Basically, they're giving me a job without a job. I accept it this time because it's true; I do as much as I can around the house.

While Connor and Brady are gaming, I watch cooking shows and try new recipes. I could probably stop learning more since I'm sure Brady and I won't starve now, but cooking brings me calm, and I love seeing Brady eat the food like it's the best he's ever had.

Brady doesn't go on one single date this summer, but it might be because the only time we see girls is when we go to the drive-in theater. Connor doesn't date either, for that matter. I still can't stop this feeling that things can't stay the same for much longer.

Starting school is nerve-racking, and even Brady seems nervous about today. It was impossible for us to be in every class together since I need a first-year foreign language and he's already taken his as a freshman. I choose French since that's what he has learned, and at least we can talk to each other because otherwise,

I can't see us using the language unless we fly to Paris or something.

I'm also in AP Literature and Composition last period, and he'll be practicing football now that he's in varsity.

Other than that, we matched up classes so we can be together, and our lockers are side by side this year. Connor is on my other side, and I don't have to worry that I'll get picked on by anyone. Not that I'm terribly concerned since most of the football players are kind of friends with me by association. All except for Derek and Nick, who still hate me as far as I know.

"You're going to be fine. I can walk you to class before going to my own."

I glance over at Brady, who is driving us to school. He doesn't look as confident as he sounds, but I try to do what he's doing and fake that I'm fine with it.

He pulls into an empty spot next to Connor's car and gets out, holding his door open for me to slide over so he can help me down without face-planting.

"I'm getting the running boards put on this weekend. They finally have the parts in."

"You think that's going to help me not face-plant getting out of this gigantic truck?"

He grins. "No, not really...but you'll at least be able to climb up inside on your own."

"Hey Brady!"

We turn to see Tessa with some other girls walking by, all staring at Brady like he's their next meal. Brady smiles and gives a small wave.

I roll my eyes at him and walk toward Connor, who is waiting for us. "Nice of her to say hi to me, too."

"I can't help it that I'm so irresistible to the ladies."

Connor catches what he says and scoffs. "Because you've been on so many dates already."

"Just wait and see; I'll be dating before you know it."

My stomach cramps, and I try to force a smile. Connor puts his arms around my shoulders. "Guess it'll be the two of us while he's off dating. Maybe I can teach you how to longboard."

Brady frowns, popping Connor's arm off my shoulders. "He's not going longboarding...it's dangerous."

"Whatever, dad," Connor jokes. "You won't know what we do

because you'll be on a date with some chick that does that hair toss thing and talks constantly."

"Dad?!"

Connor takes off running, and Brady chases him for a few yards before coming back to walk with me into school. He knows where our lockers are and directs us through the mass of kids that I didn't miss. Connor is already at our lockers, and Brady does a smack to the back of his friend's head before opening his own locker.

I'd memorized my lock combination earlier this week and open mine to stuff my bag inside. Guys and girls say hi to us—more like hi to the two guys next to me—as they walk by.

Derek is only a few lockers down, unfortunately. He gives me his typical angry look, and I sigh—yep, still hates me.

Brady and I head to class together, sitting at the table side by side. All the teachers know to just leave us together, and I'm pretty sure Dad is the one that made that clear to them.

It might be my imagination, but girls seem a lot more aggressive than they used to be. We barely get two steps down the hallways before another girl is begging for Brady's attention. He is always nice, giving them a shy smile—it kills me to see it.

By lunchtime, I leave him talking to some new girl by our lockers and walk with Connor to the cafeteria.

"Zach, hold on," Brady yells out. I turn to see him get stopped by another girl and keep walking with Connor.

"You okay?" Connor's brown eyes are full of understanding, and I wonder for a second if he knows I'm in love with Brady.

I shrug, not sure if I can lie to him about it.

We sit down with the guys, and it isn't long before Brady joins us. "You guys could have waited for me."

"Dude, no one wants to stand there watching girls throw themselves at you," Connor says over my head to Brady.

"I was trying not to be rude."

This year is going to be torture. I pick at my food and give myself a pep talk on how Brady is just my best friend and I need to get a grip on reality.

Brady leans close to my ear. "You're awfully quiet."

"Just stressed about starting school."

"Oh look, there's the freshman faggot," Derek says loud enough for the entire table to hear and probably the surrounding tables, too.

Brady tenses beside me. "Don't be a dick, Sanders."

The poor guy walking by flushes with embarrassment. He's wearing a pink shirt and jeans shorts with a pink rose embroidered on them. He's a good six inches taller than me but has the same slender build that I have. His shaggy blonde hair makes him look pretty, and when he reaches up to tuck some of it behind his ear, I see pink fingernail polish on his nails.

It hits me that I've just spotted the first gay person like me. If he really is gay. I shouldn't assume since Derek isn't known for being honest. The new guy does have this way about him that says he might be. I don't think I walk that way, but who knows.

The guy sits a few tables down across the aisle with a couple of girls that look to be freshmen, too.

Derek at least shuts up and doesn't say any more. While Brady and Connor talk to their teammates, I'm still thinking about how I'm not the only one who is gay in my school. How did the other boy have the strength to be open about it? Because I'm terrified of being *out of the closet*, as they call it.

Brady walks me to French class, and I take deep breaths as I watch him walk away. I can do this and be here without him. I am not always with him at home and manage okay, so I should be able to sit in a classroom for forty-five minutes without him.

The guy Derek pointed out as queer is in here. Not surprising, since most of the students in this class are freshmen or sophomores. He looks up at me, and I give him a smile, hoping he'll realize not everyone will judge him. His eyes flare a little, and I wonder if he can tell I'm gay.

Forty-five minutes later, I have discovered I hate French class. It's going to take me a lot more studying than my other classes. All the sounds get mixed up in my head.

Connor catches up with me as I walk down the hallway to our lockers. "How do you like French?"

"I hate it."

He grins. "Figured you would. Nobody enjoys that class."

Up ahead, Brady is scanning the hallway, watching for me as he shoves his book inside his locker. He smiles when he sees me, and I hurry to reach him.

"Did it go okay?"

"Didn't panic, so I guess it went well." I haven't had a panic attack since my birthday.

"Good, I was worried."

He's so sweet that I forget about him being just my best friend, all over again.

We have the next class and then study hall together. After that, I get dumped off at my Literature class while Connor and Brady go to football practice. Their first game is in two weeks, and they've been impatient to play. Brady made captain this summer, which is not surprising since he's a natural leader and everyone respects him.

Literature class is awesome, and I know I'm going to love it. I've already read all the books listed on the sheet the teacher hands out. However, I'll enjoy discussing or writing papers on them. A lot of the kids groan when they see all the books they have to read, but reading is my passion, and I'd live in a library if I could. Well, if Brady was there with me.

After class is over, I walk down to the lockers and get my bag, stuffing the books I need inside. Without Brady or Connor, standing at my locker makes me nervous, the noise and people beating against my anxiety. Brady and Connor are still outside on the football field, and I rush to walk out there, sinking down in my usual spot by the tree.

Brady's head turns in my direction, and he gives me a wave before getting back into the mock game they are playing.

The coach is so used to me being around, he doesn't mind when I sit in the sports locker room waiting on the boys while they shower. I always make sure to sit where I can't see anyone and work on my homework until they are done. If anyone ever finds out I'm gay, I don't want them thinking I've been lusting after them while they run around half-naked on the other side of all these lockers.

THE NEXT WEEK GOES OKAY, minus the girls that flirt with Brady constantly. Some girl named Alyssa has taken up sitting next to him at lunch. I try to block it out and ignore it; it hurts too much.

Derek has been the worst part of the week. He constantly makes comments about *the faggot*, who I learn is named Avery. Brady always tells Derek to knock it off or shut up, but I feel bad that Avery has to hear it at all. I don't know what to do about it, though, because I'm too tiny to take Derek on and even the thought of fighting brings the feeling of panic to just below the surface. I've already shown I can't fight anyone bigger than me and almost died proving it. I do make a point of smiling or saying hi to Avery when he walks by, and so do Brady and Connor. He seems surprised every time, but I can tell he appreciates it.

It's the Monday before the game, and Derek has been in rare form today, loudly making fun of Avery in the lunchroom and hallways between classes. He and Brady have already had words, and there's this tension between all the guys now.

French class has ended, and I'm hurrying down the hallway to my locker. Brady is watching, and I point to the restroom that's close by our lockers. He nods and I duck inside to go quick. I'm washing my hands when Avery comes in, giving me a quick hello.

"What do we have here? It's the *fag* and he's standing up to take a piss." Derek has come in with Nick and goes over to stand behind Avery. "I thought gays sat down like girls. You're sissies, after all."

He pushes Avery against the urinal so hard that his face slams against the porcelain and blood spurts out of his nose instantly.

I can't stand here and do nothing. "Stop it!" I'm pretty sure I'm going to die now.

Derek's head swings around to see me standing here. "If it isn't *little* Zach. What are you going to do? Beat me up?"

"Just leave Avery alone."

Nick pushes me toward Derek, and he pushes me back. Panic roars in my ears, but I try to keep control over it, or I won't be able to help Avery. "Get out of here," I tell Avery as I'm pushed back at Derek.

Nick grabs Avery before he can leave, holding him with his arms pinned behind his back. I open my mouth to tell them to let him go, but Derek slams me into the wall, lifting me up and pinning me against the hard cement with his arm to my chest. "You're not better than me now, are you?"

I hear myself screaming *Brady* without knowing I've opened my mouth. The panic has hit too hard, and I gasp for air, but I can't breathe with his arm so tight against my chest.

One minute Derek is laughing in front of me, and the next, he's being thrown into the bathroom stalls across from me. Everything happens so fast as I fall to the floor.

Derek lunges up and punches Brady in the face seconds before

Connor crashes into him, taking him to the floor. Nick lets go of Avery and tries to kick Connor, but Brady slams into him and holds him off.

Connor gets punched and then he punches Derek; they roll around until Connor has him pinned down with his knee on his back. "Stop it, dude! You've lost your mind!"

Alex and Mike push their way through the crowd of students that has formed in the doorway and take over holding onto Nick for Brady.

He rushes over and pulls me into his arms, talking me through breathing until I suck in air. I fight not to break down in tears because all I can see is Avery and the blood that is still pouring from his nose.

"Avery," I whisper, "help Avery."

Brady turns his head to see Avery and then looks back at me. "Are you okay?"

I nod, even though I'm sure that I'm not okay. Brady leaves me long enough to pull his shirt off and wad it up to hold to Avery's nose. He guides him over to sit next to me, squatting down in front of both of us. I put my arm around Avery, trying to comfort him.

By now, the entire football team seems to be in here. Brady's lip is bloody, and Connor's cheek is red and has a cut on it. I'm sure it'll be turning black and blue in the near future.

"What's going on in here?!" Vice-Principal Dellinger takes us all in and orders Connor off Derek's back.

"All of you to the principal's office now!" His gaze falls on Avery and me sitting here. "You two as well."

Brady is pissed as hell. "How about an *are you okay* since they were hurt?"

Vice-Principal Dellinger eyes Avery before answering, "Sometimes they bring it on themselves."

Brady's eyes flash and he stands in front of us. "Because he's gay?"

"Because he flaunts being gay. I don't judge for being gay, but it doesn't need to be shoved in everyone's face like they all do." He dismisses us with a hand motion. "Go to the office."

Avery's shame hits me in the face, and I can't stay quiet. "Stop it!"

I stand, holding onto Brady's arm to steady myself. "You're no better than Derek, saying those things about Avery. There is nothing shameful about who he is or how he wants to dress or act. Everyone treats him like he's the only gay person in the world, but he's not. I'm gay! Tons of people are gay!"

Connor helps Avery off the floor, and I reach out to hold his hand.

He squeezes mine and the tears in his eyes make coming out like this worth it.

"Enough! You're both going to be suspended by the time I'm done with you."

Brady keeps his arm around me as we walk past Dellinger. "By the time I'm done with you, you won't have a job. This is a zero bully tolerance school, and I'm pretty sure that includes bigotry from you."

Dellinger doesn't say a word as we leave the bathroom.

Brady is already on his cell, calling his dad. "You need to come to the school. Zach and another kid were getting hurt in the bathroom, and now we are all in trouble."

Pause

"Because they're gay."

Pause

"Okay, thanks, Dad."

We reach the school office, and Derek is standing against the wall, his eye swelling already. Nick is sitting in a chair, avoiding looking at us altogether. Connor and Avery take a seat, and then Brady takes the last one, pulling me down to sit on his lap, hugging me. "You sure you're okay?"

"No," I whisper.

"I'm proud of you for coming out. You're so much stronger than you think." He presses his forehead to the side of my face.

"I couldn't even protect myself or Avery. I had to scream for you," I murmur, rubbing the spot on my chest where Derek's arm had crushed me.

TWENTY-ONE

BRADY

Zach looks so pale and shaken, his body trembling against me. His eyes have that vacant look I haven't seen in a long time. It's like sadness and fear, yet he also seems disconnected from everything around him.

I should have been with him, should have protected him, but instead, I was talking to Alyssa. He had taken too long, and I had just gotten away from her to go see if he was okay when I heard him screaming my name. That scream won't leave my mind, so full of panic and desperation. *Fear.*

Vice-Principal Dellinger walks by us and into Principal Weston's office. I can only imagine what he's telling him. This is going to be a he said, she said type of scenario, and I'm sure Dellinger's word will be believed over mine.

We sit here until parents start to arrive. Derek's dad looks like he has a temper; he's all red and pissed off already. I've seen him at games but haven't paid much attention to him.

Connor's dad shows up, taking in Avery and Zach sitting here, and gives Connor a nod like he gets it.

Both Dad and Mom come in, and Dad's face after he sees Zach sitting on my lap is his *nobody hurts my kids* look. Dad runs his hand over Zach's hair and then squeezes my shoulder before letting Mom stand next to us.

BRADY   149

"You both okay?" she asks, worry clear in her eyes when she looks from me to Zach.

"I'm okay, Mom," I answer, but Zach just does this half-shrug.

A woman rushes in, immediately hugging Avery. I'm going to assume it's his mom.

Dad leans close so we can talk quietly. "Tell me what happened, quickly."

I relay what I know from when I walked in the restroom to find Zach being held up against the wall to what Vice-Principal Dellinger said. Dad's eyes darken and his jaw clenches, but he is utterly calm.

Principal Weston comes out of his office, Dellinger following him. "Let's move this to the conference room."

Zach slides off my lap but stays glued to my side as we all walk down to a room with a long table in it. Nick's mom joins last minute, and all the students sit down, as well as some of the parents. I keep Zach on my lap, Mom's sitting next to me and Dad behind us.

Principal Weston eyes all us boys down. "Vice-Principal Dellinger filled me in on a fight between you boys. Derek, let's hear from you first since it seems you were getting the brunt of it."

Zach flinches in my arms, and I have to bite back the urge to argue. Dad puts his hand on my shoulder, signaling for me to stay calm.

Derek looks down at us. "I was minding my own business when Brady attacked me, and then Connor punched me. He had me pinned to the floor and was acting all crazy."

Weston looks over at Connor. "Care to explain yourself?"

"We came into the restroom when we heard Zach screaming. Derek had Zach pinned to the wall, and Nick had ahold of Avery. Brady pulled Derek off Zach, and then Derek punched him. I knocked Derek down, he punched me, and then I punched him and held him down because he wouldn't stop."

Mr. Sanders makes this scoffing noise. "My son would never fight unless he was defending himself. I'm going to make sure charges are pressed against you!"

Weston holds up his hand. "Everyone, stay calm. Let's hear from Avery and Zach."

Avery looks terrified, and I can't blame him with Mr. Sanders practically breathing fire in his direction. He lowers my shirt from his nose, showing the blood has stopped pouring out and is dried on his face.

"Derek pushed me into the urinal, and Zach tried to stop him. It happened like Connor said."

"You're going to believe some freshman sissy over my son!"

"Enough," Dad interjects, his voice firm and calm in a way that makes people listen to him. "You can be upset, but you do not get to call minors names or shame them in any form. I've heard the entire story from my son, and it disgusts me that homophobia exists not only amongst our students but also in the school system."

"No one asked you," Mr. Sanders bites out. "It's their choice, and they have to live with the consequences."

Avery has tears pouring down his face, and Zach turns to press his head into my chest, letting me wrap my arms around him more.

"We are leaving until you can sort this out," Dad tells Weston. "I'm not subjecting my sons to this."

Weston puts his hand up. "Hold up. Since everyone has a different story, I'm suspending all of you for three days. You boys are off the football team. Avery and Zach, you can serve detention after school for the rest of this semester for your punishment."

Connor pushes his chair back, clearly pissed. "This is bullshit. Bullies go after two kids for being gay, and you're going to punish them?"

"We don't allow fighting in this school, and we don't know what happened. Derek and Nick have never been in trouble before, and Vice-Principal Dellinger vouched that they were the ones being held down. He also said Brady and Zach were downright disrespectful."

Dad taps my shoulder. "Come on, boys. Let's go home. I'll come back and deal with this when you don't have to hear it all."

My cell vibrates for the tenth time, and then Connor's dings again. I'm sure it's the guys wanting to know what is happening in here.

Vicki, the school secretary, opens the door to the conference room. "Sorry to interrupt, but I thought you might want to see this. It was just posted to the school's Facebook page. It's a video of the fight."

Weston motions her in. "Run it through the wall tv, please."

Derek squirms in his chair, giving Nick a look.

Yeah, you're going down, asshole.

The video is obviously from someone who was in the bathroom from the beginning. You can tell he's holding it in a door crack of one of the stalls. It starts with Avery getting slammed into the urinal and then catches everything from there, even Dellinger's exchange with us at the end.

The room is quiet for a second at the end, except for Avery sniffling.

"I'm proud of you, Son," I hear Connor's dad say.

"Brady, take Zach home. You two don't need to be here for this."

I nod to my dad and keep my arm around Zach as we walk from the room. Connor's dad sends him with us. I stop, turning back long enough to look at Avery, "Do you want to come with us? Your mom can get you from our house."

He looks to his mom and she nods. "Go ahead, honey. I'll come to get you later."

The four of us walk out together, Zach taking Avery's hand on the way. Connor tries to lighten the mood. "We all look like we're out of a Hollywood movie and just kicked ass in a gang fight."

Avery gives a small laugh. "Never thought I'd hear that one."

We reach our vehicles, and Connor says he'll meet us at my place. Zach sits next to me in the truck, tucked under my arm. He's still trembling, and I have a feeling he's going to fall apart before all this is over.

"I'm sorry you had to come out for me," Avery says quietly.

"Don't be. It's time I stop hiding away who I am."

"Thanks for helping me. Not many people would have." He sighs. "Maybe I shouldn't wear the clothes I do, but it's the only way I feel like I'm me."

Zach reaches for his hand. "I like your clothes. You should keep wearing them."

"You should." I agree, hoping Avery understands he doesn't have to change who he is.

We pull in at home, with Connor right behind me. He helps Avery down from the truck on the other side. I don't even let Zach get down and instead carry him with my arm under his ass and his legs wrapped around my back. I never carry him in this position, but he rests his head on my shoulder and lets me.

Honey comes running up as soon as we walk inside, sniffing Avery since he's new. "Let's go up to my room. We'll find you a shirt to wear."

Connor busies himself finding a shirt in the drawers where Zach keeps his stuff while I set Zach down on the bed. I kneel to take his shoes off and then his socks. "Do you want to take a shower?"

He hugs Honey, who is on the bed trying to lick him. "Yeah, the restroom floor was disgusting."

"Avery, if you want to take one, there's a bathroom down the hall. Connor can show you where it is."

They leave the room, and I maneuver Zach to the bathroom, turning on the hot water and getting him out a towel. "I'm going to get you some clothes. Call out if you need me." I don't like leaving him in there alone, but I give him some privacy.

I decide on going with pj's and one of his boxer briefs, carrying them into the bathroom to set on the sink counter. That's when I hear him crying in the shower. "Zach, are you okay?" I peek toward the glass shower and don't see him until I look down. He's sitting on the shower floor, his arms wrapped around his legs.

Stripping off my own clothes down to my boxers, I step into the shower and squat down next to him. "You're okay; I'm here."

He leans against me, crying those heart-wrenching sobs that always tear my heart out. "Why Brady? Why do people have to hurt other people? I get so tired of being scared."

Kissing the top of his head, I wish that I had all the answers. "I don't know... I really don't." I reach up for the shampoo bottle and carefully wash his hair, shielding his eyes as the water rinses it out. He lets me rub soap over his back and arms, his hands... I don't bother with the rest because I don't want to make him uncomfortable. "Come on, let's get you out of here."

Turning off the water, I reach for a towel to wrap around me and then get one for Zach, draping it over him before lifting him off the shower floor and carrying him out to the vanity counter. He sits there, clutching the towel to him while I dry his hair with another towel.

"Brady?"

I pause to look at him, and his green eyes are all teary and red. "Yes?"

"Do you ever get tired of saving me?"

He's asked me this one time before, but I know he needs the reassurance. "No..." I comb his hair with my fingers. "You save me, too, you know."

His brow furrows. "I do?"

"Yes, you really do," I answer with conviction. He has no idea how much he gives to me and how much I need him. How he fills every crevice of my heart with the love he shows me.

He wraps his arms around my waist and lays his cheek on my chest. "I love you, Brady."

I swallow hard at the intense truth of his words. When you love someone this much, a kind of pain seems to go with it. The pain of ever losing them, even though it hasn't happened yet. "I love you."

We hold each other for a minute before I help slip his shirt on over his head. I stay close but turn my back as he pulls on the rest. It isn't until he's lying on my bed with Honey that I get some clothes and hurry to get dressed.

Connor takes his turn in my shower, borrowing my clothes to change into. After rolling around on the floor with Derek, I'm sure he feels disgusting, too.

We end up sitting on my bed, the four of us. Avery is shy at first but gets talkative the longer he's here. He keeps looking at Zach and me like he can't figure out our relationship. Could be because Zach is between my legs, leaning back against me.

"Let's go raid all of Zach's desserts. I know there have to be some downstairs."

I toss a pillow at Connor's head. "All you think about is food."

"You know what they say, the way to a man's heart is through his stomach."

Zach lets out this fake gasp of shock. "Are you saying you're in love with me then?"

Connor swings his arms out dramatically. "Marry me, Zach, and bake for me—forever."

"Whatever, dork," Zach says, laughing.

Avery eyes us all. "So, are you guys like a throuple?"

I burst out in hysterical laughter. Connor totally doesn't know what a throuple is by the look on his face.

"It means the three of us are a couple—a throuple," Zach explains.

"What the hell, Brady...stop making eyes at me and telling all our secrets," Connor jokes.

His ability to never get offended over things is one of the reasons I love having him as a friend. "You know it, big boy. I want you so bad."

Connor makes gagging noises. "I love you, man, but keep your dick away from me."

Avery is watching us like we are nuts. "So I guess that's a no?"

"We are all just friends," Zach answers. "Brady is about to date ten million women...or so he claims."

Avery looks from Zach to me and then says, "Ooookaaaay then."

Zach changes the focus to Avery. "Do *you* have a boyfriend?"

"No, until you, I hadn't even met one single boy in school that was gay, too."

Zach climbs from the bed, waiting for me to follow and take his hand. "I'm sure there are more; they are just too afraid to be open about it."

We all end up in the kitchen, eating desserts and snacks. Avery and Zach get to talking about some book they've both read about a gay kid. It dawns on me that they might want to date each other, and for some reason, I don't like the idea. Maybe it's the thought of him getting his heart broken that kills me.

My parents walk in from the garage, and we all wait to hear how it went after we left. I'm not surprised that both Mom and Dad immediately look at Zach, probably seeing that he was crying. Dad glances at me, and I give a nod to assure him Zach's okay.

"How did it go?"

"Derek and Nick are off the football team. They'll be cleaning the school's bathrooms at the end of every school day for the rest of this semester."

"What about us?"

"They are giving you and Connor a three-day suspension. I told them Zach wouldn't be there until you were back. You are still on the football team and can play in the game Friday night."

"So basically, we get three days of vacation," Connor says, smiling.

"Yes, basically. They've agreed to let you do your assignments at home so you don't get zeros."

Mom comes over to hug Zach and then me. "I'm proud of you, boys."

"What about Dellinger?"

Dad frowns. "I made some phone calls to the school board, and they all saw the video. He's been put on administrative leave until the board can meet. I am sure he's going to be fired—or he will if I have anything to say about it."

I can only imagine what all my dad had said after we left. "How did Derek's dad handle it all?"

"Not well, but he couldn't exactly argue too much after seeing the video."

Connor's dad and Avery's mom show up, and they end up staying to talk for a while. As a single mother, Avery's mom seems happy to have Dad's help with the whole situation.

THAT NIGHT, we are lying in bed, and I'm running my fingers through Zach's hair as I read to him. The day has worn him out; I can see it in the way he's limp against me.

I pause my reading to ask him, "Are you interested in dating Avery?"

He turns his head. "What? No."

"Why not?" I'm genuinely curious.

Zach's face flushes pink, and he gives me a duh look. "He's not my type."

"Why?"

"Umm...think about it."

"Just tell me. He seems nice and sweet."

Zach sighs loudly. "If you must know...my type would be a top."

A top? *Ohhhhh, Zach is a bottom.* No wonder he gave me a duh look. I should have known that because everything about Zach screams bottom, or at least from what I've seen in the couples we watch online. I doubt either of us would know what a top or bottom even was if it wasn't for all the YouTube videos talking or making jokes about it. "I'm a moron."

"You said it," Zach teases. "Avery is definitely not my type, and there is zero sexual chemistry between us."

Hearing my best friend say sexual chemistry feels weird. "I bet he's a power bottom."

Zach's brow furrows in thought, and then he asks, "What's a power bottom? I never did understand what they meant by that."

Grinning, I try to explain. "Power bottom is where they want to be the bottom but boss the top around while doing it."

"So they want to be in control even though they are the one getting...you know..."

It's funny how red he is and can't even say the word. "Yes, and you're definitely *not* a power bottom."

He looks offended. "You don't know; I could be."

I snort and pat his back. "Okay, whatever you want to be."

"Fine. I'm not a power bottom."

Grinning, I go back to reading the book. Thoughts of Zach letting some guy top him keep flitting through my mind, and I push them away. I'll deal with the uncomfortableness of Zach dating and having a sex life when it comes to it. For now, any guy that even remotely thinks about looking at Zach is going to have to come through me first.

TWENTY-TWO

ZACH

Three days at home is kind of nice. Avery's mom also keeps him home, feeling like the whole thing needs to settle before he goes back. He comes over a few times to swim and watch movies with Connor and us. I think it's good for him to realize that not all jocks are mean and that he's not the only gay high schooler.

Brady refuses to let me get on my cell to look at Facebook or Instagram. I'm sure all sorts of comments are on there about me being gay. He goes into my profile, setting it to private and doing other things that he says will protect me from homophobic bullies.

Friday morning, we walk into school with Connor. Everyone is looking at me differently, and it's a harsh reminder of why I waited so long to come out. It's like I'm the new gay freak on display at a museum.

Brady's football friends are all nice to me, though, and act like nothing's changed. I wonder if Brady had a talk with them when he left for an hour last night to meet up with the team.

Avery stops by to introduce us to his friends, Sara and Misty. He seems a lot more comfortable being around all the guys than he was before.

The day goes okay. Derek and Nick now have lockers near the principal's office, or that's what I heard the guys saying. They don't try to sit with us at lunchtime, instead sitting off at a table by themselves.

Since tonight is the first game, instead of going to our last class, all the students pile onto the auditorium bleachers for the football rally. Connor and Brady have to be with the team, but Avery waves me over to sit with them. It feels good to have someone to sit with when otherwise I would have been alone.

The band plays some songs, and the cheerleaders do their skits. The principal makes a stupid speech that no one listens to, and then the coach talks about the game, trying to rile everyone up against the rival team.

Then they bring the football team forward, and as captain, Brady steps up to the microphone to say a few words to everyone. I know how much he hates being in front of people, but his eyes scan the crowd until he spots me sitting with Avery. He grins and gives me a little wave before starting to talk. "Hey everyone. For those of you that don't know, I'm Brady Wellman, the captain of Rockville's Cougars. I'm supposed to get you all psyched for the game tonight, but instead, I'm going to talk to you about what happened this week."

Principal Weston steps closer like he's going to stop him, but the coach puts his hand out for him to let Brady speak.

"Zach, this is for you. You're the strongest person I know, and I'm proud of you every second of every day. I want you to *never* be ashamed of who you are because you have the most beautiful heart, and anyone would be lucky to be even a fraction of the person you are."

Oh my God, he's standing in front of all these people for *me*. Avery takes my hand as Brady continues.

"As you all have probably seen the video, you know that two students were bullied this week. One for being gay and one for trying to stop the bullying. Bullied by guys that were bigger and stronger than them.

"How many times have you heard someone cutting another student down? How many times have you seen someone shove a student or bully them? How many times have you done nothing? We all do nothing because we don't want to be the next target. We all do nothing because we don't want to stand up alone.

"Bullies are cowards that have to cut another person down to make themselves feel better. They aren't better than us, and no one should have to come to school being scared of what might happen...of whether or not they will be judged for what they wear or how they look."

I glance around the stadium, and every student is transfixed by Brady.

"As for being bullied because you're gay…it sickens me. Aren't we the generation that vows to stop homophobia? Aren't we the generation that is inclusive and proud to accept every person regardless of gender or sexual orientation? Aren't we the generation that can change the narrative of how the future unfolds? I'd like to think we are. We are the generation that is comfortable and more open with our sexuality than any before us. We aren't ashamed of what we like or who we want to be. No one at this school should have to live in fear of being bullied or of coming out to their friends."

He pauses and lets his words sink in before continuing, "We can fight together to end what happened this week. If you hear someone bullying another student, stand up and say, *"No, we don't do that here."* Stand up together. If someone is in the lunchroom saying horrible things about another student, stand up together. If all of us stand up and say no, it *will* stop. We have the power, together."

Brady turns to motion to the guys, who all line up behind him, arms over each other's shoulders, unified. "To all of the students that are scared of being bullied or scared to come out or scared to be who they are or simply need help… You see these guys behind me? They will walk you to class or out to your car or stand beside you to show that you're not alone. We have all vowed that bullying stops here at our school, and that means we will join together to make sure you feel safe here to be who you are and never look back.

"So I'm issuing a challenge to all the students here to stand up and show that we are the generation that will be heard. We will make our high school years the years that changed lives for the better—*all* our lives."

This ripple of emotion flows through the atmosphere around the auditorium as everyone absorbs Brady's words. I wish that I could run out there and hug him right now.

Brady's voice grows even stronger as he says, "Tonight at the game, I challenge you to wear pride colors. Show that our school accepts the freedom to be yourself as our only choice. Show everyone that you are secure enough in your own skin and who you are, that you can wear whatever color you want.

"We are going to play tonight on that field, proud of all of you. We are playing for *you*, each one of you. All of you are a part of our team because we are united and proud to be Rockville Cougars!"

The entire auditorium stands up and roars, screaming and cheering over Brady's speech. Tears prick my eyes as I cheer right alongside everyone else. It's like every single person feels this surge of freedom over being united together and being a part of something bigger than all of us.

Brady steps back with the other players, and I notice Connor nudging him with his shoulder, a big grin on his face. My best friend looks my way, and I see the love he has for me. He did this for me. If we never have another moment like this, I'll cherish this forever.

Principal Weston steps up to the microphone to talk, waving his hands for everyone to be quiet, but the cheering goes on until finally he gives up and stands off to the side. It isn't until the football team has to leave that everyone files out of the auditorium.

I'm so proud of Brady and humbled over the kind of person he is. Since there's a game tonight, he's taking me home and will eat before going back. Then I'll come with the whole family to the game tonight.

He's at the lockers when I round the corner, and I run down the hallway, hugging him as soon as I get there. "That was beautiful... Thank you."

"Hey, what about me? I deserve a hug for my part."

We both turn to see Connor grinning, waiting for his hug. I move from Brady to hug Connor. "You made such a good speech. I don't know how you did it," I joke.

"You're welcome. It was better than Brady's by far."

Brady rolls his eyes and yanks me back from Connor. "I don't seem to recall that speech you made."

Connor flips Brady off. "Let's go. Zach's desserts are calling my name, and I need to fill up my energy for the game tonight."

We leave together, Connor riding with us since they have to come back anyway. Before we get home, their cells are dinging, and we discover Brady's speech is all over social media. Someone even posted it to YouTube with the hashtag *pride*, hashtag *endbullying*, and hashtag *loveislove*.

While the guys discuss the game and eat snacks, I bake some more cupcakes and cookies. Grandpa comes over and grills BBQ chicken while I make the side dishes. By the time Mom and Dad are home, the food is on the table for everyone to eat.

They watch the video of Brady's speech, and I swear that I've never seen such a look of pride in Dad's eyes than when he looks at Brady afterward. The whole family finds clothes with pride colors to wear to the game. Brady and Connor tie rainbow-colored pieces of fabric around their upper arms to show pride. I ask Meg to paint my nails a glittery bright pink, and Brady stands by us the entire time like I'm going to freak out over it. I make it through without panicking, and wearing it to the game feels like I healed a little, became a little stronger.

That night at the game is a night I will never forget. The entire stadium is packed with families dressed in rainbow colors. There are flags being waved and people with rainbow paint on their faces. People from nearby towns come to be a part of what Brady challenged, and I see more people from the LGBTQ+ community than I ever thought I would. For this being a small conservative town, it's really amazing to see.

The shocking part is when the rival players all come out with rainbow colors, too. It brings me to tears to see it all. All because Brady stood up for every kid like me and wasn't ashamed if people thought he was gay because of it.

The Cougars play like their lives depend on it. Like they are proving to us and the world that they meant every word. Brady is the driving force behind it all. He is everywhere on the field and earns the respect of pretty much anyone watching the game.

Avery and his friends sit with us, his mom, Connor's parents—they all scream right alongside everyone else. Sometimes it is all I can do just to stand here and take it all in.

We win and the crowd goes wild. Not just on our side but all the fans from the other team, too. It's like everyone just wants to be a part of this and is proud to be here tonight.

It is a night I will never forget. A night that changes who I am and erases any shame I feel for being me.

SCHOOL IS DIFFERENT AFTER THAT. I see pride colors often in the hallways. Multiple kids come out, and everyone accepts them without judgment. A few times, a bully will make a comment in the lunchroom or hallway, but all the students stand up together and make sure it ends immediately.

The time it happens in the lunchroom, the entire cafeteria of students stands up at their tables, staring at the kid who is being mean. Several of the football players go to sit at the table with the poor geeky kid who bore the brunt of the bullying. It's embarrassing to have everyone looking at you for being an ass, and bullies soon find out they want no part in being the center of that.

I don't get scared walking down the halls anymore. I struggle with the bathroom a little, but Brady always stands by without drawing attention to the fact that I still feel panicky sometimes.

Brady receives so many messages from people in the Pride community. His speech makes it to the news, and students still talk about it as if it was the best thing they ever heard. Teenagers wear what they want to school, and geeks walk the hallways like they are proud of who they are. It amazes me how one person could impact so many people.

BRADY and I are as close as ever. Sleeping with him is getting to be a slow form of torture. There isn't a morning I wake up that I don't feel Brady's hard-on pressing against my ass or against my own erection. I am getting good at making sure I have my back to him by the time we wake up because feeling him hard makes me instantly hard as well. Brady never makes it out to be anything and always just goes on like it's a normal occurrence.

February is when my happiness takes a hit, and everything starts to change. Brady and I are on our way home when he looks over at me. "Sooooo…"

I raise my eyebrow. "What?"

"Alyssa and I have a date Saturday night."

My heart drops into my stomach, and I stare out the window. "That's nice." I shouldn't be surprised; Alyssa is what most men would think of as hot. She's a bit shallow, and he deserves better.

"You'll be okay at home without me? I won't go if you need me."

My best friend is too selfless, and I know that I need to set my own feelings aside because Brady being happy is all that matters. "I'll be fine. You should go enjoy your first date."

"I'm a little nervous about it. Not sure where to take her for a first date."

"A movie and out to eat is probably the best for a first date," I offer.

"You're right. I'll do that."

I'm quiet the rest of the way home; I can't help it. To help me focus on something else, I bake and cook, then clean the kitchen better than it needs to be cleaned.

Brady sits at the island doing homework for part of it, his eyes watching like he knows I'm upset. I can't let him know how much his dating bothers me. It's not fair to him if I do because I know he'll stay home if he thinks I'm upset over it.

That night when we go to bed, I lie here thinking about how my nights of being this close to him are numbered. Brady must sense my melancholy mood because he turns the light back on and reads to me until I fall asleep.

THE NEXT DAY, we are sitting in the lunchroom when Connor finds out Brady has a date. His eyes immediately go to mine, and I see sympathy there. "You want to go sledding or bowling?"

"No, I think that I'm just going to stay home." I've never gone out with Connor without Brady, and it feels like a huge step that I'm not ready for.

"I'll come over and watch movies with you then." He gives me these puppy dog eyes that make it impossible for me to say no when all I really want to do is lie in bed depressed while Brady is gone.

"Okay, thanks, Connor."

Saturday night comes and Brady dresses up in new clothes. He seems nervous and keeps looking at me. I pretend to be fine with it until he walks out the door. Mom and Dad both give me a sympathetic, sad look, and I pray they don't know why I'm so upset. I can't handle the humiliation of them knowing I want him for more than he wants me.

Giving them a forced smile, I run upstairs and curl up in Brady's bed with Honey. I can't take the wondering of what they are doing and if they are kissing. Yanking the blankets up over my head, I try to forget about the world.

It's short-lived because a half an hour later, Connor comes in and rips the blankets off me. "Come on. I've brought Mary Poppins Returns and A Wrinkle In Time over, and I'll even watch Tangled with you if you want."

He knows I've been wanting to see Mary Poppins Returns. Sighing,

I drag myself out of bed. "Okay, but let's go to the basement and watch them on the big screen. Oh…and I'm putting on pj's first."

"Go ahead. I'll keep Honey company while you change."

I change into my Eeyore pajama outfit, not caring if Connor sees me in them right now. Brady gave them to me, and it offers some comfort.

Connor is holding Eeyore and my Tangled blanket when I come out and even carries them down to the kitchen for me. We get sodas, make popcorn, and pile desserts for Connor on a plate before taking it all to the basement.

"Why aren't you out on a date tonight?" I ask Connor once we are comfortable on the couch, with our food on the coffee table in front of us.

He reaches for a cupcake that I decorated with Winnie the Pooh's face and shrugs. "I thought it would be more fun to do this. Dating is stressful and expensive."

"I thought you liked Tessa?"

"She's pretty and nice. Maybe I'll ask her out sometime." He gives me a look. "What about you? Why aren't you dating anyone?"

"Me?"

"Yeah, you."

Dating isn't even something I've thought about. "I don't know. I think I have to get past being separated from Brady first. Besides, what guy wants to date someone who might have a panic attack?"

"If he's a good guy, he will like you more because you've gone through so much and won't care if he has to help you through a panic attack."

"Aww, Connor, you're really sweet."

A faint blush spreads across his cheeks. "Ready for this movie?"

I nod, curling up under the blanket with Honey lying against me. It might be lame, but I have Eeyore in my arms, too. Even watching movies with Connor isn't enough to keep the depressed feeling at bay.

It gets later and later, but Brady still isn't home. We are on our third movie, and I keep staring at the clock as if it'll make Brady magically appear.

"He'll be home soon," Connor says, trying to comfort me.

"I'm sorry that I'm not the best company tonight… I'll be better next time," I promise.

"It's okay, Zach. You don't have to hide it from me."

Yeah, I think he totally knows I'm in love with Brady. I move to lie beside Honey full-length on the couch, resting my head on Connor's leg. "Thank you…for understanding."

We both know what I mean, and Connor rests his hand on my shoulder. "He loves you, Zach. I know he does."

A few tears leak down my cheeks, and I close my eyes. He loves me, but he's not in love with me.

TWENTY-THREE

BRADY

Alyssa scoots over into the middle of the seat, putting her hand on my thigh. "I'm glad we went out tonight. I had fun."

"Yeah, it was fun." *Kind of.* There'd been a lot of awkward moments where I didn't know what to say. At the movie, she talked so much about every part of it that I didn't enjoy watching it at all.

Somehow, I thought tonight would be like when Zach and I go out, but it was not even remotely the same. Dating feels like work, and I've not quite figured out what the hype is about it yet.

"Brady?"

I turn to look at her because I realize that I zoned out and probably didn't hear a word she said. She leans forward to kiss me, and it doesn't feel quite like I expected. It's different. Most guys say it's like sex only with your mouth, but if this is what sex sparks feel like, then my expectations are going to be pretty low.

I wonder what movie Zach watched and if Connor made sure it wasn't a horror flick. Zach gets nightmares if he watches anything remotely scary. What if Zach forgot to take his iron supplement with supper since I wasn't there to remind him? Did he even eat supper? What if he had a panic attack without me there?

Alyssa pulls back from me. "Do you want to go park somewhere and…you know?"

She wants to have sex on the first date? Is this the norm and something I should want to do right away? I'm only sixteen and just kissed for the first time. Sex seems like a big jump. I didn't even bring condoms because I never dreamed my first time would be in the truck.

A truck Zach sits in.

I shake my head. "No, I think with it snowing again, it's best if I take you home. Plus, I have a curfew." I don't have a curfew, but it's better than saying I don't want to have sex because I'm not ready.

She seems a little upset that I'm taking her home, but I walk her to her doorstep and then make the drive back to my house.

Mom and Dad are still up, and I pause to say hi.

"How did your date go?" Mom asks.

"It was okay."

"Do you really like her?"

"She's okay."

Dad raises his eyebrow. "Doesn't sound like you had a lot of chemistry."

Chemistry…

Maybe that is what was lacking when we kissed. "You might be right. Where's Zach?"

"He's in the basement with Connor still. I think Connor brought him Mary Poppins Returns for a surprise."

Irritation skirts across my skin even though I'm being selfish. I wanted to surprise Zach with that movie; he'd been waiting for it to come out. "It's way past his bedtime…he's going to be tired tomorrow now."

Dad does his classic raise of the eyebrow. "You're out this late, and Zach is old enough to stay up if he wants. You're not his boss, Brady."

Yes, I am, my mind says to me. "I'm going to go check on him."

The basement is dark except for the TV being on. I see that The King is playing on the screen and grit my teeth over Connor letting him watch a movie with killing before bed. I come around the couch to see Connor sitting on one end and Zach lying down with his head on Connor's leg. It bothers me more than it should, seeing him take comfort from Connor. I don't like knowing he needed to be close to someone and I wasn't there.

Connor notices me and pauses the movie. "Hey, how was your date?"

"It was okay. How did Zach do?"

"He was good until about the last hour. He finally lay down and went to sleep."

"Thanks for doing this; I appreciate it."

"I didn't do it for you. I did it for Zach and because I wanted to spend time with him," he says pointedly, clearly not happy with my choice of words.

I'm not exactly sure what he's upset about, but it seems like I did something to offend him. "Zach cares a great deal about you. I'm sure he appreciated it, too."

Connor nods. "I should get home."

"Nah, the weather is brutal out there, and the wind picked up. The snow is starting to drift. Just stay the night."

"Okay."

"I'm going to carry Zach up to bed. Either you can finish the movie in my room, or we can game for a little while." I scoop Zach up, blankets and all. He mumbles Brady into my neck in his sleep. Connor grabs the leftover snacks to bring back up to the kitchen.

I lay Zach down on my bed and cover him up, smiling to see he's cuddling Eeyore. The fact that he wore his Eeyore pj's says a lot about how much he trusts Connor. The pj's are worn but surprisingly fit him still. He likes to think he's grown a lot, but I don't think it's much. I change into my pj bottoms and white T-shirt so I can be comfortable.

I'm walking out of the bathroom when Connor comes into my bedroom with Honey. "I put her outside for a minute before bringing her up." He plops down in one of my gaming chairs.

"Thank you for doing that." I watch Honey jump up in bed with Zach and settle into her normal spot.

Connor and I game for an hour, talking and laughing. As usual, Connor crashes in a sleeping bag on the floor. It takes me a long time to get to sleep, all my thoughts revolving around why I didn't enjoy the date that much. A lot of pressure comes with dating, it seems, but one thing I do know, Alyssa and I don't have any chemistry.

And Zach…it felt strange to do something without him.

I missed him.

ALYSSA ISN'T happy when she asks me about going out again, and I tell her I just want to be friends. After her being dramatic and loud in the hallway over it, with Zach's wide eyes staring at her like she is about to explode, I decide that the next girl I date will have to be sweeter.

APRIL COMES and we are all sitting around the table for Easter dinner when Grandpa starts asking questions.

"Have you boys decided what you want to do for a career yet? You only have one year left, and you should start to apply for colleges soon. Applying early for grants and scholarships is important, too, so it's best to know by the end of the summer what your plan is."

Shit. I wasn't ready to have this conversation yet, especially when I don't know if I can leave Zach for four months. All eyes are on me, waiting for an answer.

"Have you thought about it, Brady?" Dad asks. "I've seen you reading law books off and on. Thought maybe you were thinking of a law degree. You could join your mother's law firm."

"No, I'm not going to be an attorney. I don't want to sit behind a desk my whole life." I clear my throat. "I'm going into law enforcement."

Mom sets down the bowl she was holding and asks, "Police officer?"

"Yes, that is the plan." I glance over at Zach and can practically see on his face how lost he feels over this news.

Dad doesn't look unhappy about it, at least. "Are you going for a criminal justice degree?"

"Maybe? I will go to a police academy, which is about eighteen weeks. Later on, I will probably look into doing an online criminal justice degree while I work. It's nothing that has to happen right away since I can get a job without one."

Grandpa seems pleased. "What made you decide this?"

I put my hand on Zach's neck, rubbing lightly. "When Officer Andrews came, he was calm and kind and made a huge difference in how things were handled, simply because he cared. I want to have that impact. Be the one that helps people in situations like what we went through."

Zach is tense under my hand, but his eyes meet mine. "I can see you as a police officer. It totally fits you."

I relax a little at his approval of my choice. "Thanks, Zach. I also like that it's only about four months and then I can start working. Not two to four years of college, learning stuff that I'll never remember."

"Have you looked into academies? I'm sure there are waiting lists, and you'll need to get on it way ahead of time."

"I have, but I don't know which one I want to go to yet." I don't want to tell Zach in front of everyone that I'll have to go away for it.

"Sounds like you've thought this through for a while now," Dad says. "I know you'll make a superb police officer. You should talk to Chief Kuhn. See if he has any advice on what you need to do to prepare."

"I'll do that, thanks, Dad."

Grandpa turns his attention to Zach. "What about you, Zach?"

"I haven't decided yet. I was waiting to see what Brady's plans were." He looks over at me with those expressive green eyes. "I wasn't aware he already knew what he wanted to do."

Guilt hits me that I kept this from him for so long. I still haven't explained if I do this, it means leaving him for months. The nearest academy is too far away to drive back and forth. "I'm sorry, I wasn't sure if I was going to follow through with it. I'm still not a hundred percent sure."

He shrugs, staring down at the mashed potatoes he keeps pushing around with his fork. "It's okay."

"Your English teacher told me you're smart enough to get into Yale or Harvard if you apply," Mom says to Zach. "She thinks very highly of you and mentioned you should get an English Literature degree."

"I don't want to go away for school or have a big career." Zach has a determined look on his face. "I will work for a while, but eventually I hope to get married. Then I want to stay home and take in foster kids. Help the kids that don't have families and give them the love they never had, or maybe adopt siblings so they can stay together. I want to make my own impact, like you all have done in my life."

The thought of Zach with kids makes me smile. He'll be gentle and loving. They will be loved more than they ever thought possible. We could have a big house and help a lot of kids. *Except he'll be getting married and it won't be to you.* My heart does this little pang over not being a part of his plan.

My family are all smiling. I'm sure they can see Zach with kids, just like I can.

"I love that," Mom says. "You'll be a great dad."

Grandma smiles. "God knows your husband will be spoiled with your cooking. He'll think he won the lottery when you cook for him the first time."

Husband…

My stomach feels a little nauseous, and I wonder if I'm coming down with something.

Zach's eyes dart to mine and then look down again. Mom rubs his arm from his other side, exchanging a look with my Dad that I don't understand.

"You have big plans to get married and have kids, Brady?"

I know Grandma means well, but the question feels like a huge jump into the future. "I don't know… So far, girls seem a bit —aggressive."

"Aggressive? Really?"

"Yes, Mom, they really are. I can barely get from one classroom to another without them being dramatic to get attention."

Dad chuckles but doesn't say anything.

"Ask Zach. He'll tell you."

"He's right. The girls practically throw themselves at his feet and whine to get attention. Drives Connor and me so crazy that we end up leaving him behind so we don't have to hear, *Ohhhh Brady, your muscles are sooooo hot. Please marry me and have babies with me.*" He says it in this voice that sounds ridiculous, and the whole table laughs.

I flick his ear. "Haha, funny."

He pokes me in the side. "It's true. Oh, and I forgot the hair flip over and over and over." He pretends to flip hair he doesn't have over his shoulder.

"You do that pretty well." I smirk.

Green eyes narrow in on me. "Haha, funny."

LATER THAT EVENING, when we are in bed together working on home-work, Zach puts his textbook aside and swivels so he's facing me. "Why didn't you tell me that you wanted to be a police officer? We always tell each other everything."

I wince at the hurt in his voice. "Because I didn't want to cause you more stress than you were already going through, or for you to worry about it before it's even here."

"Why would it cause me stress?"

I put my own homework aside and turn to face him, taking his hands. "I haven't decided for sure I'm going, Zach. I'm waiting to see how things go."

"Things go with what?"

"With us...you? We haven't been apart much except for one date. Any police academy I go to...will be farther away. I'm going to have to live there for at least four months."

Realization dawns in his eyes. "Oh...we will be separated while you're at school."

"Yes, I wasn't sure if I would be able to leave for that long, so I didn't want to worry you about it."

He's quiet. Too quiet.

"Zach, talk to me. I don't have to go."

There are tears in his eyes when he looks up. "You have to go. It's what you want to do, and I can totally see you as a police officer. You can't change your future or not do something because of me and my baggage."

"It's not baggage and—" I almost blurt out that he is my future, but then we both know that's not true. "Maybe you can come with me?"

He shakes his head. "No, you need to do this on your own. If I'm there, you'll be worrying about me being in a new place with no one I know. I'll stay here and be okay. I'll have our family and Connor."

It bothers me that Connor will be with him, and I won't. "The time will pass quickly, and then I'll be back here to live with you. Maybe we can find a place to move into before I leave."

"Maybe. For now, just apply to where you want to go. I want you to be happy because that's all that matters to me."

"You're all that matters to me," I whisper. "I don't want to leave you if you're going to be upset or scared while I'm gone."

"I'm just going to need to start doing things without you. Get used to it and all. Like I did when you went on a date." He doesn't look as convinced as he's trying to sound.

I pull him into a hug. "We have time. No need to rush into anything."

TWENTY-FOUR

ZACH

Knowing that I'll have to be without Brady for months is enough to make me want to hurl. I swallow down the urge and try to keep the fear from my face. If you love someone, you put them first and don't hold them back. He needs to do this for himself, and I'll just have to deal with it.

Thoughts of *what am I going to do with my own life* keep rolling around in my head. I know long-term what I want: a husband, foster kids, maybe kids of our own—a home I can take care of and a family to cook for. I'm an introvert, and I don't think that will change anytime soon. Staying home with a family and having that sense of belonging somewhere is all I really want. I have that feeling with my family now, and I want to hold on to that as life goes on.

JUST UNDER TWO WEEKS LATER, we are in the second week of May, and the flowers are out in full bloom. Dad said another week and the pool will be ready to use.

It's Saturday night, and Brady is on a date with Sophie, a senior who asked him out. Connor is over and asks if I want to go on a bike ride to get ice cream. It feels like a big step for me to do this without Brady, and it makes me a little sad, too. But I'm determined to start doing things without him. I need to prove to him he can go to the police academy because I know he won't go if he thinks I can't handle it.

We bike there fine and eat our cones at the picnic tables. Connor cracks jokes to help me feel better. I make it all the way back home without any issues and feel pretty proud of myself.

Connor puts Brady's bike away, which he'd borrowed. "Want to take Honey for a walk before we watch a movie?"

"She would love that." I run inside to put her leash on, and we set out on a walk down the street. I decide to ask Connor what he's going to do after high school in hopes it might help me make a decision. "Are you going to college after we graduate?"

"I think so. The branch about fifteen minutes from here has a two-year associate's degree in graphic design. I'm going to set up my own business, creating websites for companies, designing logos…that type of thing."

"Wow, Connor, that sounds great."

"My dad owns the computer store downtown, and he said I could run it out of there until I build my clientele."

"You and Brady have it all figured out, and I haven't got a clue yet."

"Take your time. Think about what you love more than anything and try to find a job that has to do with that. You don't want to be miserable the rest of your life doing a job you hate."

The thing I love more than anything is Brady, and I'm sure there aren't any jobs that involve being around him for the rest of my life.

"I'll race you back," Connor says, taking off down the last block back home.

I chase after him with Honey, knowing full well that he's barely jogging so I can keep up. We get closer to home, and I see someone standing in the driveway. It isn't until we are ten feet away that I realize it's the monster that lives in my nightmares. My body feels frozen in place as I take in the man who made my life hell. He's thinner now and harder looking but still has that same sadistic look in his eyes.

Connor must finally recognize him because he immediately steps in front of me. "You need to get out of here!"

"Are you his new boyfriend? The devil has ahold of both of you! I will rid you of this disease, Isaac. God has ordered me to!"

Him calling me Isaac brings back too much, and I see black edging in around my vision. My body slams into the cement, but all I can think about is how I need to get away from him. "Brady…"

"Get out of here!"

I hear Honey bark, brakes squeal, and then Dad's voice—the only man I'll ever consider my dad—angry and threatening toward the man that broke me.

Connor kneels next to me. "Zach, you need to breathe for me. Please?" I see the blue sky above me as Connor says, "Brady, you need to come home now! Zach needs you… I don't know what to do."

Brady… I need Brady. I must have said it out loud because Connor responds with, "He's on his way, Zach. He's just down the road."

Dad's face comes into view. "He's gone, Zach. Try to think about your breathing and take a slow, deep breath for me. Connor, run inside and get Emily, tell her to bring his inhaler."

A panic attack and stress often bring on an asthma attack. Is it weird that my thoughts seem to be going, yet I am gasping for air?

Mom's next to me; I can feel her hand on my arm as Dad pulls me up so they can hold the inhaler in my mouth better. Blood drops on my hand, and it brings back flashes of blood on me, the monster standing over me. "Brady!" I think maybe I screamed it, but it's all muffled.

"Zach…Jesus," I hear Brady say a second before I feel his arms around me. He lifts me into his lap and orders me to breathe, doing the counting for me and using the grounding techniques. I cling to him, scared he'll let me go and the man of my nightmares will take me away.

"You're safe… I'm here. No one is going to get to you through me. He's not going to take you away."

Instead of crying like I usually do, I just go numb. Hiding away from it all in my mind and holding on to the only person I know would die trying to protect me. Crying would mean letting go, and I'm terrified to feel anything right now.

Brady moves, and I dig my fingers in even more. "Connor, can you take Sophie home, please?"

"I'll take care of her."

"What the hell happened?" I hear Brady ask as he carries me inside the house.

"Matthews was here when I pulled up… Zach was on the ground and Connor was between them, trying to get him to leave. Sit here. I want to clean up that blood and see if he needs stitches."

I refuse to let go of Brady as Dad gently wipes my forehead, keeping my eyes squeezed shut so I don't have to face the world.

"How is it possible we didn't know he was out? Jesus, what would have happened if Zach had been out there alone?"

"I don't know, but heads are going to roll for this. They are supposed to notify the vict…us before releasing him. He's not supposed to be in contact with Zach, regardless. I've already called the police."

"I can't believe the asshole had the guts to come to our house."

"We will have to make some changes for a while." Dad puts a Band-Aid of some sort on my forehead, or at least that's what it feels like. "He doesn't need stitches. It's not that deep."

"I'm going to take him up to my room and get him into clean clothes."

Brady doesn't say anything on the way up to his room, other than to call Honey to come with us. I'm glad someone brought her inside. I don't even remember what I did with her leash when I landed on the ground.

"Zach, can I lay you on the bed and get you clean clothes?"

I dig my fingers into him, holding on with this instinct that I know isn't rational. Brady doesn't force it. Instead, he leans against the headboard, still holding me close. "He's gone, baby. I promise you're safe now. Come back to me… I promise I'll be right here with you."

Baby. He's never called me baby before. It sounded like an endearment. I open my eyes to see his worried blue ones staring down at me.

"There you are." He leans down to kiss the side of my forehead that isn't hurt. "You scared me half to death out there."

We stay like this for a while longer until Brady asks again, "Can I lay you here and get you some clothes without blood on them?"

Blood? Suddenly I want them off me—*right now.* I nod and try to pull my shirt up as quickly as I can, feeling nauseous at seeing the blood. Brady tugs it off and lays me down as he scoots off the bed to get me clean clothes. I try to get my jeans off, but my fingers won't move like I need them to. Brady helps, tugging them off my feet and tossing them to the side.

"Your favorite pj's are in the dirty clothes hamper, but here's my shirt. Maybe it'll help." He helps me get it over my head and put on shorts.

"You want me to read to you?"

Nodding, I watch him take his shoes off and crawl into bed.

Curling up in the crook of his arm, I rest my head on his chest. He reads in that soft, comforting voice, his fingers running through my hair in the way I love. I turn the pages for him, trying to forget that my nightmare is free and close by.

Connor comes in and sits on my other side. He's quiet and listens to Brady read.

It isn't until Brady is done with the chapter that he asks, "Did she get home okay?"

"Yeah, I made sure to walk her to the door, too."

"I'm sorry," I whisper. I ruined his date and keep messing up his life.

Brady kisses my forehead. "You have nothing to be sorry for. I'd rather be here with you than out on a date with a girl I don't even know." He reaches over to touch Connor's arm. "Thanks for standing between them and taking care of Zach."

"If he got any closer, I was going to punch his lights out. He doesn't have his weight behind him anymore, and I could so beat the crap out of him. But once your dad showed up, I think he knew he was outnumbered."

Just talking about it is making me tremble and cling to Brady again.

Dad's voice comes through the intercom, startling all of us. "The police are here. Can you three come down, please? They need to verify that Zach is alright."

"Are you able to do this?" Brady asks.

No, but I will. I'm ashamed I fell apart when the monster was here. Brady holds my hand, and Connor stays close on my other side as we walk down to meet the police. According to his name badge, Officer Andrews is one of them, and he gives me a sad smile. "I know you don't remember me, but it's nice to see you looking well." His eyes briefly go to the bandage on my forehead.

"Thanks for saving Brady and me." I can't say any more. Brady sits on the couch and puts me between his legs, keeping his arms around me.

"Zach, we need to know what your dad said to you."

"He's not my dad! I only have one dad...and it's not him."

"I apologize. What did Mr. Matthews say to you?"

Swallowing hard, I try to force the words out. "He asked if Connor was my boyfriend, then said something about the devil having ahold of us and that he would rid me of this disease. Said God had ordered him to."

Connor nods. "That's what he said. I think if I hadn't been there, he would have forced Zach to go with him."

My whole body shudders, and I turn in Brady's arms to seek comfort from him. He adjusts me to sit sideways in his lap, holding me closer.

Officer Andrews is writing everything down. The other officer talks to Dad. "I would recommend you don't leave Zach alone at all. Make sure your security is up-to-date and set the alarm even when you're all home. We will talk to Mr. Matthews and his parole officer to see what we can do. If he makes contact again, call us right away."

Dad follows them to the door to speak privately before coming back to talk to us. "Zach, you're not to be alone outside this house, not even in the backyard. You can swim and take Honey out, but either I, Brady, or Connor need to be with you. I don't want you out front at all unless it's to get in a vehicle."

"I'd be happy to help with watching over him, anytime you need me," Connor offers.

"That would be great, but your parents need to know what is going on and have to okay it. You're all going to be carrying pepper spray from now on."

Mom is pacing in front of the fireplace. "I don't want the girls out alone either...or Honey. I wouldn't put it past him to put poison or something out there. We need to watch her."

I feel terrible that I'm putting them all at risk. "I'm sorry. I don't want any of you to get hurt because of me."

"You're a part of our family," Brady says close to my ear. "We would do anything to protect you."

Dad pins his eyes on me. "Brady is right. You're a part of this family. If this was Meg or Anna in danger, would you think twice about helping them?"

"No..."

Dad and Brady sound so much alike. They reason things out the same way.

Dad goes over how to work the alarm system with Connor and then leaves to get pepper spray. Mom orders pizza, and we all pile into the living room, including Grandma and Grandpa. Brady keeps me between his legs, a blanket pulled up around us. I still feel numb and disconnected from everything, barely even seeing the movie that's playing.

Connor decides to stay over, but they don't game. Instead, Brady reads for a while until I fall asleep.

"God told me to kill you, Isaac. It's what he wants." I look around to see that I'm tied down and can't move. Dad raises a knife above me. "It's the only way to get the demon out of you and save your soul." He sinks the knife into my chest, and blood spurts everywhere. I hear myself screaming and can't stop it. I scream for Brady to save me but know he'll never find me.

"Zach!"

I feel like I'm drowning in my own blood as I come awake and hear myself screaming.

"Zach! Wake up! I'm right here." Brady wraps himself around me tightly. "You're safe."

Anguish pours through me because this nightmare will never be over, and I can't hold back from keening with sorrow any longer. "He will kill me. I know it," I sob into his neck.

"He's not going to get close to you, I promise," Brady murmurs against my face.

I want to believe him, but fear grips me in its claws. I can't stop crying, deep sobs that hurt my heart.

"Baby, you need to calm down and take a breath." He says it sweetly, but also in a commanding tone that forces air into my lungs. "That's it, breathe again for me," he repeats, telling me so a few times until I get control over my crying. "Now listen closely… Do you trust me, Zach?"

"Yes," I half sob out, biting my lip to stop from crying all over again.

"So you're going to have to trust me when I say he will never get near you or hurt you again—I won't let it happen. You can trust me to take care of you."

There's no one else I would trust more than Brady, and I take a deep, shaky breath, letting his words sink in. Brady won't let anything happen to me. "Okay…I trust you."

He kisses my forehead. "Now sit up for me because you soaked my shirt."

I sit up with his help, and he pulls his shirt off and wipes my face with it. No wonder he sees me as a little kid. I am like one when he has to take care of me.

Connor appears by the bed with another shirt for Brady, and he has tears in his eyes, too. "Can I get you anything, Zach? A soda or something?"

"I'm sorry you had to hear that," I say, worried more about what he'll think of me than I am about my scratchy throat.

"It's okay. You've been through a lot."

Brady pulls the shirt on over his head. "Are you going to be able to sleep after that nightmare, or do you want to watch something?"

"I am scared to go back to sleep," I admit, not wanting to close my eyes at all.

Connor heads for the bedroom door. "I'll get some drinks and snacks."

"Thanks, man," Brady calls out after him.

The three of us sit on Brady's bed, watching movies for hours. I'm not sure when I fall asleep, but when I wake up in the morning, Brady is awake and staring at me. I give him a small smile and he smiles back, running his fingers gently over my cheek.

"Are you okay?"

"Yes, I feel stupid about losing it like that last night, though," I whisper back to him.

"You needed to cry it all out. I was surprised when you didn't earlier."

"Do you think I'll ever get to an age where I don't cry? I'm supposed to be a man."

That does make him grin. "It's hard to picture you as some manly man. You've got that whole twinkish, pretty boy thing going on."

"Pretty boy? Are you saying I'm pretty?"

He rolls his eyes. "Yes, I'm saying you're pretty."

"I don't think manly men want to be called pretty, but I kind of like it."

"You're silly."

"Are you two going to get up and make me breakfast since you've woken me up before noon?"

My eyes widen and I look over my shoulder to see Connor in bed behind me. "Umm…this is awkward."

Connor laughs. "You can tell everyone you slept with two guys and had your first threesome."

Brady snorts as he crawls from the bed. "Yeah, I don't think so. You just fell asleep watching a movie, and I didn't have the heart to push you out of bed. You kept your hands to yourself; I made sure of it."

"Don't lie. You know you want me," Connor jokes back.

I crawl out of bed to get clothes and take a shower. Brady comes in to brush his teeth and leans against the counter to wait for me. He never comes in when I shower; he must really be worried. As soon as I'm out, he passes me to take his own. "Don't go downstairs without me."

I brush my own teeth, keeping my eyes from straying to a naked Brady in the shower. My body likes the thought too much, and I have to escape to his room to get dressed.

Five minutes go by and Connor comes in, all showered and dressed in Brady's clothes. "Want to go down and start breakfast?"

"Brady ordered me not to leave this room."

Connor grins, shaking his head. "You thought he was bossy and protective before; I have a feeling he's going to take it to a whole new level now."

"Doesn't bother me. I like him that way." It makes me feel safe.

Brady comes out of the bathroom all dressed, snapping Connor with his wet towel before he throws it in the hamper. "You heard him; he likes me this way."

"You weren't supposed to hear that," I mutter, glaring at Connor for starting the whole conversation.

"Too late, I already did." Brady grins, which makes me grin, too.

Brady and Connor don't help make breakfast. Instead, they end up outside with Dad and Honey, talking with serious faces. I know what they are talking about and try not to think about it. Mom and I cook the food, with Meg and Anna "trying" to help, but mostly getting in the way.

After our brunch, we leave Honey with Grandma and Grandpa and head to the mall. Connor goes home because he has homework he needs to get done, promising to see us at school in the morning.

Mom is determined we get summer clothes, and I've long since learned to just let her buy what she wants because she's going to anyway. Brady, Dad, and I end up in the bookstore while the girls shop for dresses. Girls need so many clothes, it's ridiculous.

The bookstore is my favorite place to be, besides maybe the library. I could sit in here for hours and go through books in hopes of finding one that transports me to another world. Brady and Dad stick close, not letting me go through the aisles by myself like usual.

I end up buying quite a few books with my allowance, even though Dad wants to pay for them. It's a good afternoon spending time with them and is a big reminder of how much I've changed since the first time we came here.

Everything is going great until we pull in the driveway at home, and I see the monster leaning against a car parked on the street. Brady swears under his breath and puts his arm around me. I try to not even look in his direction and don't breathe until we are in the garage with the door shut.

"Why is he doing this?" Mom asks, obviously upset.

"I don't know. All of you go inside the house and stay there. Brady, you keep the door locked and don't let him in the house. Emily, call the police to let them know he's here again."

Mom grabs his arm. "You're not going out there alone, are you?"

Dad gives her a look. "Trust me." He messes with his cell phone for a second before leaving through the smaller garage door.

We all get out, Meg gripping my hand and Anna holding on to Mom's. Brady keeps ahold of my other hand as he checks to make sure the door his dad went through is locked and herds us all inside to the living room. Mom calls the police while Brady and I watch Dad out the window. I stay glued to Brady's side, trembling uncontrollably.

Dad is talking, and both men seem calm right now. Then the monster gets agitated and yells a bit, sneering as he says something else. I can't stop shaking and am grateful when I see the police pull up behind the car. It isn't long before the man I hate gets in his car and drives off.

Dad speaks to the police for a minute and then comes to the front door, where Brady lets him inside.

"What did he say?"

"Just a bunch of religious garbage and threats." Dad seems way too calm to me. "I need to make some phone calls. I'll be in my office."

Brady and I exchange looks, knowing Dad is hiding something. Mom has us unload the SUV, and I feel jittery the whole time. Every sound makes me jump, and I keep staring at the door, feeling like he's going to come through it at any second. Brady ends up carrying packages one-handed so he can hold on to me. I feel like a giant baby who needs to get over this fear, but I can't rationalize it in my brain either.

We walk over to Grandma and Grandpa's together to get Honey and watch her closely as she does her business before taking her inside.

Brady and I end up in the basement with the girls since they are scared to be alone right now. They play with barbies on the floor while Brady and I take turns reading chapters to each other in one of the new books I bought.

It's easier to feel safe when Brady never leaves my side, and I am able to relax into him. What am I going to do when he goes away after high school?

TWENTY-FIVE

ZACH

The next morning, Dad walks us out to Brady's truck before school. I'm pretty sure Brady could beat up the monster better than Dad could, but I don't say that. Brady is pretty muscular and strong—more so than most guys his age.

Connor meets us at the school to walk inside together. Brady must have talked to the football team at some point because there are always a few of them close by. Alex is outside French class to make sure I have someone with me until Connor can catch up. The day is uneventful, and so is the next one.

On Wednesday, we are outside with Honey when I look toward the woods, only to see *him* standing there watching the house.

"Brady..." I glue myself to his side.

He follows my line of sight and swears under his breath. "Let's go inside. Now." He hurries me inside, calling over his shoulder, "Honey, come."

Dad is in the kitchen and looks up when we come in.

"He's out by the woods, Dad. He was watching us," Brady informs him.

Dad hurries to the window and takes a picture of him standing there. "I want you both to stay inside this evening. I'll take Honey out before bed." He gives me a hug. "Don't worry, Zach. Everything will be fine. I promise. I've hired a security detail to watch the house until this is resolved. They installed cameras today and motion detectors. He won't be able to get in the house or on the property. If he shows up outside, the security agents are here to protect us. They are set up in the pool house, so if you see one or two men out there, that's them."

Wow, he's taking this seriously. It's a huge relief to know that the girls and Grandma and Grandpa will be safe, too. "Thank you for doing that."

"You have nothing to worry about, okay? I'm taking care of it."

"You and Brady are so much alike," I murmur, giving him another hug.

Brady's smiling when I turn around. "I'm like my dad, huh? Are you saying I'm old?"

Dad grabs him to tickle his sides. "Who's old? I can still take you down."

Brady darts away and smirks. "Only because I let you!"

With security at the house, I sleep easier than the previous nights. I still have nightmares, but it's not as bad as the first night.

THURSDAY, we are walking out to the school parking lot to go home when we see Matthews parked behind Brady's truck. He has another man with him. "That's Pastor Dan…" I back up, and the monster sees me, motioning to the pastor where I am. Brady steps between us, whistling to Connor, who's coming out of the school. Connor comes running, along with every guy from the football team who's still in the parking lot. Brady keeps one hand around me to hold me close to him as I press into his back.

They must realize they can't get through all these muscled-up football players because they leave.

Alex is next to us, shaking his head. "Guy has guts to come to school, block you in and think he's going to just take Zach."

Brady pulls out his cell, calling Dad to tell him what happened. I'm pretty sure the entire football team follows us home in their vehicles, honking and waving once we are inside.

Dad is definitely pissed the monster came to my school. He has the police escort us to school in the morning and stay until we are inside.

I am surprised when they aren't outside after school since Dad had said they would be. Brady doesn't say anything but hurries me into the truck so we can leave.

Driving down our street, we see lights blazing and multiple police cars outside our house.

"Oh my God, do you think he hurt someone?" Fear spurs me from the truck as soon as Brady puts it in park. I half fall out of the passenger side and get up to run toward the house. Brady catches me before I get more than a few feet further and places himself in front of me as we hurry together.

We pass a police car, and the monster from my nightmares is sitting in the back seat. He starts screaming at me through the glass, but I can't hear what he's saying. I jump back, though, and Brady keeps us moving away.

We see Dad by the garage, talking to police officers.

"Dad!"

He looks over at us and then says something to the officers before walking our way.

"What happened?" Brady asks before I get a chance to.

"It's over. He's been arrested for extortion and intent to murder a judge."

Brady's face goes pale. "What?"

My stomach rolls, and I lean to the side to throw up.

"Shit." Brady wraps his arm around my chest to help support me.

It isn't until I'm done and can stand upright that Dad continues. "The other day, Matthews propositioned that if I paid him half a million dollars, he would leave Zach alone. If I didn't, he would kidnap Zach and put him in a conversion camp where I would never find him. He threatened to do things to Zach...things neither of you needs to hear." Dad reaches over to rest his hand on my shoulder to comfort me.

I love him, but I instinctively sidle even closer to Brady, needing his protection.

Dad gives me an understanding look and continues explaining what happened. "While he was making threats, I recorded our conversation and then contacted the DA's office. Between them and law enforcement, we devised a plan to set Matthews up. It took us a little bit, but when he went to your school yesterday, we moved faster. He called last night to say that if I didn't follow through, he would murder me and went into great detail about how he would do it. Then Matthews said he would murder my family as well. It was all recorded. We set up the meet and videotaped him taking the money, and again, he made threats. Trust me when I say he won't see the outside of prison for a long, long time."

I sag against Brady with relief. "It's really over?"

"Yes, it's over. I'll have to testify, but with the video and recordings, he can't get out of this. We made absolutely sure to do it so all the evidence is lawful and can't be thrown out. We were just lucky he was too stupid to figure out it was a setup."

"Judge Wellman, the Chief wants to speak with you," an officer says from close by.

"Are you okay enough for me to go talk with the Chief?" Dad asks, looking hesitant to leave me.

My head turns involuntarily toward the squad car with the monster in it, but Brady adjusts his body to block my view and tightens his arms around me. My best friend always seems to know what I need and how to protect me. "No, I'm okay, and Brady will keep me safe," I tell Dad, knowing that even if he stayed, the person I would want is Brady.

Dad leaves to speak to law enforcement, and Brady takes me inside the house. It's a weird feeling knowing that the monster in my nightmares will be in prison for a long time.

Later, we find out they arrested Pastor Dan as well since he also made kidnapping threats, which were recorded. It's all over the papers, and instead of people making fun of me for being related to that asshole, they are kind and pleased the ordeal is over.

It is the last week of school until summer vacation when I figure out what job I want to get. My English Literature teacher, Mrs. Hines, has me stay to talk after class.

She motions for me to take a seat in front of her desk. "Have you thought about what you want to do after high school?"

"Yes, but I haven't figured it out yet."

"Do you see yourself happy in college? Maybe teaching or researching? Writing or becoming an author?"

"No, I don't see myself going to college for a long period of time. I'm not super social and like quiet places. My plan is to stay here in Rockville and hopefully someday have foster kids. I don't want a stressful career."

Mrs. Hines sits back in her chair, thinking for a minute. "Would you say books are your passion?"

"I would say it's my second passion for sure. I read constantly and feel like every book teaches me something new, takes me on a new journey."

"What's your first passion?"

My cheeks warm and I stammer before saying, "My soulmate."

She nods, taking me seriously. "Ah yes, love is always the first passion of a poet, and you have a poet's heart. You fall in love with words and thoughts, written down to woo your heart and calm your mind, filling up your soul with passion."

"That's beautiful," I whisper, loving how she expressed it because it rings so true to me.

"I have a job for you, and I want you to give it serious consideration."

"Alright?"

"My wife runs the Rockville Library, and they are looking to hire someone. I am sure that I can get you the job. It will be part-time for now, but Harold is set to retire next summer, and they will be hiring a full-time librarian."

First, I'm floored that she has a wife. It's cool to find a teacher that is in the LBGTQ+ community. Second, why I never considered working at a library before now is beyond me. "I would love to work in a library. It's my favorite place to go."

"Normally, I would push a student like you to pursue your PhD, but I can tell that wouldn't make you happy. Being a librarian would give you the quiet you need, and it's never overwhelmingly busy. You will also get to help kids explore the world of books, and I think you would enjoy that."

"Don't I need to have a degree to be a librarian?"

"Starting out, you won't get paid a lot, and a degree won't be necessary. And honestly, even working full-time, it's not really required. If you were to take over the library in an administrative form, then yes, you would need your Master's. But for the position coming available next summer, no, you do not need a degree. If you want to open up more opportunities at the library and further your education, our college branch offers an Associate of Arts Degree in Library and Information Technology. There's also the option of enrolling in an online program you can do from home."

"I don't even know what to say. It's all so perfect for me. It almost doesn't seem real."

Mrs. Hines smiles. "I'll tell Marcy to expect you to stop by next week to get set up."

"You really think she'll hire me?"

"Yes, for sure. She's been asking me if I have an English Lit student who would be perfect for the job, and she will be excited to get someone who's read more books than even she has."

We talk a few more minutes, and I leave for my locker. Brady is right outside the door, and I realize that school is over, and he came to find me. "Sorry, she asked me to stay behind and wanted to talk to me."

"It's okay; I was just worried when you didn't show up at our lockers." He tousles my hair. "So, what did she want to talk to you about?"

"My future career and a job she wants me to take."

"A job? Are you ready for that?"

"It's my dream job, so I have to try." I tell him everything she said about the job and online classes.

Brady picks me up and swings me around when I'm done. "It's perfect for you! I can totally picture you as the nerdy librarian."

"So you're saying my glasses will finally look hot when I work in the library?"

"Definitely," he says in a smart-ass tone.

"I'm a little worried how I'll cope without you…and what if I have a panic attack?"

"How about, in the beginning, I sit in the library reading for a couple of hours during your shift? I have some studying of my own to do on laws that police officers need to know. If you're working, I can stay in town and try to accomplish the long list of things Chief Kuhn suggested. If you have a panic attack, I'll come right away. But I think with the closure you've had, you might find panic attacks will happen a lot less."

Brady's willingness to sit in a library while I work only serves to make me fall in love with him even more. "All I can do is try it and see what happens. What kind of stuff do you need to do?"

"Chief Kuhn suggested I spend more time running or in the gym, take basic self-defense and Krav Maga classes. He also suggested I take several different firearm training courses and a trauma response class. I can do the firearm classes as long as Dad is with me."

"Sounds like you'll be ahead of everyone by the time you get to the academy." *And leave me for months.*

"I hope so. The Chief said that if I do well at the academy, he would love to hire me. It's a small town, and not many go away to a police academy and come back." He opens the door to the truck for me to get in. "I'm sure having a judge for a dad doesn't hurt, but I plan on working hard to prove myself."

"You're going to do great, Brady. I know you will."

THE NEXT WEEK, Brady drives me to the library to meet Marcy. I've already thrown up once this morning just thinking about how big this step is for me.

I love her instantly; she's so kind and easy to talk to. I've seen her here so many times, but usually someone else checks my books out.

She even insists on meeting Brady, who is sitting at a nearby table watching us. She goes on and on about the speech he made and how she was there that night at the football game, wearing pride colors and supporting the team.

For the summer, my hours will be nine to one, four days a week. I'll be checking books out for people, returning books to the shelves, assisting people with finding the books they need, and more.

BRADY DRIVES me to work every day and stays for the first hour, studying laws and codes he will need to know to be a police officer. Chief Kuhn has given him books to study that will give him an edge in the academy.

Whenever Brady leaves, Connor usually shows up for a while, and I also spot a lot of the guys on the football team. Even Avery and his girl-friends show up almost every day I work. I never feel alone because someone I know is usually sitting in here reading or on the computers.

Harold gets to do storytime with the kids and all the activities they plan with them. I can't wait to take that over if I get the full-time position. Kids gravitate toward me, and I spend a lot of time helping them find books.

At the end of my shift, Brady is always there to pick me up and take me home. If he has another class, I usually tag along to sit and watch him. His abs are so rock-hard now that I have to pull my gaze away from them more often than not. He loves Krav Maga training and is intense when he practices with the other guys.

As for his shooting skills, they're becoming sharp and easy for him. Dad takes him to the range almost every day to practice. More and more, I see that he'll be an outstanding officer with a dedication most people lack.

WE ARE SEVENTEEN NOW, and I've grown only half an inch. Brady has climbed to six foot three, and standing next to him feels like I'm this nerdy, pipsqueak kid.

He hasn't dated this summer, but he does have girls over with the guys, using his flirty smile on them.

It feels like life is finally easier, yet it's slowly inching its way toward the moment I will lose Brady. Even the thought makes my chest tight, and I find myself clinging to him more than I should. Life will change and nothing will ever be the same again.

TWENTY-SIX
BRADY

I'm not sure who is more nervous about Zach working, him or me. I drive us over to speak to his future boss, and he visibly looks sick about this job interview. He doesn't get some color back in his cheeks until after he's there and met Marcy. Watching them talk, I can tell right away that she's taken with him. Who wouldn't be after meeting him? He's so soft-spoken and gentle in everything he says and does.

Zach gets the job, which I knew he would. Luckily, it's part-time and not a huge jump into an eight-hour day apart from me. I talk to the guys in a group text, and each week, we work out a schedule to help Zach get through this summer. I always take him to work after football practice and stay for the first hour or two, depending on my classes. We don't tell him our plan, but when I leave, Connor usually shows up for an hour, and then the guys will stop by. I always make sure I'm there to pick him up from work.

So far, he hasn't had any panic attacks, and it's obvious he loves his job. He told me he just pretends he's at the library for a visit and I'm right around the corner of the bookshelf there with him.

While he's at the library, I throw myself into classes and training. Dad has been great in taking time off when he needs to be with me for firearm classes. He purchased the guns that I need to practice with, claiming we can transfer them to me when I'm old enough. I've already enrolled in the police academy that Chief Kuhn recommended most.

It's about eight hours from home, and it will be impossible to drive back for visits with the training six days a week. He's already warned me this training will feel like I'm in military boot camp and to be prepared to give it a hundred percent.

Connor has started dating Tessa, but I've not been dating at all. All my focus has been on getting ahead of my future and learning as much as I can. That, and making sure Zach is okay at his job. It's a big step for him—for both of us. I will admit that I've had to deal with some anxiety over him being at the library without me. It's one thing in the safety of our home, but he's out in public where things can happen.

It's been a good, slow start for us in being apart and gets easier as the summer goes on. We only have one blip right before school starts.

Dad is home when I pull in from picking Zach up at the library, and I can tell something has happened as soon as I see him waiting on us. Zach gives me a worried look, and I reach over to take his hand.

"Take a seat, boys." Dad motions to the stools at the island.

We both sit down and wait for him to tell us whatever it is.

"Zach, you know the trial was almost over for your…for Matthews. Closing arguments were going to be heard tomorrow, and a conviction was imminent. I think he knew he was going to prison for a long time, and well…he hung himself in his cell this morning."

Shit. Zach's staring at Dad like it's not yet sunk in, and then he starts trembling. I scoot back my stool a little and transfer him to my lap.

He slumps back against me. "He's really dead?"

Dad nods, his expression grim. "Yes, he really is."

"Can you go see him and make sure?"

My dad seems to understand what Zach needs. "I already did. They called me after it happened, and I met them at the morgue. He's dead."

"Is it bad that I'm relieved? It's like someone telling you the monster in your nightmares can't ever come alive again. He can't get out of prison or magically show up because he escaped. It's like all those fears are ones I no longer need to have."

"It's not bad." I hug him closer. "I'm relieved, too. You're free of him forever."

"Is it possible to get a DNA test and find out if I *am* related to him? Will they let you take a sample? I know he refused to allow it before, but can we try now?"

Dad leans over to rest his arms on the island counter. "I'll see what I can do."

Slowly, after the news, Zach's nightmares decrease to only a few times a month. We do get the DNA results back, and Matthews was not his father. No one knows where his mom currently is, so we can't ask her about his real biological father. Dad offers to find her, but Zach says no.

———————

SCHOOL STARTING IS A WEIRD FEELING, knowing this is our last year before moving on into adulthood. Zach and I have three classes together. Otherwise, we are split apart. Zach, of course, takes AP English Language and Composition class, which is the hardest of the AP courses. He also signs up for Poetry and British Literature. All are classes that are focused on books and will help him with being a librarian.

We meet up in the hallway and walk to lunch with Connor, who keeps going on and on about the first football game coming up. I love football, but I think now that I know what I'm going to do after high school, it feels like I'm putting a lot of energy into a sport I'll never use. I won't leave the guys, though; they make it all worthwhile.

We sit in our usual spot, Zach between Connor and me. Alex nudges my other side, nodding toward some girls sitting a table over. "Did you see the new girl? She's hot as fuck with that strawberry blonde hair and those red lips."

"Don't let Ivy hear you say that." But I do look over to see the new girl, and she has this sweet look about her. She glances in my direction and gives me a shy smile when she sees me looking at her. I grin back and wonder if maybe this is the girl that will make me want to date again. So far, none of the girls I've dated has given me any feelings I expected to have. "Yeah, she looks sweet. I think I'll ask her out."

"I'm going to the library for the rest of lunch," Zach says beside me. I whip my head back to see him throwing his uneaten lunch back into the bag.

"You okay?"

"Yep, just need a book. See you later."

Zach never goes off on his own like this at school, and something about it feels off. I pin my eyes on Connor. "What just happened? Did you say something to upset him?"

Connor rolls his eyes. "You are so fucking clueless sometimes."

"What are you talking about?"

He looks away. "Nothing. I'm sure Zach is fine."

Doesn't feel like he's fine. I eat my lunch quickly and go off to the library to find him. He's sitting at a table in the back with the book he's been reading. But instead of reading, he's staring outside the window. He has that sad expression I hate and haven't seen for a while.

"Hey…"

His green eyes flit to mine and yep, they are sad. "Hey."

"What's going on?"

"Nothing, I'm fine."

Definitely a lie, and I don't like it. Zach doesn't lie to me. I see him swallow hard and decide not to push it. Instead, I sit down next to him and put my arm around the back of his chair. "I talked to coach, and he understands I need to leave practice to drive you to the library after school."

He lifts his shoulders slightly. "I think it's time I drive myself to work. It'll be easier on you, and I need to get used to it."

"I can drive you, Zach. I want to." What is going on with him?

Zach closes his book, shaking his head. "No, I'll drive to school on the days I have to work. I need to start doing things for myself, or when you leave, it'll wreck me."

Wreck me. Two words that send sharp pains through my heart. I already feel like leaving him will wreck *me*. I know he's right, but it doesn't make letting go any easier. "Okay…if that's what you want. I'd be happy to drive you, though."

THE FOLLOWING morning when he gets into his Audi and I get into my truck, it feels horrible. I follow him to school and park next to him, but it still feels all sorts of wrong. Connor seems surprised to see Zach has driven himself but doesn't say anything.

Even though Zach said he would drive himself, I still leave football practice after last period and walk him to his vehicle. He drives off, and I worry about him every second until coach releases us.

When I leave school, I drive by the library to make sure he's parked there before heading home. He works three to six, three nights a week, and then nine to one on Saturdays. Marcy doesn't want him to work too many hours while he's still in school.

I sit at the island waiting for him to get home, doing my homework while keeping an eye on the door. He finally walks in, and judging by his face, today was as hard on him as it was on me. He rushes over, and I open my arms to hug him tightly.

What I want to say is "don't do that again," but instead, what comes out of my mouth is, "You did it and made it through."

He nods against my chest, clinging to me a little longer before letting go.

We spend the evening side by side, trying to ease some of the hurt from being separated.

THE NEXT DAY, the new girl stops by our table with Ivy, and I find out her name is Carrie. She's a junior and just joined the cheerleading squad. She has the looks of a cheerleader but seems too quiet for one.

When she gives me one of those shy smiles, I go for it. "I was wondering if you would like to go on a date with me Saturday night?"

Her brown eyes stare up at me, a mixture of surprise and excitement in them. "I would love that."

I smile. "Do you have a cell number? I can text you a time and get your address?"

She passes her cell over to me, and I send a text to myself. We spend the next ten minutes chatting about school classes and how she likes living here. When she leaves the table, I turn to find both Zach and Connor gone.

SATURDAY NIGHT, I pick Carrie up and take her to the only diner in town. We talk and laugh about everything. She reaches over to hold my hand during the movie but doesn't push for more. When I drop her off at home afterward and ask her out for the next weekend, she seems eager and happy. The fact that she doesn't try to kiss me or have sex with me makes the date more enjoyable, and I'm able to go home smiling.

Zach looks up when I walk into the bedroom, and I grin. "It was a good date. She's really nice."

"That's great. I'm happy for you." He rolls over to continue reading his book, Honey cuddled up against him.

I let him ignore me for a while, but then I grab the book out of his hand and toss it onto the floor, pulling him over to sleep next to me. He rolls over to face me and goes to sleep.

TWENTY-SEVEN

BRADY

Carrie and I date over the next couple of months. Mainly just easy dates of going out to dinner or the movies or sitting outside her house talking. We've kissed a few times, and it hasn't been anything great, but maybe it's because I've not really kissed a bunch of girls.

She's asked me about my relationship with Zach a couple of times. I've explained that we are close, that he's my best friend and very important to me.

Tonight, I've asked her to go bowling with Zach, Connor, Alex, and Ivy. Zach doesn't really want to go, but I beg and plead until he relents. He offers to drive separately, but I insist he rides with me. It's dumb to take two vehicles, and they need to be friends if I'm going to date her longer.

He stays in the truck while I go up to the door to get her, and it's not until I'm walking back that I realize he probably shouldn't sit in the middle like he usually does when someone rides with us. Last minute, I tug her hand to my side and help her climb up to sit between us.

"Hi, Zach," Carrie says, giving him this little wave.

"Hey," he mumbles, staring back out the window.

It's really weird to drive with her between us, and I keep glancing over to see him pressed as far as he can against the door. It feels wrong to not have him next to me like he usually is when Connor is with us.

I park in front of the bowling alley and help Carrie down from the truck, hurrying around to the other side because Zach is clearly going to try to get down on his own. He stumbles and falls before I can get to him. I help him off the ground and fix his glasses. "If you'd just waited for me, I would've helped you down."

"You shouldn't have to help me down while you're on a date," he murmurs, brushing by me to go inside.

"Is he okay?" Carrie asks, taking my hand as we follow him.

"Yeah, I think so. Zach…he takes a little while to get used to new people." I realize she probably doesn't know about his past like most people do. "He's been through a lot."

Connor is helping Zach get shoes, which my best friend is looking at like they are disgusting. The shoes really aren't something anyone likes to wear. It dawns on me that he's never been bowling before, and this is a whole new experience for him.

"You need help picking out a ball?" I ask him once we reach the counter to ask for our own shoe sizes.

"Connor will help me, but thanks." He barely looks at me and leaves with Connor to go through the bowling balls. Connor better not let him get one that is too heavy.

Alex and Ivy join us, and we set our lane up. When it's Zach's turn to bowl, I'm about to get up and show him how when Connor stands up to help him.

I'm pretty sure the ball is too heavy when Zach carries it with two hands. He watches Connor explain it and then tries to copy him. The ball drops hard onto the lane, along with Zach falling face-first after it. I rush up, but Connor is already helping him off the floor.

Zach's face is red, and I think he's fighting tears, especially when the guys in the lane next to us start laughing. Connor and I both give them looks to shut the fuck up. We aren't tiny, and they get the hint real quick.

"Here, let's get you a lighter ball," I say, putting my arm around Zach and guiding him over to the wall where they keep all the bowling balls.

Connor joins us, pointing to the kids' balls. "He has the lightest adult ball."

I'm sure that's why Connor went with it, not wanting to embarrass Zach by having to get a bright orange or pink ball. "Zach, lots of people use the kids' balls even as adults. Why don't you try them and see which one fits your fingers best?"

He begrudgingly tries them and ends up with the pink one. He has such small hands and slender fingers; it's not like he can help it. This time I stand behind him and help him swing his arm, talking him through how to hold his wrist and to focus on the pins. He gets a gutter ball, but at least he stays on his feet.

"Sorry if I embarrassed you," he says quietly.

"You never embarrass me, Zach." I hook my arm around his neck and kiss his forehead. "You never have to worry about that with me. This is for fun, so just try to enjoy it."

I sit down next to Carrie and pull him down on the other side of me, holding his hand to ease some of his anxiety. I know Zach, and he's clearly anxious about being here for some reason.

Connor has picked up on it, too, because he hovers on Zach's other side, cracking jokes and trying to make him laugh.

We get through a game, and poor Zach has a fifty-two for a score. Carrie bowls well, and her score is right up there with us guys. She doesn't say much to Zach, and it bothers me that neither of them is putting any effort into becoming friends.

When Carrie leans over to kiss me, I hear Zach ask Connor to show him where to get a drink. Pulling away from the kiss, I watch Connor take Zach's hand and tug him into the little arcade area. They stay in there through the next game of bowling, and when they come out, Zach is carrying a stuffed unicorn and talking animatedly to Connor about something.

Connor steers him to the window to order food, glancing over Zach's head toward me. There's something in his look that irks me, or maybe it's just that Zach isn't spending time with Carrie and me like I wanted him to.

"Do you want something to eat or drink?" I ask Carrie.

"I'll take a Dr. Pepper and some fries. You want me to come with you to order it?"

"Nah, I'll go order. Be right back."

Connor and Zach have just finished ordering when I walk up. I hug Zach from behind, tweaking his stuffed unicorn. "Won some games?"

"Connor won some games. Surprisingly, I'm not that good," he says in a self-deprecating tone.

"You were good at the racing game," Connor counters, ruffling Zach's hair.

I fix Zach's hair for him. "Sounds like you had fun."

"It was cool. I've only seen arcades on TV shows before."

His comment reminds me I've only come here with the girls I've dated. "I can't believe we have never come here together. We should have."

He shrugs. "Probably because I'm not huge on tons of people in a close area with lots of noise. It's really loud in here, and it makes me all jittery."

"Shit, Zach, I didn't even think of that. I'm sorry."

"It's okay. I've gotten used to it at school. I shouldn't let this bother me."

"May I take your order?"

My attention gets drawn to the window, and I place my order.

Zach and Connor wait for me to get our drinks before walking back to the table by our lane.

"Are you two going to play another game with us?"

"I'm not really that good," Zach says, taking a sip of his Mountain Dew.

"Only way to get good at it is by practicing." I move his soda back from the edge. "Come on, one more game and then we'll be done."

"I guess so."

We start another game but take a break when the food is brought out to the table closest to our lane. There are only four chairs, and Carrie sits on my leg without me saying anything, laughing at something Ivy is chatting about. Zach is standing awkwardly off to the side, and I feel terrible because normally, I would pull him down to sit on my lap. Ivy moves over to Alex's so Zach can have her chair, but when I look at his eyes, I feel like I kicked a puppy.

Connor nudges his arm, joking, "You can sit on my lap, Zach. I'm feeling left out."

"You just want to feel my ass," Zach smarts back, half grinning at Connor.

"Yeah, baby, you know it."

"Dork."

That Zach can laugh with Connor instead of me rubs me the wrong way. "Where is Tessa tonight?"

"She was going to some play in Pine Falls with her mom."

"Do you have a girlfriend?" Carrie asks Zach.

Everyone freezes. I can't believe no one at school told her he was gay, but then I guess a lot of my classmates have learned to be respectful of people telling others in their own time. Zach fidgets with his straw, taking a long, steadying breath.

Carrie looks at me. "What? Did I say something wrong?"

"I'm gay," Zach says in a rush, leaving the table with his glass to carry up to the window.

"I didn't know. I didn't mean to offend him."

Connor pushes back his chair. "Next time, don't assume someone's sexuality or put them on the spot. And to answer your question, no, he doesn't have a boyfriend." He leaves the table to follow Zach.

I'm blown away by his harsh tone and defensiveness. She didn't know, and she wasn't trying to be mean. "I'm sorry. Connor is protective of Zach." Like I am. And right now, I'm sitting here while my best friend feels like he just had to come out all over again.

Ivy leans forward. "We are all protective of Zach. He's the kindest person you'll ever meet."

Carrie drapes her arm around my neck. "I guess I need to get to know him better."

I'm not sure what Connor says to him, but Zach comes back carrying another Mountain Dew and sits down again. I reach over to slide his Mountain Dew away from him and push my water over. "No more sugar."

"It's just one night..."

"Not happening. Don't even bother arguing with me."

He huffs but takes a sip of my water.

Everyone is used to me bossing Zach around, except Carrie, who is looking at us like we lost our minds. "Why can't he have more soda?"

Zach gets this panicked expression at having to explain his splenectomy, so I answer for him. "Because I told him no." Relief crosses his face, but I still watch him closely to see if he's going to have a panic attack. "Are you okay?"

He gives a slight nod but doesn't look okay.

"Carrie, will you go with me to the ladies' room?"

"Sure..." Carrie gets off my lap and follows Ivy to the back hallway.

I reach over for Zach's hand, tugging him out of his chair and onto my lap, hugging him tightly. "Everything's okay; you don't have to talk about it," I whisper in his ear.

"I'm ruining your evening," he murmurs. "I can't seem to get it right tonight."

"You're not ruining it. So you're having an off night, but look how far you've come since May."

Alex chimes in, "I've seen you at work; you're doing great."

"And you can bake sweets like no one else can," Connor offers with a grin.

Zach shakes his head but smiles. "You and food."

"I can't help that I'm in love with your food."

I kiss Zach's forehead. "See, give yourself a break. You even drive to work now and haven't had a panic attack for months."

"I'm seventeen and should be past all this. It's lame."

It is hard to see him as seventeen sometimes. Maybe it's because he's smaller than everyone our age. Maybe it's the innocence he still exudes, a sheltered vulnerableness I'm not sure he'll ever lose. "I think you should stay you, and if people have an issue with it, they aren't worth your time."

Carrie appears next to us, clearly trying to figure out why I'm holding Zach on my lap. "Umm…hey," she says, looking from me to Zach.

Zach gives me one last hug, and I kiss his forehead before releasing him. He stands, awkwardly wringing his hands and stammering out, "I'm sorry…I just needed him for a minute."

Connor gets up from the table. "You want me to take you home, Zach?"

His shoulders sag in relief. "Yes, please."

"Don't forget to change your shoes," I remind him.

"I still have to pay for my games."

"I'll pay…just head home. I'll text Mom and Dad that you're on your way."

"Thanks, Brady." He sits in the chair next to me, slipping off the shoes and putting on his tennis shoes. I lean over and tie one while he ties the other.

"Don't forget your unicorn and no sweets when you get home." I know I sound like a bossy parent, but I always feel this need to watch over him.

He gives me a quick hug and runs after Connor to leave. Carrie sits down next to me, a little quiet.

"He really has come a long way," Alex says, breaking the silence.

"Yeah, he has. I should have thought about the fact he's never been here and all the loud noises."

"Is he autistic?"

"No, he's not autistic." Even if he was, it bothers me she would ask that.

Ivy tries to break the sudden tension with an overly enthusiastic, "Let's finish bowling!"

We do, and I try to get into it, but my mind keeps going to Zach at home.

On our way to Carrie's house, she brings him up. "What's the deal with you and Zach? I know he lives with you and is your best friend, but obviously, I'm missing a bunch of information."

I pull into her driveway and put the truck into park. "I'm so used to everyone at school knowing his history that I didn't think of telling you. Plus, it feels a bit like I'm violating his privacy when I talk to someone about him."

"I get that, but he was on your lap, and you two are super affectionate toward each other. Not to mention he seems younger in some ways."

"I'll give you a shortened version and not all the details." I sigh, trying to figure out where to start. "Zach came from a very religious family...cult-like if you ask me...and was homeschooled. He never went anywhere, never watched TV, had his books monitored. We met in the woods behind my house, and he was so tiny." I skip the personal part about him crying or what we talked about. "I'd just moved here, and my little brother had died not long before. Zach and I became best friends."

She's listening and nods for me to go on.

"He became a part of my family. His parents didn't feed him much, and I made sure he had food. They didn't give him love or treat him well, and he was so...sweet and fragile." I fight the urge to tear up just thinking about Zach at thirteen. "One day, Zach's mom walked out on him to move to Texas with another man. His dad beat him for it—badly. He had been beating him for a long time, but he never told me how bad it was. The next day, Zach called me. His dad had hurt him... he could barely talk." I have to pause for a minute before continuing. "I ran there while calling nine-one-one. He was a bloody mess on the floor and his dad was still—" I break off, staring out the window.

"God," she whispers, taking my hand.

"I tried to keep his dad away from him until the police came. Zach was rushed to the hospital. His dad had caused his spleen to rupture, and he was bleeding internally. He had to have it removed. Hence the not having much sugar. He almost died. My parents became his legal guardians. Zach had always been anxious about being away from me, but after that, he would have panic attacks if I wasn't with him. He feels safe with me. He's come a long way, and I'm really proud of him. We will always be close, and if he is anxious, I'm going to hold him through it. Loud noises bother him, especially sharp ones like the bowling balls hitting the lanes. When you asked why he couldn't have soda, I could see he was about to panic over remembering or needing to talk about his surgery."

"I get it now. I wish you would have told me beforehand."

"It feels like I'm violating his trust just telling you this much. It's very personal for him. Kids at school know what was in the papers. Some have seen him panic, especially my closest friends. Zach really is the sweetest person you'll ever meet. He's just more innocent than he should be at his age. He wasn't around kids or in the public school system until two years ago. I know that me holding a boy my age is different, but Zach's needs will always supersede what people think of it. He's my family and my best friend. God knows he's been through enough that he needs to know I won't abandon him simply because I'm dating."

She leans over to kiss my lips. "You're pretty sweet yourself."

"I had hoped that you two would hit it off tonight, but it didn't work out quite that way."

"We can try again, but maybe play games at your house, where he feels comfortable."

I squeeze her hand. "Yeah, maybe we can try that."

"Whatever happened to his dad?"

"He got out of jail, tried to get to Zach, threatened my family…a bunch of stuff. He was arrested and hung himself in jail. Please don't bring it up to Zach or ever call the man his dad. His dad is my dad."

"Thanks for explaining all of this to me. I'll be a lot more sensitive next time."

"Thank you, and please keep this to yourself. People have never needed to know all the details, and I don't want Zach thinking I overshared."

"I won't say anything to anyone." She starts kissing me again and shifts over my legs to straddle my lap.

I try to give in to the moment and put effort into making the kissing better. She grinds into me, and I look over her shoulder at her house. "Carrie, we are sitting in your driveway. I'd prefer not to have your parents think I'm making out with their daughter out here."

Sighing, she moves back over. "I should probably go in. Thanks for the date tonight. When do you want to go out next?"

"I have a football game on Friday. How about my place next Saturday?"

"Sure, that would be great."

After walking her to the door, I drive home and hurry inside. Meg and Anna have some friends over, and it is total chaos. I wave to Mom and take the stairs two at a time, grateful I do not have to stay with the girls.

Connor and Zach are lying on their stomachs, facing the foot of the bed and watching TV. Zach's eyes light up when he sees me, and he gives me a smile. The knot in my stomach unfurls, and I kick off my shoes, scooting him over a little so I can lie next to him. "What are we watching?"

"It's a Hallmark Christmas movie," Connor says with humor in his voice. "Someone thinks Christmas is already here, and we aren't even to Thanksgiving yet."

"I don't think it's Christmas already; I just think they are happy movies where you know there will be a happy ending. They make me feel good."

"They are sappy and unrealistic."

I reach over Zach to smack Connor. "Don't ruin it for him."

"Someday, maybe they will make one with a gay couple," Zach says with a sigh.

"They should," I agree with him, rolling on my side to rub his back.

"I'm going to head home, guys. We have some stupid family get-together tomorrow, and Mom wants me up early so I can help." Connor sits on the edge of the bed, slipping his shoes on. "Kill me now; it's going to be torture."

"Thanks for everything tonight. You made it better."

Connor runs his hand over Zach's head. "It was fun."

I get a fist bump and then he leaves. "You and Connor are getting close…"

Zach turns his head, giving me his beautiful green eyes. "He cares about me, and I'm grateful for his friendship, but he will never be you."

I'm not sure how he knew I needed to hear that, but his words make me smile. "Oh yeah? So you're saying I'm your favorite?"

He rolls his eyes. "You already know that and are just trying to get compliments now."

"Maaaaaaybeeee…" I tickle his side, and he pounces on top of me, trying to tickle me back. We wrestle until both of us flop on our backs, tired and laughing.

TWENTY-EIGHT

BRADY

Every morning that week, I wake up with the worst hard-ons of my life. We are used to it happening, and neither of us ever says anything to the other, but this is worse than before. I'll wake up to me pressing against Zach, trying to find release in my sleep. I've had to run to the bathroom to jack off every morning, sometimes twice in the shower before I even get out.

Maybe it's dating Carrie, and I just need to have sex already. Most guys in school have been having sex since they were freshmen, and I'm a freaking senior. Why am I holding on to this and not going for it? It's me that's holding back when it comes to making out, not Carrie.

Saturday arrives, and Carrie comes over for games and movies in the basement. It's the first time for her to meet my parents, and she seems nervous. Mom and Dad stand on either side of Zach, asking a few questions, but it feels awkward.

Connor and Tessa show up, along with Avery. Avery's grown a lot in the last year, filled out more. His hair has pink streaks dyed in it, which matches his current outfit of pink sequined everything. He and Zach are currently sitting on the couch, chattering back and forth while us couples play pool.

Carrie keeps glancing over at them and finally says, "They are so cute together. Maybe they'll start dating?"

Connor and I exchange looks, grinning. I shake my head. "No, they definitely aren't going to date."

We end up around the table downstairs, playing Catan. Zach does seem more relaxed, but there's still this uneasiness between him and Carrie. It's nothing specific, but I can feel it, nonetheless.

Mom brings down snacks. I think she's mainly checking on Zach. He gets a hug from behind his chair and a kiss to the top of his head. "You want me to put Honey out for you?"

"That would be great. Thanks, Mom."

"Hey, don't I get any attention?" I tease, even though I don't care.

Mom comes over to give me a hug, tapping the back of my head because she knows I'm being a smart-ass.

Zach gives me this worried expression as if I'm actually offended and he's taking too much of my mom from me. I lean over to press my forehead to his. "I was joking. I'm not upset at all. You deserve all the love Mom gives you. Got it?"

"Yeah," he whispers.

I kiss his forehead and look back at the game. Everyone is staring at us, but then Connor pulls the attention to him by asking my mom where his hug is. She laughs and shakes her head, calling Honey from Zach's side to come upstairs.

Connor leaves the table to pile a plate up with snacks and Zach's desserts. I put my hand on Zach's shoulder as I get up from the table. "I'll get yours for you."

He felt a little sick after our bowling night, and I want to make sure he doesn't have a repeat. Mom was smart and brought some fruit down with the rest. It makes it easier for him to feel like he's getting something sweet. I set down his plate along with a can of raspberry lime sparkling water for him before going back to get my own.

The game continues, and we play twice before Carrie brings out Cards Against Humanity. I've never played it before, but she claims it's fun. I can tell right away that Zach is reading the cards in shock and horror. He takes things very literally and still struggles with anything crude. His eyes are wide with people's answers, and he keeps shaking his head.

"Umm… I think I need to go make sure Honey is okay," he murmurs, getting up and running upstairs.

Avery sets down his own cards. "I'll go with him."

I flip over the cards that Zach was staring at, and one says "Dead Parents" and the other "miscarriage."

Carrie leans over to see the cards. "Sorry, I thought the game would be fun."

"It's okay. Zach has a hard time with crude or dark humor because he feels like it's laughing over hurting someone."

"I keep screwing up when it comes to him," she murmurs, collecting the cards to put them away.

"You're not screwing up." I try to help her understand my best friend and say, "With Zach...think Disney and Hallmark type stuff. He's very tenderhearted and cries during Tangled when Eugene floats away in the boat or during Beauty and the Beast when Belle is crying over not getting to say goodbye to her dad. He can't stand to see anyone hurt and loves happy endings."

Connor sits forward in his chair, giving Carrie a half smile, and continues for me. "Zach is everything that is good in this world, and maybe some people think he needs to grow up or should get used to the bad stuff, but he's had enough bad stuff for a lifetime. He deals with it in his own way...and that's by being sensitive to everyone. He feels things stronger than most, and with that, he needs the happy stuff, or he'll drown in all the wrong kind of emotions."

I stare at Connor, wondering how I missed the deep devotion he has for my best friend. I always knew he cared, but I realize now that he truly is Zach's friend, and not just because of me. It's because he truly cares about Zach.

"You said that perfectly." I kick Connor from under the table. "You're turning into a sappy, sweet guy."

He kicks me back. "I should be, as many Hallmark movies as I've watched lately. I have Tangled memorized because he watches it every time you leave him at home."

Tangled is his comfort movie when he's sad, and hearing that sends a sharp pain right through my heart. *He needs it every time I'm gone.*

"I'll have to thank Zach for that," Tessa says, hugging Connor's arm. "Connor is the most romantic guy out there. He brings me flowers and sings to me and even takes me to see romance movies most guys would die before seeing. The Hallmark movies are really paying off."

Connor grins and gives her a kiss. "Zach would love to think he had a hand in it. Tell him while dancing around and singing, and he'll love you forever."

I toss a pretzel at Connor's head. "You're making me look bad in the romance department."

"Yeah, I've never gotten flowers, and he drags me to action movies every time." Carrie nudges me with her elbow. "You need to step up your game."

Her words make me pause because I hadn't really thought about doing anything romantic with her. I thought our dates were fun just talking and seeing movies we both liked. I take Zach to romance movies because he loves them. It just feels right to see big action films with Carrie. "I'm going to check on Zach and make sure he's okay."

"We'll find a movie to watch for when you come back."

Giving Connor a nod, I head upstairs to find my best friend.

He and Avery are sitting at the table talking to my parents while Meg and Anna paint their fingernails.

Dad gives me a smile as I sit down with them. "Come up to visit the fun ones?"

"Of course. Every guy my age dreams of spending Saturday night with his parents and getting his nails painted." Meg has already started on my hand, and it looks like I'm getting glittery green today. "What? I don't get pink?"

"Zach picked pink already."

Dad holds up his hands, and they are a pukey peach color. "You were saying?"

"I love the green. It's so pretty."

Meg snickers and keeps painting. I'm sure most guys would freak over this, but it makes the girls happy, and it comes off easily.

"Next time, I want red so it matches my truck."

"It's a deal," my sister agrees, starting on my other hand.

I look over at Zach, who is blowing on his fingers to dry them. "We are going to start a movie. Are you two going to come down and watch it?"

Avery shakes his head. "My mom is picking me up. We are leaving early to go see my grandparents. It's a three-hour drive, and she wants to have most of the day with them. Four a.m. will come all too soon."

"I'm glad you came tonight."

Avery smiles. "Me, too. Winning Catan was a bonus."

I'm waving my hands to dry the paint when his mom comes

for him.

"Are you ready to come downstairs?" I ask my best friend, wanting him with me.

Zach shrugs. "Is it going to be a scary movie?"

"No, we'll find something that isn't scary," I promise.

He agrees and I give him a piggy-back ride downstairs to the couch, dumping him off with a laugh. I sit down next to Carrie, taking her hand. "What movie did you guys pick out?"

"Jurassic World," she replies.

"Isn't that scary?"

She leans into me. "No, not at all. It's a family movie."

Zach curls up on the other end of the couch under a pile of blankets. It starts out good and interesting, but then it gets scary real quick. Not that I find it scary, but I know Zach will be terrified.

Sure enough, Zach lunges from his side of the couch to me, clinging to my other side. "I can't watch!" He covers up his head, his entire body trembling with fear.

"Okay, this movie isn't going to work." I remove my arm from around Carrie so I can keep one on Zach and reach for the remote to stop it. I scroll through the movies on Netflix and pick their newest Christmas romance to turn on. "Here we go."

Zach relaxes as the movie starts with Christmas music. I'll be lucky if Jurassic World doesn't give him nightmares tonight. Zach lies down with his head on my leg and Honey curled up with him. Taking Carrie's hand again, we settle in to watch this movie.

Connor and Tessa are probably making out in the dark on the floor from the sounds of it. Carrie stays fairly quiet next to me, and halfway through the movie, Zach is asleep.

"I think we are going to head out," Connor says, helping Tessa to her feet. "We can help carry the leftover food upstairs."

I pause the movie and reach for a small couch pillow, easing it under Zach's head as I move my leg.

Carrie and I help bring everything up, seeing both of them out. She turns to me as soon as the door is closed. "Show me your room?"

My room? "Okay." It feels weird to let her come into the space that is Zach's, too. She roams around, taking it all in before sitting on the edge of my bed. Zach's Eeyore, Unicorn, and the puppy Connor got him after surgery are all lying on my bed, along with his Tangled blanket. I'm not sure if she thinks they are mine or if she just hasn't noticed.

She pats the bed, and I sink down next to her, wishing we weren't in here. One minute she's looking at me, and the next she's straddling my lap, kissing me like she's going to eat my face off.

"Ohhhh Brady, I want you," she moans, taking my hands and placing them on her breasts as she continues to kiss me.

I try to think about what to do next. Do I slip my hand under her shirt or kiss down her neck? *Why is this so freaking awkward?* I need to shut off my brain somehow.

The sound of Honey's tags jingling together brings my head around, breaking the kiss. Zach is standing there for only a second before he's shutting the door, but not before I see his face. *Shit.* I can't blame him for being upset. This is his room as much as it is mine, regardless of us calling it my room all the time. I wouldn't exactly like to come in and see him making out with a guy on the bed I sleep in.

"Does he always come into your room without knocking?"

"We can't do this. Not here in my house." I gently set her off my lap. "We should call it a night, anyway."

Zach is nowhere to be found as I walk her down to her car. As soon as she backs out of the driveway, I go to find him. His bedroom door is shut, and when I try the knob, it's locked.

"Zach? Can you unlock the door, please?" He's never locked the door before, and it's making me anxious just knowing I can't get to him. "Zach?"

No answer.

"Zach, please open the door." I lean my head against it. "I'm sorry."

I could almost swear I hear a sniffle like he's crying, but I can't tell for sure. Why did I leave him alone in the basement? It was stupid. *Stupid!* He's scared to be down there alone, especially in the dark. I rub my chest just thinking about him waking up down there and running up here to find me, only to walk in on that. It has to look like I chose something as stupid as making out, over him. Fuck, I messed up.

After waiting by his door for five minutes, I go to my room and pace, staring at my bed. Sighing, I lie down on my side of the bed and stare at the spot he always sleeps in. This feels wrong, so wrong. Not having him buried into me is like missing a part of myself. How am I going to do this for four months? Maybe it'll be easier if he's not upset because knowing he is—is killing me.

The thought that Dad probably has a key or a way to open the door crosses my mind. I hurry out of bed and run down the stairs, knocking on my parents' bedroom door.

"Come in…"

I open the door to find them sitting up in bed watching some movie. Dad immediately looks worried when he sees me. "What happened? Is Zach okay?"

"He's locked himself in his room. Do you have a key or something to open the door?"

Mom mutes the TV. "What did you do?"

"I was stupid," I groan, running my fingers through my hair. "I left him in the dark basement alone, and then he must have woken up and ran upstairs to find me with Carrie on our bed." I groan again, just repeating it.

Dad and Mom exchange one of those glances before Dad answers me. "I don't know, Brady. Maybe he wants to be alone."

"It's Zach…" I give him a pleading look. "He's upset and needs me. Just tell me how to get into his room. Please?"

He sighs, getting out of bed and walking out to the kitchen with me following. He pulls open a drawer and takes out this little piece of metal, handing it to me. "Just put it in that little circle in the knob and wiggle it around. It'll come unlocked."

"Thanks, dad." I start to walk away when he puts his hand on my arm, stopping me.

"Son, I know you didn't do this to hurt Zach…but bringing a girl into the bed you share is going to hurt him. It's hard enough for him to have you all to himself and suddenly have to share you with Carrie. Just be sensitive about it, okay? If you're going to get serious with her and be bringing her up to your room, then maybe you and Zach need to have a long talk about not sharing a room anymore."

Not sharing a room? There's no way I'm shoving him into his own room. Not having him with me is a horrible feeling.

"I'm not bringing her up to my room again, and I'm not kicking him out of my room," I say firmly.

Dad looks like he wants to say something more but just nods instead.

Running up the stairs, I hurry to unlock the door and hopefully fix this.

TWENTY-NINE

ZACH

Brady's worried voice comes through the door, but I can't open it yet. Seeing him kissing and touching his girlfriend like that hurt. Like stabbing, heartbreaking hurt. Any hope I held on to that maybe he was bi or gay and just didn't know it yet is gone. Swiping away my tears, I try to erase the image, but it doesn't work.

It was hard enough to see it, but for him to do it where I sleep…on my side of the bed even. It makes me want to vomit.

"Zach, please open the door. I'm sorry."

I want to open the door and let him in. I hate hearing him like this. But if I do, he'll be able to tell I was crying, and how do I explain that? *Yeah, I'm bawling because I've been in love with you for years, and you just stomped on my heart?* That's not going to work.

Tears leak out again, and I hug Honey, wishing she was really Brady instead. I need to get a grip and let this go. Carrie is nice, even if she is a little judgmental. I see it in her eyes every time she looks at me. She thinks I need to grow up and change. Maybe I do need to stop being such a baby about things. Is it wrong that I love Disney movies and happiness? Is it wrong that I depend on Brady so much?

Between crying and stressing, I now have a splitting headache. Stress brings back that panicky feeling I hate, as if the monster is waiting outside the door to come in and punish me. That thought sends me off the bed and into the corner, wrapping my arms around my legs.

I always waited in the corner when I knew he was coming in. As if somehow that would protect me, even though it never did.

Honey comes over to lie by my feet, but it doesn't stop the uncontrollable shivering that has taken over my body. *Stop this, Zach. He's dead... He's dead.*

The door opens, and for a second, I press into the corner, expecting the monster to come out of the shadows. A whimper escapes and reminds me of how helpless I was back then.

"Zach!"

Brady. He rushes over to me, and despite being hurt, I fling myself into his arms the second he touches me. "I thought you were him." I sob into his shirt. "I thought you were him."

"Shhh...it's just me. You're safe. He can't get to you anymore, remember?" He wraps his arms around me in a tight embrace, kissing my cheek in this tender way that brings more tears to my eyes.

"Brady...I'm sorry."

"You're shivering; let's get you off the floor." He ignores my apology and lifts me off the floor, carrying me out of the room and down to his bedroom, toeing the door shut behind us. Honey jumps up on the bed, happily settling into her usual spot.

Brady sits me on the edge of the bed, hooking my shirt to lift it up and over my head. He pushes me back so he can undo my jeans and tug them off my legs. Thankfully, I'm too upset for my dick to react to that, or it would be seriously embarrassing.

He strips off his own clothes and crawls into bed with me, moving me to my normal spot. There's something so calming about being in our normal position, with me resting my head on his arm and being pressed against him, his arm around my back to hold me there. It's the time when I feel the safest, this skin to skin, where I feel every breath he takes rise and fall in a rhythm against my heart.

"I'm sorry, Zach," Brady whispers, so much emotion in his voice that it's clear he's as upset as I am. "I'm so very sorry."

I press my lips to his chest briefly to let him know it's okay, too afraid to talk, or I'll spill all my feelings.

We lie here clinging to each other until I drift off to sleep.

MY MORNING WAKE-UP call is Brady's ginormous tool pressing against mine. Two small scraps of material aren't hiding much, and if I had to guess, I'd say his isn't even all the way inside that scrap of material. I try to move away, but he tightens his arms around me.

"Brady," I whisper.

He rocks into me, and I bite my lip so I won't moan. "Brady!"

His eyes open, and it takes him a second to realize the issue. "Fuck...sorry." He loosens his arms enough for me to roll onto my back while he rolls to his stomach.

We lie in this position, neither of us saying anything, letting our bodies cool down and get the raging hard-ons under control.

After a few minutes, he rolls back on his side and reaches over to run his fingers down my face. "I'm sorry about last night."

I don't even want to think about last night. "She probably thinks I'm some weird perv that came into your room."

"No, she doesn't. I should have never let her convince me to show her my room or left you in the basement. I thought she just wanted to see it quick."

"It's okay," I whisper, wishing he would let it go.

"Zach?"

Turning my head, I meet his intense gaze.

"Don't ever lock the door on me again," he says firmly and a little pleadingly. "It freaked me out not being able to get to you."

"How did you get in?"

"I asked Dad for a key or something to get your door open. You scared me half to death seeing you in the corner hiding and shivering."

I close my eyes, letting his fingers skim over my forehead and cheek in a pattern that calms me before answering. "He used to send me to my room and wait for hours to punish me. I would hide in the corner, praying he would forget or not see me. That somehow it would save me..."

Brady has tears in his eyes when he tugs me over into his arms so I can rest my head on his chest. "It'll never happen again. He's gone, and I would never let anyone hurt you."

If only that included him because he has the power to hurt me far more than anyone else, and it's a pain much worse than what the monster dealt out.

"Just fyi, your girlfriend is a little dark," I murmur, trying to break this emotion before I buckle under it.

He gives this half laugh. "Dark?"

"Yeah, the cards were dark...like awful dark...and then that movie!

Who the hell thinks that dinosaurs wanting to rip your body apart aren't scary?"

His chest rumbles under my ear. "I don't know, Zach. I don't know."

Maybe it's what happened last night, but we spend the day glued to each other. He reads to me and then I read to him, all while snuggling with each other. We take Honey on a walk, holding hands. At supper, Brady keeps an arm draped over the back of my chair, his hand resting on my shoulder. The only time we aren't together is when we shower, and God knows I need privacy for that. Being this close to him is this constant push against my control to not be turned on by him.

Watching Brady drive to school the next morning, I memorize every line of his face, his kind eyes, and the way he looks over at me. I love him more than life itself, and I have to put my own feelings aside when it comes to his happiness. Because seeing him smile is everything to me. If Carrie is what he wants, I need to make an effort to become friends with her. I don't want to come between him and his future. No matter how much I want it to be me, it needs to be the person he wants it to be.

I do great right up until lunchtime, when she walks over to our table and I remember that she probably thinks I'm a perv. My face turns red, and I duck my head while I eat, hoping I magically become invisible.

Connor steals one of my strawberries, drawing my attention to him. "What has you so red in the face?"

I lean up, cupping my hand to his ear and whisper, "I walked in on Brady and Carrie making out..."

He pulls back, his eyebrows raised, and then leans in to ask, "Where at?"

"Brady's room. She has to think I'm some weirdo walking in on them."

Connor is quiet and actually looks a little red in the face for a minute. Then he puts his arm around me and steals another strawberry. "I wouldn't worry about what she thinks," he whispers.

"What are you two over here whispering about?" Brady pipes in from beside me.

"Nothing you need to know about," Connor snaps back.

Brady eyes Connor, and they seem to be having some sort of stare-off. I wave my hands between them until they look at me. "I'll give either one of you a hundred dollars if you let me have your brownie."

Brady rolls his eyes at me and Connor laughs, followed by a big no from both of them.

"I'll sell you mine," Alex offers. He's sitting in front of Brady and slides his brownie over.

Brady slides it back. "Nope, not happening."

"You know…someday I'm going to grow a foot, and then you won't be able to boss me around anymore," I huff.

Brady bursts out laughing, along with everyone else close enough to hear. "You keep dreaming because if you get past five foot five, I'll be shocked."

I'll be shocked if I get past five foot three at the rate I'm going. I'd be thrilled with five foot five.

I DON'T HAVE to work this evening and sit outside for Brady's practice. Their last game of the season is this Friday. Then football will be over for him for good. It's a weird feeling knowing I'll never see him playing out on the field again. Having football finished is one step closer to him leaving, and I'm not ready to say goodbye.

THE NEXT SIX weeks fly by, and suddenly it's Christmas vacation. I have my own money from my job to buy presents with this year. Brady and I spend time at the mall shopping, and of course, an hour of it is spent in the Disney store. Brady's gifts I order online so he won't know about them.

After what happened with me locking my door, Brady has moved all my stuff from my closet and drawers into his. He's moved anything that made my room mine and has declared his room *our room*. I've been forbidden to use the old room again, or he's taking the door off the hinges. I can't tell if he's being serious or joking about that part.

Carrie and I haven't really seen much of each other. Brady hasn't brought her over again, which I'm not upset about. They've mainly done dinner and movies, and only on Saturday nights. Everything is going really well, even though every time Brady goes on a date, it's hard for me.

I think I've grown a little, but I'm too afraid to measure, in case it's not true. My jeans seem shorter, and Mom says she'll get me some new ones after Christmas.

Christmas with my family is perfect. Even though we celebrated Christmas together before, it still feels new to me, and I love every little thing we do. From decorating the tree to baking sugar cookies with the girls, to listening to Christmas music and watching movies.

We always spend New Year's Eve as a family. Connor comes over, of course, and this year he asks if he can bring Tessa. His parents are coming also since they've become good friends with Mom and Dad. Somehow, Alex and Ivy get invited. Then Carrie is suddenly coming, and I resolve myself to being the odd man out again. Even Meg and Anna each have a friend coming this year.

I would invite Avery, but he's spending it with his close friends. I like him, but we will never be besties.

The day of, Carrie asks if her parents can come along since they don't have any place to go. It feels like they must be getting serious if her parents are coming. Brady almost seems uncomfortable about it but is too nice to say no. Mom and Dad ask what they are like, and he admits that he's never met them before. They've dated for months; how can he have never met them?

I help Mom make all sorts of food, appetizers, and tons of desserts throughout the day. When it gets time for people to start arriving, I escape up to our room to read a book. I'd rather be anywhere but downstairs where there are that many people.

Connor shows up a little while later, sitting on the edge of the bed to talk to me. "Why aren't you downstairs?"

I let my book flop down so I can see his face. "Because there are so many people down there. It's going to be loud, and I'm the only one without a date or friend."

Understanding is there on his face. "That sucks, but you can hang out with me."

"No offense, but watching you and Tessa suck face isn't exactly my kind of party."

"Is this really about there being so many people, or is it about Brady having Carrie and her parents here?"

Connor has never once openly said something about how I feel, and my eyes widen that he does so now. "It's about me not wanting to come down. You know I get anxious with noise and people, especially new people." I look away for a second and then admit, "Plus, seeing Brady with her parents will feel like I'm watching him with his future in-laws. It makes me want to puke."

"If it makes you feel any better, her dad is annoying and very loud."

"See, you just proved my point of why I don't want to go down there."

He sighs, patting my thigh before standing up. "Okay, but if you change your mind, you can sit on my lap all evening."

I chuck a pillow at him. "No, thank you. I'm not having Tessa kill me."

His laughter follows him out the door.

An hour later, Brady comes in and tosses my book to the side. "You're coming downstairs. I don't want to bring in the new year without you."

"I don't want to be around everyone," I grumble, picking up my book from where he tossed it.

Brady snatches it away again and hides it behind his back. "The adults are in the living room. Our friends are in the basement, and the girls are at the table doing some artsy craft thing with their friends."

"No, I hate being the extra all the time. You can all make out with your girlfriends, and I'll just stay up here reading a book."

"Zach...come on. You can even sit on my lap while we play games and be my partner."

"Your girlfriend isn't going to want me sitting on your lap."

He throws the book to the side and scoops me up off the bed. "My girlfriend will have to get over it." He refuses to let me down, even when I kick my feet trying to get away. "Come on, Honey."

The traitorous dog trots after us as if Brady is the boss, and she doesn't have to save me. He carries me down and directly to the basement steps, saving me from seeing everyone else.

Connor notices him carrying me over and grins. "I see he told you no, too."

"Yep, and kicked and screamed like a little girl when I didn't give him a choice." Brady sits down where they are playing Catan and swivels me on his lap so I'm facing the table.

"I did not scream like a little girl."

"You're pouting like one right now," he teases me, reaching around to play some cards.

"It's sulking, not pouting. Big difference."

Connor pokes me in the side until Brady smacks his hand. "Stop poking him."

Leaning back against Brady, I watch everyone play but stay quiet. Being close to Brady is worth just sitting here. Carrie looks at us many times, and I wonder if she wants to claw my eyes out. Because if Brady was my boyfriend, I'd never let another guy sit on his lap.

"If you're tired of sitting on his lap, I can trade you," she says after the game is over and they are starting another one.

Brady answers for me. "No, he's fine where he's at."

I really think that we've gotten so used to being touchy and close with each other that he forgets not everyone thinks this is normal. After me locking myself in the room, he seems to be a lot more protective and wants me close.

Honey starts bugging me to go outside, and I try to move Brady's arm from around me, but it's like trying to move steel. "Honey has to go outside. You have to let me go."

He relents, letting me up. "We need to get some refills on snacks. Let's take a break."

I lead the way, following Honey up the stairs to take her outside. Brady and the rest descend on the kitchen for more food.

I let Honey into the backyard and go over to the kitchen to join the others, giving her a minute to do her business. Brady is making me a plate of healthy food and has one small glass of Mountain Dew for me.

"Thanks, daddy," I spout off to him as I take it.

"Oh, you're in for it now," he says, chasing me around the island until I hide behind Connor.

"Sorry, it was a joke!"

Connor faces Brady, acting all tough. "To get to him, you'll have to go through me first."

Brady laughs and then uses his bossy voice. "Zach, come here."

Without thinking, I move out from behind Connor to stand next to Brady.

Connor throws his hands up in the air. "I was trying to protect you."

"It was sweet, too, but he used that damn bossy tone." I almost say daddy tone to irk Brady, but he gives me this look that makes me shut my mouth.

Everyone is ready to head back downstairs. Brady is holding my plate, and all I have is my glass.

"I have to get Honey."

He nods. "Hurry up then; we'll wait."

Honey is at the patio door, and I let her in, tail a wagging.

"You must be the gay boy that my daughter has to put up with."

My head whips around at the man's harsh voice and words, only to find him standing not even two feet away from me. The monster in my dreams melds with him…same body build, same balding head, same look in their eyes. My body feels frozen, like I can't move or talk.

"I've heard all about you…screwed-up gay boy taken in by a wealthy family. I'd be remiss as a Christian not to tell you that your choice is a sin, one you'll pay for later. You need to stay out of their way…or you'll drag that boy to hell with you."

He's back… He's not supposed to be back.

"Get the fuck away from him!" I see Brady's furious face as the room spins, and it feels like slow motion as I go down, my arm flinging out as I hit, my glass flying from my fingertips. The sound of glass shattering and yelling is drowned out by the sound of me gasping for breath.

My mouth tries to form the words, but my lungs won't expand to make them. Familiar arms pull my body close, and I hear Brady's voice ordering me to breathe. My vision starts to go black around the edges, narrowing more and more.

"God damn it, Zach! Breathe!"

The fear in Brady's voice forces air into my lungs in a painful breath. My inhaler is pressed between my lips, and Brady orders me to breathe again. He starts counting and doing grounding at the same time. He rubs my hand over his cheek. "Feel my face, Zach. It's me."

"Brady?"

"Yes, baby…come back to me. You're safe."

"He wasn't supposed to come back again," I gasp into his chest. "He wasn't supposed to come back…"

"He's not back, Zach. I promise. No one is going to hurt you."

Realization hits me that I've lost it in front of everyone. I'm so fucked up and never going to be free from my past. Sorrow rips through me, and I can't stop the sobs that pour from my soul.

THIRTY

BRADY

*Z*ach's cries tear my heart out, and my own eyes fill with tears as I hold him to my chest. His entire body is shaking in my arms as he clings to me. We had come so far, and it was all undone by a homophobic asshole we invited into our home.

Everyone heard what he said, his booming voice so loud and grating. Connor about punched him and only didn't because Alex held him back. I have no idea where he is or what Dad did because all I can see is Zach. It took so long for him to take a breath that I was worried we would have to call nine-one-one.

"Brady," I hear him sob again.

"I'm here, baby." I want to get him out of this room where everyone can't see him, but there's glass everywhere.

"He was supposed to be gone," Zach gasps out between the crying that is wracking his body.

Fuck. How did I not know her parents were religious homophobes? She never said anything.

Dad and Connor are cleaning up the glass. I can see tears in Connor's eyes, too.

He comes over to help me up while I'm holding Zach, and I carry my best friend through the kitchen to the stairs, ignoring Carrie's *I'm sorry* as we walk by. We can talk later. All that matters right now is Zach.

Connor follows me, opening the door to the bedroom and standing in the doorway as I sink down on the bed. "Can I do anything to help?"

"No, he isn't going to calm down until we are alone. Make sure that asshole is gone for me."

"I will. I'll be downstairs if you need anything." He shuts the door, and I turn all my focus onto Zach.

"Zach, it's just you and me. No one else." He's shaking so hard his teeth are chattering as he cries.

Laying him on the bed, I pull away and he starts to freak out. "Baby, I'm right here. Just let me get these clothes off you." I tug his shirt off, trying to hold him close as I pull his pajama pants off. It's hard to get my own shirt and jeans off with him clinging to me, but I think if he can feel me skin to skin, it'll bring him out of this faster. Scooting him over, I crawl into bed and gather him to me in the position we always sleep in. He starts to calm almost instantly, his shuddering sobs quieting down to soft cries.

"Shhh…you're okay. Match your breaths to mine."

He calms more as I feel his chest expand with mine, over and over until he's quiet. My legs are wrapped around his, and my body heat seems to have finally seeped in to warm him from the shock.

I'm not sure how much time passes as we lie here quietly together. I know that he's okay when he presses his lips to my chest in one of his brief kisses. I kiss his forehead in return and loosen my arm around him so I can run my fingers over his forehead and cheek in the way he likes. He tilts his head up so I can see his red, puffy, but beautiful green eyes. They are sad and pool liquid just looking at me.

"I messed it all up again," he whispers.

"No, you didn't. It's been a long time since you had a panic attack…almost seven months, I think. Every time, they get farther and farther apart."

"Why did he say that to me? I've never done anything to him." A tear escapes down the crease of his nose to drop onto my arm.

"Because he has serious issues and is stupid. It had nothing to do with you and everything to do with him."

"I wasn't trying to get in the way of your relationship… I only want you to be happy."

I can tell he's going to start crying again if he keeps going. "You didn't do anything, baby." I kiss his forehead again. "I love you. That's all I want you to concentrate on right now. *I love you.* You're safe and

I'm not upset with you and you did nothing wrong. Your family loves you and Honey loves you. No one outside of that matters. Except for Connor maybe, because he'd throw himself in front of a bus for you."

"I love you, Brady," he says, with so much feeling it sends shivers over my skin.

I watch him as his eyes close, and he gives in to the fatigue that always follows. I fully expect him to wake up and stay up half the night watching movies to avoid nightmares. Leaning back from him, I reach over to grab the jeans that I took off and fish my cell from the pocket. I move back, and he buries himself into me.

Dad is the first person I call.

"Brady, how is he?"

I keep my voice low and quiet. "He's sleeping right now. I think it's best if he doesn't come back down, and I'm not going to leave him."

"I agree. We sent everyone home but Connor. He's worried sick about Zach."

"You can send him up here."

"I think your mom is going to peek in on you both. She's been pacing and worrying about him—we all are. I hate seeing him go through this."

"Me, too. Did Carrie say anything when she left?"

"No, I think she knew we were all upset, and she needed to leave. I don't know if she has the same views as her parents, but if she does..."

He doesn't have to say the words that she won't be welcome here. "I know, Dad. I think that relationship is over after this."

"I'm sorry, Son. Are you going to be okay?"

How do I feel about it? I wait for some kind of sadness or emotion to hit me, but nothing comes. Other than regret I put Zach through this. "Yeah, I didn't love her, Dad. We were just dating."

"I kind of guessed it wasn't anything serious." I hear Mom say something in the background. "Your mom is on her way up there."

"Okay, thanks, Dad."

"Love you, Son."

"Love you."

It isn't but a minute before Mom walks into my room, coming up behind me and peeking over at Zach. "He looks exhausted," she whispers.

"Panic attacks wear him out."

"Do you need anything?"

"Maybe send some bottles of water up with Connor. Otherwise, I'm just going to lie here with him. He'll probably be up half the night, so please don't wake us up in the morning."

"I won't." She rests her hand on my arm. "I'm so proud of you, Brady. You're so gentle with him and show a strength that is so much like your father. We know we focus on Zach a lot because he needs us, but we see the man you're becoming and love you so much."

"Thanks, Mom. I'm very grateful that I have you and Dad for parents."

She pats my arm lightly and leaves the room.

Connor comes in, carrying some water bottles and looking hesitant. His eyes go straight to Zach, and he sits down on the bed behind my best friend. His gaze shifts to me. "Will he be okay?"

"Yes, he's embarrassed and upset over everyone seeing him like that."

"It's not his fault. Our friends care about him, and it's hard for all of us to see him go through a panic attack."

"Did her dad leave right away? I missed it all."

Connor scoots back to the headboard, resting his legs on the bed. "Your dad showed him the door and tossed his coat out after him, threatening to call the police if he didn't leave immediately. Her mom rushed out after him."

"Did Carrie say anything to you?"

"No, but then it would be hard for her to explain when everyone is pissed off at her dad. I mean…I get that he's a bigot and all, but she had to have told him something considering what he said."

With everything that happened, I hadn't thought that far yet. Connor is right; she must have said something to her dad. Did she tell him everything I told her in confidence? Anger simmers inside of me, but I push it down. If I tense up, Zach is going to feel that tension. "I'll talk to her and find out."

"Are you going to stay with her?" He sounds like the thought would be incredulous.

"No, there is no way I would subject Zach to that reminder of what happened all the time. Not to mention there would be no future together. I would never be able to step foot in her house without wanting to punch her dad out."

"I didn't think you two seemed that close, anyway. You ate at separate tables at lunch most of the time. Never saw each other on week-nights. There wasn't that sizzle between you at all."

Sizzle. I'm back to the lack of sexual chemistry. If I'm honest with myself, it's a relief to know I won't have to try so hard to force that part of our relationship.

"I need you to teach me what you do with Zach when he's like this. The breathing thing and senses or grounding, whatever you call it."

I glance over at Connor and see how serious he is about it. He means for when I leave Zach to go to the academy. "How am I going to leave him, knowing this might happen and I won't be here? I don't know if I can do it."

"You have to do this for yourself, Brady. It's what you want to do with your future."

Zach's my future. I inwardly shake my head at my own thoughts. "What if it happens and he won't come out of it?"

"I'll do what you teach me, and if that doesn't work, I'll call nine-one-one. People who have *no one* have PTSD…and it may not be ideal for him, but he will get through it. It's not any different if it happened at work while you weren't there. You can't always be a minute away for the rest of your life. Besides, he rarely has them, and you can't sit around waiting for the next one just because it *might* happen."

"I know you're right, but it's going to be really hard to leave him." My chest hurts just thinking about it.

"I'll be here with him while you're gone and will take care of him, trust me."

I do trust Connor to be here for Zach. He's proven over and over that he cares about my best friend. "I trust you."

"Have you thought much about where you're going to live? Is he going to stay here while you're gone? Are you getting an apartment? If he won't be staying here, then maybe I should move in with him while you're away."

"I thought an apartment maybe…or buy a house. I'll have to talk to him and see if he wants to move that month before I leave or if he wants to stay here."

"It's weird hearing you say 'buy a house' at our age."

"Maybe it is, but I know I want to stay in this town. My family is here, and my job will be here. There's really no reason to waste money on an apartment when I know my future is here."

"How do you think Zach will adjust to moving into a new place?"

I run my fingers over Zach's cheek. "He'll be fine as long as he's with me. We've known for a long time that we would live together after high school."

Connor looks like he wants to say something but doesn't. We bring in the new year lying on my bed, talking about what he wants to do in the future and about the academy. Zach wakes up shortly after midnight from a nightmare, and we end up watching movies until five.

IT's JUST past noon by the time we wake up and crawl from bed. Zach's eyes are still red, but he looks better than last night. I sit on the counter in the bathroom while he takes a shower, and he does the same while I take mine. He's too quiet; it worries me.

I know that I need to talk to Carrie and not let this go, especially since school starts back tomorrow. Connor finds out I'm going to leave to talk to her and hangs around to stay with Zach.

I can tell Zach doesn't want me to go, but he doesn't say anything.

Since I texted ahead, Carrie runs out to get into my truck when I pull up in front of her garage. I drive to a parking lot, and we sit here in silence for a few minutes before I decide it's best to just get on with it. "Did you tell your dad about what I told you in confidence?"

She flushes guiltily, giving me my answer.

"Why would you do that?"

"You're so focused on Zach all the time...and he's gay," she mutters, averting her eyes from mine and staring out the window.

"What does him being gay have to do with it?" I'm getting pissed and try to rein it in. "Are you homophobic like your dad?"

"No, I don't judge...but I don't accept that it's right either. It's his choice, as long as it doesn't affect me."

"That is the dumbest bullshit I've ever heard. You don't judge, but you don't accept? Is saying it that way supposed to make you feel better about yourself?"

She shrugs. "It is the way I was brought up."

"Don't you think you're too old to use that as an excuse?" I rub the back of my neck and try to figure out how I missed this about her. She seemed genuinely sad about Zach's past when I told her.

"My dad doesn't want me to see you anymore."

Glancing over at her, I wonder how she thought I would want to see her anymore. "I don't want to see *you* anymore. I'm all about acceptance. About loving people for who they are...*acceptance*. I'll never understand your fucked-up sense of self-righteousness."

Flinching, she turns to glare at me. "How do you want me to respond? I tried to ignore that he was gay, but it's impossible with the way you two are together. Not to mention the fact that we've been dating for months and never had sex. You don't even seem that into kissing...and making out with you; it's pathetic. That orgasm that you thought you gave me? I had to fake it. I thought it would get better, but it didn't. I should have never listened to Dad to keep going."

Ouch. How could I have been so blind to her true personality? She always seemed so sweet and shy. We got along great and talked so much. "Why did your dad want you to keep going? It makes no sense that you would date someone because of your dad."

"We are poor, and he heard that you had a trust fund from one of his friends and thought you would be able to take care of me...help them out, eventually."

"Jesus Christ, you really are a fucked-up family." I put the truck in drive, ready to have her gone. I'd never once considered someone would date me for my trust fund, especially since so few people know about it.

She's quiet until we are in her driveway, and she's about to get out. "I'm sorry. I never meant to hurt you."

"Just get out. You and your family can stay away from me and my family."

As soon as she's out of the truck and walking up to her porch, I back out and drive home, wanting to be away from her.

Dad sees my face when I walk in the house. "Didn't go well?"

"Her dad was having her date me for my trust fund."

He's upset, I can tell by the look on his face, but his words come out calm, like always. "Son, you're going to find greedy, shallow people throughout your entire life. It happens. You can't control people and what they do, only your reaction to their behavior. Don't give them a single part of you, not even your anger. Feel it for a moment, but then move on. They are of no meaning or value in your life. They only have power if you give it to them, so don't. It's over and done with. Learn from it and move on."

His words settle on my shoulders, and I let out the anger I was feeling. "You're right, thanks, Dad. You always seem to know what to say."

He gives me a hug. "I wish that were true, Son. There are times when even I have to wing it or struggle over something. I'm human, like everyone else. I'm always here, though, and will help you to the best of my ability."

"You do more than you know. Sometimes I think about the impact parents make on their kids and how it influences their whole lives."

Dad nods his agreement. "You have Grandpa to thank for teaching me how to be a good dad. I know you'll be a good dad, too, someday."

Zach's plan for foster kids flits through my mind. "I'm going to check in on Zach."

He's on my bed reading a book when I open the door, and his eyes light up seeing me. I smile, loving the way he can change my mood in an instant.

"Bro, how did it go?" Connor is in one of my gaming chairs, watching YouTube.

"It's over. I want nothing to do with her from now on."

His eyebrows shoot up. "Didn't go so well, huh?"

"Not really."

"I'm sorry, Brady. I know you really liked her," Zach says in a sad, quiet voice.

Did I?

"It's not a big deal, Zach, really. I didn't love her."

"Oh…okay. Did you break up because of me?"

I sit down on the bed next to him, putting my arm out so he can curl up at my side, and he does. "No, we broke up because she has issues and apparently only wanted my trust fund. But I would have broken up with her for you and had no regrets."

Connor makes a choking noise. "Are you kidding me? Your trust fund? What is this, Riverdale teenage show of shallow idiots?"

Laughter escapes from my chest over the way he says things. "Seems that way."

"Well, you have us, and we don't care about your trust fund," Connor reassures me.

Zach kisses my shirt, laying his head down on me. "I'd love you if you had nothing and would try to take care of you."

My heart constricts almost painfully, and I hug him tightly, kissing the top of his head. How am I ever going to leave him?

I can't lose him.

THE REST of our school year goes by too quickly. Zach hasn't panicked since the incident and seems to have recovered. He's increasingly anxious about me leaving. He never tells me he is, but I know him too well not to notice.

My dating is kept to one or two dates per girl because I don't want a repeat of what happened with Carrie. If I don't feel chemistry, then I move on. So far, I've not felt it with any of the girls.

It's a month before graduation when my parents ask me to sit down with them and talk about the future.

"We know your plan is to stay in Rockville, but we wanted to talk to you about where you're going to live. Have you put any thought into whether you're going to live here, rent an apartment, or buy a house?"

I've been putting this off for far too long and need to really consider it. "I want to buy a house. Just haven't decided if it should be before or after I get back from the academy. I guess that I'm running out of time to buy one beforehand."

"That's what we want to talk to you about," Dad says. "Grandma and Grandpa have bought a winter home in Florida. They are getting too old for the harsh winters here and want to downsize. They don't need a big house up here for only four months a year and want to stay in the pool house during the summers. It's set up to be an in-laws home and will be perfect for them. They are going to sell their house, and we wanted to check with you before putting it on the market."

My grandparents' home is huge and has always been way too big for them. I knew they wanted to be close to us to help with Zach when everything was happening, but now I'm not surprised they are ready for Florida and a downgrade.

I've always loved their home with its warm, brick exterior. The house was only built shortly before we moved here. It's bigger than my parents' home, with six bedrooms and a master that I could stay in forever. I know Zach will eventually find someone else, but I can't help but think it would be perfect for his dream of raising kids.

"I know it's a lot of house for someone your age to even consider. Please don't feel pressured. We felt like it was only right to check with you first. With being next door, we would be nearby if you ever needed us."

What I think my dad is trying to say is that they would be close by if Zach needed them. Especially if I'm going to be gone for months. They don't have to convince me because I think the house is perfect. "I want it. It's perfect, really. Honey can still be with someone if we aren't home, and she'll have the fenced-in yard. The house is beautiful, and I love that it's next door. Zach will feel more secure there with family close by. It really is perfect."

"Your grandparents are moving a lot of their furniture to their home in Florida. They never did have the house completely filled up, and most of the bedrooms are empty. We can't finalize anything until you're eighteen, but they have decided to start moving next week."

It's a surreal feeling to know that I'll be buying a house next month. Life is suddenly moving so quickly, and it's a little scary. It would be even scarier if I didn't have the trust fund coming soon, too. I'm very grateful for what I've been given and don't want to take it for granted. So many don't have this, and I can only imagine how scary it would be to start with nothing. "I'll talk with Zach and let him decide if he wants to move before I leave or when I get back. Connor has offered to stay with him while I'm gone if we do move."

"Whatever he wants, we will support him."

Dad and I talk about more details and pencil some things out before I climb the stairs to talk to Zach.

He's reading like usual and lays the book down when he sees me. "Everything okay? Dad seemed serious when he asked to talk to you."

"Everything is fine. Grandma and Grandpa bought a home in Florida and are selling their house next door."

He sits up and gravitates to my side where I plopped down on the bed. "They are leaving? How can they just leave? I'll miss them…"

"They are going for the winter. You'll still see them all summer long because they are going to stay in the pool house when they are here."

"What about Christmas?" he asks, his voice breaking slightly.

He's taking this harder than I'd have thought. "I'm sure they will fly home for Christmas." I take his hand, holding it in mine. "Zach, I'm buying their house for us. It'll be close to Mom and Dad, and Honey won't have to readjust. We can have our own home, and yet you'll be able to walk over to be with Mom and Dad anytime you want."

His eyes are like saucers, wide with shock. "Are you being serious?"

"Yes, dead serious. Mom and Dad want you to know that you can live here for as long as you like. You do not have to move if you don't want to."

"My home is with you," he says instantly.

I grin, knowing he was never going to live here without me. "The question will be...do you want to move before I leave or stay here and move after I leave? Connor has offered to move in with you while I'm gone so you won't be alone. Either way, I'm fine with it."

He jumps off the bed and starts pacing. "Am I allowed to decorate? Like paint and stuff?"

This I didn't expect. "We can paint whatever you want...buy furniture. Make it our own."

I spend the next hour hearing all about the bookshelves that should be put into the family room so it's partly a library and how he really wants some kind of dishes he saw once. I just let him talk because if he's excited about decorating, he's not worrying about me leaving.

THE NEXT MONTH flies by in a blur of things to do. We help Grandma and Grandpa move some belongings to the pool house, which is now freshly painted and has new flooring put in. The movers pack up most of their stuff to take to Florida, and Mom flies down there with them to help unpack and get them settled before flying home.

Cleaners come in and thoroughly clean our new house from top to bottom. We could have cleaned it ourselves, but mom insisted we have it professionally done so we can concentrate on finals.

Graduation day feels like this milestone in our lives, and it's hard for me to enjoy it when I know that I'll be leaving in five weeks. *Five weeks.* I stare over at Zach in his graduation gown and cap, hoping to hell I can survive four months without him.

THIRTY-ONE

ZACH

Brady is staring at me with the same expression I must have right now. It's a mix of uncertainty, fear, and sadness over him leaving. I'm not sure I'm going to survive it, but I'm trying not to let it show.

Mom and Dad have a graduation party back at their house for our closest friends.

Toward the end of the party, Dad catches me alone in the kitchen and asks if I can come to his office with him.

"What's wrong?" I ask nervously as he takes a seat across from me.

"Nothing is wrong, but I wanted to talk to you about your previous house."

Swallowing hard, I remind myself that *he's* dead and I'm okay. "I don't understand?"

"Do you want me to have Brady come in while we talk?"

I nod, worried that I'll do something stupid and ruin yet another party with a panic attack.

Dad texts Brady, and a few minutes later, he comes in with a questioning look.

"I was going to talk to Zach about Tom Matthews's estate, and I think he needs you to be in here."

Brady takes the chair next to mine and pulls me over and onto his lap. "I thought everything was over and done with? Why are we even discussing anything to do with that man?"

"When he died, the divorce was already finalized, and even though you're not his biological son, he's on your birth certificate. Everything he owned went to you. I didn't say anything before now because it takes a while to get things through the system and settle an estate. His house was auctioned off, so was his vehicle, and then there were his savings and a retirement fund. Now that it's settled, you have a check for two hundred and thirty-six thousand dollars."

A range of emotions fill me, and I'm not sure what to say. Some of it is anger over knowing he had savings or a retirement plan when all I ever heard is how they couldn't afford clothes or shoes for me. "I don't know if I want his money. It feels wrong."

"I have enough money. He doesn't need it," Brady tells his dad.

Dad moves a pen around on his desk, and I know he's about to impart some of his wisdom. "I think you should take the money. The man put you through hell, and it's only fitting that you should have it. He would hate it, which is a bonus. But mainly, I think you should use it for your life plan. You want to help foster kids and give them a home, so use the money for something good like that. Kids are expensive, and maybe you won't need it, but maybe you will. Maybe one will need help with college. Maybe you decide you want a child who is biologically yours, and surrogacy is expensive. Don't throw away money that could help you or help someone you love. Bring something good out of what hurt you so much in the past."

He always knows what to say to put things in perspective. The monster would hate it if I spent the money on Brady or foster kids. "Okay, I'll take it and use it to give to others."

Dad gives me one of his fatherly smiles. "It might bring you some healing to see happiness come from it."

THE NEXT DAY, Brady and I go through our house…his house, trying to decide what colors we like and what needs changed. It's a newer home, and everything is up-to-date for the most part. He wants shelves and other various stuff done to the garage. I want built-in bookshelves that match the wood trim and floor. He wants a grill and I want patio furniture that we can relax on. He wants new flooring in the kitchen and I want a stove that is made for someone who cooks a lot.

We are in the master room when I put my hand on his arm to get his attention. "Brady?"

"What?" He stops measuring the window to look at me.

"Umm…are we still sharing a room, or should I pick one upstairs?"

He frowns. "Why wouldn't we share a room just because we are moving?"

"What if you want to bring home a date or get a girlfriend? You'll be this bachelor…"

"We will cross that bridge when we get to it, but we aren't there yet."

We are almost eighteen and sharing a bed. How can we not be there yet? Not that I want us to be because sleeping apart will be really hard. But I don't argue because I *want* to be close to him. I feel like we are on this edge, and soon, one of us is going to have to fall off it.

Brady and I get all sorts of paint samples and pick our colors. We spend two days painting the living room before he calls a service to paint the rooms we want done.

I think we should have done it all ourselves, but our painting job doesn't look that great either.

After the painting is done, Mom helps us shop for window coverings and Dad spends an entire Saturday with Brady, hanging them all.

Harold isn't retiring until the end of July, so right now, I'm not working as much as I will be. It's a good thing because I want to spend as much time as I can with Brady before he leaves.

Brady's new flooring gets put in the kitchen and my stove arrives. We buy a new fridge and put all the shelves in the garage.

We pause to celebrate Brady's eighteenth birthday, and then he spends a day with his dad trying to straighten out his trust fund and transferring money to where he wants it. He has a meeting with an accountant and does something with a portfolio. I have no idea what all goes into it, but his dad is with him and Brady seems a little overwhelmed when he gets home.

Every day I feel a little sicker and life a little less bright. We go shopping and pick out furniture for his bedroom and the main living room. Brady leaves it up to me to stock the kitchen and bathroom. So while he's buying tools for his garage with Connor, Mom and I are shopping to stock the main things we need. I know he told me to let him pay for it, but I use the money that I now have to buy this stuff. It feels like the kitchen is mine, and I want to help buy things for our home.

My birthday comes and goes, but I don't feel any different being eighteen than I did at seventeen. The only difference is the Wellmans are no longer my guardians. I'm just me.

A WEEK BEFORE HE LEAVES, our bedroom furniture arrives, and I put the clean bedding on so we can sleep here tonight. We pack up all our stuff in our old room and move it over to the new one. Brady hangs our TV up but decides to wait to hook up the gaming consoles until he gets back. He isn't sure if he wants them in the bedroom or in the family room.

The whole day feels weird, almost as if I'm moving into a new home with my boyfriend or husband. That night we take turns showering in our huge ensuite bathroom. It has this big soaker tub that I can't wait to take a bath in.

The bed is a king-size and feels so much bigger than our last one. Brady said it has to be big because he plans on getting another dog, and we will need room for it.

The following day, we go grocery shopping, and I make us our first meal to eat, just the two of us. Brady gets this odd look on his face as we eat and it continues through washing dishes together. I don't know what he's thinking. Maybe he's just dreading the weekend as much as I am.

We ignore the house needing to be done and spend the next five days swimming, reading, watching movies, and taking walks together. Connor has left us alone, but I think it's because he knows we want this time together.

THE NIGHT before our last night, I wake up to Brady's hard-on pressing against my ass and his lips on the back of my neck, kissing slowly. My body hums with want and need; every press of his mouth on my skin is setting me on fire. I try to move, but his arms are holding me tightly. He has to be sleeping because I know he would never do this awake.

"Brady?"

His teeth graze my neck as he continues to kiss me, rocking his hips in a way that makes me moan. Oh God, I'm about to lose it, and I can't let this break up our friendship.

"Brady!"

His breathing changes and he lifts his mouth from the back of my neck. "Fuck…sorry."

"It's okay, but do you think maybe you need to go take care of that mammoth thing before it hurts someone?" Humor is the only way to deal with this, or else I'll cry over how much I want him.

"Mammoth, huh? I think I like that description."

"You would."

He moves away from me, slipping out of bed. "I'll…errr…be right back."

As soon as he shuts the bathroom door, I groan and grab my own dick. I'm used to him having a hard-on or rubbing against me without realizing he's doing it, but kissing me? Kissing feels so intimate and not his body's natural response. It's more.

It takes an embarrassingly short time for me to come all over my hand. I hurry to wipe it off with my shirt and throw it in the hamper. Needing to steady myself before he comes back, I walk out to our kitchen to wash my hands and get a cold water from the fridge.

Honey decides she needs to go outside, and I end up standing at the door waiting on her.

"Zach?"

"At the patio door," I call out over my shoulder before turning back to watch for Honey. From the reflection in the glass, I see him in the kitchen getting a drink from the fridge. His eyes are staring my way with that same odd expression on his face.

"What is she doing?"

"I don't know. She's been out there forever, and it's too dark for me to see her." I lean out the door and call her again, but nothing.

He comes over, leans out the door, and uses that damn bossy voice of his. She comes running in, and I determine she has selective hearing.

"Traitorous dog," I mutter.

Brady locks the door, grinning way too proudly over it. "It's all in the tone. You have to sound more…dominant."

"Yeah, because I'm so dominant and all…that should be so easy," I quip in a smart-ass tone.

He laughs. "Mhmm, sure."

We end up back in bed, and I lie with my head on his arm, trying not to cry over the fact that we only have one more night after this. "I'm going to miss you."

"I'm going to miss you, too," he whispers back, wrapping his arms around me tightly.

THE NEXT MORNING, Connor comes over, and we move Brady's old bedroom furniture into the first bedroom upstairs. Connor brings all his stuff from home, unpacking it and putting it away.

He and Brady spend some time together outside talking. It looks serious, and I wonder if they are discussing me.

Brady spends time with our family, saying their goodbyes now instead of in the morning. I think they want to give us some privacy for our own goodbyes.

It's when Brady is packing his suitcases that I start crying. I know it's not manly, but I can't help it. He pulls me into his arms, neither of us saying anything. This is so painful already, and he hasn't even left yet. I eventually move away to help him pack, but I'm barely holding on by a thread. I'd planned ahead and asked for a few days off before and a few days after he leaves. I won't be in any condition to be around people.

Connor leaves, saying he'll sleep one last time at home and will be back tomorrow. I'm grateful he's not taking this last bit of time away from me.

Brady and I both push around our food and barely eat anything for supper. We spend our evening in bed, cuddled up together. I cry too many times, and he holds me, telling me we can get through this.

He falls asleep at two, and I lie here watching him, unwilling to waste one second of our last hours together. I memorize every moment and try to hold on to the feeling of him holding me.

How am I going to do this?

I have to do it for him and his future. It's selfish of me not to want him to go, and I keep reminding myself that all I want is his happiness.

It doesn't make it any easier, though. This is hard and painful, excruciatingly so. I finally crawl from bed and shut myself in the bathroom to cry ugly, horrible tears. Brady comes in and sits on the floor with me. I move to rest my head in his lap, crying out in pain that isn't going to end. His fingers run through my hair over and over, his other hand holding mine. I tug it to my chest to hold close, wishing that I wouldn't have to let go.

"Baby…you have to stop crying, or you're going to make yourself sick." His voice sounds torn and shaky.

"I'm sorry," I sob, clenching his hand tighter.

"Come here." He tugs me up into his arms, holding me while I get control over myself.

When I am finally quiet, neither of us moves. We just stay this way, clinging to each other until I hear the alarm go off. We both flinch at the sound.

Somehow we make it through him getting dressed and loading his suitcases into the truck. He leans against it and holds me for these last minutes. I think I'm numb or in shock; I don't know. But when he leans down to kiss my cheek and whispers, "I love you," I manage to keep control.

"I love you, too, Brady. Be safe."

He nods, getting into his truck and shutting the door. I see him take a deep breath and close his eyes for a second before putting it in reverse and backing out of the driveway. I stand here watching his truck disappear, with tears rolling down my face.

Five years together and now he's gone. I feel like my very soul just drove away, and it breaks me into pieces.

THIRTY-TWO

ZACH

Walking back into the house, I go straight to our bed and pull the blankets over my head. Crying my heart out and then crying some more. The sorrow is all-consuming, and I let it take over.

I lose track of time and just stay in this position. Mom comes in and sits next to me on the bed, her hand rubbing my arm. "What can I do to help?"

"Nothing… There's nothing anyone can do."

"He's going to come back, Zach. You have to be strong and get through this; I know you can do it."

Yanking the covers back over my head, I hope she stops because right now, I can't hear all the stuff I should be feeling. I only know how much it hurts.

"I'll put Honey outside for you and let her back in before I go home."

I can't even say thanks because if I open my mouth, sobs will come pouring out.

It's late afternoon before I stumble to the bathroom to pee and then go straight back to bed again. I hear Connor's voice seconds before I remember he is going to live here now. Why did I agree to this when all I really want is to be alone?

"Zach?"

I don't answer, and the covers get pulled off my head.

"Jesus…you look like shit."

"Just leave me alone to die."

"Yeah no, that's not happening. Did you eat anything today?"

I yank the covers over my head again.

"I'll take that as a no. Did you drink anything today?"

Hearing him ask me about food and drinking reminds me of Brady, and I start to cry all over again.

He leaves the room and comes back, forcing the blankets down and pulling me up into a sitting position. "Drink this."

"I can't drink…I'm crying," I sob out.

"Take a drink, or I'm going to dump it down your throat." He waits for me to take a few deep breaths before handing me the bottle of water. I drink half of it and hand it back.

"Do you want to watch Tangled?"

"No."

"Do you want me to read to you?"

I want Brady to read to me. "No. Just leave me alone to drown in my sorrows."

He grins, the ass. "I see you're going to be melodramatic about it."

Groaning, I flop back on the bed and roll to my side, ignoring him.

At least he leaves me alone for a while.

Brady doesn't call, but I'm assuming he's getting settled into his temporary apartment. It hurts, though, that he doesn't take the time to check in.

Connor comes in periodically to make me drink and to take Honey out. I refuse to eat or move from the bed or even shower.

Brady calls the next night, and I pretend I'm not dying inside. He says he's settled in and starts classes in the morning, and I tell him I'm okay. It's a brief call and only makes me cry more once we hang up.

On the third day of me lying in bed—a total mess—Connor comes into my room and forces me up. He starts a bath and tells me if I don't get cleaned up, he'll throw me in clothes and all. I can tell he's serious and decide to just get it over with. I have to work tomorrow and need to be able to function on a basic level.

I'm in the bath soaking when he brings in clean pj's and leans against the counter. "Don't even think of crawling back into that bed. You're eating something if I have to force-feed you."

"I'm starting to hear a theme here," I mumble.

"Yes, a theme of *you're going to at least eat and be clean.*" He leaves the bathroom with a stupid, determined expression on his face.

I finish washing my hair and body, rinsing off. It does feel better to be clean. Not eating for three days has made me weak, but I get dressed and brush my teeth. Walking out to the kitchen, I see that Connor picked up meals from the diner. We have to sit at the island because we don't have a table yet. I pick at my food, eating some and tasting nothing. I do drink a sparkling water when Connor pushes it my way with a look.

Brady doesn't call this evening, and I cry three-fourths of the night because of it. I probably look like a zombie at work, but I do my job with a fake smile.

THE NEXT MONTH seems to go the same. Me, lying in bed depressed, barely eating anything, barely sleeping. Going to work and coming home. I'm on autopilot, and nothing seems to jerk me out of it.

Brady calls every other evening and tells me about the academy. He sounds good and excited about his days there. I think it hurts even more to know I'm dying, and he's just fine.

It's the end of July, and I'm about to start full-time when Connor comes into my room on a Saturday morning and rips all the blankets off of the bed.

"Get up."

"No, and give me my blankets back."

"Zach, you get out of that bed, or I'm going to beat your ass. Your choice."

I crawl out of bed, staring at him. "What is wrong with you?"

He's definitely pissed if his flushed cheeks are anything to go by. "I'm done watching you cry yourself sick all the time. You've lost weight and look like death. I know you love Brady, and this is hard for you, but you have to find yourself without him."

"I don't know how," I whisper, scared to admit he's right.

"By getting up and starting to live again. Trying new things and making new friends."

"But I don't want to... It's too hard."

"You're doing it. You need to do it for yourself." Connor gives me a sympathetic but determined look. "You can't keep waiting around for Brady to want you the way you want him."

I flinch because it hurts to hear that truth. "I know," I say in a small voice.

Connor pulls out his cell phone and taps on something before showing me the screen. It's Brady at a bar with some chick, taking a selfie with her. Both of them are smiling. It's not a picture he posted, but one she tagged him in. Stella O'Malley is her name. It's painful to see, and I rub my hand over my chest.

"You have to stop this, Zach. You are worth so much more than loving someone whom you can never be with. You're worth so much more than wasting away in this house until he comes home. How can you ever expect him to see you differently if you don't find yourself without him?"

The image of him smiling won't get out of my head. "Okay, but I need your help to get started."

"I can do that." He gives me a hug. "It's okay for you to miss him and love him, but no one is worth you not eating or sleeping over."

Brady is worth it, but I don't say that. "I'll try harder, I promise."

"Get dressed; you're coming to the gym with me."

I groan. "That's your solution? Me at a gym?" I motion to my weak, skinny body. "Have you seen me?"

"Yes, I've seen you, and you'll feel a million times better if you work out. You'll build some muscles and get some abs. You'll look hot, and all the guys will want you."

A burst of laughter erupts from my chest. "I think that might be far-fetched there."

"Go get dressed. You're going."

I'M in a pair of shorts and a T-shirt, standing in a gym with a bunch of sweaty men and women. I look like a mouse amongst lions, and they are going to eat me alive.

Connor starts me on a training regimen. Running, weights, and more. It's hard, and my body aches when we are done, but he tells me it'll get better.

And that's how our routine starts. Every day, we get up early and go to the gym for two hours. When we leave there, we go home to shower, and I make us a healthy breakfast before I head to work and he heads to school.

Working full-time at the library is amazing. I have taken over all the activities with kids and get to read to them every day. We have movie nights and fun activities to keep them wanting to read. I throw myself into work, and it's easy to smile when I'm with the kids. I work Monday through Friday, eight to four, except on the days that we have an evening activity, then I work until eight. I get the weekends off unless I have something planned and need to be there.

After work, I drive home and cook us supper, or sometimes we eat at Mom and Dad's house. Connor and I watch movies together, go on walks, or I read while he studies. Tessa comes over on the weekends when she's back in town, but she's away at college during the weeks.

Brady and I still talk every other night. He's never brought up the girl and mostly talks about the cool things he's learning. I never talk about the gym, keeping that just for me, but tell him about my work.

I've grown a couple of inches, I think. I still haven't measured, but I did go get some new jeans. I'm also still skinny as a rail, but Connor promises me I'll start to see a difference soon.

Now that I'm not wallowing in self-pity, I find I enjoy decorating the house. I'll admit that I want it to feel like our home, but I really do love putting a room together. Brady pays all the house bills online, refusing to let me pay a dime. He even gave me a credit card to use for anything I might want to buy. But I use my paychecks and the money I have in savings to buy stuff for the house.

I've roped Connor into hanging pictures more than he likes, but he does it for me. I pick one room at a time and make it look homey, personalized to fit us. The bookcases are done and get put in on one side of the family room. They are beautiful, and I start filling them with books that I love. Comfortable, oversized, brown leather couches get added to the room, along with accent colors and other furniture that speak of comfort. I buy a kitchen table and new stools for the island bar. Changing out the lights makes it seem warmer. The beautiful plates I've wanted forever get added, and I match everything to them.

Connor helps me with buying a pool table for the basement. I get a huge sectional and comfy overstuffed chairs, as well as a big screen TV and surround sound, although Connor picked out those. There's a small kitchen and bar down there that I add stools, too, and I change out the countertop to something that doesn't look like it's this weird, retro style. Wood countertops give it a warmer feel and set the tone for the entire basement.

I also buy us patio furniture and even a massive grill for Brady. I decorate our room and personalize that, too. Every inch of the house gets worked on, except for three of the bedrooms upstairs. The other two closest to Connor's bedroom get made into guest rooms where people can sleep if they stay over.

Two months into using the gym, I finally see that I have muscles showing. I feel better about myself, even if I hate exercising. I can't say that I want to do this forever, but it's helping me clear my mind every morning and focus on the day.

My hair has grown a few inches, and it's hanging over my ears more than it ever has. I guess it goes with the whole *I want something different and need to find things I like for myself* plan.

On a spur-of-the-moment decision, I take a painting class and learn I love to paint. I'm fairly good at it, and slowly pictures I paint get added to the walls.

Brady should be back in one month. I keep focused on that. All I have to do is make it to the end of October, and he'll be back. I can't wait to show him the house and for him to see how much I've changed.

THIRTY-THREE

BRADY

Driving away from Zach was one of the hardest things I've ever had to do. I keep wanting to turn around and drive back, but I know I'll regret it. I want to be in law enforcement, and I have to do this to get there. I'll be able to protect Zach even better when I'm an officer.

I arrive late at the furnished apartments where students are staying. Mine is a two-bedroom, and I know that I have a roommate but not who it is yet.

I'm exhausted by the time I carry everything inside, and even though I want to call Zach, I know if I do, I'll turn around and drive back home.

My roommate must not have arrived yet because the place is empty of any clothes or bags. I pick one of the identical rooms and unpack my bags. I brought clean bedding from home and put it on so I can go to sleep.

Lying in bed alone is another reminder of how empty I feel without Zach. How can I sleep without him curled up with me? Laying my hand on the bed beside me, I wonder if he's okay. Is he sleeping or as miserable as I am? Tossing and turning, I finally give up at four and go out to our tiny living room to watch TV.

The door to the apartment opens a little after eight, and in walks a woman carrying bags.

"Hey," she says, setting them all down on the floor next to the couch.

"Hi…you must be my roommate?"

"Must be. I'm Stella O'Malley." She offers me her hand, and I stand up to shake it.

"Brady Wellman, nice to meet you."

She scans the small apartment. "Which bedroom is mine?"

I point to the door on the left. "They are identical, so I just picked one."

"Fine by me. I think we will be too tired to care where we sleep."

I hope that I'll be so tired I can turn my mind off and sleep. "You need help carrying anything up?"

"This is it. I packed light since they are providing uniforms." She picks up a couple of her bags, and I lean over to get the rest, carrying them into her room after her. Our rooms are the size of a walk-in closet with barely enough space for a bed and small desk.

"You want to get some food? I have a feeling this is the last day until Sunday that we'll have time to do anything. We should probably buy some groceries, too."

"Sure," I say, glad to have something to do.

We go for breakfast and talk about the academy. She's twenty-two and already went for a criminal justice degree. We keep talking as we shop for groceries, anything easy for two people who can't cook. I'm so used to having Mom or Zach cook for me that it's eye-opening to realize I'm going to have to survive on microwave meals and cold meat sandwiches.

The day goes by with us getting to know each other. She tells me about her family, and I share a little about mine. I don't talk about Zach, because quite frankly, I'm not sure if I can keep it together and not cry if I do. I don't want her first impression of a fellow recruit to be that he's an emotional wreck.

THAT NIGHT I barely sleep again and end up on the couch watching TV for most of it. We both report to the academy at seven a.m. for paperwork and uniforms. The first day is a lot of meetings and learning what they expect of us.

I manage to get two hours of sleep that night, hugging a pillow and pretending Zach is with me. The fatigue sucks, but I drink some fancy coffee that Stella swears will keep me awake.

After that, I don't have time to think. Every part of my day is filled with learning or pushing myself physically. Chief Kuhn said this academy would feel a lot like the military, and he was right.

For three weeks, all I do is concentrate on getting through the day. I'm still not sleeping well, and I am borderline falling apart from exhaustion. I call Zach every other night, and he doesn't say much but sounds okay. He never mentions that he's struggling like I am, only that he misses me. My anxiety over his well-being is always here. Is he taking his iron? Is he having nightmares? Is he sad?

Connor texts or talks a few times a week with me, always saying he's taking care of Zach and to just concentrate on the training. I know I shouldn't be upset with Connor, but part of me hates that he's taking over for me. Like I've been replaced, and that's probably why Zach doesn't seem that upset.

Stella walks into my room at midnight, sitting on the edge of the bed. "Saw your light on and door open."

"Yeah, couldn't sleep."

"You never sleep and look like shit. Our training officers are beginning to notice, and that's not the kind of attention you want. You need to sleep."

"I know. It's just I'm used to sleeping next to someone."

"Oh... Do you want me to sleep next to you? It might help?"

"We probably shouldn't. I am too tired to be in a relationship right now, and I don't want you to get the wrong idea."

She laughs and pats my shoulder. "Cute, but you're not my type. I'm into girls."

Relief spreads through me, and I'm not even sure why. I might have been worried she would start to like me, and I'm too sad for anything.

When I don't say anything, she gets a worried look. "You aren't homophobic, are you?"

"God no! My best friend is gay. You can look me up on YouTube, and you'll see the speech I gave in high school about accepting others. I think you being a lesbian is awesome."

Grinning, she lies down next to me. "No wonder we get along so well. I requested a male roommate because I didn't want any girls freaking out that I would want them, but I was a little worried the guy would come on to me. You've been a perfect roommate. So what do you say? You want me to try and sleep next to you? See if that helps?"

"As long as you don't get pissed if I wake up with morning wood. It happens sometimes, and I can't control it."

"I won't get mad, but it sounds like you have some serious sexual tension and need to get laid."

"That's the understatement of the century, but I think I'll pass on girls while here. They're too much work."

"God, don't I know it. Emotional and needy. The last girl I took on a date cried because they put cheese on her salad."

"Are you sure you want to be a lesbian?"

"Yes, dick does nothing for me. I tried it once to see, and there was no…you know that feeling when you kiss someone and there are fireworks? That wasn't there. It was about as exciting as when I got my first pap smear."

I've never felt fireworks, or I'd understand better. "Never had a pap smear, but I'll take your word for it."

"Now, what do you need…to spoon me or hold hands or cuddle?"

There's no way I can cuddle with her like I do with Zach. "Let's try spooning."

She flips over, and I scoot closer, wrapping my arm around her. It doesn't feel like it does with Zach, and I almost pull away, but the exhaustion screams at me to try. Closing my eyes, I picture that Zach is next to me and that the warmth I feel is him. That it's his chest that is rising and falling; that he's safe and okay. She smells totally wrong, and I know it isn't him, but it does help, and I find myself giving in finally.

It's amazing what sleep does for a person. Stella sleeps next to me every night that week, and I feel ten times better with more energy. To my surprise, I haven't woken up with a hard-on even once.

That Saturday night, she claims we deserve to go out and takes me to her favorite pub, O'Malley's. I get to meet her dad, who owns the place, and a couple of her brothers. We play darts and pool, eat some food that isn't microwaved, and chat with her family. There are times when I feel that pang of Zach not being here, but I need to stop being a downer, and I try really hard to enjoy myself. Stella takes a selfie with me, claiming she's going to scare all her friends into thinking she's suddenly into men. I laugh as she takes another photo.

. . .

FOR THE NEXT two and a half months, she sleeps beside me unless she has a girl over. More often than not, I wake up facing away from her, and we aren't even touching. We go to O'Malley's or some other pub-type place on Saturday nights, and I get to meet all her friends. All of them accept me into their little group without question. Melody is dating Harry, and they seem happy together. Dixie is a lesbian and has a friends with benefits arrangement with Stella. They aren't exclusive, though, because I've seen both of them with different girls. Willow and Candace are flirty, and I can tell they would like it if I asked them out, but I don't want to cause discord if I date one and not the other. I don't really feel like dating at all.

There are times when everyone is talking or laughing that I feel so alone.

I miss Zach.

THIRTY-FOUR

ZACH

It's the middle of October when he calls me on FaceTime, which is the first time he's done this. I answer and almost cry at getting to see his face. Drinking him in, I can see that he's cut his hair shorter and has a five o'clock shadow. He is smiling, and I try to smile back.

"Hey…"

"Hey, it's great to see your face," he says.

"Yeah, yours, too." *Don't cry. Don't cry.*

"Your hair is longer?"

I run my fingers through it, messing it up. "Thought I'd try something different."

"I like it." His face doesn't match up with the "I like it."

"How's everything there?"

He rubs the back of his neck; my first clue there's a reason he's FaceTimed me. "Everything is great. I'm at the top of my class, and the instructors have been teaching me more than I ever thought possible."

"I'm happy for you. I knew you'd do amazing."

His smile falters. "Look…I know that I am supposed to come home in two weeks…"

My heart stops and I wait for him to crush me.

"…but they've asked me to stay on for another eight weeks to take their K-9 program. I spoke with Chief Kuhn, and he's all for it. They are going to purchase the dog I work with, and he'll come back with me to be the first K-9 unit in Rockville."

"That's great, Brady. You'll be perfect for that." Two more months and he acts like it's nothing.

"I hope you're not upset? I know you were counting on me coming home in two weeks."

"Nope, it's fine. I'm keeping busy, and Connor keeps me company." *He's not you.* I'll cry if I don't get off this call. "Look, I need to go. I'm going out tonight."

"Going out? With who?"

"Just some friends I met." I'm going to hell for lying.

"Okay, I can let you go… I really miss you."

I dig my fingertips into my leg to keep from crying. "I miss you, too."

He doesn't say I love you like usual, and I hang up the phone so I can give into the tears.

Connor comes in a little while later and lies on the bed, facing me. "I'm sorry. He just called to tell me."

"I thought I was doing so well, but it just hit me hard. He didn't even seem to care he was breaking my heart all over again."

"I think he cares about hurting you…and what's this about you going out tonight with friends? He asked me what friends, and I had to say I didn't know, which he wasn't happy about either."

"I lied. I couldn't cry in front of him, and I didn't want to sound pathetic, so I said I was going out with friends." I swipe some tears from my cheeks.

"Okay, this is what we are going to do. It's time for *Operation Get Zach A Date.*"

"A date?"

"Yes, a date. You're eighteen years old and have never been on a date. It's time to get out there and give Brady a taste of his own medicine."

I know he's talking about the pictures posted on Instagram in the last month where several girls have tagged him. They are usually in a bar or club, smiling like they are having a blast.

"How do I find a date?"

Connor sits up, excitement on his face. "I know! I met a guy at college that I'm sure would help you. He's gay and fun. He's definitely up on the whole gay dating scene. He's also really nice, and I'm sure he would help you if I asked him."

"Alright, are you thinking he'll date me?"

"Umm no...he's a bottom like you for sure...or maybe vers. He's a twink. All the pictures of guys he dates are like big, muscular men. They aren't twinks."

"Got it. I'm not into twinks either. Actually, I've not been around many gay guys, so I don't really know what I'm into, but I'm assuming since I'm into Brady, it's not twinks."

"Okay, so let me talk to him tomorrow, and we'll get this going."

"Wait...how did you know I'm a bottom?"

He rolls his eyes. "Have you met you?"

I reach over and pinch his arm. "That was mean."

"Hey!" He rubs the spot that I know doesn't hurt. "I can't help it if it's true."

CONNOR FOLLOWS through and says Kelly will be over on Saturday to see what he has to work with. I have no idea what that means, but I use it to get through the week and not think about Brady staying away longer.

Tessa is visiting for the weekend, and she seems as excited as Connor about this new *Operation Get Zach A Date*.

I'm nervous when Kelly is supposed to show up. He's not from this county, but the one over from ours. I'm not sure what I was expecting, but in walks the most confident person I've ever seen. He has coal black hair that swoops over to the side. Striking blue eyes and a sharp jawline and pouty red lips that draw your attention to them. He's a few inches taller than me, but definitely a twink. His style is designer clothes, but they aren't too flashy, though, more just really stylish and cool.

He takes one look at me and presses his hand to his heart. "Oh my God...I'm going to make you look so hot. You are *gorgeous*...just hiding behind those glasses and baggy clothes."

I look behind me, swearing he's not talking about me. When I look back, he's grinning.

"You're adorable."

I point to myself. "Me?"

"Yes, you. Let me help you get some confidence and find your style. I promise there won't be a gay man around that won't want to do you."

"I'm not sure I want them all to want me," I murmur, a bit scared at the thought.

"You're a virgin, aren't you?"

I'm shocked he asked me that but can't keep from blurting out, "Maybe."

He grins. "Okay, so let's go. I already booked an appointment for you at my hairdresser's and spa."

Connor insists that he and Tessa go along to Pine Falls. I think he's worried I'll have a panic attack doing all these new things. Kelly agrees but tells Connor that he doesn't get a say on what he does to me.

Connor and Tessa decide to sit at a cafe next to the beauty salon, with the promise that Kelly will call them if needed. He nods his agreement, and I'm left alone with him to do with me what he wants.

The hairdresser and Kelly discuss hairstyles and colors. They show me pictures of what they think will look good, and I pick the one that feels like me. I've never done anything like this in my life, but I love the hair on the guy in the picture.

When they are done, I barely recognize myself in the mirror. Instead of drab brown hair, I now have blond highlights throughout. It's not that bleached hair look, but it's lightened up immensely and looks vibrant. They cut the sides shorter but not *short* short and then left the top long but styled. The hairdresser shows me how it can swoop across my forehead to get one hairstyle or how to use this paste to create a wavy, heavy top quiff. Not that I know what that is, but I like both styles. Kelly promises to help teach me them at home.

I think we are done, but no. My eyebrows get plucked a little, just enough to make them look cleaner, the lady says. She also goes over makeup with Kelly, and they choose some for me to take home. I can't see myself wearing makeup, but Kelly makes me promise to try it just once before I say no.

Then he loops his arm through mine and takes me over to the spa side. "Now, I know this is personal, but how much hair do you have on your body?"

"Umm…I have zero chest hair and a little leg hair, but it's so light that you can barely see it."

"And what about your other hair?"

It dawns on me what he's asking, and I feel my cheeks heat up. "I have a little bit of hair there."

"This is going to suck, but I need you to trust me, okay? Men like their twinks hairless, especially adorable, pale twinks like you. But we don't do this for them; we do it for us because being smooth and soft feels amazing. If you don't like it, you can let it grow back, but trust me, it'll give you more confidence in yourself. "

"Hairless?"

"Don't look so scared. It's worth it to get this done. You'll love it once it's over."

I'm terrified when a lady takes me to the back, and then I proceed to have an area waxed that I never thought I would. She claims I have less hair than most, and she doesn't have to do my butt-hole. I stare at her like she's lost her mind. Do guys really wax their asses? Is that my future? She's lucky I didn't scream bloody murder and have a panic attack. My legs get waxed, which hurts like hell, and I swear I'm just going to shave them at home. I didn't think being hairless would make a difference, but they feel smooth and silky with no hair, plus all the lotions she rubs on them. Next, I get a pedicure and manicure. Kelly orders red for my toes and clear for my fingers.

He grins at me as we walk out of the spa. I've just spent a small fortune, and he made me set up another appointment in eight weeks.

"Did they have to bleach your asshole?"

My mouth drops open at the question and how open he is about personal things. "What?"

"Usually if your asshole is really dark, they will tell you that you need to get it bleached."

"People actually do that? I feel violated just getting waxed."

"Yes, if you want your asshole to be pretty."

"Well, she didn't tell me it needed bleached and said it didn't need waxed either."

"Wow, you must have a pretty asshole."

I stop on the sidewalk, staring at him. "I've never even talked about my asshole. This is crazy."

He laughs. "Better get used to it because tops will be licking it, fingering it, and fucking it. Your asshole is going to be the center of attention."

I'm not sure if I should be turned on or scared to death. "That's a bit terrifying."

"Oh God, you have so much to learn." Kelly hooks his arm through mine and moves us forward toward the cafe.

When Tessa and Connor see me, I don't think they recognize me at first. Then Tessa squeals and Connor just stares at me like I'm an alien.

"Is it that bad?" I ask him.

"No, you look hot…really hot."

"Thanks, I think."

Since my makeover took hours and hours, we are all starving and dine out at a place I've never been before. It's definitely not a small-town diner. I swear a couple of guys look at me, but then I think maybe I'm just being weird.

On the drive back to our house, Kelly makes me call and schedule an eye appointment with my optometrist for next Saturday morning. He is coming along and will help pick out glasses, plus he wants me to get contacts.

At home, he shows me how to put eyeliner on and some other makeup that makes me look even younger than I already do. I'm not sure I'll wear it, but the eyeliner does draw attention to my eyes.

Kelly goes through my clothes, tsking at every single thing. He gets to my underwear and about passes out. "Oh honey…no no no no."

"What's wrong with them?"

"Everything is wrong with them. We have to get some ordered *now*."

We sit at the island with my laptop, and he opens my eyes to the world of men's underwear. They cost more than I ever thought I would spend on underwear. I use some of my savings, figuring nothing would piss *him* off more than to know his money went to sexy underwear. I buy Calvin Klein, Versace, Addicted, Andrew Christian, and more. Kelly has me order low-rise trunks, briefs, and these ass-revealing scraps of nothingness called jocks.

Connor comes up behind us and almost chokes himself to death on the soda he was trying to swallow. "Holy shit…why even wear them if your asshole has nothing over it?"

Kelly pats him on the arm. "Why do women wear crotchless panties if they just have a hole where their pussy is?"

He runs his hand over his face before walking away. "Forget I asked."

Grinning, Kelly goes back to showing me things I need to order. It's kind of strange changing things up, but it also feels like I can be more comfortable in my sexuality.

During the week, Kelly and I text back and forth. We get along like we've always been friends. There's an ease between us that I think we both feel. I learn little bits about him through our texting, like how he'll be twenty-one in January and is getting the same graphic design degree as Connor. He may be super confident, but I can tell he's really sweet, too.

SATURDAY, he comes with me to my eye doctor appointment and helps me pick out new glasses. My contacts and glasses will be ready in about a week. Tessa is not back this weekend, so Connor comes along to the city to be a self-appointed bodyguard.

I feel kind of sorry for him because he has to follow us from store to store as Kelly has me try on so many different clothes. Kelly wants to see what looks good on my ass or what styles I like more than others. I never knew tight jeans, but not too tight, were so important. I feel like every pair he has me buy is low-rise enough to show the band of my underwear or the curve of my hip and hug my ass for everyone to look at. He claims that's the point, but it's going to take some getting used to.

We order pizza for supper and eat in the family room together. When we are finished, Kelly goes online to some type of clothing place that has crop tops and tight shorts that he claims would look hot on me at a club. I finally just hand over my credit card and let him order what he thinks I need.

Brady calls while Kelly's here and asks who is talking in the background. When I tell him one of my guy friends, he gets really quiet. I can hear a girl laughing in the background at his place, but I don't ask who she is because I don't want to know.

When he hangs up, I struggle not to cry and lose the battle. Kelly sits next to me, hugging me and trying to offer some comfort.

"I hate to say it," Kelly says, "but every single one of us has to learn that falling in love with a straight guy never works. It's just torturing ourselves until our hearts break."

"I know. I just love him so much."

"And he lives here with you?"

"Yeah, it's his house, really. But we've been pretty inseparable for five years and always planned on living together."

"If this is his house, it's awful nice of him to give you the master bedroom."

Connor lets out a snort from the couch. "They share the master bedroom and sleep in the same bed. Have for years."

Kelly gives me wide eyes. "And he's straight?"

I shrug. "He thinks he is."

"I think I need to hear this whole story."

So as much as it's hard for me to talk about, I sit here telling the whole story of us—how we met and all that happened. I cry through some of it but manage to go on. I can tell Connor learns things he didn't know before, but we've been friends long enough that he deserves to know me.

When I'm done, Kelly gives me a hug. "I know that wasn't easy to share, but it helps me understand you better. You're amazing to go through all that and turn out to be this sweet, soft-spoken guy that is so kind to others. I didn't really understand how you could be so innocent at your age, but now I get it."

Connor reaches over to squeeze my hand. "Thanks for sharing all that. I knew a lot, but not in that detail or how you and Brady became so close. It explains a lot I didn't understand. It's no wonder being away from him has been so hard and why you love him so much."

"I'm not sure the guy is straight. I've never heard of a straight guy being quite so affectionate and all in like he is."

"I don't know. I would think if he was bi, he would know it by now."

"I've met men in their forties who just figured out they were gay. Sometimes they don't see what's right in front of them." He scoots down a little so I can lay my head on his lap. "Anyway, it's his loss. Any guy would be lucky to have you."

"I agree. You deserve someone who wants you as much as you want them," Connor says, giving me this steady look.

"Thanks, both of you."

THIRTY-FIVE

ZACH

The following weekend, Kelly takes me shoe shopping—who knew you needed different shoes for different outfits? He also helps me pick out a coat for winter and socks and sexy pajama bottoms that he swears will draw a man's eyes to my ass.

My contacts and glasses have come in, and we pick them up on our way home.

That night, we are sitting in the family room together, just chatting about their classes and all our shopping, when I keep noticing Kelly checking his cell.

"Is everything okay?"

He bites his lip and shrugs slightly, but I think if he talks, he's going to cry. He looks up, and I see tears in his eyes.

Seeing Kelly like this makes me tear up, too. I scoot off the couch to the floor next to him and wrap my body around his. "What's wrong? You can lean on me."

He leans back into me and sighs. "Today is my brother's sixteenth birthday. I've tried calling my mom and texting, but she refuses to answer. Now I think she's blocked me. I love my brother, and there's no way for me to tell him happy birthday. We were always so close. I just wanted to let him know I still care."

"She blocked you?" Connor looks as upset as I feel.

"Yeah, my parents kicked me out when I was sixteen. A girl at our school took a picture of me making out with a boy at a party and posted it to her Instagram. Her mom is friends with my parents, and she forwarded it to my mom. My parents flipped out and literally threw my stuff out on the lawn."

I hug Kelly tighter, losing the battle with my tears.

Connor moves from his chair to the floor in front of us, taking Kelly's hand. "Was it because of religion, like Zach's parents?"

"No, my parents aren't even remotely religious. My dad is a farmer and hunter. He's that ultra-masculine guy that wears camouflage and thinks deer hunting season is the reason he exists."

It's really hard to picture stylish Kelly being a farmer's son.

"I grew up wearing work boots and flannel. Driving a tractor was something I learned when I was twelve. Gifts for Christmas were typically more camo and rubber boots. It was all great for my three brothers, but it wasn't for me. I knew I was gay really early on but tried to hide it. Dad would get pissed if he saw anything gay on TV and called gay men sissies. He was real good about making gay jokes or saying things like 'if any of my boys become gay, they will be dead to me.' I didn't want to lose my family, so I tried to keep my gay from showing."

"I'm sorry, Kelly," I whisper, kissing his cheek.

"He never suspected you were gay?" Connor asks. "I mean, you practically scream gay when I look at you."

Kelly rests his head against mine. "Nope, he never suspected a thing. You have no idea how hard it was to go outside to feed calves when all I really wanted to do was go shopping with my mom and baby sister."

I get this picture in my mind of Kelly outside doing farm work, all miserable and sad. "Aww...I hate that you had to feel that way."

"It's in the past now. I honestly try not to think about it too much, or I'd miss them more than I can handle. My siblings are all younger than me, and Dad expected me to take over the farm one day." Kelly sniffles. "I could have handled it better if he'd just yelled and screamed, but he refused to talk to me or even look at me. I don't exist to him anymore."

Connor scoots closer and ends up hugging us both. "I don't know what's wrong with people and why they do this to their kids. I'd die before I turned my child away for being who they are."

"I wish that was how all parents are, but they aren't. I've not spoken to my family for four years. At least when they threw my stuff out, it included the money I had stashed away from my allowance and birthdays. After they kicked me out, they had their attorney contact me to file emancipation with the courts. I went along with it because I didn't want to live in a group home. I'd have rather been on my own than with a group of kids that hated me. The process is fairly quick when everyone agrees to it."

I rub Kelly's back gently, trying to comfort him so he can continue.

"During that time, I dropped out of school and took on three jobs. Moved into the crappiest, cheapest apartment I could find. Once I got a handle on everything, I obtained my GED and started to think about my future. I tried to put aside as much money as possible so I could start college and not work myself to death while going. I knew there was no way I could work full-time and keep up with classes.

"For a while, one of my jobs was at an expensive boutique, and the owner gave me a lot of clothes that didn't sell fast enough, which is how I got most of my fabulous clothes. She was there for me whenever I needed someone. Unfortunately, she closed the shop last year and moved to Cali. Besides my little group of friends, she was the only person I've had since my parents kicked me out."

"You have us. We'll adopt you," I say in a rush, determined that Kelly will never be without family again.

"Aww, Zach, you're the sweetest," he replies, turning his head to kiss my cheek.

Connor squeezes us both in his arms. "We can be a family together."

Kelly leans over to kiss his cheek, too, and I swear Connor blushes.

"So how did you end up at a party kissing a boy, anyway?"

"Oh...it was our neighbor's son. He often helped us bale hay or went fishing with us. Whereas I liked clothes and shopping, he loved hunting and the outdoors. I had no idea he was gay, but I had been crushing on him forever.

"So we ended up at this party in town, where I drank a little too much and so did he. We got to talking, and he confessed he was gay. I came out to him, too...and we ended upstairs in a bedroom. One thing led to another, and neither of us noticed that someone came in and took a picture. After our parents found out, he told me he loved farming and his life too much to give it up. So he told his parents he was drunk and didn't know what he was doing—that I took advantage of him. He went back into the closet and is still there as far as I know."

"Wow, what a douche," Connor grits out. "I get that people need to come out in their own time, but to tell them that you took advantage of him is such an asshole move."

"I know, but I'd already lost everything and didn't have it in me to say any different. I wasn't as strong back then as I am now. He was someone I was attracted to, but it wasn't like I was in a relationship with him. Although, I so wanted to tell his parents that I wasn't the one sticking *my* dick in his ass."

His humorous tone makes Connor and me both smile.

"I think you were really strong back then," I tell him. "Not many teens your age would have made it on their own and worked so hard. I think you're amazing and special and deserve tons of love. I'll be your family and love you no matter what."

Kelly half laughs, half cries. "Dammit, you just had to say something so sweet and make me cry."

"Don't cry, or you'll make me cry," I choke out, trying not to full-out bawl.

Connor rolls his eyes at both of us, but I think his eyes look a little glassy, too. "Okay, you two. We are going to make hot fudge sundaes and binge-watch the Mandalorian. I've heard it's funny."

That's exactly what we do. Kelly and I snuggle on the couch under a big blanket, eating ice cream. Connor joins us, holding a huge bowl of buttered popcorn. We cuddle and watch the show but eventually turn it off so we can talk and laugh. It's a perfect night and brings all three of us closer together.

I FINALLY BREAK down and let Connor measure me. I've made it to five foot one. It's still short but better than four foot ten. The gym is paying off, and I'm starting to get abs...maybe. Connor says since I have practically zero body fat, they can show up quicker. I wouldn't say they are defined into a six-pack, but there's a hint of some kind of pack there. My shoulders, arms, and upper chest are all looking like more than just a skinny boy's. I never want to be super muscled up, it's not me, but I want to look like an adult and not a twelve-year-old.

. . .

I THINK Connor and I both live for the weekends when Kelly will come over and spread his energy all around. This Saturday, he takes us to a sex store. I feel like I'm doing something illegal when we walk inside.

"Okay, so first things first. Let's find you a harness."

"Harness?"

Connor shrugs like he has no idea either.

"Yes, a harness. Sometimes gay clubs will have leather or kink night, and having a harness is a must. You can wear them on any night at a club, a lot do. They are sexy as hell on a twink, and the bears will love you in them."

"Gay club?"

"Oh honey, I'm definitely taking you to a gay club. I've been easing you into all this, but we are going to start meeting guys next weekend."

I take Connor's hand, totally scared just thinking about it. He squeezes it gently. "Don't worry; you can do this. I'll even come along to make sure you're okay."

I have to take my shirt off in the store, and Kelly buckles on some different harnesses until he finds one he likes. It's apparently called an H-harness, but then he decides I should also get a shoulder harness. I don't argue with him, but it's hard to picture me in a harness going anywhere.

Next, he makes Connor stand on the other side of the store while he explains prepping beforehand. All about lube and butt plugs and dildos. I'm in over my head as he piles on everything I need to be ready for my first time. I hide the thing you douche with on the bottom of the pile so Connor won't see it. Condoms get added as he lectures me on the importance of never letting a top convince you he doesn't need one.

He also talks about something called PrEP that I need to get on if I'm going to be hooking up. I decide to hold off since I haven't even kissed a guy yet.

IT'S Sunday morning when Connor comes into my bedroom and sits on the bed with me. I can tell he's upset and scoot over to hug him. Well, basically, he hugs me because I'm so much tinier than him.

"What's wrong?"

"Tessa broke up with me."

"What? Why?"

"She said that the distance was too much, and she can't keep driving home all the time with how much homework she has."

I know how hard it is to be away from the person you love. "I'm sorry, Connor."

"Not your fault. I could feel her pulling away this last month and kind of expected it."

"Do you want to spend the day eating sweets and watching movies?"

"Yes, but you're not allowed to have more than one dessert."

"Fine, it's a deal."

We wear pj's and lie in bed all day, watching a wide range of movies. I even suffer through two action movies, just for him. We also watch romance, Disney, and even a gay movie that I'm pretty sure he cries over.

We do take a break so Connor can call one of his friends about an assignment due.

While he's busy, I call Brady.

He answers the phone immediately. "Hey…you okay?"

"Yeah, I'm okay. Just missed you."

"Miss you, too. Less than five weeks left."

Feels like forever. "When do you start work once you're back?"

"I'll have about three weeks off before I start. I want to spend time with you."

He has no idea how much I needed to hear that. "I can't wait."

"Are you having fun with your friend? What's his name again?"

"Kelly? Yeah, we've become pretty close. I think you'd like him."

"Is he gay?"

"Yes, why?"

"Just wondering."

"You should call Connor and talk to him."

"What's wrong?"

"Tessa broke up with him, and he's pretty upset. He might talk to you about it more than me. I don't know."

"Shit…yeah, I'll call him. I thought they'd be the ones to make it."

"People change and move on."

He gets really quiet on the other end.

"Brady, are you okay?"

"Yep. I should go and call Connor. I'll call you in a couple of days."

"Okay…stay safe."

"You, too."

He hangs up before I can say I love him. Why is everything changing? I feel like he's pushed me away since he left, and I'm not even sure he'll want to share a room with me when he gets home.

Connor comes back in after a solid twenty minutes of me feeling sorry for myself. "Brady called. He said you told him."

"I thought you might need all the support you can get. You two were always so close."

"It helped. Thanks."

I MAKE sure to spend tons of time with Connor this week, giving him the same pep talks he gave me. I even try to mimic his voice if he doesn't listen, and that usually makes him laugh hysterically, which is the point.

This Thursday is Thanksgiving, and I invite Kelly to go with us since I'm his family now. I spend the morning helping Mom cook and listening to the girls chatter on about boys at school.

Dad comes in, and as usual, he reminds me so much of Brady that it makes me homesick.

"So you're actually bringing a boy to dinner?"

"Yes, Dad, Connor and Kelly are both coming."

"But Kelly is gaaaaayyyyyy?" Somehow he makes gay a long word that rises at the end, like it's the best thing in the world.

"Yes, he is, but we are just friends. He's helping me get more stylish."

Mom smiles and tucks a piece of my hair back into place. "I think he's doing a great job. I love your hair and these clothes. I can't believe how different you look."

Me neither. Just wearing jeans that fit perfectly has changed my look more than anything. I have a stylish shirt on right now that fits my body just right.

My whole business wardrobe has changed, too. I have fitted dress pants that look like something I'd see a model wear, with shirts and jackets I would have never dreamed of buying. I didn't even have to spend as much as you would think because Kelly is unreal at finding deals on everything.

Connor yells from the front door that *he's heeeeeere*, like it's a great announcement, and we all smile. I hurry to meet him and Kelly, bringing Kelly in to introduce him to my family. They immediately love him, and Kelly fits right in with us like he's always been here.

Mom goes to take pictures, and I realize she's going to send them to Brady. "No!"

Everyone's eyes go to me. "Don't post any pictures of me. At all. I want to see Brady's face when he sees my makeover for the first time."

"He's not even going to recognize you," Meg says. "I didn't when you came walking in with your hair all done…no glasses, and those clothes."

Kelly squeezes me from the side in a happy hug. "He does look even more adorable now. I'm so proud of my work."

"Can you give me a makeover?" Mom asks, smiling.

He eyes her clothes and then her hair. "Absolutely, you should be rocking your forties and turning heads. I can take you to see Lux on Saturday. He'll squeeze you in if I call."

"Be prepared to be waxed in places that hurt," I murmur.

Dad raises his eyebrow and then shakes his head. "I don't want to know."

Connor shudders, drawing Kelly's attention to him. "I think you could use a makeover, grumpy bear. You need to up your ante now that you're single."

Connor eyes him like he's lost his mind. "Are you saying this hotness can't get a date all on its own?"

"Do you want a date, or do you want all eyes on you?"

He sighs, giving up. "Fine, you can do me over, too. I have to admit Zach looks like a model now. A tiny one, but a model."

I smack his arm. "I grew two inches this year!"

"Still tiny."

Kelly gives me another squeeze. "Don't worry; your size will only draw more guys to you. I can't wait to take you out Saturday night."

We had decided not to go out tomorrow night because Black Fridays are insane with traffic. "What are we doing again?"

"We are going to a small house party with some of my friends. I think we should start small and work our way up to the gay club."

Dad gets this "oh dear God, I don't want to know" look when he hears gay club.

I try to reassure him. "Don't worry; I won't drink there."

"But we may have to give him a shot beforehand to loosen him up a little," Kelly adds in.

"I've never even tasted alcohol."

"Honey, you can't be eighteen and not even have tasted it."

Honey comes over to him like she was called, wagging her tail. Kelly bends down to baby talk to her. "Of course I called you, baby girl. You're the most adorable, beautiful dog in the whole world."

Connor does this chuckle but stifles it when Kelly glares at him.

Shortly after dinner, Brady calls to wish everyone a Happy Thanksgiving, and Mom puts him on speaker.

"What are you doing for Thanksgiving, Son?" Dad asks.

"I went to a friend's and had lunch with her family. We just got back to the apartment."

Ouch. I swear everyone here gives me a sympathetic expression. Everyone is quiet for maybe a bit too long because Brady clears his throat and asks, "How is Thanksgiving going there?"

Mom answers, "It's been lovely. Connor and Kelly came over, and we've enjoyed having them."

"I see... Glad you're having fun."

I know my best friend, and he definitely sounds off. "We miss you," I add, wishing he was here.

"I miss you guys, too. One month left. I can't wait for you to meet Ruger."

Ruger is the German Shepherd he's training with, and he will soon be a fixture in our home. "I hope he likes Honey."

"He will. He likes female dogs—a lot."

Kelly lets out this small laugh.

"Well, I should go. Stella wants to watch a movie."

It's the first time he's even said her name in conversation. My stomach hurts. What if he decides not to come home at all? What if he brings her with him?

"Okay, Son. Thanks for calling."

"Yeah, bye everyone."

I'm going to cry. "Excuse me, I think I need to check on something at home." I rush out the patio door and run to my house. *His house.* Shutting myself in our bedroom so I can cry.

Why do I keep doing this to myself?

I know he doesn't want me that way, but I keep letting myself get hurt. I lie on the bed, grabbing Eeyore to hug him to my chest.

A minute later, Kelly comes in without knocking. He crawls onto the bed and cuddles with me. "I know this hurts, but you're going to get through it."

"I don't know if I'm ready to date. My heart still belongs to him."

"How about you just work on making friends and having fun? When you're ready, we can move on to sucking dick and frotting with some guy. No one said you have to give your heart away. Then we can find you the big D, and your ass will help you get over Brady."

I laugh; I can't help it. "What is frotting?"

"Jesus...my sweet little baby virgin. You don't know anything, do you?" He wipes some tears off my cheeks. "Frotting is where two guys face each other and thrust their cocks together...or one holds both cocks and jacks them both off together. It's quite hot, and there's nothing like feeling someone's cock move against yours while they're gripping tightly."

My body definitely feels hot now. "Okay...I definitely want to try that. How did I not know about frotting?"

"Because you watch sweet couples on YouTube instead of porn. You really need to invest in some premium porn. Don't watch the free shit. Cockyboys is the best, trust me. There's this top on there—Austin Wolf. I'd climb his body and let him have his way with me, over and over again."

"Alright, I'll look it up and watch some." I'm not sure why I never looked at porn before. Probably because of the monster's voice in the back of my mind saying porn will send me to hell. I push the voice away and promise myself I'll watch porn later.

"Do you want to go Black Friday shopping tomorrow? We can fight the crowds and buy sexy clothes at great sale prices."

I already have a ton of clothes, but he makes me want to experience new things. I've never gone Black Friday shopping. "Are the crowds going to freak me out?"

He bites his lip and then gives me a serious look. "They might, but you'll never know if you don't try. If they do, we'll come back here."

"Okay, then I want to try."

"Try to think of it as these aren't people you know. They don't care about you or matter. They are all just trying to get deals and shop for stuff. It'll be good practice before going to a bar or club because there are a lot of people in them."

"What are you two planning now?" Connor asks from the doorway.

Kelly grins at him. "Hope you're not doing anything tomorrow because we are going shoooopiiiiiing!"

"Kill me now," he mutters but walks into my room to flop down on the bed beside me. "Can you at least promise to feed me every two hours?"

"Ohhh, is grumpy bear going to bite if he doesn't get food?"

"Yes, I'm definitely going to bite and roar. It'll be ugly, and someone will get hurt."

"I supposed that we can stuff you full of food every two hours then. You'll be like our two-year-old who needs snacks to stay happy."

I giggle at the horrified look Connor is giving Kelly over being compared to a toddler.

Connor pokes me in the side. "You're supposed to be on my side."

Kelly reaches over to poke him. "I've always wanted to poke a bear."

Even Connor can't help but laugh over that one.

I'm realizing it's good to have friends of my own. Friends that want to be with me, not because they are friends with Brady, but because they are *my* friends.

THIRTY-SIX

BRADY

In the last month, we spend a week learning about police dogs and get to tour the adjoining facility where they train officers with dogs. I love it and spend a lot of time talking to the training officers in hopes that at some point, Rockville will want a K-9 unit.

My hard work last summer pays off because I can outshoot all the other recruits. Physically, I have a lot more stamina, especially since I'm sleeping every night. It's all going great until they offer me a spot in their K-9 program.

Zach. Two more months feels like forever to wait to see him. He'll be upset, and I'm not sure I can do this to him. I speak to Chief Kuhn, who jumps on board immediately. It seems they've been wanting to add a police dog to their force and even have the money set aside to buy the dog.

I wait for Stella to leave before I call Zach on FaceTime. I want to be able to see his face and tell if he's okay or not.

Seeing him for the first time in months, I have to swallow back so many emotions.

He's studying me, his expression serious. He looks different. His hair is so much longer, and he looks a little older if that's possible in three months.

"Hey, it's great to see your face."

"Yeah, yours, too."

"Your hair is longer?" *Duh, why did you even ask him that?* I don't like change and want him to stay the same.

"Thought I'd try something different," he says, messing with his hair.

"I like it." *I hate it.* I don't want him to be different when I go back.

"How's everything there?"

Fuck, I don't want to do this. "Everything is great. I'm at the top of my class, and the instructors have been teaching me more than I ever thought I would learn."

"I'm happy for you. I knew you'd do amazing." He looks like he knows I'm about to give him bad news.

I might as well get it over with. "Look...I know that I'm supposed to come home in two weeks, but they've asked me to stay on for another eight weeks to take their K-9 program." I keep explaining, but his face doesn't change. He doesn't tear up or get upset.

"That's great, Brady. You'll be perfect for that."

His response is not what I expected. "I hope you're not upset? I know you were counting on me coming home in two weeks."

His green eyes look away from me. "Nope, it's fine. I'm keeping busy, and Connor keeps me company."

He's replaced me and doesn't need me anymore. My chest hurts at the thought.

"Look, I need to go. I'm going out tonight."

My Zach is going out? Since when? "Going out? With who?"

"Just some friends I met," he says nonchalantly.

He used to tell me everything, and now I don't even know who his friends are. It's not like you've been telling him about Stella and her friends, my subconscious screams at me. "Okay, I can let you go."

He gives me his beautiful eyes again, and I swallow hard. "I really miss you."

"I miss you, too."

Fuck, I can't do this. I end the call, but I swear I saw hurt in his eyes before the screen went blank. I immediately call Connor.

"Bro, what's up?"

"Hey, how is Zach doing?"

"Nice of you to check in on me," he quips.

"How are you, Connor?" My tone might be a little sarcastic.

"I'm doing great, thanks for asking."

"Now, how is Zach doing?"

"He's doing good, keeping busy."

"Who are the friends he's going out with tonight? Are they safe?" I feel sick that I'm not there with him.

Connor is quiet for a few seconds and then answers with, "I didn't know he was going out and don't know with what friends."

"What do you mean you don't know what friends? You're supposed to be making sure he's okay at all times!" I'm being unreasonable but can't seem to help it.

"He's fine, Brady. You'll be home in two weeks, and then you can see so for yourself."

"About that...I'm staying for an extra two months to take their K-9 program."

"Fuck...did you tell Zach that?"

"Yes, and he seemed fine with it. I don't think he cares."

Connor grunts. "I need to go pick up the pieces, bye Brady."

The call ends before I get another word in. *Pick up the pieces?* He sounded pissed at me.

It's driving me crazy that I'm too far away to go check on Zach. I feel helpless and frustrated over here.

Homesick.

Two more months... I can make it two more months.

Two weeks later, I'm sitting on the couch while Dixie and Stella attempt to cook spaghetti. It's going to be burnt and taste terrible, but they are having fun trying. It's lonely watching them together, and I call Zach.

There's someone talking in the background, and Zach sounds distracted, or maybe it's distant. We've hardly talked in the last two weeks, and I miss him.

"Who's there with you?"

"One of my guy friends," he replies.

Guy friends? He really is fine without me. I don't know what to say to him, and when Stella starts laughing loudly, I tell him goodbye.

How am I going to fix us when I get back? I want things to be the same as they were. What if he and that guy are dating? I should be happy for him, but instead, I worry that he'll get hurt or the guy won't be good enough for him.

I hate this.

. . .

It's the Sunday before Thanksgiving when Zach calls me out of the blue. I hurry to answer the phone, worried something has happened.

"Hey...you okay?"

"Yeah, I'm okay. Just missed you." He sounds like my Zach.

"Miss you, too. Less than five weeks left." I want it over with now.

"When do you start work once you're back?"

"I'll have about three weeks off before I start. I want to spend time with you."

"I can't wait."

I can hear the smile in his voice. I know I shouldn't ask, but I can't help myself. "Are you having fun with your friend? What's his name again?"

"Kelly? Yeah, we've become pretty close. I think you'd like him."

Close. *Close as in sex close?* "Is he gay?"

"Yes, why?"

My stomach hurts at the thought of him replacing me. "Just wondering."

"You should call Connor and talk to him."

I can tell something has happened. "What's wrong?"

"Tessa broke up with him, and he's pretty upset. He might talk to you about it more than me. I don't know."

"Shit...yeah, I'll call him. I thought they'd be the ones to make it."

"People change and move on," he says quietly.

Does he mean us? Is he even going to want to be my best friend when I get back? I feel sick.

"Brady...are you okay?"

No, but there's nothing I can do about it. "Yep. I should go and call Connor. I'll call you in a couple of days."

"Okay, stay safe."

"You, too." I hang up and throw my phone across my bed and watch it topple off the side. Guilt hits me that I didn't even tell him I love him.

Groaning, I crawl from the bed to retrieve my cell and call Connor.

Thanksgiving is hard for me. I've always been with my family, and I miss them so much. I'm more homesick than I ever thought I would be.

Stella comes into my room and pulls my ear so I'll sit up.

"Hey, what was that for?"

"Get up; you're coming to Thanksgiving with me."

She refuses to take no for an answer, and I spend the next few hours with her insane family. They are all very animated people with huge personalities. It must be the Irish blood that makes them all so energetic. I can understand now why she chose to stay in an apartment instead of just driving over to the academy.

I wait until I'm home to call my family, but it only makes me feel worse. Kelly had dinner with my family? They must be really serious if Zach brought him home for a holiday meal. I even heard him laugh, and he sounded...I don't know...cute.

All these thoughts are driving me crazy. I just want to see Zach and hold him. I want to be close to him again. I want him to tell me everything and for me to be able to just be me. He's the only person I'm completely myself with. I have to get that back because his friendship means everything to me.

I spend the next week trying to think of what would make Zach happy...something he loves. It finally pops in my head, and I start making plans. First, I call his boss to make sure he can take off the time. She agrees he can and promises to keep it a secret. Then I call and make reservations and buy plane tickets. I plan everything out for us.

It gives me something to do and look forward to and is exactly what I need to help get me through this last month.

When the last day arrives, Ruger and I pass our testing with flying colors. We are really close, and I know that he'll be a part of my family. Zach is going to love him.

Stella knows that I'm taking a vacation as soon as I get back, although she doesn't know about Zach yet. I feel guilty not telling her about him, but he's mine, and I didn't want to share him or try to explain why we are so close. Maybe it's because of what happened with Carrie, but I feel like everything with Zach is private...personal.

She loves Ruger and offers to keep him while I'm on vacation. It's a better plan than asking my parents to watch an intense police dog that doesn't know them. Stella and I will meet halfway when I get back.

It isn't until I'm on my way home that my heart gets lighter. I can't wait to see Zach and my family. I can't wait to lie in bed and read to him. I can't wait to eat real food and see him smile while he cooks something.

I just want to be home.

Everyone is expecting me to come home on Monday, but I'm going to surprise them. Saturday traffic is heavy, but I should get home before supper. Zach is going to be surprised when I walk in the door, and I can't wait to see his face.

THIRTY-SEVEN

ZACH

Kelly ends up staying the night so we can leave at the crack of dawn. He has mapped out all the deals and what times they start. He is like a military drill sergeant when it comes to shopping for sales.

Black Friday is truly insane and a total eye-opener that I've been living in a small town my whole life and haven't experienced a lot of things.

He finds designer clothes at obscenely low prices, and I end up with more outfits than I need. We also find great deals for Christmas presents, and I check everyone off my list. True to his word, Kelly gets food for Connor every two hours, but he also makes sure to tease *grumpy bear* the entire time.

There are a few times that the crowds and noise make me break out in a cold sweat of anxiety. Connor and Kelly must be watching because every time I get that way, we spend time outside the stores getting fresh air and letting me calm myself.

It's an exhausting but fun day. Kelly makes everything fun with his humor and energy. Kelly and Connor are in the family room right now, going through all the clothes he forced Connor to buy. I believe Connor is getting a lesson on what to pair with what and how his old jeans need pitched. I grin at the groan I hear Connor let out while stirring the chicken fettuccini alfredo I'm making for supper.

Sauce almost gets on my crop top, and I hurry to find an apron. I've discovered that I love crop tops. They make me feel sexy, or at least as sexy as I probably will ever feel. I'm wearing one with a gray pajama bottom that hangs on my hips.

As always, Brady is on my mind, and I can't wait for him to see the new me. Not really a new me, but the me that's been hiding away for so long. I feel a little nervous that he won't like this me, but there's also no one in the world I want to share this me with more than him.

The three of us eat supper together, and I even drink a tiny bit of the wine Kelly brought over. Connor sets up Brady's gaming system in the family room, and I hope that he'll be okay with it in here when he gets home. We spend the evening playing Mario Kart and Monopoly, with lots of laughter between the three of us.

SATURDAY, Connor and I hit the gym while Kelly sleeps in. He has taken over one of the guest rooms on the weekends, and it feels natural to have him sleep at our house. When we get back and shower, Kelly is all business again as he herds Connor and Mom into my SUV. We let Connor drive because—as Kelly points out—he's a grumpy bear if he doesn't feel in charge in some way.

I know they are going to be a while, and I spend hours in the book store finding books for the family room shelves. They text me when they are done, and I drive back over to get them.

Mom walks out looking ten years younger with her new hairstyle. It has highlights and lowlights, cut in this choppy way that is going to make Dad crazy. Her makeup is so much better now, too, and I'm speechless seeing her.

As for Connor, his new haircut makes him look older and classier. Sexier, too—at least according to Kelly. Connor seems happy with it.

"I didn't get waxed, in case you were wondering," he tells me. "I draw the line at someone touching my man bits."

Kelly reaches over to pat his head. "Grumpy bear roared and tried to bite over it, but that's okay. Bears are supposed to be hairy."

Connor turns ten shades of red over his obvious reference to *gay bears*. Mom is oblivious, thank God.

Connor smacks Kelly's hand away. "I'm not that hairy, I'll have you know."

"Don't worry; you'll be a daddy bear in your forties."

He chokes on his drink, and Kelly has to pat his back, all while I'm dying laughing in the backseat.

"I'm going to guess by bear, he doesn't mean an animal," Mom says, sending all three of us into hysterical laughter.

Over lunch, I can tell Mom falls in love with Kelly as much as we have. I'm pretty sure she's going to adopt him into the family and love him forever. I'm sad his own mom hasn't accepted that he's gay and doesn't talk to him anymore, but I think he just gained one if he wants her.

Mom learns what shopping truly means when Kelly takes her to all his favorite stores. He even gets her to buy sexy lingerie and stuff, during which Connor and I go to a different store because we don't want to know.

It's such a long day that we barely get home in enough time to get ready for meeting his friends. Dad sees Mom and his mouth drops open. I grin when he thanks Kelly for doing this. Dad declares they are going on a date tonight, just the two of them. I can't remember the last time they went on a date, and it makes me happy. Connor carries all Mom's stuff in and then hurries back over here to shower.

Kelly picks out an outfit for me, helps put a little makeup on, and styles my hair. He gets ready himself and then has to redo Connor's hair because he's not happy with it now that Connor has showered.

I'm nervous when we get to his friend's house in a town about fifteen minutes away. I've never been to this town, but it's a little bigger than Rockville.

Kelly doesn't knock, just leads us inside to meet everyone. Stacey is a raven-haired goth girl who is with Hanna, a blonde girl-next-door type. Bane is the typical college guy with a swimmer's body and dimples, and then there's Craig, who is a stocky, older-looking guy with a beard. By older, I think like thirty. Liam is tall and hot, with muscles and a flirty smile, probably mid-twenties. He reminds me of Brady a little in the easy way he carries himself.

Everyone is really friendly and genuinely wants to get to know us. They are open about their sexuality and don't mind talking about it either. I find out Stacey is trans and bisexual. Hanna is a lesbian, and Bane is bisexual. Craig and Liam are both gay.

"We can already tell you're a gay little twink," Stacey says to me with a smile.

"Is it that obvious?"

"Yes. You checked out Liam the second you saw him…so yes."

My cheeks burn with embarrassment, but Liam winks at me. "Don't worry; I like it when gorgeous twinks check me out."

Gorgeous?

Kelly waves his hand. "He doesn't think he's hot."

Everyone looks at me like I've lost my mind. "What? I'm not hot. I'm just a skinny, geeky boy."

Bane's eyes flare and he leans forward. "Umm…you're like crazy hot. Your ass…and fuck…those eyes. They won't know if they want you on your knees to suck or to fuck."

Connor leans over to fan some air into my face. "Breathe, Zach."

"I'm trying to…"

The others laugh and show mercy by focusing on Connor. Hanna studies him. "So you're straight?" She tilts her head. "Or not."

Connor shrugs. "Actually, I've never told anyone I'm straight. People just assume."

My head whips over to him. "Wait a second… What do you mean?"

He gives me an apologetic look. "I'm sorry. I wanted to tell you, but I thought Brady would never let me stay over if I told him I was pansexual."

Part of me is angry he didn't tell me. Out of everyone, I would have supported him. But then I remember the agony I went through to accept who I was and to tell even Brady. Plus, he has a point. Brady probably wouldn't have let him over to sleep in the room if he thought Connor might have been attracted to me.

I scoot over to sit on his lap, hugging him. "You don't have to apologize to anyone. It's yours to tell who you want, when you want. But I'm glad you finally came out to me."

He hugs me back. "Thanks, Zach. I always knew you would understand. I never lied about it, just never told anyone either."

"Aaaaww…look at grumpy bear being all sweet." Kelly comes over to pile on his lap, too, kissing his cheek.

"You two are embarrassing me in front of everyone," he grumbles. "Go cuddle or something."

Kelly grins, kissing his cheek again. "There's my favorite grumpy bear…about to roar."

Connor rolls his eyes, but I see a hint of a grin.

Kelly and I do sit on the couch together and cuddle.

His friends are all smiling over the exchange and offer Connor a lot of support. A few of them share their coming-out stories, and only one of them was a good experience. I've never felt so accepted in a group of people my age or close to my age. I'm not the only one that's gone through trauma, and they've all not only survived it, they've become stronger together.

THAT WEEK we meet up with all his friends for supper at a bar they love that has an awesome atmosphere. I think Connor is letting go more and being himself with everyone. He really hits it off with Bane, and they spend a lot of time talking about gaming stuff.

I feel like things are going great, and even though missing Brady is a constant, I am learning more about myself and what I like.

THIRTY-EIGHT

ZACH

The following Saturday morning, Connor persuades Kelly to go with us to our gym instead of the gym he usually goes to. Afterward, we eat breakfast at the diner, undoing all the running I just did. My body has really transformed over the last five months. I actually look like someone who spends time in the gym. I don't have these buffed-up crazy muscles, but I'll admit my body does look fit.

As we pull into the driveway at home, I notice a vehicle at Mom and Dad's house. The woman standing by it looks familiar.

"Stop," I tell Connor before he parks in the garage.

"What's wrong?"

I get out before he's even in park and start walking over to her. Mom and Dad come out of the house as I get about ten feet from the woman. It's *her*...after all this time. The man she ran away with is standing behind her holding the hand of a little girl, who has to be close to three years old.

"Isaac, it's so good to see you," she starts, giving me a big smile.

Shuddering at the use of my old name, I bite out, "My name is Zach. Why are you here?"

"Zach, you've grown up so much, I can hardly believe it." She steps closer, but I put my hand up for her to stop.

Connor and Kelly are now by my side, offering me some support.

"Why are you here?"

Her smile falters a little. "Can't I come to see my son?"

"I'm not your son. You left me with that monster, knowing damn well he would beat me for you leaving. You let him hurt me. What kind of mother does that?"

"I did the best I could. Legally, I couldn't just take you away to another state. He would have forced me to stay."

"I don't want any excuses. Just leave me alone."

"You have a sister," she says in a rush. "Isabella."

"I hope you protect her better than you ever did me."

The man speaks up from behind her. "Be nice to your mother. We couldn't take you with us."

I stare at the man and can see some resemblance between us. "Are you my biological father?"

Joy's eyes widen in surprise. "How did you know?"

"Well, is he?" My breathing has a wheeze to it as my chest rapidly rises and falls. I ignore it, needing their answer.

The man nods. "We suspected you might be."

Rage pours through me. "You knew I was your son, and you left me with an abusive asshole to raise me?"

"I wasn't in a position to raise a child."

Yet they had another one and handled that fine. I press my hand to my chest, the feeling of tightness getting worse. "I don't want to hear it. You need to leave, *now.* You both disgust me."

"Wait…we know you got all of Tom's money. I was his wife for years and deserve half of it. We really need the money right now since Trey is out of work. You don't want your sister to be homeless, do you?"

"You both need to leave," I hear Dad say.

"I can't believe you. You didn't come here to see me because you care. You came for money. What is wrong with you? What was so wrong with me that you couldn't love me? I don't understand. Why?" That feeling of panic is already pushing against me. Partly because of them, but partly because it scares me that I can't seem to get a full breath.

"Even ten thousand would help," she rushes out.

I back up, needing to get away from them. How could they not love me? I did nothing to them. I never did anything wrong. "Brady," I gasp out as I go down, the impending panic attack taking over.

"Zach!" I hear Connor yell.

Brady… I need Brady. He would protect me from this and make it okay. He would make her leave and hold me until I felt better.

"Breathe, Zach, please breathe."

But I can't do it. When I try, it's like trying to suck air through a tiny straw.

I vaguely hear Dad's voice say, "Call nine-one-one," before the darkness takes over.

Brady—

"He had a severe asthma attack brought on by stress. Since they had to intubate and put a tube in until we could get his breathing under control, we want to keep him here overnight. We were able to take his tube out, but his oxygen levels still aren't great. Our biggest concern is preventing pneumonia from setting in since he can't fight off infection the same without his spleen. My guess is that his asthma hasn't been under control lately, and this just exacerbated it."

The man must be talking about me. My throat feels like someone scraped it with a knife. I try to open my eyes, and it becomes apparent real quick that I'm in the hospital. Everything comes back to me, and a tear leaks from my eye. I want Brady so badly, it hurts.

"Zach…you're okay. Dad and I are here, Connor and Kelly, too."

"Water," I croak out.

Mom lifts my oxygen mask so she can hear me, and I repeat it. Once the water coats my throat, I look around to see Kelly and Connor standing next to my bed.

Tears start because the person I need is Brady. I must have said his name out loud because Mom brushes her hand over my head. "I'll call him. He'll come."

"No, you can't. Don't tell him this happened," I gasp out, a wheezing sound coming from my chest. "Promise me."

"He'll want to know, Zach."

"No! He needs to finish school, and I won't be the reason he has to leave. I'll get through this on my own." I'm getting out of breath, and Mom puts the oxygen mask back on.

"Okay, Zach, we won't tell him."

Closing my eyes, I try to hold on to the sobs I know will overtake me. The nurse comes in and asks them all to leave while she does her assessment.

It's a relief when they leave because it means I can finally let go without Mom and Dad seeing me fall apart. The sobs pour from my chest in painful cries that hurt to hear. The nurse touches my arm and exits my room.

"Brady...I need you so much. I can't do this without you." But he's not here to hold me or tell me that I'm safe.

"Honey..." I feel Kelly crawl into the bed behind me, wrapping his arm around my front. "You can do this. You're so strong. Think of all you've done for yourself. The gym...the kids at the library...your sexy crop tops...the house you've made beautiful...all of that is you."

"I miss him so much," I sob. "Every second of every day I feel like I'm missing part of me."

He must be able to understand me through the mask because he presses his cheek to mine. "I know you do, but I promise it will get better. Love is painful. That's how you know it's love. Cry it out if you need to, but you're not alone. Connor and I are here for you. You're not alone."

I do cry it out, with him curled around my back and Connor holding my hand. Crying aggravates my asthma, and I hear the nurse say they are giving me something to help. Then everything goes blurry and their voices fade.

I WAKE up to Kelly and Connor sitting next to my bed in chairs. Kelly is resting his head on the bed and holding my hand. Connor notices my eyes are open, and he puts his hand on Kelly's shoulder.

Kelly pops his head up and moves to sit on the bed next to me, brushing hair from my eyes. "Do you need some water?"

I nod and then realize the face mask is gone; now it's just the tubing that runs under my nose. Sipping the water helps, but my throat is still scratchy when I ask, "How long?"

"It's about midnight. They kept you calm until your oxygen levels came up more. The steroids are working, and you're breathing much better."

"Sorry I lost it before." It's embarrassing they saw me like that.

"Don't be sorry. Now it's over, and you'll be out of here in no time," Kelly says, offering me a radiant smile that warms my heart.

"Will you stay at our house with us?" I need the happiness and laughter he brings.

"Of course I will. That guest room is like a five-star hotel next to my apartment." He gives me another sip of water. "Plus, grumpy bear needs me to cook for him while you're resting, or he'll starve."

"I can get takeout, you know," Connor counters, sounding offended.

Kelly reaches over to cover his mouth. "Don't pretend you don't need me. You know you do."

He rolls his eyes and pries Kelly's fingers off his mouth. "Oh yes, I will die without your food."

"Good boy."

Connor glares at Kelly. "You're going to pay for that one. You're also getting a nickname as soon as I can think of one."

His head gets patted. "Okay, daddy bear."

Connor's answering groan makes me grin.

Kelly's expression brightens even more when he spots my attempt at a half smile. "I knew we could cheer you up with our banter." He directs a smart-ass smirk at Connor before leaning over to kiss my cheek.

"I love you, guys." I think I meant to say it with humor, but it comes out serious.

"Aww, our sweet little baby virgin loves us."

Connor lets out this laugh, and even I might laugh a little.

"We love you, too," Kelly adds in for both of them.

CONNOR AND KELLY stay the whole night with me until Mom and Dad come back here in the morning. After my friends leave for home to shower and pick up clean clothes for me, I'm left alone with my parents.

Dad positions a picture of Brady next to my bed where I can easily see it and hands me Eeyore. "Thought these might help you."

I stare at Brady's smile and pretend for just a moment that his arms are around me, holding me. A sharp pain through my heart reminds me of how much I miss him. Hugging Eeyore to my chest, I move my gaze to my dad. "Thanks, Dad…they do help."

Mom takes my hand, both of them exchanging looks for a second, and I know they are trying to decide if they should tell me something.

"What?" I ask.

Dad sighs and steps closer to lay his hand on my shoulder, offering support in a physical way. "We don't want to upset you but also want to talk to you about your…about Joy."

I'd been avoiding even thinking about her since I woke up. "Did she leave after…"

"Yes, they left when the paramedics arrived. She has tried to visit here at the hospital, but we asked her to leave."

There isn't any part of me that believes she actually came to visit because she cares. This is about my inheritance. "Do you think I should give her some money?"

"No, Son. They are adults and can take care of themselves. You are not responsible for them or their actions. If you give them money this time, they will just come back and ask for more later."

The image of my little sister fills my mind. "I feel guilty because of Isabella."

Dad nods. "I can understand you wanting to help your sister, and maybe someday, when she's older, you will be able to have a relationship with her. But for now and for the sake of your own health, I think it's best that you don't let them into your lives. Your mom and I will support whatever decision you make, though."

After this incident, I don't think my body can handle being around them. "How do I even keep them away?"

"First, I'll have a talk with them about staying away," Dad says.

Mom squeezes my hand. "And if that doesn't work, you can get a restraining order against Joy and Trey. It'll keep them from showing up at your work, too. Your Dad and I can help you file the paperwork. We feel given your past and the health risks when you have a panic attack, the courts will grant your request."

The reminder of my panic and that fear of not being able to breathe during an attack sends my heart rate up. The machine near my bed beeps rapidly, making my anxiety impossible to hide.

"Zach, take some deep breaths and focus on something happy," Mom says softly.

My eyes move to Brady's picture, and I am able to calm myself down again. "Whatever we have to do to keep her away," I murmur, wanting this whole episode to be over. "As long as Isabella is okay."

"Let me take care of everything," Dad says firmly. "There are plenty of programs that provide assistance for situations like theirs. If they are even telling the truth and are as bad off as they say. I wouldn't be surprised if it was all made up simply because they want money. Regardless, I don't want you to worry about anything to do with them. I will handle all of it."

Tears fill my eyes as I stare at both of my parents. "I don't think that I've ever told you both how grateful I am for you taking me in and loving me. You changed my whole life...you and Brady. I love you both, and you will always be my mom and dad."

Mom's eyes glisten as she moves closer to hug me. "We love you, Zach. You're ours and always will be."

Dad leans down to kiss the top of my head. "You are my son and have been since the moment I saw you."

"Aww...Dad..." I swipe some tears from my cheeks and barely keep from full-out crying. His words make me think about why they moved to Rockville. "Do you think Owen knows how grateful I am that he gave me his parents to love me?"

Mom smiles, brushing hair back from my eyes. "I think he knows, and I think he loves you as much as we do. When I look at you, I see the gift he gave us, and it heals all the pain and sorrow that came with Owen dying. His gift helps me remember the good memories of him and his never-ending love for every person he met."

Unable to keep from crying, I sit forward and hug my mom. I feel Dad's arms wrap around both of us and his ever-present strength seeping into me. "Thank you, Owen," I whisper to the boy who gave me the miracle of love.

THE DOCTOR RELEASES me from the hospital early that afternoon, with instructions for doing breathing treatments every six hours, checking my oxygen level, and taking a couple of different medications for the next week.

Once we get home, Connor and Kelly lie on my king-size bed with me, watching movies and picking on each other like little kids. Honey has been glued to my side, happy to have me home and seeming a little worried about me.

Brady calls to check in, sounding perfectly fine as usual. I manage to keep it together and not tell him what happened when all I want to do is cry and beg him to come home.

I have to take Monday off work and see my asthma doctor. He

clears me to work as long as I keep up with my medications and breathing treatments. My daily inhaler is now changed to something stronger. I have to go back next Monday for a final check-up, but hopefully, then this will all be over.

Connor refuses to let me go to the gym all week, but he does drag Kelly with him.

Kelly is like this bright spot in the house. He and Connor ride together to classes, except one day a week when Connor has a later class. I'm beginning to think I should get them together because they are perfect for each other.

Connor has taken up calling Kelly baby bee, and when Kelly annoys him, he makes a buzzing sound. Kelly only pretends to be annoyed. I can tell it doesn't bother him a bit.

That Saturday night, all our new friends come to my house for their little weekly get-together. We eat Chinese food and talk about everyone's week. They know I had a bad asthma attack, but Kelly didn't tell them why.

We end up in the basement, where some of them play pool while the rest of us play cards with a movie on the big screen TV. When they find out there's a swimming pool, this place becomes the designated house for Saturday nights during the summer so everyone can swim. All I can hope is that Brady will love them as much as I do.

Later that night, when everyone leaves, the three of us are in the family room with the fireplace going. I'm reading a book aloud to them, and it hits me that I'm happy in this moment. I lower the book and look at Kelly. "I think you should move in here."

"What happens if Brady comes back and doesn't want me living here?"

"If he doesn't want anyone living here, then you and Connor can get a place together. I don't really expect Brady to have an issue because he'll love you. Plus, he's sweet and kind. But think about it…if you stay here, then you can save all the money you normally spend on rent and if you end up moving in with Connor later, you can have a nicer apartment if you share rent. You save money riding to school together. It's the perfect back-up plan. But I really want you both to stay here for now."

Kelly looks over at Connor. "What do you think, grumpy bear?"

"I think you should move in here, and we'll find a place if Brady has a problem with it. But only if you cook for me if we have our own place, baby bee."

"It's a deal, daddy bear."

Connor tosses a pillow at Kelly's head, who simply takes it and stuffs it under his back. "Thanks, I needed that."

"Brat. Maybe your new name should be baby brat."

Kelly smirks. "Suits me, I think."

THIRTY-NINE

ZACH

Now that we have all gotten to know each other and I'm more comfortable, they decide we should go to our first gay bar. I'm a nervous freaking wreck because of the noise and all the people that will be there.

Connor and Kelly promise that they won't leave my side the entire time we are there. Since it's my first time, I wear jeans and a gray fitted T-shirt. Connor dresses the same.

We were told it'd be hot in the bar and to only wear a jacket until we get there, then leave it in the vehicle.

Kelly wears a crop top and tight glittery pants that draw your attention to him. He looks hot, really hot.

"If I was a top and into twinks, I'd totally do you."

He grins at me. "Thanks. Next time, you're dressing sexy, too. Nothing's hotter than a twink dancing in a crop top or harness."

I bite my lip. "I don't know how to dance."

He stops short and herds me into the family room, ordering Connor to play some sexy music.

Kelly starts dancing, and he can make his body move so sensually that even Connor's eyes are glued to him.

"Okay, just feel the music and let your body flow with it."

I try and it's horrible. "I can't do this. I have no rhythm."

"Yes, you can. Close your eyes and stop thinking." He puts his hands on my hips and helps me find the rhythm. "Feel the music and let it bring passion to your body...like you're moving and touching, making love with it. Don't think about what you look like. No one else matters."

Drawing on the passion I feel for Brady, I try to picture his body in front of mine and that feeling of wanting him. Kelly moves his body against mine, and it gets easier the longer we dance together.

"Okay, fuck—I think you two got it," Connor says, turning the music off.

Kelly grins at me. "You'll do fine as long as you don't overthink it. We'll practice some sexy moves and dirty dancing this week. Next Saturday, you'll melt the dance floor."

"That might be a stretch, but thank you."

He gives me a hug before strutting past Connor. "Okay, horny bear, let's go."

"You are *not* calling me horny bear!" Connor yells after him, but Kelly just blows him a kiss as he backs out the front door.

"I'm so fucked trying to keep guys off you two," he grumbles as he follows.

Nerves set in, but I'm excited, too. I'll be at a place where everyone is like me and will accept me for who I am.

We drive into the city to a bar called Feel Free. The parking lot is packed, which makes me even more nervous. I can't afford to have another panic or asthma attack right now and use my inhaler before we even get out of the vehicle. Connor shoves it into his pocket to take inside with us, and then we join up with the rest of the crew who just pulled in.

The bouncer checks our IDs and lets us through the door. It's darker inside, but with lots of rainbow-colored strobe lights to make it so you can see.

There are guys dancing on one side, and it's hot as hell just to watch them dance suggestively together. On the other side, there are high-top tables and then booths around the wall. The bar is long, with men leaning against it and talking. Kelly keeps ahold of my hand as we find a longer high-top table we can all sit at.

We order drinks and food. I think it's to give me a chance to get used to the atmosphere. Guys stop by to talk to Kelly, and he introduces them to us every time. They don't stay long and move on to talk to other guys.

Kelly puts his arm around me, leaning closer. "Do you see all the guys checking you out?"

"What?" I glance around and see nothing. "You're delusional."

"Oh honey, you're so innocent—it's adorable." He tilts his head towards the booths off to the side. "The bear over in the corner has his eyes glued to you."

I look and sure enough, the guy gives me a nod and a smile.

"And that tall, hot guy at the table over there—wants to fuck you senseless."

I follow his gaze, and there's a good-looking twenty-something guy watching me. "Maybe they are looking at you," I suggest, still feeling like there has to be some mistake.

"Would you like to dance?" A man stands at my elbow, staring at me intently.

Kelly leans over. "He's not hooking up tonight, but thanks."

The man nods and walks away.

"Did that man really want to hook up with me?"

Liam laughs. "He was hoping you'd suck him off in the bathroom for sure."

"Eww…bathrooms are dirty."

That earns me a kiss to the cheek from Kelly. "You're precious, Zach. Don't worry, you'll find the right guy when you're ready."

The food is good, and I'm handling the noise better than I thought. I feel safe with my friends close.

"Okay, it's time to dance. We'll all stay with you. If a guy dances with you, he might try touching. Tell him no or move his hand away… unless you want him to touch you, then anything goes. If a guy asks to talk, it might mean he wants to find the bathroom or a private corner or even a car to get off with you."

"Don't leave me alone at all," I plead, feeling more nervous now that he said all that.

Connor puts his hand on my lower back. "I'll be right there with you."

"You going to dance with us, grumpy bear?"

He stares down at Kelly. "Yes. I *can* dance, you know."

Kelly grins. "Okay, daddy bear, let's see what you've got."

The dance floor looks full, but we somehow find an area to dance.

Kelly puts his hands on my hips and talks me through my jitters, helping me to let go and dance. It's so much more fun than I ever thought it would be. All of them aren't afraid to dance up close to each other suggestively but don't mean anything by it.

Kelly and I dance together, and Connor keeps shaking his head at us.

Liam dances behind me, and fuck, it's hot to feel him rub against me. I don't feel like he'll touch me or that he'll want anything; it's just everyone enjoying dancing together.

Connor *can* dance and when Kelly dances close, he gets this look that tells me he is attracted to Kelly even if he doesn't want to admit it.

Some other men want to dance with us, but my friends are good about keeping me in the middle. Connor has pushed back a couple of guys, shaking his head at them when they seemed determined to dance with Kelly and me. I'm positive Kelly would have danced with them if he weren't here with me.

I have no idea how long we dance, but when we leave, I'm exhausted and smiling. I'm definitely going to dress in a crop top next time because it's so warm in there and also because I want to feel like I'm doing what I want to do.

Being me.

Connor drives us home, with Kelly and me in the back cuddled up together. "Thanks for tonight," I whisper, kissing his cheek.

He smiles, brushing back some of my hair. "You're welcome."

THAT WEEK we do practice dancing. He shows me some dirty dancing that could about make me come in my pants. Connor can't handle watching us and has to leave the room, adjusting himself as he goes. It makes Kelly laugh and call him horny bear for the rest of the night.

Since Brady will be home on Monday, I spend time after work every day cleaning the house from top to bottom. Making sure everything is perfect for him. Honey even gets a trip to the groomers so she'll be all pretty and smell good.

Friday, I go to the store and buy food to make all his favorite meals next week, stocking the fridge with everything he might need.

I'm actually feeling a little sick about him coming home. He may not like me anymore, and then I'll have to deal with that heartbreak.

It's been two months, so Saturday morning is spent getting my hair cut and highlighted again, going through the waxing part, getting a manicure and pedicure. I want to look good for Brady, to show him that I can be more than a geeky boy with no style and baggy clothes.

When we get back, I spend a little time with Mom, Dad, and the girls. Mom asks where I'm going tonight, and I tell her when the girls aren't around. I think she's happy that I'm getting out and doing things.

Tonight we are going to So Cocky, a bigger club than last time, with a DJ that Kelly loves. Clothing is more risqué in this club, and he claims I better come out in something sexy. Wanting to really let myself be free tonight, I take extra care with getting ready. Showering, shaving my legs since I skipped waxing those. I slather lotion on until my skin is even softer than before. I've found that I really like my body hairless and smooth; it makes me feel good. Kelly styles my hair, and I manage my makeup on my own. I even put on some colored lip gloss.

For the outfit, I pick Calvin Klein low-rise trunks, the sexiest pair of low-rise stretch denim that leave nothing to the imagination. You can see the hint of my Calvin's at the top of my jeans. Then I put on a white crop top that shows my middle without raising my arms.

Kelly comes in and does a whistle. "Love it."

"Help me find some shoes, please."

He goes through the shoes we bought and picks out these green suede ankle boots with an inch and half heel. "The green will match your eyes...and I love the hint of green eye shadow you put on. So subtle, but it makes your eyes pop, especially with the eyeliner. Might want to put your lip gloss in your pocket or have Connor carry it for you."

He finds me a sherpa-lined jean jacket to wear there and reminds me to put on the cologne I picked out when we went shopping.

Connor is wearing jeans and a black Henley, with black boots. Kelly gives his approval and remarks, "You look like a sexy top."

We leave early because we are going to Liam's to pick him up on the way. He's old enough to drink and doesn't want to drive home.

Instead of eating at the club, we meet up at their favorite restaurant and eat there first.

The club is hopping by the time we get there, and this one has a place you can check your coat into. It costs us money to get in, but it's more upscale and worth it.

Kelly was right; the DJ is playing the kind of music that makes you want to dance even when you're not on the dance floor. I get asked to dance by four guys before we even make it to a table.

Kelly keeps grinning at me and motions to the guy I just turned down. "Do you still think you're not sexy as hell?"

I look down and have to admit that my body does rock in this. My waist is so tiny that it looks good…I think. "I think I look sexy."

Maybe.

"My sweet little baby virgin is growing up," he teases, wrapping his arm around my waist.

Kelly and I are really huggy, touchy-feely. I think he's attractive and could turn anyone on, but we have this bond that isn't sexual at all. However, the men in the club seem to have their eyes glued to the two of us hugging and keeping close to each other. Connor looks like a grumpy bear now for sure and practically hovers.

"Did you two have to dress so…"

"Sexy?" Kelly supplies him with the word.

"Yes, sexy."

"Why, yes, we did." He twirls in a circle to prove his point. He's wearing a black fishnet crop top with black stretch jeans and black-heeled ankle boots. With me going light and him going dark, we make quite the pair together.

We stay at the table long enough for the legal alcohol drinkers to get a couple of shots down and then go out on the dance floor. Kelly and I dance close together, with our other friends around us. We've gotten so much closer since my trip to the hospital, and I consider him my best friend next to Brady.

Connor goes with us when we take a bathroom break, which Kelly tells him is cute. I'm positive Kelly has hooked up with guys in a bathroom before and knows how to handle himself. We wash up and reapply our lip gloss before handing them back to Connor.

"Why do I have to carry everything in my pockets?"

"Because your jeans aren't as tight, grumpy bear. Besides, a top should be willing to do that for two gorgeous bottoms."

He rolls his eyes and opens the door for us to walk out. We get a drink to rehydrate and then go back to dancing. I see Connor check his cell and then whisper something in Liam's ear. He nods, and then Connor leans over to us. "Have to take a phone call. Stay with Liam."

"Okay, daddy bear," Kelly answers, rubbing his hands down Connor's chest. He swallows hard and walks away from us.

We both laugh and keep dancing. A couple of songs later, they put on one that drips sex, the perfect one for us to dirty dance to. There are so many guys watching, but I ignore them, smiling and laughing as we dance against each other. It feels good to just let go and be free.

FORTY

BRADY

Traffic is way worse than I imagined, and I get stuck behind an accident, which involves all vehicles at a standstill for two hours on the highway. My stomach is doing flip-flops at the thought of seeing Zach in just a few minutes as I drive down our street.

I pull into our driveway and see a car parked by the garage that I've never seen before. Connor's vehicle is in the garage, but Zach's SUV is gone. Great, he's probably not even home, and I lived for this moment to see him.

Grabbing my bags, I carry them into the house from the garage. The living room has so much more done to it than when I left. It's perfect. I couldn't have designed it better myself. My bedroom has changed, too. It's warm with colors and pictures, little touches that make it feel personal.

I drop my bags and call for Honey, but she doesn't come. She must be at Mom and Dad's, and I hurry out the patio door and over to their house.

Honey comes running to me the second I walk inside, and I bend down to love all over her. "I've missed you, girl."

"Brady!" Mom rushes over to hug me. "We've missed you so much. It feels so good to see you standing here."

"Wow, Mom…you look great." Her hair is more stylish, and she looks younger, and her clothes are hipper than what most girls my age wear.

"I know, right! Kelly helped me do a makeover. He's so good at it!"

Kelly.

He really has become someone in Zach's life.

"Where is Zach? I was trying to surprise him."

"Oh, he went with his group of friends to a gay club in Pine Falls. They probably won't be back until late."

A gay club?

"Zach is at a club?"

"Yes, he went last weekend to a smaller gay bar and handled it well, so they went to a bigger club tonight. He was pretty excited to go dancing again."

"Zach doesn't dance."

"He does now. Kelly has been helping Zach practice all week."

"Sounds like Kelly is at my house a lot."

She narrows her eyes at me. "You mean your and Zach's house because it's his home, too. And yes, Kelly moved in a couple of weeks ago."

I feel sick, and...some other emotion I don't recognize. How could he ask someone to live there without talking to me first? Have they been sharing our bed? "What club are they at?"

"So Cocky...but Brady, please be careful not to ruin this for him. He's worked so hard these last six months to get to this place, and he needs you to love the new him."

"I won't hurt him, Mom." But I am going to let him know how upset I am over him not talking to me about Kelly.

Sending a text to Connor, I head to Pine Valley. He doesn't answer, and when I get closer to the club, I pull over to text him again. This time he texts back that he'll call in a minute. I start driving again and accept the call as soon as it rings through the vehicle's system.

"Brady? What's so urgent?"

"Are you at So Cocky with Zach?"

"Yes?"

"I'm almost there."

"Why do you sound so pissed?"

"Because of a lot of things. Zach—Kelly—all of it."

"You need to stop and cool down before you do something stupid that will hurt Zach."

"I'm pulling into the parking lot now. See you in a minute." I end our call and step out of my truck, shoving my keys and cell into my pockets. Before I can go two feet, Connor is in front of me.

"You're not going in there like this and ruining his night."

"Ruining his night? I come home early to surprise him, and he's at a gay club? He always said he needed me, but he sure as hell took being apart from me well. He's not even been upset or cared at all. Now I find out he's moved a guy in without even telling me? If we are so close, you would think he would tell me he's fucking some guy in our bed!"

I'm more pissed because it hurts that he doesn't care. I push Connor, and he pushes me hard up against the truck.

"You are so fucking stupid, and I'm sick of it. You think that he didn't care or wasn't hurting? You claim to know him so well, and yet you're so fucking blind it's not even funny."

I try to push him away, but he slams me back again. "You're going to listen to me before you go in there and crush him. After you left, Zach did nothing but cry in bed for almost three days straight. He didn't sleep or eat, and I barely got him to drink water. For the first month, I forced him to shower and function, forced food down his throat, or he wouldn't eat. Zach was like walking death, with no will to do anything. He lost so much weight, it was scary. He went to work and came home to lie in bed under the covers. And he was crushed that when he talked to you, you didn't even seem to be upset at all."

My chest feels like someone stabbed me. "I didn't know…"

"Of course you didn't know. He tried to sound happy so you wouldn't come home. He loves you more than he loves himself and would have done anything for you to stay in training. After that first month, he saw that picture of you at the bar laughing with that girl, and it broke him even more that you were out having fun while he was dying inside. I was done watching him half kill himself over missing you, and I told him he had to start living—that he had to find himself without you. Maybe the picture was good because it helped me get through to him."

"What picture? I never posted a picture," I protest.

"You didn't post it, but the girl tagged you in it—therefore, it was on your Instagram. Regardless, it hurt him. So every morning, I took him to the gym, and he focused on working out. He threw himself into decorating your house. He wanted you to love it and to make it feel like a home. He wasn't great, but he was better. He actually ate and took care of himself, at least. But don't think for a second that he wasn't missing you. It's like he was only half a person."

Connor doesn't give me a chance to say anything and continues. "Then he got the call—that you were staying two more months, and he crashed. He lied to you about going out with friends because he had to get off the phone before he lost it. I had to watch him cry his heart out all over again. And who picked up the pieces? I did. I'm so sick of watching him wait for you to fall in love with him and never giving himself a chance to love someone else. Sick of it."

I don't know how to process all this and latch on to what he said in the last part. "What are you talking about? Fall in love with him? I love Zach."

"You're so fucking blind!" He swings his arms out in exasperation. "He's been in love with you since the day he met you. You crushed him when he saw you making out with Carrie on your bed. I wanted to fucking punch you so hard that day when he told me what had happened. You crushed him every time you went on a date with a girl, and who was there to help him through it? *Me*.

"So when you crushed him again by not coming home, it was time. It was time for him to stop pining over you and start looking for someone to love—someone who could love him in return. I asked Kelly to help him, and he has changed Zach's life. He helped him find his own style. Taught him things about being gay that he didn't know. He introduced him to a group of queer friends who have become our friends as well. He has been there for Zach every step of the way, and so help me God, if you ruin their friendship, I'll never speak to you again!"

"Friendship?" Intense relief hits me at hearing that word.

"Yes, friendship. They are both twinks and bottoms and absolutely fucking adorable together. They can laugh and be gay together. Kelly has taught him how to dance and shown him how to be sexy and confident in himself. They can cuddle and laugh and dance together and yet are only friends. It's what Zach needed."

It's killing me to think about Zach moving on from me. I want to hold him all night long and for things to be the same as before. "He didn't have to move him in without talking to me first."

Connor shakes his head. "You know what prompted Kelly to stay with us? Zach's biological mother showed up, along with his biological father and his sister. They wanted money from him. They didn't care about him or regret leaving him; they just wanted money that they thought he owed them.

"Zach stood up for himself, but then the stress gave him a severe asthma attack. We had to call the squad in, and they had to intubate him, or he would have died. When he woke up in the hospital crying for you, he told us not to call you because what you were doing means so much to you and he wouldn't pull you away from it. But he needed you, he cried for you and cried for you. And you know who got him through it? *Kelly*. He lay in that bed with him and talked to him about how strong he was and how far he'd come and that he'd get through this, too."

I sag back against my truck, fighting tears. Zach almost died and still tried to make sure I was happy. That's how he's always been. I let my own stupid pain of him not saying anything rule over what I know about Zach. He's the most selfless person in the world. To know he lay there crying for me makes it hard to breathe.

Connor continues. "Zach needed that to make it, and he asked Kelly to stay while he was recovering. Kelly took over and got him through it. And the three of us fit together. We laugh all the time, and Zach asked Kelly to just stay there. He sleeps in a guest room upstairs next to mine, not with Zach. No, Zach sleeps in your bed, cuddling your pillow like he wishes it was you.

"He made prior plans that if you had a problem with it, Kelly and I would move in together and share an apartment. But of course he thinks you're the best person in the world because he was like *oh Brady is so sweet and kind, he won't care if you stay here.*"

"I'm sorry... Kelly was over for Thanksgiving, and I just assumed they were dating if he brought him to a holiday."

"He brought him because Kelly doesn't have any family willing to talk to him. They kicked him out and disowned him because he's gay. Zach wanted him to have a family to be with. You know...because he cares about people."

I'm a fucking idiot. I should have just talked to Zach about everything. "I know he does."

"You claim to care about him, but you sure didn't show it while you were gone. You could have FaceTimed him a couple of times a week. You could have spent more than two minutes on the phone with him. You could've read to him over the phone. You could have made this so

much easier on him. I know you were busy, but if you truly love him…
you should have shown it."

He's right. I knew it would hurt too much, so I shut him out. I took
the selfish route. "I never meant to hurt him."

Connor sighs. "I know that, but you can't go into that club and hurt
him again. He won't recover from it, and you'll lose him. Do you get
that? Zach's scared you won't like his new style or hair. He's scared you
don't want him close anymore. He's scared that he's finally being free
enough to explore things and let more of himself out, and you won't
like that part of him. He lives and breathes for you."

I live and breathe for him, too. Doesn't he know that?

Connor is oblivious to my agony at hearing that Zach is scared over
me not wanting to be close anymore. He pins his eyes on mine, a determined expression on his face. "So stay the fuck out here until you can
get a grip on yourself, and then and only then can you come inside to
see him. You may think he and Kelly are too close, but you're going to
have to put aside your feelings and watch them together. You'll see that
he's found a friend that he needed. You always had me and Alex and
all the guys. He's only had your friends. Kelly is *his* friend. Don't ruin
that or so help me God, I'll take Zach away from you myself."

Connor turns around without another word and walks back toward
the club. I sit in my truck for a full five minutes, trying to process everything he said. *Zach is in love with me?* How did I not see that, or is it even
true?

If I do nothing else, I need to make sure he knows I like him as he
is now. I'll figure out the rest later, but I can show him I've missed him
and love him. Opening the door to the truck, I walk to the club
entrance and pay the fee.

I just want to see Zach.

FORTY-ONE

BRADY

The club is dark, but not so dark that I can't see around me. I scan the bar area to find my best friend, but he's not at any of the tables. Moving toward the dance floor, I'm a little shocked at how sensual all the dancing is. The song has this seductive rhythm to it, and the men are practically having sex on the floor.

I spot Connor dancing behind this twink with coal black hair. He's what most would call hot and has this fishnet crop top on. He looks up at Connor and says something that has Connor grinning. I'm surprised to see Connor sexy dancing with a guy.

The black-haired twink has another twink in front of him that he's dirty dancing with. They are literally the sexiest couple on the floor, and every man around me is watching them. The other twink is the light to his dark, with blondish-brown hair, a white crop top, and a perfect body underneath. I'm straight, and even I feel a little turned on watching him. Maybe it's the way his small waist curves or the sexy way he moves his body.

Another man steps in to dance behind the lighter one and rubs against him. He tries to edge away, and Connor moves to push the man back, shaking his head no. Connor, three other guys, and two girls form a circle pretty much around them, all dancing and laughing.

I still haven't spotted Zach, and I don't understand why Connor isn't with him. What if he's alone in the bathroom with some creep and needs help? I walk closer to get Connor's attention and mouth, "Where is he?"

Connor points to the light twink, and my heart stops for what feels like an eternity. Just then, Zach turns his back to who I'm guessing is Kelly and dances with his ass to Kelly's front. Kelly slips his hands over Zach's stomach, and it looks sensual as hell.

How can that be Zach?

His hair is lighter and styled like something you'd see on an Instagram model. He has eye makeup on and no glasses. And his body...it's tight. He's filled out with some muscles, but yet still has this almost soft, feminine curve to his waist that draws every eye to it.

His jeans...I don't even know what I'm thinking right now because the man dancing on the floor is stunningly beautiful. He's not my Zach anymore; he's this vibrant, gorgeous, hot guy.

The song changes and it seems like everyone knows it because they begin to clap to the beat. It tells them to put their hands in the air, and Zach is laughing. Then the song screams for everybody to jump. His whole group of friends starts jumping, all of them grinning and having fun.

I don't even know what to do now and lean back against the wall to watch Zach dance. He's grown so much more confident—unless a guy approaches him, then he looks a little terrified. Kelly says something to him when Zach shakes his head at another guy. Zach says something in Kelly's ear, and then Kelly puts his arm around his waist.

They are adorable together. I'll admit that Connor was right about that. Being close to the same size, and their contrasting looks...not to mention it's obvious they care about each other.

While observing, I see guys leaving with other guys down the hallway to the restrooms. I see others in the corners definitely doing more than just kissing. The thought of Zach trusting some stranger not to hurt him scares me half to death.

When the next song ends, his group must be calling a break. Zach is holding Kelly's hand, who is making Connor laugh over something. I step out into Zach's line of sight, and when he looks up, it takes him a second to compute that it's really me. Tears fill his eyes almost instantly, and then he's running toward me, jumping into my arms and clinging to me. I hold him close, choking back my own tears at finally having him in my arms again.

We don't say anything, just hug each other as tightly as we can. I finally move to kiss his cheek and forehead, staring into his liquid green eyes. "Surprise."

"I missed you…"

"I missed you, too. I couldn't just sit at home and wait. I had to come find you."

Zach buries his face in my neck, and his soft sobs rip my heart out all over again.

"I'm home now, and I'm not leaving you ever again," I murmur next to his ear.

Connor and Kelly are in front of us, watching with worried eyes.

"You must be Brady," Kelly says.

"You must be Kelly," I answer, trying to keep the bite out of my tone.

He lays his hand on Zach's lower back. "Honey…" I think he feels that Zach is crying because Kelly pins his blue eyes on mine. "Take him home; he needs to be close to you for a while."

Connor digs into his pocket and hands over Zach's inhaler to me. "I have his keys and will drive his vehicle home. We have to drop off Liam first. Just take care of him."

Nodding, I carry Zach out of the club. His legs are hooked around my back and his arms looped tightly around my neck. By the time we get to the truck, he's shivering and only lets go long enough for me to lift him inside. I climb in and start the truck, blasting the heater as best I can with his body glued to my side. It takes some work for me to get the seat belt around him and snapped in. I reach over and grab my coat, putting it over him to help keep him warm. "You don't have enough clothes on for winter."

"My coat is inside." He says it so softly I can barely make out his words.

I send Connor a text asking him to bring Zach's coat home. Then I slide my arm under the coat and around Zach's bare stomach, holding him closer.

No words are spoken all the way home. He just clings to me, his small body trembling under my hand.

As soon as I park inside the garage, he's unbuckling his seat belt and trying to squeeze onto my lap.

"Hold on. Let's go inside." I open the truck door and slide out, turning around to help him down. He looks like he's going to beg me to carry him but then walks in front of me into the house.

Mom must have brought Honey over before they went to bed because she comes running to greet us. Zach gives her a pat but keeps walking to our bedroom and then into the bathroom. I lean against the bathroom doorway, watching him wipe off the makeup that has smeared from his tears. I can't really get over how different he looks now. He's taller, but then my eyes travel down to his boots with heels, and I figure that has something to do with his height. Never in a million years did I think Zach would wear boots with any type of heel. Hell, I've never even seen him in boots. He always wore his Converse or tennis shoes.

He's looking at me in the mirror, and Connor's words about him being in love with me play over and over in my mind.

"I'm going to shower." He takes a deep breath. "I just need a few minutes to process that you're home."

"Go ahead; I'm not going anywhere."

He nods and I leave him alone, even though I don't want to. Walking over to his drawers, I go to get him some clothes and stop short. His plain boxers are gone, and in their place, there is an assortment of underwear that I never thought Zach would own. I pick up something with straps that doesn't look like underwear at all. There are briefs and little, tight boxers. Why would he need all these?

Because he's planning on having sex with a guy and wants to look sexy.

Jesus, this is really happening... He's going to be dating and hooking up. I shut the drawer, figuring maybe he should pick out his own. I don't want him to be embarrassed that I saw all his new stuff. Although, I'll probably be seeing it anyway when he's sleeping next to me. Things will be different now. Hell, I'll have to get used to seeing Zach...in a whole new light.

Kicking off my shoes, I walk into my closet to get some pj's I left here and have to pause to take it all in. Where before Zach's side of the closet was mostly bare and only held a few things, now it's full of clothes and shoes—so many that they are spilling over onto my side. Shaking my head, I grab some pj bottoms and carry them out to get some boxers from my own drawer. My boxers look plain and old next to his, and it crosses my mind that maybe I need to upgrade my own.

While Zach is showering, I unpack one of my suitcases and put my clothes away. He comes out of the bathroom with a towel wrapped around him, glasses on. He looks a little more like my Zach with the glasses, but these aren't as clunky as his old ones. He seems nervous and has a hard time looking at me.

"I'm going to shower real quick." I pick up my clothes and disappear into the bathroom. After a long day of driving, it feels good to shower. I get dressed and then go into our bedroom to find him gone.

Walking out to the kitchen, I see him standing by the patio door, drinking a bottle of water while staring out into the darkness. He's wearing a pink crop top with pink bottoms that hang off his hips. His underwear must be almost nonexistent because as low as his pj bottoms are, I can't see them. My cock stirs and I shake my head. I do really need to bite the bullet and get laid.

He opens the patio door and lets Honey in, explaining why he's out here. When he sees me standing behind him, his eyes light up for a second before worry dims them. I don't like that he's unsure of me now.

"Want to go to bed? I can read to you."

Tears fill his eyes, and he moves to wrap his arms around my waist. "I missed that."

Connor is right. I'm a total asshole. I could have read to him on FaceTime or Skype. I could have helped him through the last six months. Kissing the top of his head, I keep an arm around him all the way to our room.

There's this feeling of coming home when I crawl into bed next to him, holding my arm out so he'll cuddle up to me. He does and we both let out an audible sigh of relief.

He takes off his glasses, handing them to me to lay on the side table. "Are you sure you're really here?" he whispers.

"I'm sure and I'm not leaving again."

"Where is Ruger?"

"He's staying with a friend for the next two weeks, and then I'll meet up to get him."

Zach runs his fingers over my chest absentmindedly. "Why not just bring him home with you today? I bought him a bed and toys, his own bowls."

My skin tingles where his fingers touch, and I shift a little. "Because I just didn't." I can't really tell him why or it'll ruin his Christmas present.

"I have something to tell you…"

"What is it?"

"Don't get upset, but I asked Kelly to move in here. He was here all the time, and I needed that. If you don't want them here, he and Connor will get an apartment together. They both don't mind and will move out if it's not okay."

"For now, it's fine. I don't want people living with us forever, but they can stay for a while."

His body relaxes into me. "Thanks, Brady. You'll love Kelly once you get to know him. He's really special."

I'll wait to see what he's like before I agree with that. Zach is so trusting; he could be missing that Kelly is using him.

I run my fingers through his hair like I always do, and he closes his eyes. "I like your hair. You look beautiful."

One second he's fine, and the next he's on top of me, burying his face in my chest to cry. I rub my hands up and down his back, letting him get it all out.

"I thought you wouldn't like it...me...now," he says through his sobs.

"Oh, baby...you know I love you no matter what you look like." Connor was right about Zach being scared I wouldn't like him, the new him. Seems like Connor knows Zach better than me at the moment. I don't like that thought at all.

He doesn't cry more than a few minutes and then just lies here all quiet on top of me. I reach over to pick up the nearest book, probably one he's already read, but I start reading anyway. I thought he would go to sleep, but he lies here listening. When he starts to yawn, I set the book aside and declare it's time for sleep.

Zach crawls off me and stands next to the bed to strip down. He's wearing tiny black briefs that mold to everything. Looking away, I strip off my own pj bottoms and join him back in bed. We gravitate to the same position we've always slept in, and it's the best feeling in the world. "I've missed sleeping with you," I whisper, kissing his forehead.

"I've missed this, too. It's the only time I feel totally safe." He turns his head to kiss my arm before laying it back down again.

Maybe all my worries were for nothing, and things will go back to the way they were, as if I never left.

. . .

My cock throbbing wakes me in the morning. It's so hard that it's painful. I haven't woken up like this in…six months. Zach is so buried into me, his leg between mine, that I have to extract myself carefully so I won't wake him up.

Heading to the bathroom, I take a long shower and rub one off to get the release I need. It's been so long since I came this hard. I hope Zach didn't hear me from the bedroom.

He's gone when I come out of the bathroom, and I hurry to get dressed so I can find him. He's not in the kitchen, but I hear quiet voices down the hall. I walk down the hallway and peer into the family room.

Kelly and Zach are on the couch sitting side by side, cuddling. They haven't seen me, and I step back into the hallway so I don't disturb them.

"How are you handling him being back?"

I halt my departure at Kelly's question.

Zach answers, "I love having him back, but I'm scared, too. When I'm close to him, all those emotions are right there…and I can't go through what I did when he left, not again. It hurt too much. I need to stay separate in some ways to protect myself."

Ouch. It hurts to hear him say that he needs to keep some distance from me.

"I know you love him. You'll always love him. You just have to figure out how to love him without being in love with him. Be close and keep the special relationship, but put yourself first and keep yourself open to new experiences."

"It is not that easy. Every time a guy comes up to me, I feel like I'm going to freak out on him. A panic attack doesn't sound like an awesome first time."

"I don't think a random hookup for your first time is the best idea. A lot of guys don't want to take their time with a virgin, and trust me when I say *prep is everything*. We just need to find someone you can trust to get you through all your firsts. Help you gain some confidence when it comes to having sex."

"Yeah, because I know so many gay guys," Zach says in a sarcastic tone.

"What about Liam or Bane? They both would gladly help you out."

Like hell. Zach isn't just going to ask some guy to help him have sex.

"No, if things went badly, it would ruin our group. I'm not risking that."

"What about Connor? I'm honestly surprised you two haven't hooked up already."

"I didn't even know he was pansexual until you did, and it would never work. Brady would kill Connor if he touched me."

Yes, I really would. And what the fuck, Connor is pan? Why wouldn't he tell me?

"He wasn't kidding when he said if he'd come out, Brady would have never let him near me."

"Okay, so Connor isn't an option, either."

"He needs a bratty type," Zach says, humor in his voice. "Maybe a baby brat that teases him constantly."

"Pfft, we fight all the time."

"It's not fighting; it's banter and a whole lot of sexual tension. Just admit it, he's your type. Maybe you can stop watching Austin porn and have some of the real deal."

Connor and Kelly do have this sexual chemistry now that I think about it. Zach is definitely trying to play matchmaker. It eases my urge to kill Connor for possibly lusting after Zach for years.

"Oh come on, tell me when you watch Cockyboys that he isn't the best one on there. Fuck, he can top like a dream. All those 'good boys' he gives out, and the way he always strokes them to make sure they are hard and enjoying it. Slow and hot."

"Okay, okay, stop or we are both going to be too horny…and some of his…err porn…is hot. I like to watch tops who are sweet and say sweet things. Do you think tops are really like that, or is it just in porn?"

"I've been with some amazing tops. There are a lot of assholes out there, though. They seem nice, but all they want is to use your mouth or hole, and they don't care if you enjoy it. It's only good when they actually want you to have pleasure as well."

"I'm sorry you've crossed paths with some of the bad ones," Zach says in a quiet voice.

"Oh, my sweet little baby virgin, you're just too tenderhearted for random men. We'll find someone who won't give you a bad experience. Just be patient. We can start with a dating app—not a hookup app because it would be dangerous for you to meet up for sex—but we'll find one where it's relationship stuff."

Dating app? All the stuff Kelly said scares me half to death. Zach could be abused or hurt. I rub the back of my neck and walk back down to the kitchen. I should feel guilty for listening in, but I don't think this is something Zach would share with me. Connor was right again. Zach needs a friend like Kelly.

Kelly calling him sweet little baby virgin makes me smile. It fits Zach perfectly.

FORTY-TWO

BRADY

There's a coffeemaker on the counter that we never had before. Neither of us drank coffee, but I drink it now. Kelly or Connor must be a coffee drinker, too. I pick a flavor and shove a mug underneath to start brewing a cup.

Looking around, I take in the house and all the changes. The kitchen has reds and yellows, some blues. He's made it look like someone loves cooking in here. The kitchen table fits perfectly, and every little touch adds accents of colors. There are paintings on the walls, and the splashes of colors match the accent colors in the room.

I think about the first moment I saw the family room and how it was exactly how I would have wanted it.

Comfortable.

I wish I would have looked at the bookcase or taken in the Christmas tree I vaguely saw by the window.

Zach has truly made this house a home for us. I didn't expect it because he never used the credit card I gave him. He must have used his own money for all of this. I have all this money, and he used his for our home.

Connor comes in the kitchen with his shirt off, his hair all messed up from sleeping. He's gotten really muscled up and might even be bigger than me now, not quite as tall but bigger.

"Where are Zach and Kelly?" He pulls my mug out, which is done brewing, and sets it over by me before starting his own.

"In the family room cuddled up on the couch."

"Figures." He glances at the clock on the microwave. "Bet they won't last much longer without wanting breakfast."

"You all have a routine down…"

"We do, except for Sundays. We don't usually go to the gym on Sundays."

"What time do you go to the gym in the mornings?"

"We leave here at five and get home at seven. It's on Sugar Street and only a few minutes' drive from here."

I was so looking forward to spending three weeks sleeping in and not having to be anywhere, but it looks like part of that time will be spent at the gym—at five in the morning.

The urge to ask Connor about him being pansexual is right on the tip of my tongue, but I can't do it. He'll tell me in his own time, and I need to respect that. It makes me wonder if all the times he stayed with Zach or watched over him, he might have wanted him in a romantic way.

Kelly and Zach descend on the kitchen, shooing us over to the island stools. Connor turns on some Christmas music as I watch them start to cook. Zach gives me some shy smiles every once in a while, but then Kelly will make him laugh over something. Kelly never stops moving and is like this ball of energy. He dances around the kitchen and then forces Zach to dance with him. I can't take my eyes off Zach, with his new everything and the way he loves his best friend. I used to be the only best friend he had, but now he has someone without me.

Connor has been watching them too, and is trying not to smile at their antics. "Do you think you could maybe finish breakfast so we can eat? I'm starving here."

Kelly leans over and pinches Connor's cheek. "It's cute that you think we are nineteen fifties housewives here to serve you, grumpy bear. Now shush it, or you're not getting anything."

I laugh at their playful exchange.

Connor rolls his eyes. "I don't think you're nineteen fifties housewives; I think you're nineteen fifties husbands."

Kelly flips him off but is grinning. "It's a good thing I know you're joking, or I'd beat you with this frying pan."

Connor smirks. "I'd like to see you try."

Kelly picks up the skillet, and Zach takes it away from him. "Okay, you two, get along, or I'm giving you both a time-out."

I'm guessing this is the norm for Connor and Kelly. Zach is definitely right about the sexual tension between them.

"Like you could put me in a corner."

Zach eyes Connor down. "I may not be able to, but Brady will if I ask him to."

Connor looks at me and I shrug. "If he asked me to, I couldn't say no."

"Why is it three against one? Someone has to be on my side!"

Kelly laughs. "Aww, it's so much fun to poke the bear."

"You're a bottom; there's no way you're poking anything." Connor crosses his arms, happy with his comeback.

"I could try being vers just once...so your ass isn't safe from me," Kelly deadpans.

Connor has no response other than to turn ten shades of red.

Zach gives an abrupt laugh and then hugs Kelly from the side. "Stop teasing him. He can't handle it before he has eaten."

"He started it!"

How we ever manage to finally sit down to eat is beyond me. Connor and Kelly never stop teasing each other. They need to fuck already and put themselves out of their misery.

After breakfast, Zach and I clean the kitchen while the other two go off to game. Then Zach shows me all the rooms he has done. Every room is perfect, and he practically glows when I tell him so. Our house is homey and beautiful, everything I wanted. For never having any experience, Zach has really outdone himself with the decorating.

"Where did you get the paintings? They look like they were done by the same artist."

"Those are mine. I know they aren't the best, but I thought it would make it more personal."

"You painted them? They are really good. I didn't even know you could paint."

"I took a painting class while you were gone to try and...anyway, I learned a lot and found that I enjoy painting."

I know he was going to say "try and cope" or something to that effect. Again, I'm reminded of how much he suffered without me. "You should paint more often."

"It's fun once in a while, but I'd rather read a book."

Kelly yells for Zach, and I follow him to the family room.

"You ready to set up that app? I think I have the perfect picture of you, one I took last week." He's scrolling through his cell, looking at pictures.

Zach hesitates and then takes a deep breath, sinking down next to Kelly. "Okay, let's do this before I freak out and change my mind."

Kelly starts asking him personal questions for the app, and I feel a little like throwing up. I can't sit here watching this and leave them to it, grabbing my coat and sitting outside with Honey instead. It's cold out, but the sun is shining, giving warmth enough to make it okay to sit here.

All I can think about is Zach and what he and Kelly are doing in there. He can't trust any of those guys; I don't care how much he gets to know them online. Maybe if he was experienced like Kelly, but he's not. He needs someone that absolutely won't hurt him physically and will take it slow.

You could do it.

Out of nowhere, the thought pops into my head, and I almost laugh out loud but then mull it over. I could do anything for Zach. I may not be gay, but it's not like my cock doesn't get hard around him. I'm sure that somehow we could make it work, even if it was early in the morning when I wake up. He could practice kissing, blow jobs, and even sex. He's been through so much and would do anything for me… I can help him with his firsts. *How hard can it be?*

Now that the idea has taken root, I can't stop thinking about it. I think about it all through lunch with Mom and Dad. I think about it while unpacking the rest of my stuff. I think about it when Zach and I take a nap together in bed, with him buried into me.

It consumes me so much that it's all I can focus on. All four of us spend the evening in the family room, with Zach reading aloud, and then we watch a movie. Zach and Kelly cuddle for part of it, but then he lies down with his head on my leg so I can run my fingers through his hair like I used to. Kelly lifts Zach's legs onto his lap and holds his hand while we finish the movie.

MONDAY MORNING, the alarm goes off too early for me, but once Zach bounces out of bed, I drag myself up to join him. Connor and Zach are wide awake to go to the gym, whereas Kelly and I groan numerous times about being up so early.

I start to wake up once we're inside the gym. They pick treadmills in a row and start running before I can even get mine turned on. I've been working out and running during my academy training and fit in with them easily. I'm surprised at the stamina Zach has and how ripped he looks when he's lifting weights. I hope he doesn't get any more muscular because I like his body soft the way it was.

Zach makes everybody eggs and toast when we get home, with a bowl of fruit on the side. I'm told that normally Connor and Kelly would go off to classes together, but they are currently on winter break. They do have plans to leave and go do some last-minute Christmas shopping.

Zach showers and changes into these fitted dress pants with a button-down shirt and a sharp jacket over it. His hair is styled so it waves back on his head and makes him look even more model-like.

Kelly fixes it a little and then hugs him. "Alright, son, you're ready for work."

Zach laughs, kissing his cheek. "You and Connor have fun shopping."

I walk him out to the garage and pull him in for a hug, kissing his forehead. "Be safe today."

As soon as the garage door closes, I hurry to my bedroom. If I'm going to bring this up to Zach, I need to know everything. I spend the entire morning watching YouTube videos on how to be a good top and what bottoms need to do to prepare. I watch horror stories and good experience stories. I research toys, lube, prep, and anything else I can think of.

At noon, Connor and Kelly still aren't home, and I eat a sandwich for lunch while googling Cockyboys since they mentioned it. It's a premium porn site, and I eye Zach's laptop by his side of the bed. It's password-protected, and it takes me only one second to decide on typing in Brady, and it works. He really needs a better password; every one of us can probably guess that one.

He has Cockyboys in his favorites, and it has the password saved, so I don't have to type it in again. Fuck, this *is* some premium porn. I've never seen porn look so...professional and clear. They must pay a fortune for good cameras.

He has some marked under his favorites, and I start watching them.

They are definitely ones where there's a strong top and a twinkish bottom, with very clear roles between them. I picture me topping Zach like that and start to get hard. Something is seriously wrong with my cock.

I shouldn't be picturing my best friend like that without his permission. As soon as I take Zach out of the equation, my cock goes down.

From there, I go back on my own laptop to read articles that give even more advice on how to make it amazing for your bottom. It explains in great detail how to find the prostate and what it feels like.

By the time Zach gets home, I'm more determined than ever that I can do this with him. He comes in and gives me a hug.

"What did you get up to today?" he asks as I follow him into our bedroom. He's stripping off his clothes as he goes.

"Just lay in bed watching YouTube all day…nothing much."

Zach throws his shirt in the hamper but hangs up his jacket in the closet. He strips out of his dress pants in front of me like it's nothing, and I guess it should be nothing because we do it before bed all the time. This just feels different.

"You deserve a day of nothing," he says, slipping on some yoga pants and a crop top.

"You love crop tops, don't you?"

He turns to look at me. "Yeah, I do. They make me feel…like me… or like maybe at some point, I can be sexy."

"You are sexy, Zach." How can he not know how sexy he looked on that dance floor, or how sexy he looks right now with the curve of his hip showing and that trim waist of his?

His eyes widen, and he rubs his hands down his thighs like he doesn't know what to do. "Uh…thanks, Brady. That's sweet of you to say."

I try to help him make supper, but I'm not very good at it and end up just leaning against the counter, listening to him talk about his day.

"Do you think that you could bring Honey to the library for me tomorrow…at about ten o'clock? I have a group of preschoolers coming in, and the theme is dog rescue. If you can't, I'll come home and get her. It would just save me time if you're not doing anything."

"Sure, I'll bring her over." It'll also give me a chance to see him more.

Connor and Kelly come through the door from the garage,

carrying bags of whatever they bought. They eat with us, telling us about their shopping trip and teasing each other constantly.

Kelly pauses at one point and turns to Zach. "I forgot to ask you, did you get any messages today?"

Zach takes a drink, clearly avoiding an answer that I want to know as much as Kelly.

"Zach, come on…tell me," Kelly pushes.

"I got like two hundred messages while at work. It's insane. Half of these guys are like sixty years old. Are they nuts?!" He sets down his glass. "And at least a third of them started their message with a dick pic." He shudders. "I'm scarred for life now."

Kelly sighs. "So much for it being an app for relationships and not hookups. I'll go through them with you this evening. Maybe there will be a few nice ones in there."

No no no no no. I need Zach to stay off the app until I have a chance to talk to him.

Connor and Kelly do the dishes tonight, and Zach goes in to soak in the bathtub. All night, I wait for the perfect time to talk to him, but it never seems to happen.

He and Kelly narrow down the guys on the app to two that seem decent. Zach claims he'll message them tomorrow, that he's too tired tonight. And he must be because as soon as he curls up to me and I try to talk to him, he's asleep. He digs his leg between mine, and it dawns on me that it's silky smooth. He's been shaving his legs. They feel good on mine, and I think I like it.

THE NEXT MORNING, Kelly opts out of the gym, saying he can only handle it a few times a week. He does make breakfast so it's ready when we get home. He and Connor go back to bed while Zach gets a shower and dresses. I find my eyes studying his legs now, and they look as smooth as they felt.

After he leaves, I take a shower and relieve this need I constantly seem to have now. I visit with Mom, who is off work for the holidays, before taking Honey over to the library.

Zach has about fifteen kids sitting on little chairs in front of him, listening to him read a book about Madeline Finn reading to a shelter dog named Bonnie. I stay in the back, watching him read and how the kids look at him. One little boy starts crying for some reason, and Zach holds him in his lap while he finishes the book. He reads two more books before talking to the kids about their own dogs or pets, drawing them into a conversation. Every kid seems to want to be near him, and several take turns on his lap.

Zach sees me standing in the back and smiles, motioning for me to bring Honey up. He tells the kids about how Honey is a rescue dog and how much we love her. Then we both kneel on either side of Honey and let the kids take turns petting her. Honey eats it up and is so gentle with them.

Zach ends up leaving me, going off with some of the kids to help them find books. He's amazing with them and does it all with ease. He magically has tissues and wipes noses, talks to parents, and obviously loves every second of it. The kids adore him and follow him around. I hear *Mr. Zach... Hey Mr. Zach... Mr. Zach, can you help me?* It's nonstop, and yet I can tell that he's happy.

The kids are cute, and one little girl plants herself on my lap, petting Honey and talking to her like the dog understands every word. And maybe she does.

By the time all the kids leave, I have this vision of Zach when he's a little older, taking care of foster kids and giving them all the love they will need. He's going to be a great dad someday.

"Thanks for bringing Honey over," he says to me after he's seen all the kids out.

"I enjoyed it. The kids love you."

He shrugs, blushing a little. "It's my favorite part of the job. They are so innocent and full of life. I want them to learn about all kinds of books."

He wants them to have what he didn't have.

We talk a little longer before he has to get back to work, and I have to take Honey home. Seeing Zach at the gym and the library or even the club...it's all making me see him differently. He has a past and things he still needs support with, but he really has become stronger and found himself. He's amazing, and I don't think he understands just how special he really is.

FORTY-THREE

ZACH

"Hey guys, sorry I'm late." I set the bag of Chinese on the counter. "I stopped by the store to get groceries since I won't have time tomorrow."

Brady and Connor get up to bring the groceries in while Kelly and I put them away. We take our plates of Chinese into the family room, and I sink down on the couch with mine.

"Are you off work tomorrow?" Brady asks.

"Yes, we are closed now until next Monday. They used to stay open more, but it's a small town, and everyone wants to be at home for the holidays. I would have taken off tomorrow anyway since we are baking all day."

"Mom won't care if you bring that much to Christmas. Don't kill yourself baking too much."

Kelly swallows his bite of food and tells him, "It's for the LGBTQ-plus community center in Pine Falls. We are helping with the food for their Christmas Eve party for the kids. Our group is going to volunteer for it, and each of us has a few kids assigned to us that we've bought gifts for."

"I'd like to help, too. I didn't even know there was something like that there." Brady's eyes meet mine, and I know he's thinking of how I could have used a place like that when I was younger.

We sit around talking until Connor has eaten all the remaining food, and then I escape to take a long, hot bath. Being up at four-thirty in the morning and then on my feet all day, I'm tired by the time supper is over.

Brady is sitting on the bed when I come out of the bathroom. He has this serious look on his face, and I immediately go over to sit down facing him. "What's wrong?"

"Nothing's wrong. I want to talk to you about something." He looks nervous, which is making me nervous.

"You're not leaving again, are you?" I hug myself at the thought and pray he doesn't break me all over again.

"Noooo, I'm not leaving you again." He hooks my hips and brings me closer.

"Okay, then just tell me because you're scaring me when you're nervous like this." A million scenarios are running through my head right now.

"I overheard you and Kelly talking about how you need someone you can trust to help you get through all your firsts."

My cheeks are instantly hot, and I groan. "You're not supposed to know about these things."

He frowns. "Why not? We used to tell each other everything. I was the person you would talk to about these things, even if they were embarrassing."

"Because this is one of those things I don't think you want to know about. What am I supposed to say? *Hey Brady, I need a guy that will let me give him a blow job for the first time even though I'll suck at it?* No pun intended."

He half grins but then gets serious again. "Yes, that's what you're supposed to say. It's always been you and me. I know you and Kelly are close, but if you're worrying about something, I want to help."

"How in the world are you going to help, Brady? Go out and find someone for me? Message these men on the apps and find out who's not a serial killer or a rapist?"

"I want you to delete the app for now and not meet some guy on there to have your first time with. What if he hurts you? You could get seriously hurt if the guy isn't careful, especially because you've never had sex before."

I can't believe we are having this conversation. "You think I don't know that? I'm scared enough as it is, but if I never meet anyone, I'll end up being a forty-year-old virgin who works at a library and never gets to experience anything."

"I know…which is why I want to be the one to help you." His blue eyes are imploring me to let him help.

It's hard enough for me to think about being with anyone but Brady, but hearing him say he wants to help is making me want to cry. "Again, I'm not sure how you can help. If you want to meet the guy first, it's going to be kind of awkward to explain that the man I sleep with wants to screen them before we have sex. Like that doesn't sound crazy."

Brady rubs the back of his neck for a few seconds before answering. "No, that's not what I meant. I want to be the person you trust to help you with your firsts."

He's not saying what I think he's saying, is he? "I don't understand…"

"I want you to use me to try it all and learn everything. If it's me, then I know you'll be safe. I'll make sure we do everything right so you don't get hurt and can get the experience you need to be able to date easier."

I sit here staring at him, trying to figure out if I'm dreaming or in an alternate universe. "Am I in a dream right now…or a prank?" I look around to see if Connor is going to jump out and say *gotcha.*

Brady cups my chin, bringing my gaze back to him. "It's not a dream or a prank; I'm being serious. I can't handle the thought of you being hurt, and this is something I can help with. You can trust me, and we can get through it together."

And he thinks me having sex with him so I can date other people won't hurt me? I'm going to be devastated to have been that close to him, only to have it taken away. How would this ever work? Straight guys don't have sex with other guys. "But you're straight?"

"Yes, but we can still make it work. I get hard in the mornings next to you. We can use that. Besides, I think if someone puts their mouth on your cock, it's going to get hard, right? You're the most important person to me, Zach…and nothing should be embarrassing or shameful between us. We can do this together."

Part of me immediately wants to say yes because he's giving me the chance to be with him intimately. Something I've dreamed about forever. But the other part of me knows if I agree to this, I'm going to get hurt, and I might not ever recover from it. "I don't know, Brady. There are a lot of factors that could make this a terrible idea. What if it ruins our friendship? And how do we end it? I give you so many blow jobs and we have sex twice and boom, we never talk about it again?"

"It won't ruin our friendship. We won't let it. And as for it ending… we can communicate like adults. We'll do this until you're comfortable with sex, and then we can sit down to discuss ending it."

He makes it sound so reasonable, but it screams disaster. "I don't want to have sex with someone who is just having pity sex with me. How is your dick even going to be hard when you're with a guy?"

"Jesus, Zack, it's not pity sex. It's me giving you something you need, and I love being that for you. And it's not just a guy, it's you. If it doesn't work, then we can call it quits, but let me at least try to help you with this. Please…" He gives me this look of almost desperation. This really is important to him.

"I don't know, Brady. Once we've seen each other naked and your dick has been in my ass, I'm not sure we will ever look at each other the same again."

"Maybe not, but can you say that if this was me who needed help like this and you knew I was going to go off…meet up with some stranger that is bigger than me… What would you do?"

"I'd want to be the one to help you, but that doesn't make it a great idea."

"Why are you fighting this so hard? You know that no one will take care of you and make it good for you like I will. I'd die for you without hesitation. I can do this."

I know he'd die for me. Memories of him protecting me from the monster, of lying in a hospital bed with me, of him holding me while I cried after a panic attack…all come flooding back. He's proven to me over and over he would do anything to protect me. He'll do everything he can to protect me through this, too. "Okay, I'll consider it. Just give me a night to think on it and make sure I'm okay with it. I don't want to do anything to hurt you in any way either."

"Fair enough, but please don't message guys on the app until you make a decision. I worry about you."

"Okay, I won't. I'll let you know as soon as I decide." I could be kissing Brady…actually kissing him! I have so many butterflies in my stomach that I feel a bit light-headed. "Thanks for offering this. I know it couldn't have been an easy decision for you."

He runs his nose down mine and then kisses my cheek. "It was an easy decision to help you. I even spent all of yesterday doing research on how to do it right without hurting you."

"You researched how to have sex with a guy?"

"Yes, I watched gay porn, and I watched videos on how to be a good top. What to do, what not to do. I want to do it right."

Just knowing he watched gay porn makes me feel a little too hot. "You really *are* serious about this?"

"Yes, I want this to happen. Just you and me."

"I'll make a decision; just give me a little time."

He nods and I leave him alone in the bedroom, needing to get some space so I can think straight. I throw on a jacket and a pair of shoes and go out to sit on the patio. Honey runs around the yard, but it's so dark that I can barely make out where she is at.

What do I do?

Take a chance that my heart won't break at the end? Savor every second of Brady touching me? I'd be giving my virginity to my best friend, who I've been in love with forever. I would always have that to remember and hold on to.

I sit out here until I'm shivering and yet am no closer to a decision.

Kelly shows up and squeezes into the chair with me, covering us both with the blanket he brought. "What are you out here thinking so hard about? I can tell something is bothering you."

"I'll tell you, but you can't tell Connor."

"I won't tell a soul…so spill it."

"Brady just told me that he wants me to use him to do all my firsts with. That he doesn't want me going off to meet some guy that might hurt me."

"Wait…what? He wants to have sex with you?"

"Yeah, all of it."

"I'm confused. Isn't he supposed to be the straight one?"

"Yes, but he claims he can still do it. I wake up every morning with his ginormous, hard dick pressed against me, so maybe he can. I don't know."

Kelly shifts a little. "He's hard every morning, and it doesn't bother him that he's pressed against you?"

"I'm used to it, and it's not like he's awake. I even woke up one time to him kissing the back of my neck and moving against me in his sleep."

"Honey…straight guys don't kiss other guys in their sleep. Trust me."

"They must because he's straight. We sleep together every night, and when he's awake, all he does is hold me. He's never once tried anything."

"I don't know, Zach. Sometimes, guys like us know early on, but I've met guys that were married twenty years and then divorced, only to figure out they were gay. I know it's not likely, but it's possible he hasn't figured himself out yet."

"I don't want to have hope, or it'll make it worse. I don't know what to do. Getting to experience all my firsts with the man I'm in love with sounds like I've won the lottery. But knowing it's just him helping me and doesn't mean more…and in the end, I'll have to accept that's all I'll get—it's going to hurt like hell. What if I can't recover from it?"

Kelly wraps his arms around me, and I snuggle into him. "Ultimately, it's a decision you'll have to make for yourself, but don't let fear guide you. Maybe it's a gift to have this with him. Maybe it'll hurt, but you can recover from it. You have done so much without him these last months, and you would survive being hurt again. You need to ask yourself if you really think it would ruin your friendship or not. That's the most important part."

Deep down, I know it wouldn't ruin our friendship. Even if it hurt, we would cling to each other and get through it. "It wouldn't ruin our friendship."

"I don't know Brady well, but honestly, watching you two see each other when he came to the club…it was intense. There's this love that is almost tangible in the air around you two. He loves you; anyone can see that. And here at home, he watches you all the time. It's like you're the center of his universe. If you hadn't told me he was straight, I would have thought you were a couple that were truly in love."

Don't even think about getting your hopes up!

"I know he loves me. He's my home…always has been. Even the thought of dating someone and moving on *hurts* because he's my person."

"Sounds like you already know what you're going to do. I can't say it'll end well, but you know I'll be here for you every step of the way. You won't be alone."

"Thanks, Kelly. I hope you know how much I love you. You've become my best friend, and I am so grateful for you."

He hugs me tighter, kissing my cheek. "Aww, you're so sweet. Don't ever change. Not many people are so open and show emotion, but you give it all. It's beautiful to see. And I love you, too. You and I were meant to meet and will be friends for life. I can feel it."

We sit here together for a little while longer before going inside. I know that I'm going to end up saying yes, but I don't think I'll be able to sleep tonight if I know it's definitely going to happen. What if Brady wants to do something the second I tell him? I need to mentally prepare for this and find a way to guard myself a little.

Brady doesn't pressure me for a decision, and we don't talk about it. He reads to me, and when it's time to sleep, we get into the same position as usual. The only difference is that my body wants to get turned on and respond to him now that it knows I'll be allowed to touch him soon.

"What's wrong? You can't seem to hold still."

I flip over so my back is to him. "Nothing's wrong."

"Then why aren't you facing me?"

"Because my dick is hard, okay? Now that it knows you might touch it, he's not listening to me anymore."

"Oh, I guess that's a good sign…that he wants you to do this."

"He definitely wants to do this," I mumble, trying to will it to go down.

"So you're saying I turn you on," he says with humor.

"Yes, Brady, you turn me on. Now can we stop talking about being turned on, or I'm never going to get any sleep. I'm tired and have a long day of baking tomorrow."

He does stop talking but runs his fingers softly over my forehead and down my cheek until I relax and fall asleep.

FORTY-FOUR

ZACH

The light from the windows wakes me from a deep slumber. My eyes flutter open, and the brightness abruptly shows me I somehow slept in. I try to sit up in a panic, but Brady tightens his arm around me and won't let me up. I must have rolled over during the night because I'm facing him again.

"Go back to sleep," he says in a sleepy voice.

"I was supposed to go to the gym. Connor must think I ditched him!" I try to move but can't.

"I texted Connor and told him you were sleeping in. Now go back to sleep."

"You what?" I twist enough to see the digital clock, and it's after nine. "What happened to my alarm?"

"I turned it off. Now go back to sleep."

It's too late; my mind is already thinking about all the desserts we need to bake. I haven't even wrapped the presents I bought yet. "Brady?"

Blue eyes open to glare at me. "Can't we sleep until ten just once during my time off?"

I went six months wanting him to come home so I could lie next to him, and now I'm trying to rush off? "We can sleep," I whisper, burying myself even closer to him.

Brady's steady, slow breaths of slumber always bring this peace to me. There's a familiarity in it that feels like coming home. Comfort.

I don't sleep, but I lie here soaking up this feeling of him wrapped around me, of feeling safe and protected. In my life before Brady, no touch ever felt like this. It was so easy for him to hold me when I was crying in the woods that first day. Touch was something Brady grew up with, but for me, that moment was everything. The beginning of knowing love.

Kelly's knocking on the door a little after ten wakes Brady. He glances at the clock and then down at me. "Did you sleep anymore?"

"No, but I rested here with you."

He kisses my forehead and then untangles our bodies so I can get up. I think about telling him right now that I'm going to say yes to him helping me, but Kelly knocks again, and I have to hurry to throw clothes on.

Kelly and I start mixing up cookies as soon as I'm done eating a Pop-Tart and drinking some juice. We have a list of desserts we are baking, and I've never been so grateful for our big, beautiful kitchen. Kelly can cook some meals, but he hasn't baked a lot yet. He's hilarious trying to figure out how to dip peanut butter balls into chocolate to make buckeyes. Every single one he screws up seems to disappear in Connor's mouth, who is hovering for any chance at sweets.

Brady is sitting on a barstool paying bills like the mature adult he's become. Sometimes I feel like he's way older than us, with how mature and thought-out his actions are. I didn't think he was paying attention to me until I sneak a buckeye and he clears his throat behind me. "No more after that one."

I look over my shoulder, and he's staring at me with a pointed look. "You weren't supposed to see that."

"I know, but I did." He goes back to typing something on his laptop like his bossiness is just fine.

Kelly nudges me with his arm and whispers, "See, I told you he watches you all the time."

It makes me smile, knowing that he does. I missed him and his bossiness.

We have a fun day of baking together. Kelly keeps me laughing with his singing and dancing. He even gets Connor to dance in the kitchen with him. Their dancing is definitely not PG, and Brady exchanges a look with me.

You'd have to be blind not to see that they are attracted to each other. It dawns on me that Brady doesn't know Connor is pansexual, and yet he still gave me that look.

Does he know?

I give him a questioning look, and he answers with a quick nod as if he knows exactly what I'm asking. I would feel him out about it later, but I don't want to share what Connor should tell Brady himself.

After supper, Brady helps me wrap the gifts I bought for the kids. I can tell he's waiting for me to give him my answer, but he hasn't asked me about it yet.

THE NEXT MORNING, the beeping of my alarm brings me out of a deep sleep, only to feel Brady's hard length digging into my hip. He stirs but doesn't move away like he normally would. Which only makes my body respond by getting hard, too.

My face is pressed to his chest, and I can't see his eyes, but I can feel the change in his breathing. He's thinking about what we might be doing soon.

The alarm is really starting to annoy me, and I finally slide my leg from between his. As soon as he moves his arms, which were banded around me, I roll over to crawl across the bed. Turning the incessant beeping off, I scoot off the edge and hurry into the bathroom to shower, needing some release before being around Brady all day. I wonder if he's getting off out there while I'm rubbing one off in here. The thought makes me coat the shower tiles with my cum and then sag against it to catch my breath. If we do this…when we do this, I'll be in a constant state of arousal, and it's going to be so embarrassing.

When I come out of the bathroom with a towel wrapped around my waist, Brady is sitting on the edge of the bed. He gives me this stupid grin, as if he knows what I was doing in the shower. I flush but don't say anything, pulling out some hot pink briefs to wear. I might as well be rocking some color underneath the jeans I'll be wearing today.

"You fell asleep last night during the movie. We didn't get a chance to talk."

I turn to see his eyes silently giving me a pleading look to put him out of his misery and give him an answer so he can stop wondering. "Sorry, I didn't mean to."

"And?"

I walk over to stand between his legs, wanting to be close enough to see his deep blue eyes better. "And my answer is yes, but you have to promise me that this won't ruin us, and if you at any time decide you don't want to do this, you'll tell me right away."

"I promise to do both of those things. I want us to take this slow… no rushing."

Cupping his cheek with my hand, I run my thumb gently over his skin. "Okay, then I guess we are doing this."

"Yes, we are."

There's this long, silent pause.

Well, this is awkward already. "When are we starting this?"

"Tonight, we don't have much time before we need to leave for Pine Falls."

Tonight…

Great, I'll just walk around with a hard-on all day thinking about it. Inwardly groaning, I move away from him to get dressed in the closet. Kelly said to dress casual, so I pick jeans and a comfy red Henley for some Christmas color.

We take my SUV, but Brady drives, talking to Connor in the front while Kelly and I are snuggling in the back. His eyes meet mine in the rearview mirror, and I give him a smile.

The LGBTQ+ community center is bigger than I'd pictured it being. We arrive before the kids and spend the morning helping to set up tables and chairs, hanging more Christmas decorations, and preparing games for them. Our whole group is here, and I get to meet quite a few volunteers that are really nice. We seem to be the youngest volunteers; the others vary in ages from thirties on up to sixties.

Brady sticks close to me, which makes it easy for me to relax and enjoy myself. Several of the guys mention we are a cute couple, and instead of correcting them, Brady just smiles and says thank you. I raise my eyebrow at him, and he ignores it.

Then the kids start to arrive, and I forget about everything but them. Most are teenagers, but there are some younger ones, too. Some look so sad and defeated that it breaks my heart. Some are happy and excited to be here. There's one boy in particular, with the remnants of a black eye, who is here with his foster mom. He has to be about eleven or twelve. I ask Heather, who runs the center, what his story is, and she tells me his name is Wyatt. His homophobic father found out he was gay and went into a rage, beating him for it.

Wyatt's family wants nothing to do with him, so now he's in foster care.

I struggle to get my emotions under control. Brady tugs me into a hug, having heard the story with me. *Why does this happen?* It makes me sick. We aren't any different from anyone else. We love and hurt the same as a straight person.

I end up spending most of the day by Wyatt's side. He talks to me about what happened and how he feels, and I share some of what happened to me so he doesn't feel alone. He starts to come out of his shell the longer he's here and even smiles. It's an unforgettable day of games, food, presents, and even some music and dancing at the end, because Kelly gets them all going.

Before we leave, Wyatt's foster mom takes down my phone number and gives me hers. I've promised to come meet Wyatt here on some Saturdays so we can spend time together. It's hard to watch him leave, and when he runs back to give me a hug, I choke up and have to blink back the tears. If I could put him in a bubble and protect him from the world, I would.

Brady and I walk out to our vehicle together, and he breaks the silence by saying, "Is there anything Wyatt could have done wrong to deserve that?"

I give him a horrified look at his question. "No, of course not. He's so young and easy to love. Nothing he did could make him deserve that."

Brady stops to meet my eyes. "Exactly, that was you back then. You always thought you did something wrong. Sometimes, I think deep down, you still believe you were somehow to blame. Tell yourself what you would tell Wyatt."

His words sink into me, and I struggle not to cry. Brady wraps me up in his arms, pressing his lips to my forehead. "You were so tiny and sweet...easy to love."

"Thanks, Brady," I say with feeling when I can finally talk again. He's right. I have questioned what I did wrong to make them do to me what they did—so many times. But now I see myself like I see Wyatt, and I know I did nothing wrong. It wasn't even a tiny bit my fault.

I'm quiet all the way home and go in to take a shower, changing into pj's. Brady bypasses me to the shower, and my brain switches gears to what we are going to do tonight.

Are we going to just kiss? Do more than kiss?

Since it's Christmas Eve, we all put coats and shoes on, slipping out the back door and walking over to Mom and Dad's house. Honey greets me and wants all my attention. We'd left her there all day since we were going to be gone. Hugs are exchanged all around, and then we pile into the living room for a Christmas movie, popcorn bowls in hand. Brady sits on one end of the couch and I snuggle close, leaning against him. Kelly lies with his head on my lap and his feet on Connor's, who has squeezed into the only space left on this couch.

Halfway through the movie, Anna curls up in front of Kelly. The whole family has accepted him as one of us. He needed a family, and I'm happy that we've become that for him.

The movie ends and we sit around talking for a little while before walking back home. We will open our gifts early tomorrow morning at their place, as is tradition. Brady has already brought all our presents over there a couple of days ago.

When I walk into our bedroom, there are so many butterflies in my stomach that I feel a little sick. I shut myself in the bathroom and take some deep, calming breaths, trying to center myself. It doesn't help, so instead, I stand here staring in the mirror and give myself a pep talk about how this is just him helping me. We are just friends, and this doesn't mean more to him. After telling myself that a dozen million times, I brush my teeth and use mouthwash since I'm going to be kissing him.

Kissing Brady.

God, my world has tilted on its axis for sure. Brady comes in and starts brushing his teeth, too. We give each other nervous looks in the mirror.

Brady and I end up on the bed facing each other, with me begging my body to cooperate and not to throw up over nerves.

"We can do this," Brady assures me, using his fingers to comb some hair back from my eyes.

"I'm nervous."

"Why? It's just you and me. We can start with just a kiss tonight."

"Because I'm afraid that I'll embarrass myself," I admit.

"Nothing to be embarrassed about. We all suck at kissing at first, but that's why we are doing this...so you can practice."

Feeling my cheeks heat up, I try to explain it to him. "I'm afraid that you won't even have to touch me and I'll...you know..."

"Oh…" He shrugs. "So what if you do? I'm not going to laugh or be upset."

"Okay…" *Ohgodohgodohgod, this is really happening.*

Brady scoots back a little, sitting against the headboard of our bed. "Come straddle my lap."

My dick is already getting hard just knowing what's about to happen. I move to position myself on his lap like he wants as he stretches his legs out behind me. His hand comes out to lightly grip the side of my neck just under my ear, his thumb resting on my cheek. As he leans forward, I have to close my eyes, and then I feel his lips ever so softly press on mine. *It's Brady,* my soul whispers to me. His lips lift and press again, sending shivers all over my body. The next time, I open my mouth a little and kiss him back. This may not mean anything to him, but I decide to pour all the love I can into what we're doing…into this kiss.

It's Brady.

FORTY-FIVE

BRADY

Zach's lips are soft under mine, letting me kiss him lightly. His lips part and he mimics my kissing with his own. I thought it would be awkward and weird to kiss a guy, but it just feels like…Zach. Natural and beautiful, this feeling of us breathing each other in. I'm not sure which one of us deepens the kiss, but when I feel our tongues meet and he lets out this whimper of need, it's like someone sends a jolt of electricity through my body. Every nerve ending is begging for more, and I give it to them by wrapping my arms around Zach's back and drawing him closer. Fuck, we kiss like we are starving for each other, tongues dancing together and soft moans escaping from him.

Something inside of me whispers, *so this is what it's supposed to feel like.* This is why people love to kiss.

Zach rocks into me, and I feel his erection rub on mine, which is so rock-hard that I know if he keeps going, I'm going to come. I don't stop him or want to stop him; hearing his breaths and whimpers of need makes me want to give him everything. I just keep kissing him, my hands sliding down to his hips and encouraging him to take what he wants. He breaks away from the kiss with a gasp and then buries his face in my neck to moan as he comes. That moan releases something inside of me, and I start to come with him, streaks of pleasure like I've never felt taking over as I let go.

Zach is trembling in my arms, but totally limp, too. I try to catch my breath, needing to make sure he's okay. Running my hands over his back, I turn my head to press gently against his. "Are you okay?" There's this fear inside of me that I'll mess this up and hurt him.

"Mhmm," he mumbles in a sleepy voice.

"Was it good?"

"Mhmm." He presses his lips to my neck briefly.

I grin over how relaxed he is and ready to fall asleep on me. "We need to get cleaned up, and then you can sleep."

He sits up slowly, his cheeks flushed with what I think is embarrassment. "Did I kiss okay for the first time?"

He kissed better than any girl I've ever kissed before. "You were perfect. Quit worrying."

"Did you really come?" His eyes move down to take in my cum that's all over my abs and his stomach. When it gets hard, my cock doesn't stay in the confines of my boxer briefs or pajama pants. "Umm…yeah, I guess you did." His green eyes are wide as he touches where I came on his stomach.

"Come on, we both need to change." And I need a moment to think about all this.

Zach tilts his head to the side a little, studying me with worry in his eyes. "You aren't going to freak out and be mad at me, are you?"

His quiet tone, filled with fear, brings my arms back around him. "No, Zach, I'm not going to freak out or be mad." Normally I would kiss his forehead, but now I give him a light kiss on the lips. Things are changing, and it gives me this funny feeling in my stomach.

He nods, slipping off my lap to get a clean pair of underwear out of the drawer. Mine didn't get anything on them, and I just strip out of my pajama pants, wiping my stomach off with it before chucking it in the hamper.

Honey is asleep on her side of the bed, and I make a mental note to shut her out of the room the next time. It's weird knowing a dog was watching us, or maybe she wasn't since she hasn't opened her eyes or moved.

Zach comes out in some gray briefs and crawls into bed, assuming our normal sleeping position with me. He's asleep in minutes, but I lie here forever, thinking about what happened. *Why did this feel so different from kissing girls?* I've never gotten hard kissing a girl, much less came from it. Even when Carrie straddled me and rubbed herself against me, I didn't get hard. But with Zach, I was so turned on just from kissing him and hearing his moans. I don't know if it's knowing I'm bringing him pleasure that did it or just that we are familiar with each other? I know that I'm not gay because I've never once seen a guy in the locker room or on TV and wanted them. Never gotten hard over them or had thoughts of them. I'm not sure why my body responded to Zach, but I want to do this again. I want to give him whatever he needs. My head starts to hurt as I try to figure out what is wrong with me, and finally, I manage to turn it off so I can fall asleep.

CHRISTMAS MORNING COMES EARLY when I hear a knock on the bedroom door a second before Kelly comes in to jump on the bed. He snuggles in behind Zach, kissing his cheek.

"Why are you in here?" I groan. "It's too early to get up."

"It's Christmas and we have to get over to Mom and Dad's house," Kelly says happily. He's taken to calling them Mom and Dad, too, which my parents seem to love.

Zach shifts, rolling over in my arms so he can cuddle with Kelly. "Good morning."

"Morning…now get up so we can start the day!"

I roll my eyes at Kelly's exuberance, and he reaches over to flick me. "Hey!" Before I can flick him back, Zach sits up to block us from each other.

"Okay, you two…try to remember it's Christmas and all about love today." Zach stretches. "Also, Brady is mostly naked…so if you don't want to see that, you might want to go bug Connor until he gets dressed."

"Hmm…that's a difficult decision. Brady is pretty hot." Kelly leans around Zach to wink at me.

Connor takes that moment to show up in the doorway. "Having a threesome without me? I'm so hurt."

Zach motions him in. "It's your job to take Kelly out and babysit him until Brady gets dressed."

Kelly laughs. "Yeah right, like he could keep me from doing anything."

Connor drags Kelly to the end of the bed by his ankle and picks him up to throw over his shoulder, smacking his ass lightly. "You keep believing that."

Instead of screaming, Kelly winks at us with a grin. "Oh no, don't carry me, daddy bear!" he exclaims dramatically.

"You're older than I am, brat." I hear Connor say as they disappear out the door.

Zach scoots out the other side of the bed to get a quick shower. I think about going in to shower with him, but I don't think we are ready for that yet. He comes out with his hair done and a towel wrapped around his waist. When he sees me still sitting on the bed, he motions with his hands at me. "Get out of bed and hurry up…presents!"

Grinning, I get out of bed and hurry to get ready. I can't wait for him to open his Christmas present. He has no idea what's in store for him today.

Kelly has pancakes ready for us when we come out. Now that Anna and Meg are a little older, we don't have to open presents at six in the morning. But still, Zach and Kelly cram down their food like we're in a race for our lives. Connor grins at me over their heads as they chatter about what Christmas movies we are watching today. I shake my head, grinning back.

We make our way next door, where everyone is up and ready, except Grandma and Grandpa. They show up just in time, bringing Honey in with them since she was done running around the backyard.

Meg passes out all the presents to the right person, and then we take turns going around to open up a gift. It's my favorite part, getting to watch people's faces as they open their presents.

Kelly just keeps looking at everybody. It dawns on me that he has the same expression as Zach when he came to live with us and had his first real Christmas. Zach was right; Kelly is special and does fit in here. I'm glad he asked him to live with us for now. I watch him open up the gift from my parents. Inside is a laptop that I'm sure is top of the line.

Kelly stares at it and then looks at my parents. "These cost a fortune…"

Mom gives him a smile. "You're in graphic design and need one for school that isn't breaking all the time. They said this one will do every-thing you need. They downloaded the top programs for you, too."

"Thank you, I don't know what to say…"

I have never seen Kelly speechless before, but he is right now. He's about to get up and hug them when Dad motions to the card. "Open that first…your gift isn't over."

He opens the envelope and then reads the card before studying the paper that fell out when he opened it. Zach puts his arm around him because anyone can see he's struggling not to cry.

"Why? Why would you do this?" He loses his battle with the tears.

"Because you're special and a part of this family, and because we can and wanted to," Dad answers.

Mom and Dad must really think the world of him if they are doing this after only knowing him for such a brief time. He does have a way of making everyone love him. Plus, it's obvious Zach adores him, and they are going to be inseparable. It confirms the decision I made earlier this week was the right one.

I have no idea what my parents did exactly, but my guess is they gave him some money, and it wouldn't surprise me if they paid his college tuition. It's what they would have done for Zach or me. Connor's parents paid for his, or I'm sure my parents would have helped him, too.

We go around opening up gifts, and I wait until everyone is done before handing Zach his present. He gets off the floor and sits on my lap to open it. Moving the tissue paper, he pulls out a red fanny pack with Mickey Mouse ears on it. "This is cute, thanks, Brady."

"There's more." I nod to the box.

He reaches in and pulls out Mickey Mouse ears to wear and slips them on his head. Next, he brings out two T-shirts that have the outline of Cinderella's castle with the words "My First Disney Trip" on them. One is his size and one is mine. He stares at them and then looks at me. "I don't understand…"

Mom has figured it out and is smiling already.

Zach takes out the red folder on the bottom, setting the box aside before he opens it. His eyes get huge as he reads the flight itinerary I printed out and then leafs through the Disney packet they mailed me. His eyes are filled with tears when he looks up at me. "You're taking me to Disney World?"

"Yes, we are going to Disney."

He throws his arms around my neck, hugging me tightly. "Oh my God, I'm going to Disney! It's like my biggest dream! I'll get to see Space Mountain and Cinderella…and the parade…and Mickey Mouse!"

I don't think I've ever seen him as excited as he is right now.

He pauses. "Wait… I have to work on Monday."

"No, I called your boss over a month ago, and she knows you won't be there."

"You planned this while you were away?"

"Yes, I wanted to do something with you before I started work. We leave later this afternoon."

His face falls. "I can't go then."

"Why not?"

"Because I promised Kelly that I would spend the holidays with him. I'm not breaking my promise."

"It's okay, Zach. Connor and I can spend it together. I want you to go enjoy your vacation," Kelly says, giving him a smile.

"No, I'm not breaking my promise. I know what it's like to need someone."

I lean over to whisper in his ear. "You might want to check the folder for how many tickets are in there." Thank God I booked two more flights after seeing how attached he was to Kelly. I had to sneak a look at Kelly's license when he left his wallet on the counter, just to get his info for it.

He flips through the folder and pulls out all four tickets, then waves them at Kelly. "We are going to Disney!"

Kelly just sits there in shock for a minute until Connor nudges him with his foot. "You mean I'm going to Disney, too?"

What ensues next is total chaos. Zach and Kelly are jumping around like idiots. I swear Disney turns them into little kids.

Kelly hugs me when they finally calm down. "Thank you, Brady. I've never been anywhere before."

"You're welcome. Once I saw Zach and you together, I knew he wouldn't leave you behind. Your seats aren't right with us on the plane, and I could only get one extra room, so you and Connor will have to share. It has two beds in it, though."

Kelly gives Connor a saucy grin. "You have to share a room with meeeeeeeeeee."

"God help me," Connor mutters, but he doesn't look that upset about it.

I'm not sure how much money Kelly has, but I want to make sure he knows he doesn't need any for this trip. "It's an all-inclusive trip to Disney. You don't need to worry about paying for food or anything."

He smiles, a flash of relief on his face, making me glad I said something. Disney is super expensive when it comes to food. "I didn't have time to get you both shirts, but we can get some when we get there."

Zach comes back over to crawl in my lap, laying his hand on my cheek. "Thank you, Brady. It means the world to me that you were planning this while you were gone...that you were thinking of me."

I don't think he has any idea how much I've thought of him and missed him or what I would do to make him happy. I'd give him the moon if I could.

FORTY-SIX

BRADY

Zach and Kelly end up in the kitchen helping Mom prepare food, with Grandma sitting at the island. The girls are trying to help, but at eleven and thirteen, they are getting in the way quite a bit.

Connor is standing by me, watching them talk excitedly about all the things they are going to do. He leans over. "You do realize they are going to be like little kids running around Disney until we are exhausted?"

"Yes, I do. But I'll admit I'm excited about going, too. It's been a long time since we went on a vacation." With Zach, we didn't take our yearly vacations because Mom and Dad didn't think he could handle it, especially with his panic attacks and anxiety over being around a lot of people. I don't think any of us felt comfortable with the idea, but now I think it's time.

Dad makes sure to talk to me after our big turkey dinner, reminding me about Zach's asthma and to have a plan if he should have a panic or asthma attack. I decide I should talk to Connor and Kelly about it, and as soon as Zach is busy with Mom, I sneak them away to Dad's office to discuss it. We are all in agreement on not letting Zach alone at all and making sure whoever is with him is carrying a spare rescue inhaler. We are also going to watch for situations that might scare him and try to keep him between us. Maybe we are being overprotective, but the last thing I want is for him to feel like he ruined our vacation because he had a panic attack.

Zach has a hard time hugging Honey goodbye, but my parents and grandparents both promise him they will spoil her until we are back. Anna has offered to let Honey sleep with her, and that helps Zach feel a little better.

We all hug one last time and then carry our gifts back to our house. Now is when the madness begins. Zach and I are in our room with my two suitcases lying open on the bed. He's trying to google what the temps are in Florida right now. It looks like it's going to be fairly warm for most of the trip. He texts a screenshot of them to Kelly and then starts packing way too many clothes.

"You realize that you'll probably buy Disney shirts while you're there and not even wear this stuff," I say.

"You're probably right." He takes out a few shirts to set aside. He opens his bottom drawer to get socks out, and I see boxes of what look like sex toys from a distance.

"What are those?"

He flushes and tries to close the drawer, but I pull it open again, squatting down to see what he bought.

"Kelly dragged me to a sex store to buy things he thinks I need for...you know."

I've read a lot about prep and figured I'd have to stop somewhere to get things, but it's all here. I take out the lube, butt plug, and before I can grab the douche bulb, Zach snatches it up and hides it behind his back.

"You're not supposed to know about prep stuff; it's mortifying," he huffs.

"I'm going to be sticking my cock in your ass, Zach. I think you need to get over being mortified. I've read all about prep and know what goes into it. Not everyone decides to douche beforehand, but I think it'll make you more comfortable with what will happen. Especially the first time."

He covers his face with his free hand, groaning. "Oh my God, we cannot be having this conversation."

I stand up to toss the lube and butt plug into my suitcase. "Pack the box you're hiding in your suitcase. I don't know if we will get to that while we are on vacation, but bring it in case we do."

Zach hides it under some clothes. "Does it feel hot in here?"

He's so adorable the way he gets all flustered over being embarrassed. I lean over to close the drawer and spot leather. Picking it up, I try to figure out what it is. "What is this?"

"It's a harness that you wear to gay clubs on leather night or kink night or some wear it any night. Kelly insisted I will need one when we go out to them."

I hand it over to him. "Try it on; I want to see."

"You realize we are in a hurry."

"Yes, so do it quickly."

He strips off his shirt and puts on the harness, adjusting some buckles to make it fit tightly. I stand here staring at him, trying to decide what I think about it. The leather on sweet, innocent Zach makes him have this "I'm a bad bottom boy, come dominate me" look. I'm not sure that's what it means, but it's where my mind goes. Actually, my mind goes to all sorts of places I never thought it would.

"Are you done staring at me?"

"Yes, but you're crazy if you think I'm letting you go to a club dressed like that without me. You'll have men all over you." Men who'll want to hold on to that harness and do…things to him.

He takes it off, stuffing it back in the drawer and closing it. "I highly doubt men are going to want to date me if I bring you to the club as my own personal bodyguard."

Fine by me.

Now that we've brought up sex, I really want to kiss him again and see if last night was a fluke thing. If we had time, I'd so find out, but we are already going to be pushing it.

Zach and I are going to check in our luggage, but both of us are taking backpacks. We stuff some books, travel paperwork, and Zach's inhalers into them. We also pack our chargers, earbuds, and my iPad.

Connor and Kelly wheel their suitcases in, which they borrowed from my parents. Each of them has a backpack as well.

"Are your parents going to be upset that you're not visiting for Christmas?" I ask Connor.

"No, Dad took Mom to Hawaii to celebrate their silver anniversary. They knew I'd be with you guys and that it would be okay."

Everything seems to be working out. I double-check that we have our tickets, that everyone has their ID on them, and then text Dad. He had offered earlier to take us to the airport, and I know it's hard for him to see Zach go on a trip. The trip to the ER this last time really scared my parents, and it's only been a month since it happened. I don't think anyone would have told me if I hadn't asked Dad about it after learning from Connor. Dad made it sound worse than Connor, and I'm still pissed that no one called me and that I wasn't there for Zach when he needed me.

Dad drops us off and I see him hug Zach extra long, saying a few words to him. He hugs me next, telling me quietly, "Please take care of him and be careful."

"I will, Dad."

"Take care of yourself, too. Love you, Son."

"Love you, Dad." I have the best dad in the world.

Zach is nervous going through the airport. We checked our luggage in at the curb and thankfully only have our backpacks. It makes it easy for me to keep an arm around his back while he holds Kelly's hand. I try to steer us clear of people as much as possible.

I paid for first-class tickets, knowing he would freak being closed in by strangers. Connor and Kelly are two rows up from us, where we can't see them.

Zach is as close to me as he can get while still wearing his seatbelt. I put my arm around his back and kiss the top of his head. "You're going to be okay. It's only a two-hour flight, and we'll be there."

He's terrified during the take-off, but then settles down and even looks out the window. For the last hour, he sleeps with his head resting on me.

The descent is harder on him than the take-off, and I have him use his inhaler because he sounds a little wheezy after we land. I ask Kelly to sit with him while Connor and I get the luggage. I'd reserved transport, and we are soon on our way to the Four Season's Resort. I might have gone all out on this vacation, but I wanted it to be perfect and to know it'd be a safe place for Zach.

Zach's and Kelly's mouths open in shock as we pull up. It's cute how they cling to each other as they walk inside—as if this is too good to be real. I did manage to get us side-by-side suites, at least. Each room has a balcony where we can sit outside if we want.

We decide to drop our stuff in our rooms and eat in the restaurant downstairs before retiring to our rooms for the night. It's been a long day, and we are all tired.

Kelly and Zach stare at the prices on the menus, and I can tell they are nervous. I finally put down my menu to address the both of them.

"Look. Everything at Disney is expensive. I picked this place and wanted this trip. I don't talk about my trust fund much, but I can afford to do this and not have it make a difference in the amount of money I have. So I don't want to see worried faces or second-guessing on costs. This is a Christmas present, and you're going to enjoy it. I'm paying for everything, and I like being able to do this for you guys, so stop worrying. I'm sure this won't be the last time we come here because Zach is going to fall in love with this place. Now pick what you want from the menu so we can order because I'm starving."

That seems to do the trick because they both pick out what they want, and we stuff ourselves with food.

Back in our rooms, Zach and I take turns showering. Dad calls to make sure we made it here okay, and I talk to him for a few minutes.

Zach and I don't even bother with pj bottoms or shirts, instead crawling into bed in our underwear. He's wearing these low-rise trunks that he seems to prefer; this one is purple.

As soon as we cover up in bed, Zach gravitates to my side like he always does. I wait about all of three seconds before I lower myself to kiss him. I know instantly that last night wasn't a fluke because I feel a heat between us that could easily ignite the fireworks I didn't think existed. This time I'm on top and can control our movements more. We are both seeking friction, and when I rock against him, he moans into my mouth. Fuck, I could come right now just from that sound. Pulling back, I stare down at his heated eyes and red, swollen lips.

Deep down, I feel this shock inside me over wanting to touch him and make him come. I want to see his heavy-lidded eyes and hear his moans. What the fuck is happening to me?

Holding myself up with one hand, I slide the other between our bodies slowly, watching him as I rub my fingers over his trunks, tracing the head of his cock and then down its length.

"Ohhh...Brady," he moans, arching up into my hand.

I keep stroking and rubbing, cupping his cock through the fabric and squeezing gently.

"Stop...you're going to make me come too fast," he begs, his chest rising and lowering in rapid succession.

I know he's embarrassed to come fast, but I love that he's so turned on that he can't control it. It's so fucking hot to watch his eyes with this desperate, needy look of desire. Moving my hand up slightly, I trace the edge of his trunks, and his eyes flare with anticipation.

"Are you going to come for me when I touch you?" My voice sounds husky. A sound I've never heard before.

"Yes…I won't be able to stop it," he whines, digging his fingers into my back like he's trying to hold on.

"Good, I don't want you to stop it." I slip my fingers underneath the waistband and down to caress him. He's so hard, yet his skin feels soft under my fingertips. My eyes stay on his, memorizing the way they glaze over when I touch him. My fingers curve around his cock, and I gently grip it like I would my own, running my finger over his slit. A few strokes and a long, deep moan comes from his mouth, his body tightening up as he lets go. I rub him through the orgasm until he shudders and goes limp.

Watching him come has my own cock leaking, and I kneel up to free it, stroking myself as I stare at the cum on his stomach—the evidence of how much pleasure I gave him with barely a touch. But it's when I look up at his eyes and find them on my cock, still hungry and wanting, that I can't hold back any longer. "Fuck," I growl out, jetting hot streams of cum on his stomach. Mixing his with my own.

I've never felt such an intense orgasm, and I try to get some control over my shaky limbs, coming down from the high. I'm doing good until Zach runs his finger through some of my cum and lifts it to his mouth to taste. His eyes close and he sucks his finger until it pops from his mouth, letting out this *mmmm* sound as if he fucking loves it.

Fuck fuck fuck fuck. I want my cock in his mouth and to come down his throat. I'm already getting hard again just watching him. I take a deep, steadying breath and remind myself that this is Zach and I need to take it slow with him. Pulling my underwear back up over my cock, I get off the bed, praying he won't notice my shaky legs. He needs to think I know what I'm doing and that I have control over this. "Stay there," I order, rushing into the bathroom to get a warm washcloth and towel.

His eyes never leave my face as I wipe our cum from his stomach gently before drying it with the towel. I take them back to the bathroom and then crawl into bed to pull him into my arms.

"Are you okay?"

"I think so. Maybe a little embarrassed that I came so quickly."

"I like the way you respond and how turned on you get."

"You taste good," he says in almost a whisper.

Fuck. I kiss his forehead and will my cock to stay down. "You'll get to taste more soon."

"Umm…Brady?"

"Yeah?" I run my hand up and down his bare back slowly.

"I changed my mind about the sex part."

What? "Why? We already talked about this." Why am I so upset?

"Because your dick is huge and is going to wreck me," he whispers.

My body relaxes and I can't help but grin. "It's going to be fine. Trust me. I'm not going to just ram it in the first time we do any ass play." I never thought I would even utter the words ass play. "We'll start with fingers, maybe the butt plug. I'll stretch you carefully until you're ready."

"But it's huge!"

"I thought bottoms were size whores, or at least I read that somewhere."

"If they are, they've probably never seen your dick before," he says under his breath.

"Oh, come on, it's not that big. Stop worrying about it and trust me." I honestly think he doesn't know what is considered big.

He's quiet for a minute and then whispers, "I do. Thank you for doing this with me, Brady. It means more to me than you can know."

He's so sweet it makes me want to curl around him and protect him from the world. I wrap him tightly into me, smiling as he slips his leg between mine like he always does. "Thank you for trusting me."

After that, his body relaxes and he falls asleep. I struggle to quiet my mind and fall asleep, though. *What is going on with me?* I'm turned on by Zach, and I don't understand why. Is this a long-term thing, or am I going to lose interest? I don't want to hurt him by promising him something, only to find out that this is all a fluke thing.

I dated Carrie for months and was never turned on. Now that I know what I should have been feeling, it's even more apparent to me that I'm broken when it comes to sex. I'm not gay or I'd be attracted to men. I'm not sure I even like women. The more I think about it, the more I realize that I never have been attracted to women like the other guys. I dated them because that's what guys do in high school. Even then, I barely dated compared to my teammates. Most girls, once they figured out things weren't going to get hot and heavy, didn't care that I never called them again.

The one time I tried to go further with Carrie, I didn't like it. I'm not really sure why guys like going down on a girl. It did nothing for me. She'd tried to give me a hand job, and I did get hard, but it didn't feel right or last long. I think she was offended I went limp and didn't come, which is why I tried oral on her to make up for it.

I rub my hand over Zach's soft skin, and just touching him calms me. He has such a beautiful heart, and I never want to hurt him. I need to keep perspective of why we are doing this and not let him too close because I don't understand my own body right now and can't promise him anything.

"I love you, Zach," I whisper, closing my eyes to get some sleep. Tomorrow Zach and Kelly will be running around at full speed. I smile at the thought before falling asleep.

FORTY-SEVEN

ZACH

A faint showing of the sun lightens the room enough to wake me up. I'm instantly wide awake because today we are going to see so many things that I've dreamed of seeing. Brady is still asleep, which is no surprise. He loves to sleep in and probably thinks this vacation means sleeping in until noon—never going to happen. I fully expect Kelly to be knocking on our door before eight, and I have to agree we should get an early start.

I still can't believe I'm here, but mainly I can't believe what's happening between us. Somehow I thought when he said he'd help me with my firsts, it would be more…clinical. He would let me practice mild kissing or giving a blow job. I'd imagined it being more instructional and friend-like. Instead, it's everything I dreamed it would be with Brady. There's this intensity to it, this feeling of passion. All the love between us is very much a part of every touch and kiss.

I don't understand Brady or what is happening. Straight guys don't get hard over kissing a guy, do they? Since that first kiss, he's watched me with an almost feral look of hunger and want. He's turned on by what we are doing.

The expression on his face when he watched me come and how he jacked off in front of me… All of that wasn't what I think a straight man would be like.

It feels natural between us, an extension of the love and closeness we already have for each other.

I can't get my hopes up, though, or expect this to turn into more because he didn't offer more, and I don't want to get hurt. Okay, more hurt than I already will be. I need to talk to Kelly about how intense and aroused Brady is. Maybe he'll understand it better.

And I need to stop obsessing about it right now because the answers won't magically appear. Today is about Disney and happiness, fairytales and magic.

Unable to lie here any longer, I carefully maneuver out of Brady's arms and hurry into the bathroom. I'm dressed, shoes on, and have my fanny pack filled with what I need, and Brady still isn't awake. There's a knock on the door and I grin, knowing it has to be Kelly.

He's standing there smiling, looking as excited as I am. "You ready to do this?"

"Yes, but Brady isn't up yet."

"Neither is Connor." He looks as bummed as I feel.

"We could go down and eat breakfast while they are sleeping...and then see if they have a T-shirt and fanny pack for you in their shop. I have Brady's card, and we can go wild." I'll use my card, but I don't want him to feel bad if I pay for it. Brady has already told him he'd be buying him those things.

He claps his hands, and I sneak out of the room, shutting the door quietly behind me. Laughing, we hurry to the elevators and take one down to the main floor to find a restaurant. There are several, but we get a table at Ravello and order breakfast.

"Do you think this is real, or are we dreaming?"

Kelly grins. "I think that if we are dreaming, I don't want to wake up."

"Me neither." I stare out the window at the sun, marveling at how beautiful it is. "Remind me to get some sunglasses."

We've decided the Magic Kingdom should be the first park we visit on our trip, and the map is currently between us on the table. We mark which rides we absolutely have to go on and study it so we know how to get there.

Our food comes and we eat while trying to decide where to start first, Tomorrowland or Adventureland.

About halfway through breakfast, Brady and Connor show up at our table. I look up to see Brady scowl at us, and Connor's expression isn't much better.

"What's wrong with you two?"

Brady pulls out his chair to sit down before leaning over close to my ear. "Don't leave the room without me again."

I think he's actually pissed at me. "We just came down to eat breakfast so you could keep sleeping."

"Next time, wake us up," Connor says, giving Kelly the same look Brady gave me.

Brady is never mad at me, and I don't know how to handle it. Tears form in my eyes, and I duck my head so I don't have to see how upset he is with me. "I'm sorry… We were just excited," I say, hating that my voice cracks.

Brady sighs, reaching over to cup my chin and tilting it so I'm forced to look at him. "I'm sorry if I seemed upset with you. I'm not mad at you; I was *worried*. Disney World is a big place, and I'd feel better if you two have one of us with you all the time. Especially after your last asthma attack…I worry about you."

I nod, wishing now that I'd woken him up.

"At the very least, you two could have left us a note where you were going," Connor adds. "We woke up and didn't have a clue where to find you."

Kelly rolls his eyes. "You do realize we both have cell phones, and you could have just called us."

Brady takes mine out of his pocket, sliding it over. "You forgot yours by the bed."

Connor gives Kelly another death stare. "And I tried calling yours, and you didn't answer."

Kelly digs his phone out of his pocket and then grins. "Oops, it's on silent."

That makes Connor roll his eyes. "Better not do it again, brat."

"Oh yeah, daddy bear? What are you going to do to me if I do?" Kelly is grinning way too big.

"Spank your little ass like you deserve." He tries to sound serious, but it doesn't work.

"I'm definitely doing it again now," Kelly mouths off to him.

They have a stare-off that crackles with sexual tension, neither one of them breaking away.

The server showing up to get Brady's and Connor's orders is probably the only reason they aren't having sex on the table right now. I think Connor keeps forgetting that he hasn't told Brady about being pan yet.

As soon as the server leaves, Brady reaches over to take my hand, his eyes on the map between Kelly and me. "I see you two have been busy."

"Yes, we've marked down all the rides and attractions we have to go on, and the best way to fit it all in," I answer, handing over the map so he can see.

He studies it and passes it over to Connor to look. I think they are both more excited than they let on because they eat quickly so we can leave. We do stop by the little shop first and get some Disney shirts for all of us. I find sunglasses and Kelly picks out a fanny pack. Back up at our rooms, Kelly and Connor change shirts, and Brady decides Kelly can carry my spare inhaler, which I think is silly. I have one with me, and it's not like this fanny pack is going anywhere.

We finally take the shuttle to the Magic Kingdom and our day at Disney begins. It truly is my every dream come true. Every attraction is so happy and gives me that same feeling as when I watch Disney movies. Brady either has his arm around me or has ahold of my hand. I'm sure every person we pass thinks we are a couple. Although, more often than not, Kelly is on my other side, holding my hand. They try to pretend they aren't watching me for signs of panic or asthma issues, but I can tell they have formed some sort of pact together.

Brady has almost kissed me on the lips several times, and I think Connor is picking up on the change between us. He's given Brady some weird glances throughout the day.

When Connor and Kelly want to go on the Haunted Mansion ride, Brady and I sit on a bench nearby. I know it probably won't be that scary, but I still can't make myself go on.

Brady tugs me onto his lap when he sits down, and I lean into him. "Are you having fun?"

I look into his eyes to make sure he sees how sincere I am. "I've never had so much fun. It's as happy as I always dreamed it would be. I love it." I look around at all the smiles and happiness. "You know, when I saw my first Disney movie at your house...it was Tangled...and then I learned about this place. All I could think about was that if I could come here and just feel that magic for myself, then maybe I would have my own fairytale. Maybe, like Cinderella, I would find love and happiness even though my family didn't love me. I would lie in bed at night and dream of this, trying to escape, or maybe it was hope… I don't know. But being here now…with you, it's everything I thought it would be."

Brady leans closer to press his lips to mine. It's a sweet, gentle kiss that says he loves me. I can feel it flow into me, as if it's my next breath and my next one again. Love has this way of almost tangibly causing pain in this feel-good hurt kind of way.

His mouth lifts from mine and then kisses my forehead. Emotion is thick in my throat, and I need to be closer to him. I turn my body so I can hug him tightly, burying my face in his neck. He embraces me back, giving me the feeling I was craving by holding me to his chest, his arms tight around me.

"I love you, Brady."

"I know, baby. I love you, too."

It's the first time he's used baby as an endearment when I'm not having a panic attack or crying. Hope flares inside of me, and I don't snuff it out successfully this time. We stay in that position, neither of us moving. I needed this… Maybe I will always need this.

"Is Zach okay?"

I hear Connor's question and raise my head to see Kelly sinking down on the bench next to us.

"He's fine," Brady answers for me, easing up on his hug so I can move.

Connor is standing in front of us, and I give him a wave. "I'm fine. Just needed to be held for a minute." I sound like such a freaking baby…*needed to be held for a minute*… What eighteen-year-old says that?

Kelly brings in humor like usual. "I need to be held, daddy bear. You going to hold me?"

Connor rolls his eyes but grins. "I'll hold you down while I spank you."

"Bring it," Kelly taunts, his eyes daring Connor to follow through.

"Okay, you two. Save it for the hotel room tonight," Brady mutters, helping me off his lap.

I think Connor has finally realized that Brady knows he's not straight. He doesn't say anything, but I can tell he wants to talk to Brady about it. I'm sure it'll happen when they are alone.

The rest of the day is full of laughter, amazing food, meeting Disney characters, and rides. We do some shopping toward the end of the day, buying souvenirs and little gifts for the girls. Brady has already told me he wants to bring the whole family next time.

We stay till the very end to see the fireworks and light show. All four of us are exhausted and have sore feet by the time we get back to the hotel.

Kelly and I give each other a hug before parting to our own rooms. Any previous thought of staying up to swim is gone with the fatigue I'm feeling. I just want a shower and then bed.

Brady calls Dad to check in since he's texted to ask how everything is going. I talk to both Mom and Dad for a few minutes, reassuring them that I haven't freaked out over the crowds and that my asthma is okay. I hand the cell back over to Brady and go into the bathroom, stripping down and stepping into the shower.

Even though I'm tired, I take the time to shave my legs to keep them smooth. Is Brady going to want to do more tonight? I'd like to last longer than five seconds and decide to get off now so I can keep from coming so quickly if we do anything.

Laying one hand on the wall to support myself, I stroke my hard length slowly, letting my mind think of Brady and how he moved his hand over my dick. I'm close to release when I feel Brady behind me, pressing into my back and kissing my neck.

"Put both your hands on the wall," he orders in that low, sexy voice he used last night, too.

My hand regretfully loosens around my dick, and I rest it on the wall next to my other one.

I'm naked in the shower with an equally naked Brady. What is happening to my life?

Brady's lips press under my ear, sending shivers over my body. His strong hands feel down my chest, lower and lower, until he's encasing my erection in his palm. I can feel how hard his dick is against my back, his chest and body—so much bigger than mine—enfolding around me. Our size difference always makes me feel safe. He's stronger and bigger, a physical reminder that he can protect me.

My thoughts zero in on the pleasure he's giving me as he starts to stroke my length slowly.

"During this...your cock is mine to touch and only mine," he growls against my neck.

"Brady," I whimper, "you're going to make me come."

He stops stroking for a minute, kissing my neck and shoulder slowly.

I barely catch my breath before he moves his hand up and down in this way that feels so good. Every time I get close to release, he stops and then restarts. Finally, I can't take anymore and become a babbling, pleading mess.

"I've got you, baby," he says near my ear, stroking me faster and not stopping. He sends me barreling off that cliff into sheer pleasure as I come and come until I can barely keep my legs under me. His arm bands around my waist to hold me up so I don't fall. His lips and tongue move over my back as I feel him jacking off behind me.

"Please, let me taste you," I beg before I even think about what I'm saying.

He groans and moves away his arm so I can turn and sink to my knees. Staring up at him, I open my mouth and stick out my tongue, begging for it. There's so much raw desire on his face as he gazes down at me kneeling here. *At me kneeling for him.*

"Fuuuuuuck," he growls out, his body tightening as he starts to come. He lays the head of his dick on my tongue as hot, thick jets of cum shoot into my mouth. I swallow several times, moaning over getting this gift from him, a taste of him. If I thought his eyes were full of desire before, right now, they are a million times more intense. I run my tongue up his slit, trying to get every last drop before swallowing again.

"Jesus...baby, I've never seen anything as hot as you kneeling there with your tongue out, begging for my cum." He runs his hand over my head in this loving way that melts me. "Come on, let's get you off the floor." He helps me stand, and I immediately hug his body, needing to be close. He must understand because he keeps one arm around me while he washes his hair, letting me glue myself to him until he's done.

Brady stays close as we towel dry off and brush our teeth, keeping one hand on me almost constantly. Neither of us talks as we get into bed and lie together like we always do. I'm pretty sure it only takes seconds before we are both asleep.

FORTY-EIGHT

ZACH

Brady and I sleep in and don't wake until Kelly is knocking at our door. He pulls away to slip jeans on to let Kelly in.

"Good morning," I hear Kelly say from the other room. "Where's the baby of this family? Still in bed?"

"Yes, he's sleeping," is Brady's grumbly reply.

Baby of the family?

Kelly never ceases to make me laugh over the stuff he says. "I'm awake," I call out.

He comes in to bounce on the bed next to me, looking so happy that he makes me smile. "Get up! Time's a wasting!"

Now that I'm awake, I am eager to get the day started, too. Scooting off the bed, I go through my suitcase to get a pair of jeans and grab one of the Disney shirts we bought yesterday.

"You could put some pants on around other guys, you know."

I turn around to see Brady covering Kelly's eyes, giving me a pointed look. Kelly is grinning and says, "Ohhhhh…somebody is possessiiiiiiiiiiive."

"It's not any different from wearing a bathing suit around him. Besides, he's seen me like this before…and it's Kelly," I explain, thinking Brady is being silly, but loving his possessiveness anyway.

"Just go put some clothes on."

Kelly pulls Brady's hand down long enough to wink at me. "Ohhhhhh Zach, you're sooooo sexy in those Calvin's that I can hardly keep from ravaging you."

Brady flicks his ear. "Where is your daddy bear? He needs to keep his brat in line."

Kelly laughs. "He was trying to find a snack because he's starving. You know he can't go this long without food."

Brady and I hurry to get dressed and ready for our day at Disney's Animal Kingdom. We head downstairs, where Connor has ordered breakfast for us, and eat quickly. There's so much that we want to see today, and we map out what is important.

We spend the day visiting animals that I never thought I would see, going on attractions that make my heart race, and more. We go on Avatar Flight of Passage, and it's a little bit terrifying but awesome at the same time. I might be a little afraid of heights. Brady has me use my inhaler afterward because I sound wheezy. They use the excuse of wanting to eat after that, giving me a chance to sit down.

After supper, we watch the Finding Nemo show. I still can't believe I'm here and can't stop smiling.

We get back to the resort at around seven-thirty, and Brady gives me this look that makes me squirm. He makes an excuse about me being tired and needing to rest, even though I never said I was tired. Kelly gives me a wink, knowing exactly what is going on.

Brady orders some room service while I'm showering. I thought maybe he would come in for a repeat of last night, but he doesn't. He takes a shower after me, and the room service comes while he's in there.

He's ordered us some strawberries with chocolate fondue, potato skins with cheese, and fried zucchini.

Brady comes out in pajama pants and no shirt, giving me this smile that melts me. I suddenly want to skip the food and just do whatever he's willing to give me tonight.

"Let's eat on the balcony."

I nod, and we carry everything out there. Brady gets some bottles of water for us, and we sit together on one lounge, me between his legs and leaning back against him. Brady keeps reaching over to take food off the plates next to us and feeding me a bite before taking one for himself. I don't think he's trying to be romantic, even though it is. I think it's simply Brady being who he always is with me. He likes to take care of me, and I'm starting to realize that all the times I was worried he would get tired of saving me, he really wanted to and wasn't doing it because he had to.

"Did you have fun today?"

I swallow the bite of zucchini so I can answer. "It was amazing. Can we bring our whole family and Honey here with us and just stay forever?"

"I'm not sure that would work. Honey would miss her backyard, and I would miss our comfortable new bed."

"I suppose." I open my mouth to take the bite of strawberry he's offering me.

"Besides, we have Ruger coming soon. He's a bit intense and needs to be working."

Right now is when I want to ask him about Stella, the girl he spent Thanksgiving with, but I can't get out the words. If I say something and I don't like his answer, I don't want to ruin this between us. I want to savor every second until it's over.

"How old do you want to be before you become a foster parent?"

Whoa, that's a heavy question out of the blue. I picture myself in the future and try to think of how old I should be. "I don't know, really. When I get married, I want time with my husband to just be us and do things together. So depending on when I get married…sometime in my mid-thirties I could see fostering? But then I think things can change, and if I met a child that needed me before that time, I would foster him or her." I look back at him over my shoulder. "I won't feel ready in the near future if that's what you're asking. I don't want to mess it up and need to become a responsible, older adult beforehand."

"You're very responsible, but I think you're right to wait until you're older. What about getting married? How old do you want to be for that?"

Where are these questions coming from? "I don't think age matters. If you love someone and want to be with them forever, then why wait? But some guys don't want to get married, and they want to just stay partners. I guess it would depend on who I was with and what he wanted as well." *I love you and want to stay with you forever.* I so want to blurt it out but don't. "What about you? When do you see yourself getting married and having kids?"

Brady is quiet for a few minutes. "I'll know when I get there," is his reply.

Neither of us says anything for a bit, looking out at the lights in the darkness surrounding our balcony. Eventually, Brady and I take the plates inside, turning off the balcony lights as we go.

We brush our teeth and strip down to our underwear. Brady goes back into the bathroom, bringing out a towel to set on the bed. He seems nervous, which is making me nervous.

"Brady, we don't have to do anything tonight. I'm not going to be upset if you don't want to," I say quietly.

His blue eyes are intense as he steps closer. "I want to. I'm just worried about making it good for you. If we are going to have sex at some point in the near future, we need to start doing…certain things. I don't want to embarrass you or rush you. I'm trying to do this right."

I should have known he would be worried about being perfect for me. I'm not even sure how he's doing this in the first place, being that he's straight and is talking about having sex with a guy. Most guys would be running from the room if they thought they were getting anywhere near their gay friend's ass.

Stepping forward, I wrap my arms around his back and press my body close to him. "This is just you and me." I use his own words on him. "It doesn't have to be perfect because it's just between us."

Letting out a long sigh, he presses his lips to the top of my head. "Okay, then we should try some new things tonight."

Anticipation dances across my nerves at whatever is about to happen. I've dreamed of sucking Brady off so many times and wonder if that's what we are going to try.

He moves away from me to his suitcase, and I sit on the edge of the bed, trying to stay calm. "Brady?"

"Hmm?" He has the bottle of lube in his hand, making me swallow hard.

"I know that I'm not going to be good at it like the girls you've been with, but can I give you…a blow job?" Blow job sounds so crass, and I wish I had said it some other way. "Please?"

Brady frowns for a second before he meets my gaze, and there's heat in his eyes now. "You really want to?"

"More than anything," I blurt out too quickly. "I can get better if you give me a chance."

He brings the bottle of lube over to set on the side table next to the bed. Hooking his thumbs into his boxer briefs, he tugs them down his legs, letting his erection spring free. He's already semi-hard and getting harder by the second. I haven't touched him there before, and I want to more than anything in this moment.

Brady scoots over on the bed, propping his back up on the pillows, all while keeping eye contact with me. "Get naked and come here."

I try to get my briefs off too fast and trip, almost doing a face-plant. Brady is grinning by the time I crawl over to him. Taking off my glasses, I hand them to him because his arms are long enough to reach the side table.

Right now, I'm straddling the end of his legs, and I really want to be between them. "May I lie between your legs?"

He nods, pulling his legs out from underneath me and moving them to my sides. My hands are shaking as I crawl closer. I've wanted to do this for so long, more so than him touching me. I want to give him pleasure and taste him and then do it all over again.

Lying down with my arms over his thighs, I look up to see him watching me with hooded eyes. He wants this. He really does want this.

Leaning closer, I inhale Brady's scent. It's all him, the essence my body and mind know like it's a part of me. I'm scared I'm going to do this wrong, but I decide to give it everything I have and show him what doing this for him means to me.

FORTY-NINE

BRADY

Zach is between my legs with such a look of reverence as he nuzzles my balls before licking and sucking them into his mouth. I'm so hard, and it feels too good. I want his mouth on my cock now. "Zach, get your mouth on my cock...now," I grit out, clenching my teeth as my cock leaks precum and bobs against my stomach.

His green eyes meet mine as he licks up my shaft, raising his body up to lick the precum and take the head in his mouth to suck. He only sucks the head, almost like he's nursing it and trying to get more of my taste in his mouth. It's so fucking hot to see his eyes hungry for more, begging me for more.

"Zach," I half order, half beg, needing more of his mouth.

He pulls off to lick the sides, worshiping my cock ardently. Right when I open my mouth to growl at him for more, he wraps his lips around my length and takes it in deep until the head bumps the back of his throat.

"Fuck...oh fuck, that feels good," I moan. His mouth is wet and hot as it bobs on my cock. He tries to take me deeper and struggles not to gag. Again and again, he tries until tears leak from his eyes. He's trying to please me and do this for me, but I don't need more. I just need him. I wind my fingers through his hair, gripping enough to pull him off a little. He tries to sink down more, thirsty to suck me, and moans when I let him take me a little deeper again.

Fuck, his glistening green eyes and his whimpers as he looks at me, my cock sliding in and out. I can't hold on anymore and start to come, bucking up into his mouth.

Zach swallows and swallows, but some of my cum leaks out the corners of his mouth and down my cock. As soon as I relax from the sheer intense release, he moves to lick every last drop of cum from my cock and balls. These little, soft sounds coming from him are telling me how much he wants every taste I'm willing to give him.

I'm reeling from the way Zach gave to me. He wanted to give me pleasure, to worship and treasure what I was offering him. He thinks being able to suck me off is a gift, one he desperately longs for.

He nuzzles my balls again, but then this look of uncertainty flits across his face. I reach down to yank him up into my arms, wrapping him close and kissing his mouth a few times. "Baby, that felt so good. You gave me so much pleasure, thank you."

"I'll get better," he says in this tiny voice that grips my heart.

"I'm not sure I can handle you any better. Your mouth is already hot as hell, baby." I roll us over so he's beneath me and kiss him more aggressively until he's kissing me back, forgetting all his insecurities. Easing my hand down his stomach to touch him, I'm surprised when Zach breaks our kiss and pulls my hand up.

"Uhh…I already came," he says, ashamedly. "I'm sorry."

"You did? When?"

He closes his eyes. "When you came. It's just…you sounded so turned on, and I love giving you that… It made me come."

Grinning, I kiss his lips and nip at them when he barely responds. "You came hands-free?"

He nods, opening his eyes to look at me. I have read that some guys can come hands-free, but it's not the usual. I think it's hot that I can turn him on so much he can come without even touching his cock.

"That's hot," I murmur against his lips, my hand slipping between us to wrap around his cock. He gasps at the feel of my hand and within seconds is almost hard again. It actually works better if he's come once because I need him to last long enough for me to stretch him some or at the very least for him to get used to having something in his ass.

Leaning back from him, I kneel between his legs and reach over for the bottle of lube. Zach's eyes widen, his cheeks pinkening as he realizes what I'm going to do. I'm more nervous about giving him a blow job than I am about fingering his ass. What if I'm as bad at this as I was at going down on a girl? What if I hate it and hurt Zach's feelings? He thinks I'm this experienced sex expert, and I hardly have any experience.

He gives me this trusting look that says he loves me, and I swallow back my fears, determination settling over me. I can do this. "If you need me to stop, tell me… I'll stop immediately. I want this to feel good for you, not hurt. Pain means we need to stop, okay?"

He nods, biting his lip while he watches me pour lube on my fingers. I lean over him to kiss him until his tongue is dancing with mine, whimpers escaping as our mouths touch.

"Bend your legs up," I order as I leave his mouth to kiss down his stomach. He does, but I can feel his body trembling over what I'm about to do. My fingers find his hole and I circle them around, just rubbing lightly to help him relax. I try to remember everything I've read so I can make this good for him.

His cock is at my lips, and I push all my insecurities away and just give in to what feels right. As my mouth sucks him in, I press my finger to his hole and slowly push inside. Zach's cock is smaller like his twinkish little body, and I can easily take him all the way in. I think his cock is perfect, straight and hard, sexy as hell. He tastes like Zach, innocent and sweet. Moving my mouth up and down on his cock, I slowly insert my finger in and out with the same rhythm.

"Brady…oh God…fuck please…" Zach babbles and moans, barely keeping his body still.

The harder he gets in my mouth, the more it turns me on. I reach my finger around inside of him, searching for the spot that will bring him more pleasure. I know I've found it when he lets out this incoherent moan of pleading, his body arching up into my mouth like he's been zapped. Rubbing that spot makes his cock even harder, and I feel his hands in my hair as he begs. "Ohgodohgod…Brady please…please I need to come…please Brady…oh God…fuck…"

My finger moves over it again, and I take his cock all the way in my mouth with a moan of my own over hearing him. His body bows as he comes in my mouth, his cries of ecstasy turning into sobs. I swallow down everything he gives me, unsure if I like the taste or not, but wanting every part of him.

Hearing all his moans and pleading has me ready to come again, but Zach's soft sobs are saying he needs me more. I slowly pull my finger from his ass and move up beside him to gather him close to me.

"Shhhh…you're okay, baby," I croon to him. If I hurt him, I'm never going to forgive myself.

Zach only cries for a minute before he grows quiet but still clings to me. "Sorry," he whispers. "It felt so good. I never knew it could feel like that."

My body releases the tension it was holding. Thank God, I didn't hurt him. "You liked it then?"

"It was…perfect. I didn't expect you to give me…you know, or swallow. You didn't have to do that for me."

"I wanted to." It's true, I did. I even liked it and got hard over doing it. It wasn't anything like the oral sex I had with Carrie, and whereas I felt yucky with her, this felt empowering and amazing. It was Zach and just another part of him, an extension of the love I already have for him. Where in the fuck does this leave me now?

We lie here snuggling together, with me stroking his bare back and periodically kissing his shoulder or neck. Finally, I figure we're both going to fall asleep if I don't get up, and I force myself to move away from him. Picking up the towel, I use it to wipe any remaining lube from his ass. Then use the clean side to wipe his cum off the sheets from when he came the first time. He hasn't moved, and I leave him to wash my hands in the bathroom.

I manage to get him to sit up and drink some water before he collapses back on the bed, his eyes closed. Joining him, I smile as he buries close and digs his leg between mine. Too tired to dissect my sexuality anymore tonight, I ignore everything and just sleep.

"Brady?"

Zach's voice pulls me from sleep, and I become aware that I'm pressing my morning wood into him. Normally I would move back, and there's something hugely satisfying about being able to shift against him instead.

He licks his lips, his green eyes darting to mine with a begging look. "Please?"

Fuck, his soft plea about makes me spill my load right then. I raise my arm from behind him to brush hair back from his eyes. "You don't have to ask permission, baby. Whenever you want to suck me off, you can… I'll love it."

He eagerly scoots down to take me into his mouth. I grip his hair for a second to get his attention. "Try not to come."

His eyes are saying that he'll try, but he refuses to pull off my cock to answer me. His need to give me head is a drug that I'm fast becoming addicted to.

Fuck, Zach's warm, wet mouth feels so good around my aching cock. Why didn't we ever do this before? I'm not going to last long even if I wanted to, not with the sounds he's making. I grip the sheets with my hands, trying to hold on to my restraint while he bobs his head, his hand jacking me at the base in the same rhythm. The next time the head of my cock hits the back of his throat, I lose control. He moans as he gulps down everything I give him.

Even after I start to go soft, he's licking slowly, in this almost lovingly way that threatens to undo me.

"Zach, come here," I order, my voice husky and low.

He crawls up my body, kissing and dragging his tongue across my skin every few inches as he goes. When he reaches my lips, I roll us over so I can devour his mouth with the passion he ignites in of me. I lose track of how long we kiss because it's fire and love melded into this raw, clawing need between us.

My brain's demand for oxygen makes me break away from the kiss, my chest heaving as I stare down into his shocked, green eyes. His lips are swollen and red, cheeks flushed, and soft pants are coming from his mouth.

"God, you're beautiful," I whisper, tracing my finger over his lips.

Zach's eyes tear up at my words as he swallows hard.

There's a knock at the door, and he starts shaking his head. He's still hard between us and hasn't found his own release yet.

The knock comes again, sending me off the bed to slip on my pajama bottoms. Zach grabs his glasses to shove on as he runs into the bathroom. As soon as he's away from prying eyes, I go to answer the incessant knocking.

Kelly is practically bouncing with anticipation for the day, and Connor is leaning against the wall, looking mildly amused and bored at the same time. I'm seriously regretting having them come along right now.

"Can't you two ever sleep in? Or I don't know, call before you come knocking on our door?"

Kelly brushes past me to come in, and Connor shrugs. "You try keeping that one from doing something he wants. It's impossible."

"Tie him down next time...anything."

Kelly turns to give Connor a wink. "You heard him...tie me down next time."

Connor grins. "You never know, brat. Maybe I will."

"Where is our baby?" Kelly peeks his head into the bedroom.

"He's in the bathroom."

Zach comes out right then, wearing pajama pants only. I'm fairly certain he has nothing on underneath them, but at least he isn't hard anymore. Either he took care of the problem, or it went down on its own. His lips are still red and swollen, and his cheeks look almost scratched. I reach up to feel my face, confirming that my stubble did that to him.

Kelly rushes over to give him a hug and then looks back at me with this knowing grin. I can only hope Connor doesn't notice, or he's going to be asking a barrage of questions I don't have answers to.

Connor nudges me with his elbow. "So, what's the plan for today?"

Before I can answer, Kelly pipes up. "It's warm outside. Maybe we could go swimming instead of going to a theme park? They have an adult-only pool, lazy river...water slides."

Zach gives me this hopeful glance, and that's all I need to agree. "Whatever Zach wants to do. This is his Christmas present. A lazy day here, swimming and relaxing, does sound nice, though."

Zach nods, eliciting a squeal from Kelly.

We get dressed to go down and eat breakfast, both of us giving each other side glances frequently. This new sexual element to our relationship has changed things between us. I've always been hyperaware of where Zach is at all times, but now I not only want to be close to him, I want that added intimacy and passion, too. I also want sex, badly. I've never really cared before now, but with Zach, I want to be inside of him and connect with him on that level. My thoughts just keep going around and around on what it all means.

Before heading back up to our rooms to change, we stop by a hotel shop to buy bathing suits. The only person who remembered to bring one was me. Kelly is picking out these skin-tight briefs and holds one out for Zach.

I reach out to snatch it up, hanging it back on the rack. "No, not happening."

Zach smiles at me. "Why not?"

He knows exactly why not. "Because I said so." I point to some trunks that are tighter, but not skin-tight. It's a happy medium between the baggy swimming trunks and the tiny briefs that Kelly is holding.

Kelly is grinning way too big at my expression. "Oh, you two are adorable together."

Thankfully Connor is checking out and doesn't hear him. "Glad you think so. Maybe *daddy bear* should see what you're planning on wearing."

"Maybe he should," he quips, taking the ones he wants up to the checkout.

Connor's face when he sees them is comical, but I doubt he gets any say over it. I turn my attention back to Zach, who is trying to find his size in red trunks.

I put my hand on his back. "You're not upset that I said anything, are you?"

He shakes his head, pulling out the one he found. "No, I like that you don't want to share that part of me with the world. If you wanted to, I think I would feel...dirty." He looks up at me with those beautiful green eyes. "Someone seeing me like that feels wrong because it's personal...between us. Ours...yours, if that makes sense."

I lean over to press my lips softly to his cheek, so close to his mouth. "It makes sense, baby." *He's mine.* How many times has that thought run through my head over the years? *My Zach.* He's always been mine. Now I'm feeling this possessiveness even stronger, and I'm not sure what that means for the future. Will I ever be able to watch him with someone else? A sharp pain spreads through my chest at the thought.

"Besides," Zach says, "if I really wanted to wear them, I know that you'd accept my choice."

He's right. If Zach ever wanted to do something, I would never stand in his way. I might be bossy, but I would respect Zach's decision if he told me no.

"Come on, you two," Kelly calls, breaking the moment.

Zach stands on his tiptoes to kiss my cheek before running up to pay for his trunks.

I'm so in over my head right now. I pick up some sunscreen off the shelf and follow him. The last thing we need is Zach sunburned on this trip.

FIFTY

BRADY

The day is sunny and beautiful. It's hard to picture the cold winter back home when we are soaking up warmth and sunshine. We spend the morning swimming, floating numerous times in the lazy river, and going down the enormous water slides. It takes a lot of coaxing to get Zach to go down them, but they finally let him go down with me, and after that, he loves it.

We order lunch out here and take naps on comfy two-person lounges. Connor has given us some weird looks but hasn't said anything. It's just now that we've been touching each other sexually, there's this intimate feel when he sits on my lap or holds my hand. I'm positive every person who's seen us out here thinks we are a couple, especially when Zach curls up against me to nap. I have picked a lounge with an umbrella to keep the sun off him, and we've applied sunscreen several times, but I still don't want to take any chances.

Connor and Kelly are in a lounge next to us, quietly talking to each other. I see Connor roll on his side, running his finger down Kelly's nose before brushing it over his lips. I close my eyes, feeling like I shouldn't be seeing this, and let myself doze off with Zach.

After a relaxing couple of hours, we swim some more and float around the lazy river until we are hungry again. We head up to our rooms to shower with the plan to meet in half an hour to go up for supper. I've already made reservations at Capa, the rooftop steakhouse where we can eat on an outdoor terrace. It seems like the perfect place after our day together.

Once we are inside our room, I follow Zach into the bathroom. We don't have much time and I shouldn't do anything, but I still find myself following him into the shower. No words are spoken as we wash each other, needing the touch more than anything verbal. I soap up his hair and help rinse it out. He's too short to help with mine, but he wraps his arms around my middle and kisses my chest while I do it. We are both hard, but this closeness between us is more important.

I finally break the silence. "Did you come this morning?"

He shakes his head no.

Taking a seat on the shower bench, I pull him over to straddle my lap so I can kiss him, wrapping my hand around his cock to jack him off. I feel his small hand grasp mine to do the same. I don't care about getting off right now; I just want to give him what he needs.

Breaking away from his mouth, I kiss down his neck and nip his shoulder. "I wanted you all day, baby. Do you have any idea how much I want to be inside of you?"

He whimpers, his eyes glazing over as he looks at me.

"You want that, don't you? My cock pushing inside of you until I come and fill you up."

"Brady…I…I…" His body tightens as he starts to come, his hand falling away from my cock as his pleasure takes over.

"That's it, baby… I love it when you come," I murmur, putting my arm around his back to support him.

He collapses on me the second he comes down from the high, and I barely get to press my lips to his shoulder before he's scooting off my lap to kneel between my legs.

"Zach, you don't have…" I trail off as he takes my cock in his mouth. I love watching him suck me, wanting to please me. I think I'm going to last longer until he angles his head so he can look up at me while he sucks. There's so much love in his eyes that it makes me shoot my load in his mouth with a low groan. Zach swallows it all before I pull him up into my arms to hold him close.

"I love you, baby," I whisper in his ear.

"I love you more than anything," he says quietly.

We stay wrapped up in each other for another minute before getting out of the shower. Then it becomes a rush to get ready before Kelly is beating on our door. We dress up for this dinner, and Zach looks hot in his fitted dress pants and button-up shirt. He wears his glasses after the chlorine bothered his eyes today. His hair is styled back and looks…sharp. I'm discovering the hot, smart nerd look really is my thing, at least on him. I've never thought any other guy was my thing.

Kelly knocks on the door as we are slipping on shoes, and I take Zach's hand to leave. Out in the hallway, Connor and Kelly are waiting, dressed up a little more, too. None of us are fancy, just casual dressy.

Dad calls on our way to the elevators, and I can tell he's worried about all of us, but mainly Zach. After reassuring him and handing Zach the phone for a minute, we end the call. I ask an employee walking by if they'll take a picture of us, and we all smile big for it. I text it off to Dad, hoping that helps, and immediately get a cheerful reply.

Sitting out on the terrace is amazing. We all order steak, but try some different foods on the menu that we never would have otherwise. The coolest part is when we see the Disney fireworks while eating dessert.

I really want time alone with Zach, but Connor and Kelly end up following us into our suite to watch a movie. At least housekeeping changed the sheets and made the bed today, making it easier for me to feel comfortable with the idea of us all watching the movie from it. Zach changes into pj bottoms and a crop top, and Kelly borrows a set to wear, too. They cuddle in the middle with Connor and me sitting on the outside of the bed.

Zach and Kelly insist on watching a Disney movie since we are at Disney but are asleep thirty minutes in. Connor looks over at me and tilts his head toward the balcony. I nod, easing from the bed and putting a pillow behind Zach's back. Connor covers them both up with a blanket.

Connor and I sink into the lounge chairs, staring out at the night sky. It's been a while since we've had time to talk by ourselves.

"I guess you've figured out that I'm not straight," he says hesitantly.

"Kind of hard not to when you and Kelly are eye fucking each other all the time."

He does this strained, short laugh. "I know that I should have told you I'm pansexual. I'm sorry I kept it from you."

I look over at him, seeing the regret on his face. "Did you like Zach all that time? Lust after him?"

He shifts uncomfortably in his chair. "Yes and no, I was attracted to him because he's the sweetest and kindest person. I wanted to date him…thought I was in love with him. Every time I wanted to approach you about it, you would make a comment about how any guy would have to come through you first. I knew you would never let me over if I said anything. I didn't lust after him; it wasn't like that. I cared about him."

Reining in the anger I want to feel, I try to understand. "All these years, you've been in love with him?"

"No, I wanted more with him right up until the incident with his dad. He wanted you and only you. When he screamed for you, it hit me that it was always going to be you. Even if we dated, if something happened, he would want you. You're all he sees. He's never once seen me as anything but a friend. I let go of my crush and started dating Tessa. I will always love Zach and be there for him, but I am not in love with him. I can never be what you are to him. Even when you left, he didn't see me like that. You have his heart and always will."

Would I have been okay if Connor had told me he wanted to date Zach? The thought of them together makes me feel ill. Connor would have treated him like he deserves. Better than this fucked-up situation of me not knowing what I'm going to like sexually in the future.

"Is that why you always stayed with him while I was on dates? Because you wanted him?"

"No, I stayed with him while you were out because I cared and saw how hurt he was by it. I didn't want him to be alone. Watching him go through a panic attack…it changes a person. He deserves to have someone watching over him all the time."

"What about Kelly? Sometimes I can't tell if you two are going to kill each other or rip each other's clothes off."

Connor grins. "Kelly has made me realize that Zach and I probably wouldn't have been the best match. I've found that I like some sass and fire. The brat drives me crazy, but he has a big heart. He would kill to protect Zach; he loves him as much as the rest of us do…if not more. I think I need Kelly's confidence. It draws me out of my comfort zone. Plus, he makes me laugh all the time."

"So, are you two pursuing anything together?"

He clears his throat, shifting again. "Things have been getting a little hot…and I am hoping they'll develop, but he keeps holding back for some reason."

"Have you talked to him about it? Asked him out on a date?"

"Well, no," he admits.

"Maybe he thinks you're just looking for a hookup, and he isn't interested in only that? Ask him on a date. You could take him somewhere while we're on vacation. Let him know you're looking for more. You were always so romantic with Tessa. You should know what to do."

"Tessa was easy; she's a girl. You throw flowers and a romantic movie at her, and she'll melt. But Kelly…he's more complicated than that. He's special, and I don't want to just bring him flowers. I don't want to mess it up."

I can tell he really wants this to work out. "You're already messing it up by not making an effort to start a relationship. Ask him on a date and bring him something you know he'll love. From being around him, I'd say he'd love anything you give him."

"I'll figure it out." He looks over at me. "What's up with you and Zach? You've seemed different together."

Fuck, I can't tell him the truth, or it'll ruin this trip when he tries to kill me. "Nothing is up. We are just needing to be close after being separated for six months."

"When he saw you in the club and ran to you… I've never seen love like what you have for each other. It's beautiful."

His words remind me of something Dad said to me a long time ago. Something to the effect that Zach is pretty much my whole heart. "Zach is everything to me."

"You better not leave for a while. I don't think his tender heart could take it so soon after going through all that."

"I'm not leaving him again," I promise, adamantly. "I can't go through it again either. I know that I didn't show it enough, but being away from him those six months nearly killed me."

"Is it sick for me to be a little happy that you suffered, too?"

I reach over to smack his arm. "Yes, that is sick."

He smacks me back. "You weren't the one who had to watch him suffer. If it hadn't been for Kelly, I'm not sure he would have made it through okay. Kelly swooped in and saved us."

It's difficult to hear, but I have to accept that I did this to all of us. "Kelly is special. He might be more energetic and confident than Zach, but he's kind and sweet, too. He brings out the protective streak just like Zach does."

"Yeah, he does. He thinks he can take care of himself, but I want to follow him around in case he can't. I don't think he'll let me, though."

"Aww…look at you all fallen in love," I tease, grinning at him.

"Shut it, Wellman."

I scoff. "Oh, bringing out the last name. You must be serious now."

"Be nice to me, or I'm telling Kelly, and trust me, you don't want him mad at you."

Laughing, I shake my head. "I really don't want him mad at me, but shame on you for using him to fight your own battles."

We talk and laugh, catching up on the last six months. It's late when Connor scoops Kelly up to carry him back to their room. I open the doors and make sure he gets into their suite okay, before going back inside to strip down and lie with Zach.

He mumbles my name as he does his usual burying into me and slipping his leg between mine.

"I love you, baby," I whisper.

FIFTY-ONE

ZACH

We aren't even awake yet when Kelly starts knocking on our door. Brady groans at the sound, but both of us crawl from bed to shove pants on.

Kelly is soon bouncing on the edge of our bed, hurrying us along. "Where are we going to today?"

"Up to Zach!" Brady yells from the bathroom.

I'm kind of tired and don't feel like running around a theme park all day. Kelly must notice because he takes my hand, pulling me down to sit next to him. "Want to just stay here? We can swim or go to their little boutiques. If you're tired, we can just stay in the room and watch movies."

"I don't want to stay here if you all want to go somewhere."

Connor is leaning against the doorway. "What are you two whispering about?"

"Zach and I have decided to stay at the hotel and relax today. You two can go off to do your thing if you don't want to."

Brady's head pops around the corner of the bathroom door. "You two stay here? Alone? I don't think so."

Kelly throws his hands up in the air. "Why not? I'm older than you two are, and we aren't leaving the hotel. It's perfectly safe for the two of us to hang out here without you two."

Brady comes further into the room, putting his shirt on before standing in front of us. "Because you two are tiny and too sweet for your own good."

"Fine, why don't you big, strong men—who guard us from certain death—go protect us by hiking down to the wilderness and foraging food for breakfast. Kill some coffee beans or something."

Connor chuckles, but Brady just rolls his eyes.

I think I hear "brat" muttered as they leave to get us breakfast.

Kelly and I lie back on the bed to talk while we wait.

I finally get up the nerve to ask him, "How do you deepthroat without gagging?"

He grins at me. "Aww, my sweet little baby virgin is growing up."

"Kind of… I want to make it good for him, but his dick is huge, and I can't do it."

"First of all, you need to relax when you do it. If you're stressing about gagging and being perfect, it's only going to make it worse. Relax your body—relax your throat. I can't say that word enough—relax relax relax. You have to train your gag reflex not to fight it. Try taking him deep and just holding still, all while trying to ease your throat's response. Stay that way for five to ten seconds if you can, teaching your reflex not to react."

"Okay, I can do that."

"Some guys will practice with a dildo. They'll do it a few times a day until they can do it easily. Once you've conquered that, then you start adding in movement. If you get really good at it, then you can start swallowing…contracting your throat around them. That drives them crazy."

"It sounds like this is going to take time," I lament, thinking about how Brady isn't a forever thing.

"It doesn't take that long unless you have a really strong gag reflex. If you ask Bane, he'll tell you that he threw up on the first guy he tried it with."

"I think I'll pass on that story." My stomach feels a little nauseous just hearing Kelly talk about it.

"How are things going with you and Brady? Is he having a hard time doing things because he's straight?"

I roll over to face Kelly. "No, not at all. He's as turned on as I am… unless he's faking it. His eyes when I give him head are like he's about to ravage me." My dick starts to get hard just picturing Brady's heated eyes. "He told me he can't wait to be inside of me."

My cheeks heat up as Kelly stares at me openmouthed.

"Did he give you head, too?"

"Mhmm…while he fingered…you know."

Kelly sits up and I follow, watching him think about it. "Okay, there's no way he's straight. I've met a lot of straight guys who were bi-curious, but none of them ever wanted to return the favor or would have gone near my ass."

"I don't know, but when we kiss, it's passionate and everything I've ever wanted." I reach over to take his hand. "I don't know what's happening. I thought this would be more instructional with him helping me learn things. It would be easier to keep perspective if it was. Instead, it's hot and he's majorly turned on. How am I supposed to keep my heart out of it and be okay when it ends?"

Kelly tugs me to sit between his legs so he can wrap his arms around me. "I wish I had the answers for you. All I can tell you is what I see from the outside, and what I see is that Brady loves you more than a friend loves a friend. He looks at you like you're his world. You both hug and touch like lovers, not friends. I didn't get to see much of your relationship before his plan, but to me…he's in love with you."

"If he is, he doesn't know it. He's seemed a little lost at times after we do something."

"Of course, he's going to feel a little lost. He thinks he's straight, and yet he is turned on by you. He's probably trying to come to terms with it all. Give him time and don't push him. Sexuality isn't black and white; maybe he needs time to figure it all out."

"I don't think I can bear the rejection of him not wanting me like this anymore," I whisper. "For me, it's just another way I get to love him. It's beautiful."

"Aaaww, you're so sweet," Kelly croons, kissing my cheek. "Maybe it'll all work out. I can't see him leaving you, honey. He barely lets you get two feet from him. Not to mention he looks like he wants to rip the throat out of any guy that so much as looks your way."

"He does not."

"Yes, he does! There was a girl that checked you out yesterday, and he even gave her the evil eye."

I laugh, wishing it were true. "He *is* pretty protective. But I don't want to get my hopes up. He has only ever dated girls and wants a family one day."

He hugs me tightly. "Gay couples can have families, too. Whatever happens, I'm here for you."

The guys show up with coffee and bagels, except Brady sets down a juice for me. He takes in Kelly, who's holding me between his legs, and gives me a raised eyebrow as if to ask if I'm okay. I nod and scoot off the bed to join them. We sit at the little table eating, but as soon as I'm done, Brady motions for me to sit on his lap. He forgets Connor is right here and presses his lips lightly to the back of my neck. Connor gives us a speculative look but doesn't say anything.

After we change into suits, we have fun at the lazy river and swimming. Kelly and I end up on a shaded, two-person lounge while Brady and Connor swim some more.

I finally decide to ask him about Connor. "So, are you and Connor a thing? You both seem to like each other."

He raises his sunglasses on his head and turns to look at me. "We have a date tomorrow."

It comes out almost as a whisper, and he looks so serious.

"Wow, a date. That's exciting." I reach over to rub his arm. "Why do you look so terrified?"

"Because I really like him. I've never dated anyone seriously. I've hooked up with guys from clubs or had a few guys I dated a couple of times, but it was mainly for sex. I've never dated someone I'm friends with and liked like this."

I try to reassure him. "Connor is the best guy and would never do anything to hurt you. If he's asked you on a date, it's because he wants a relationship. He's always taken care of me when Brady wasn't around. That's the kind of guy he is."

Kelly sighs, staring out at the lake nearby. "That's what scares me. What if I'm bad at relationships and hurt him?"

"I don't think you're bad at relationships. Look at our friendship and how you've stepped up to take care of me. You are great at helping people be the best version of themselves, inside and out. My whole family adores you and you belong with us. They may not be sexual relationships, but I don't think you'll have a problem with the sexual part. You and Connor are already friends… You can do this."

"You think so?" He bites his lip like he's thinking.

"I know so. Besides, how will you know if you don't try? If you let Connor pass by, you'll regret it later. And you know if things don't work out, I'll be here to pick you up, just like you would me."

Kelly blinks a few times and sniffles. "I've had friends but no one like you before. You've changed my life, Zach. No matter what happens with the guys in our future, we will always have each other."

"Always. You can be my best man when I finally get married. I'll let you babysit my kids even."

Kelly laughs, lightening the mood. "You're crazy if you'd leave your kids with me, even if we will be way older. Can you imagine me with kids? They'll be on a sugar high and get to do whatever they want."

"True. Connor can babysit all of you."

He flicks me playfully. "Jesus, you're marrying me off already!"

"Nah, just wanted to get you laughing, and it worked."

"What are you two over here giggling about?" Brady sits down by my legs, towel drying his hair.

Connor is standing at the end of the lounge, staring at Kelly with hungry eyes. They are both crazy if they think staying friends is even an option.

"We were discussing my hot date tomorrow," Kelly says.

Connor smirks. "Hot seems like a fitting description."

Brady moves to squeeze in next to me. "What are you two doing on this hot date?"

"He won't tell me anything."

"Because the day is a surprise."

"Day?"

Connor gives us this shy look before sitting down on the end of the lounge. "Yes, day. I have the whole day planned, just the two of us."

What would it feel like to go out on an official date? Here I am kissing and being physical with Brady, but I have never even been on a single date in my life. It's a little depressing I don't know what it's like to be picked up for a date. Or will I be expected to pick the guy up for the date? It just feels more natural to not be the one planning or being in control of it all.

Brady leans close to whisper in my ear, "What are you thinking about?"

"Nothing." The last thing I want to talk about with Brady is how I long for a guy who wants to date me and be boyfriends. I long for *him* to officially ask me on a date and want to be boyfriends. I want to be able to kiss him in front of others and know he's proud that I'm his.

"Why do you look so sad then?"

I shrug, trying to smile so he'll leave it alone.

"Don't worry, Zach, you'll get asked on a date before long." Connor is giving me an understanding look, but inside I'm cringing that he said it front in of Brady.

Kelly takes my hand. "I'll take you on a date, honey. We can pretend to be boyfriends."

"I'm fine, you guys. I don't need a date." I scoot down to the end of the lounge and get up to walk over to the pool, diving in before I do something stupid like cry.

Kelly joins me a few seconds later, hugging me in the water. "I'm sorry Connor said that in front of Brady. He doesn't know what's going on between you."

"It's okay." Looping my arms around his neck, I sneak a look at Brady. He's sitting on the edge of the lounge, staring down at the cement, lost in thought. He looks sad right now, and I can't stand seeing it.

Connor swims over to us, and I leave Kelly with him so I can go make things better with Brady.

He sees me coming and moves his arm so I can sit on his lap, immediately hugging me to him.

I sag against his chest, tired and a little hot from the sun. "I love you, Brady."

His eyes soften, and he reaches for my towel to run over my wet hair. "I love you, baby."

Yawning, I close my eyes for a minute to rest them.

His fingers run over my forehead. "Are you tired?"

"If I say yes, will you escape to our room with me and make out?"

Brady practically pushes me off his lap to help me stand, grabbing our towels and phones. Taking my hand, he yells out to Connor and Kelly as he's already walking toward the hotel. "Zach is tired, and we are going to go take a nap. See you guys later!"

Kelly grins at me, giving me a small wave. I'm sure he knows exactly why Brady wants to "take a nap."

Back in our room, Brady leads me into the bathroom. "Put some eye drops in. Your eyes are getting red."

They are irritated right now. The chlorine seems to bother my eyes for some reason. While I'm putting eye drops in, Brady starts the shower for us. He disappears into our room for a minute and comes back to step into the shower.

Brady's washing his hair when I get in the shower with him. His dick is hard, which makes mine hard, but he seems to be concentrating on getting us clean. From the expression on his face, I think he likes to wash my hair for me. He soaps up a washcloth and runs it over my chest, moving to wash every inch of my body.

"Turn around and put your hands on the wall."

I turn around and place my hands on the shower tile in front of me, my stomach all butterflies now.

He washes my back and then goes lower to rub the cloth between my ass cheeks. He's going slow in this way that says he's trying to turn me on, but I was aroused the second I saw him hard. The washcloth moves away, and then I hear the snick of a bottle cap. Brady's arm comes around my front, his hand stroking my length a few times while his lips find my shoulder. I feel his fingers rubbing against my asshole, causing my body to tremble with anticipation for what comes next. He must have brought the lube into the shower because his finger is coated in it when he pushes the tip inside me.

Every thought fades as his finger goes deeper and heat flushes my skin. "Brady…"

His arm comes up to my chest, pulling me from the shower wall back against him, holding me here. Brady's mouth is kissing my shoulder and up to my neck, sending shivers over my skin, but it's his finger pushing in and out that has my legs quivering.

"Relax for me, baby," he murmurs, nipping my neck.

Taking a deep breath, I try to relax my body for him.

"That's it… Keep relaxed." He pulls his finger out, and then I feel two pushing slowly inside me. It burns a little as he stretches my hole, and I gasp, raising my hands to clutch his arm at my chest.

"Relax, baby…I've got you." He continues to murmur words of encouragement in my ear as he moves his fingers deeper.

The burn subsides to pleasure, and he must know it feels good because he starts to fuck me with his fingers. Moans and pleas fall from my mouth incoherently. I need more. I start to move my hand down to stroke myself, but he immediately stops me with, "Do not touch yourself."

"Please…I need to," I whine, desperate for any friction on my erection.

"No. I love seeing how hard you are, so turned on. Your cock jutting out from your body just begging to come."

A low moan rips from my chest at his words. I'm so close to coming and so hard that it's painful. "Brady...please."

His answer is to angle his fingers to touch that spot, and I swear I see stars. He rubs it again and again until I can't take it anymore.

"Oh God, I'm going to come...Brady!" I moan, my body tensing up at the tingles traveling from the base of my spine to my dick.

Brady groans. "Fuck yes, come for me, baby."

His fingers stroke over that spot of heaven again, and I'm lost, spurting out cum as the pleasure consumes me.

Brady's fingers ease from my ass when I sag against him, panting wild breaths and trying to keep my legs underneath me.

"Fuck, get on your knees, baby... I need you."

The tortured sound in *I need you* helps me to regain my senses. He guides me lower down to my knees, and I turn quickly to face him, taking him in my mouth to suck him off. His length is so hard it's like velvet steel, and I barely get to suck it before he's coming in my mouth. I suck and swallow until there's nothing left to give me.

Brady sinks down to his knees in front of me, pulling me between them to hold me against his chest. His hand cups my cheek as he lowers his mouth to kiss mine. Our kisses are gentle and sweet, *reverent*.

Fatigue hits me, and I can barely keep my eyes open. I think orgasms suck the energy from my body because I feel limp and exhausted right now.

Brady tugs me up from the shower floor. "Come on, let's get you to bed for a nap before you fall asleep on me."

He helps me dry off, and then I sit on the counter while he dries his body. He washes his hands, a reminder to me that his fingers were just in my ass. I think I fell into an alternate universe where Brady plays with my ass, or maybe I'm dreaming. My eyes close and I hear Brady chuckle a second before he's carrying me to bed.

"Go to sleep, baby," he whispers when we are cuddled up together under the blankets.

FIFTY-TWO

BRADY

Zach is sleeping already, his chest slowly rising and falling against mine. His soft, even breaths reassuring me that he's okay. I always worry that what we do will cause him an asthma attack or hurt him somehow.

Every time we are together like this, it's more powerful than the last time. We connect on a deeper level, something that is beautiful and scary all at once. Fuck, watching him come hands-free is the single most erotic thing I've ever seen. Just seeing him hard because of me is enough to drive me crazy. Add in his moans and begging, and I can barely keep my head to make sure I do everything right for him.

I close my eyes and can see him on his knees in front of me, his face flushed with desire. Those green eyes saying he loves me and wants to give me everything.

I'm terrified of hurting him.

Today, I purposely looked at other men while they were swimming, trying to get turned on by them.

Nothing

I felt nothing. I looked at women in their bathing suits, and I felt nothing. I can notice that a person is good-looking or attractive, but it's not a sexual attraction. I simply think they are pretty or whatever, with zero interest in touching them. Just the thought of kissing them brings back that dreaded feeling when I went on dates and had to kiss the girls. God, I'm so messed up when it comes to sex stuff. Every time I kiss Zach, I wait for that feeling to come and ruin this.

What happens when his firsts are over and he goes on a date with some other guy? Will we be able to sleep next to each other without getting turned on and touching each other? I should have never started this because when it ends and he dates someone, I'm not sure how I'll deal with it. I'm not gay and can't promise him anything more.

Knowing he's sad over not getting to date affected me more than I want to admit. I would take him on an official date if I could promise him forever because Zach will be the type to want forever from a relationship. In a way, we have dated for years because I've taken him to the movies more times than I can count. Sat under the stars or went to get ice cream together. All the things we would have done if we had been boyfriends.

I rub my hand over my forehead. I'm so confused over my body's reactions to Zach. There is no denying that I am turned on by him.

Not able to take any more thoughts on it right now, I close my eyes to sleep with him.

WE WAKE a couple of hours later to Mom calling us to check in. Zach and I exchange a look, both of us remembering the shower together. Talking to Mom ends up being a speaker phone conversation with the entire family. Kelly and Connor knock during this, and I'm forced from bed to get pants on to let them in. I throw pj bottoms at Zach before I get the door, making sure he has enough time to put them on before I open it.

Kelly and Connor pile on the bed to talk to the family, too. Hearing everyone laugh reminds me of how blessed I am to have such a close family.

The four of us get ready to go and make the drive into Orlando to the dinner theater with knights jousting and putting on a show. It's something different that none of us has ever seen, and we even get to pet the horses before we leave. Seeing Zach experience new things makes me happy, and I want to travel with him to see more places. I know he's dreamed of seeing Ireland and Scotland, and now I want to take him there. I never cared about my trust fund before, but with Zach, I'm even more grateful for it because I want to give him the best home and take him to new places.

Connor and Kelly stay in our room until Zach is asleep, canceling out any chance of repeating what we did earlier. But they will be gone all day tomorrow, and I can't wait to have time alone with Zach, just the two of us with no interruptions from our friends.

Morning comes and we have breakfast with Kelly and Connor. Kelly looks nervous; I've never seen him this way before. Connor looks a little nervous, too, for that matter. Zach gives them both hugs, stepping aside with Kelly for a minute so they can whisper to each other.

"Check in with me every once in a while and let us know you're okay."

Connor grins. "Yes, Dad, I'll be careful and will check in. Don't worry. I'll be watching Kelly and making sure we are safe."

"I do sound like my dad, don't I?"

"Yes, you do, but it's not a bad thing. Your dad is pretty awesome."

Zach and Kelly join us, and we see them off before heading back to our suite.

Inside our room, Zach kicks off his shoes and is already stripping out of his jeans. "What do you want to do today?"

"Nothing. I want to lie in bed with you all day and do nothing."

He does this little swirly dance of happiness that makes me grin. "Can we order room service instead of going out?"

I unbutton my own jeans to slide down my legs. "Yes, whatever you want."

"Can we soak in that big bathtub with bubbles?"

"Whatever you want to do, baby." I toss my jeans on a chair and tug my shirt over my head.

He's already in the bathroom turning the water on. I carry my cell into the bathroom and turn on soft music. Maybe I can't give him a date right now in the sense he's looking for, but I can make everything special for him.

Once he climbs in the tub, I turn off all the lights but the dimmest one and then join him. It feels so natural to have his naked body between my legs and lying back against me. He leans his head to the side so I can kiss him. It's soft and sweet, but there's this underlying passion that will break free if we let it.

"Brady?"

"Hmm?"

"Do you think we could rescue a kitten?"

It's so out of the blue that I let out a small laugh. "Where did that come from?"

He raises my hand from his chest up to his mouth and tenderly presses a kiss to my palm. The way he shows love makes me want to give him whatever he wants, and more. "Kelly used to have a cat growing up that he loved. He hasn't seen her since he was kicked out, and I've seen him looking online at the rescue cats at our shelter. So I was thinking that adopting a kitten would be nice for us."

I roll my eyes at the *for us*. What he means is that he wants to get Kelly a kitten that will live with us. I should have known he would want to do something for someone else. He never asks for anything for himself. "Where are you going to put a litter box that the dogs can't get into it?"

"I'll put it in the little room by the garage where we keep shoes and brooms and stuff. We can put a baby gate a few inches off the floor so the kitten can get through, but the dogs can't."

He must have been thinking about this for a while. "You do realize that Ruger can clear a baby gate like it's nothing."

"Oh."

He sounds so disappointed that I relent like I was going to the second he asked me. "I'll train him not to go in there. We can adopt a kitten."

For Kelly.

"Maybe we could let Kelly name it since he misses his cat so much."

I poke him in the ribs, and he jerks to the side, looking up at me.

"Do you really think I don't know this kitten is for Kelly?"

"Umm...well," he stutters, and then he grins. "You still said yes, though."

"Yes, and yes, Kelly can name his own kitten."

He reaches up to lay his hand on my cheek. "You're really sweet, Brady."

I'm just a sucker for wanting to make him happy all the time. "You better hope Connor is on board with this because if they move out together, the cat will be his, too."

"I don't want them to move out," Zach says in a small, quiet voice. "They are our family."

Turning my face, I kiss the palm of his hand. "I know, baby... It's nothing you need to worry about right now. I know how attached you are to Kelly, and they can stay for as long as they want to." After seeing him with Kelly, I can tell that when they decide to move out, it's going to be really hard for Zach.

He kisses my arm in that sweet way he always does. "What did he plan for them today? Do you know?"

"He's taking Kelly to see the ocean. He has other things planned, but I don't know all the details."

Zach shifts in the water to face me. His green eyes begging me for whatever he's about to ask. "After this bath, can I...can I suck you off, please?"

My already semi-hard cock becomes rock-hard at the thought. "You know you don't have to ask, baby." I hook my arm around the back of his neck, bringing his mouth to mine. This time our kissing is wild and passionate, our very breaths an extension of each other.

Zach starts rocking into me, these little whimpers escaping into my mouth. My hand drifts down to his ass, and I rub his hole, inciting another low moan from him. The more erratic his breathing becomes, the more I want to be inside of him. I want him panting from me thrusting inside of him.

I break my mouth away from his. "Baby...wait, don't come yet."

He lays his head on my shoulder with a groan. "Please, Brady, I need to."

Holding on to him, I stand, lifting him up with me to step out of the tub. He slides down my body until his feet are on the floor, taking the towel I'm offering him.

"Dry off and go get in bed. I'll be right there," I promise him, drying myself off quickly. He disappears around the door frame as I reach into the shower for the lube and hurry after him.

Zach moves to suck on my aching cock the second I'm in bed, but I stop him. "Lie down, knees up."

He obeys, lying on his back and hooking his knees to hold them up for me. His face flushes red from embarrassment, but as soon as I run my finger over his perfect hole, he starts begging. "Please, Brady...stop teasing me and fuck me already."

Zach rarely says fuck, and it sounds naughty coming from his mouth. "I've got you, baby." I lube up my fingers and slide one inside of him easily. He's not going to last long, but I want him to last long enough for me to stretch him out good with two fingers. Easing the one out, I reinsert two slowly. I can tell from his face that me being inside of him isn't going to happen today. He's not ready, and I refuse to risk hurting him because we rushed it.

My fingers are deep inside of him when I take his cock into my mouth, sucking and fingering him until he comes. Fuck, those moans have me so close already, and when he gets on all fours to suck me off, I barely last any time at all. I'm glad we are doing this together and don't have to be embarrassed about coming so quickly.

We stay tangled up in each other the rest of the morning, with me reading to him or us watching a movie. Sometimes we simply lie here, quietly running our hands over each other. I try to memorize every touch of his skin on mine, to keep close to my heart forever.

Lunch is room service, with Zach in one of his pajama pants and a crop top. He has on his nerdy glasses that I love, and his hair is an utter mess. I've never seen him look more beautiful than sitting next to me eating french fries and laughing over something I said.

Smiling, I reach over to smooth some hair back from his glasses. He pauses, staring at me with his head tilted slightly to the side. "What are you thinking about?"

"How beautiful you are…"

Tears form in Zach's eyes, and he sets his plate to the side before crawling into my lap. I set my own plate down, so I can hold him.

"You really think I'm beautiful?"

I kiss his forehead and then his eyelids, the tip of his nose. "I think you are the most beautiful person I've ever seen. Especially those dark green eyes of yours." A tear escapes down his cheek, and I kiss that, too. "You are beautiful, baby." I lay my hand over his heart, hoping he truly sees how beautiful he is, inside and out.

We start kissing, which leads to us naked with Zach underneath me and both of us rocking into each other until we come.

A nap follows, and then we lie on the balcony together on one lounge with Zach sprawled face-down on top of me while I read to him.

"I love when you read to me."

There's so much emotion behind those words that my breath catches. I set the book aside and run my hands over his back, up under his crop top to hold him. I don't even know what to say back because nothing seems to fit the moment.

"I don't think I can handle it if you leave me again. It was like a part of me was missing. My heart hurt."

Tears fill my own eyes at his quiet words that reflect the pain he felt when we were separated. I know that pain because I felt it, too. "I'm not leaving you again. I promise."

"You can't promise that," he whispers, moving his head to press his lips to my chest.

Yes, I can. I don't think I can physically walk away from him, knowing I won't see him for months. I can't do it again.

"Read to me some more, *please?*"

I pick up the book and find my place to resume reading. Zach relaxes into me even more, and all I can think about is that I never want this between us to end.

We stay out on the balcony until dark and then order room service for supper. Zach turns on music and dances around the room like a nerdy ballerina, making me laugh. When his twirl almost ends in a face-plant, I join him so I can catch him if he falls.

After we eat, we take a walk out by the lake and around the hotel grounds. I'm careful to keep us in well-lit areas where people are close by.

"I'm thinking about starting some type of LGBTQ-plus community in Rockville," he says as we are walking.

"Really? Where at?"

"I was thinking that maybe I could start out having a meet-up at the library once a week. If enough people come, then I can start planning things. We could go bowling one week, or maybe have a carry-in at the community park, or maybe if we get big enough, we can use the town's community center. I don't know… I just think there needs to be a way to make everyone feel like they aren't alone in it all. I don't mean just for kids either. I think adults should be able to come, too. Our town is so small, it should include both. Marcy and Mrs. Hines would be great role models to kids."

"It's a great idea, Zach. You know I'll help in any way I can."

"Thank you. I might need you to be there. I'm trying to be strong, but if one of their parents came in upset, I'm not sure if I could keep from having a panic attack."

I hate that he still has to worry about that. "I will be there with you every step of the way, but I think you would keep it together. Remember when you and Avery were in the bathroom? You didn't fall apart; you kept it together until we were alone; you were strong for him."

He kisses my arm like he's done a million times, but it never gets old and I love it. "I'm not that strong. I always end up screaming for you to come save me."

"You *are* strong, but I love that I can be the one to save you." I lean over to kiss the top of his head.

"Now you're going to be saving everyone as a police officer."

"It's a small town. The majority of my work will be saving kittens and walking old ladies across the street."

"You'll do more than that. I'm worried about you getting hurt."

I stop, turning to face him. "I'll be fine. I'll have a training officer for six months—and Ruger. He's pretty intense and will do anything to protect me."

"What if he doesn't like me?"

"Everyone loves you, Zach. Ruger will probably attach himself to you and ignore me."

Zach taps his finger to his lips. "I'll bake him homemade dog treats."

"Don't spoil him. He's a police dog and doesn't need babying."

He's already started walking again, his mind clearly on baking dog treats. I grin and hurry after him, happy that he's moved on from worrying about me at work.

We make our way back to our room, and I barely get inside the door before Zach is on his knees in front of me, undoing my jeans to tug them down. I lean against the door and watch him lick up and down my cock, getting it wet before sucking on the head slowly. He's already explained what Kelly said about deepthroating, so when he takes me down his throat and holds me there, I try to stay as still as possible. It feels so good that it's hard not to thrust my hips forward. He pulls off and makes a slight gagging noise before doing it again. "Fuck baby, if you keep doing that, I'm going to come down your throat."

He moans around my cock, which vibrates and drives me crazy. I run my fingers through his hair, gripping lightly to pull him off before I come and angling his head so I can see his eyes. He lets me fuck his mouth, but I make sure not to go deep enough to make him gag. It's his eyes begging for my cum that bring that intense pleasure, my body tensing as I unload every last drop in his mouth.

I pull up my jeans enough that I can pick him up off the floor and carry him into the bathroom so we can shower. We undress and I get the bottle of lube to take in with us.

"You know that I don't expect you to get me off every time I do that for you," he says as we wash each other.

"I know, but I like to make you come. Besides, I keep fingering you because I want to be inside of you but don't want to hurt you."

Zach gives me this shy grin. "Oh…then finger away."

In the shower, we kiss for what feels like hours, and yet it's not long enough. "I want to see you get yourself off," I say, pressing two fingers into his hole to stretch him more.

Watching him touch himself, moving his hand up and down over his cock, is almost as hot as watching him come hands-free. I watch how he likes the grip and how fast he goes. How he twists his hand as it moves over the head of his cock. Memorizing all of it so I can do it for him next time. All I have to do is rub my fingers over his sweet spot, and he can't hold back from coming.

Zach and I end up back in bed, cuddled up together to watch a movie. Today was perfect. I loved getting to spend time together, just the two of us. I love our friends, but being with Zach in our own quiet way always brings me a calm that I crave. I've missed the days where we would do nothing but read in our treehouse or lie in my bed talking for hours.

I move my head to kiss his lips, tightening my arms around him. "I love you, baby."

He smiles, his eyes sparkling with happiness. "I love you, Brady."

FIFTY-THREE

ZACH

Brady is still sound asleep when I open my eyes the next morning. The soothing feeling of his chest rising as he breathes almost makes me drift off again. Yesterday was a dream day with him, and I've lost all perspective on his plan of firsts. How can he only want firsts when being together is so perfect?

Now that he's kissed me and loved me in this physical way, I don't think I can just shut it away when he's done. *What am I going to do?* We are going to have sex and then all my firsts will be over with and he'll move on.

Inwardly groaning, I roll over and crawl out of bed to get dressed. Brady and Connor want to spend the day at Universal Studios, and I'm positive Kelly will be rushing over here as soon as possible.

I'm completely ready and even have my fanny pack on when Kelly knocks on our door. Brady growls, raising up on one arm to look at me.

"Come back to bed," he says sleepily.

The knocking resumes, and Brady gets a grumpy look on his face as he maneuvers to the edge of the bed. I run back real quick to kiss him, and he traps me with his arms, prolonging the kiss a little longer before letting me go to answer the door.

Kelly is holding Connor's hand, a clear sign that everything went well.

"Good morning, you two, how was your big date yesterday?"

Connor's cheeks turn red as he tilts his head to Kelly. "You'll have to ask him."

Kelly grins, stepping up on his tiptoes to kiss Connor full on the mouth real quick. "It was the best date, and he was soooo romantic."

That brings a grin to Connor's face. Kelly gives me a long hug and then gravitates back to Connor's side. It's really cute to see them together like this.

We talk for a few minutes until Brady is ready and then take the elevator down to get breakfast. Brady and Connor are googling Universal Studios and trying to decide if we should go there or somewhere else. They watch a YouTube video for all of thirty seconds before Brady clicks his cell screen dark.

"I was thinking we should go to Epcot today."

"I thought you two wanted to go to Universal Studios?"

He shakes his head. "Nah, this is your Christmas present, and I think you would enjoy Epcot more."

Something is going on from the looks Connor and Brady are exchanging.

"We can go to Universal Studios, I don't mind," I offer.

Brady reaches for my hand. "No, it's best if we pick a Disney theme park."

"Why?"

"Because you'll be scared at Universal Studios and won't be able to go on the rides, and I'm not leaving you alone while we go on them," he explains.

"I can stay with him while you and Connor ride them," Kelly interjects into the conversation.

Connor is the one protesting now. "There is no way in hell we're leaving you two alone at a theme park. It's not happening."

"We would spend the entire time worrying about you two," Brady adds in.

"Is it really that scary?" I ask.

Brady opens his cell to show me the mummy ride, and I would in fact be terrified, even though I know it's not real. "I'm sorry that I can't handle scary things. I can try for you?"

"No, it's going to be Epcot," he says firmly, with that stubborn look on his face that means it's pointless to argue.

Epcot *is* a lot of fun, and we try all sorts of foods we've never had before. I want to ask Kelly about how it went yesterday, but they never leave us alone, so I can't. Connor and Kelly are holding hands, hugging, and kissing—a lot. I love seeing them both so happy with each other.

We get back to the hotel to shower before meeting up to eat our evening meal. Brady is on the phone talking with Mom and waves me on to shower by myself, much to my dismay.

I'm combing my hair when he comes into the bathroom to shower. He seems to be lost in thought while he's in there. I put on a little makeup for a change but leave my hair to swoop down over my forehead.

Brady gets out of the shower, towel drying off before joining me at the sink. He rubs his hand over his five o'clock shadow. "You want me to shave?"

"I don't mind when it scratches me, but it's up to you." I like when he leaves a little burn behind, reminding me for hours that he's kissed me.

"Get your butt plug and wash it," he says before I leave the bathroom.

"Umm…oo-okay," I sputter, my face already turning red.

Retrieving the box from his suitcase, I wash it thoroughly with Brady watching while he brushes his teeth.

As soon as I'm done, he orders, "Put your hands on the counter and stay here."

Resting my hands on the vanity counter, I turn my head to watch him reach into the shower for the lube. He comes back to stand behind me, where I can see him in the mirror. There's something very erotic about seeing him behind me with heated eyes.

"Scoot your feet back a little closer to me."

I do, which arches my back and sticks my ass out more. Brady runs his hands down my back to my ass, squeezing a cheek and inciting a moan from my mouth.

"Are you okay with me using the butt plug on you?"

We both know I don't care, but he seems to need to hear it. "Yes." Anything that helps get us to having him inside of me.

"Do you think we can have sex tonight?" I plead, my eyes meeting his in the mirror.

"We will see later… Maybe you wearing this through supper will help get us there." He leans forward to press his lips to my shoulder. "I couldn't live with myself if I hurt you."

I turn my head to kiss him, and he groans into my mouth as our tongues clash. His hand cups my cheek as he deepens the kiss, showing me just how much he wants this, too.

Brady pulls his mouth away to kiss down my neck to the top of my back. I hear the lube bottle open behind me, and then his fingers are pressing against my asshole. It's still tight, but I welcome the burn because I know pleasure is only seconds away.

His eyes are watching me while he fingers me, using two fingers to rub over that spot that feels like heaven. I'm so hard and needy, but as soon as I open my mouth to beg, he pulls his fingers out. "Brady... please?" I want to remove my hands from the counter and touch myself, but I know he doesn't want me to, and I want to make him happy.

"No, I don't want you to come yet," Brady murmurs in that husky voice he gets when he's turned on. He reaches around me to pick up the butt plug, coating it in lube before it disappears behind me. "Relax, baby."

It's different, feeling something other than his fingers being pushed inside of me. It gets tight but then eases. I can feel it, though. It's not something I'm going to be able to forget about and ignore.

"We need to get dressed, or we are going to be late for our reservations."

My mouth falls open in horror, but he only smiles while he washes his hands.

"You're not serious, are you? I can't go out when I'm this hard!"

His smile turns into a smirk. "Yes, I'm serious. Wearing a plug will go easier if you're turned on."

I huff. "Where did you learn that?"

"YouTube. I watched videos on what bottoms said would make it easier. What to do, what not to do. I read a bunch, too."

"I think they're wrong. Getting off will make it so much easier."

He swats my ass lightly as he moves away. "Don't whine."

"I'm not whining!" Okay, maybe I do sound like I'm whining. "Brady! This isn't fair!" I follow him into our room, feeling the plug in my ass as I walk.

Brady is going through his suitcase to find clothes and looks over his shoulder at me. "It's completely fair because I'm hard as a rock right now and want nothing more than your mouth on my cock, but I'm going to suffer through dinner right along with you."

Now I feel bad for whining about it. "I'm sorry. I shouldn't have complained. We can suffer together."

"I promise when we get back, I'll make you come...twice."

It's getting so hot in the room that my whole body feels flushed. "Stop turning me on, Brady!"

He laughs, sliding his boxers on while watching me. "Better get dressed, or Kelly and Connor are going to see you naked with a plug up your ass."

I hurry to find clothes, wondering the entire time how I went from missing him so much that I felt like part of me died, to having him torture me with a butt plug. I pinch my leg just to make sure I'm not dreaming, and it hurts more than I thought it would.

Kelly and Connor show up just as we finish putting our shoes on. Brady takes my hand until we are out in the hallway, then moves it to the small of my back. I don't think he realizes how intimate we look together now. It's just natural to be this much closer together. Connor is noticing, though, and he keeps giving me concerned looks.

There are times while we are eating that I can't keep from squirming. Brady always gives me heated eyes when I do, knowing exactly why I can't keep still. He puts his hand on my leg at one point to help calm me, and it does.

Kelly and Connor are giving each other intense looks of their own. I bet they don't have issues having sex. It brings home how grateful I should be for the way Brady takes his time with me because most dates wouldn't want to deal with me being a virgin.

I think Kelly notices that I've barely eaten anything, but I've watched a few videos, and they all say to eat minimally if you're going to have anal sex. I wish I would have asked him for last-minute advice on how to make it better for the top.

After dessert, Kelly and Connor come back to our room to visit, and when Connor and Brady disappear out onto the balcony, I finally get a chance to talk to Kelly.

"How was the date? You and Connor are all huggy and kissy now."

He cuddles up with me, kissing my cheek. "It was perfect. God, he's so sweet and treats me like I'm important to him. He opened my door for me and asked if I was cold or if I was hungry. I never thought I would be the type of guy that liked that, but I did."

"Connor is a great guy, and I knew he would treat you right."

"He listened to me and didn't get on his phone to text other people. I can't tell you how many times I had a date that just looked at his phone the whole time." He stares off with this dreamy stare that makes me smile. "He didn't make the date about getting a blow job either."

Kelly's previous dates must have only wanted to hook up. I can't even imagine how that would make me feel.

"Don't get me wrong, I have used guys for hooking up plenty, but Connor makes me want more."

"You two look like you finally did something about that sexual tension that's been going on for the last two months."

He lets his head fall back against the pillow, staring up at the ceiling with a smile. "Yeah, we did and it was fucking hot as hell. Connor has never been with a guy before, but he wasn't shy about it at all. I swear he may not look like a daddy bear, but he is all roaring top and bossy as hell."

I wrinkle my nose. "I'm not sure I want to think of Connor that way."

Kelly laughs. "Oh, my sweet little baby virgin. You're still so innocent and adorable."

"I'm not as innocent as I was," I mumble, feeling the plug in my ass as a reminder.

"Why do you look so nervous?"

I peer around him to make sure Connor and Brady are still talking where they can't hear us. "Because Brady said we might try having sex tonight," I whisper.

"Ohhhh, that's exciting!"

"He said *maybe*. He doesn't want to hurt me."

"You need to stop being so nervous, honey. Brady will take care of you. I've never seen anyone so in tune with another person as Brady is with you."

Leaning closer, I rest my head on Kelly's chest. "I know, but I want to make it good for him, too. I don't want it to just be about me."

"Honey, he gets to stick his cock in your tight ass. Trust me when I say it's not going to be just about you."

"How can I help make it better?"

Kelly runs his fingers through my hair absentmindedly. "Well... we've talked about prep. You'll want to do that beforehand and then take a shower. When he goes to push inside of you, bear down and he'll go in easier."

My nose wrinkles at the thought. "What if an accident happens or it gets embarrassing?"

"That's why you prep, but you have to remember that it's butt sex, and sometimes embarrassing things do happen—*to all of us.* You both just have to laugh it off and go on."

"I don't know if I could laugh it off... I'd be in tears."

"Honey, not everything can be perfect. If the guy is sticking his cock up your ass, he better be able to laugh off any mishaps." He rests his head against mine. "I know that Brady would never make fun of you or be upset. You need to quit worrying and just enjoy it."

I know he wouldn't either. "I know, it's just I'm this virgin and don't know what I'm doing, and he's all experienced. What if I can't live up to what he's had before?"

"Zachary Phillips, I don't want you comparing yourself to anyone else!"

"Zachary Phillips?"

"Well, I can't use your last name because you hate it. Zach can come from Zachary, so I'm giving you that whole name. Plus, I saw your middle name at the hospital was Phillip...so Zachary Phillips is what I'll use when you're bad."

I move my head to look at him. "When I'm bad?"

He smirks. "Okay, not when you're bad...just whenever I need a full name for emphasis."

Zachary Phillips... "I like it. Do you think I could change my name permanently?"

"I'm pretty sure you can. Dad would know."

Kelly calling him Dad makes me smile. "I'll ask him. I'll need a new middle name, though."

"Hmm...Zachary Kellan Phillips."

"Kellan?"

"It's my full first name. You can be named after me...like we are family."

Tears fill my eyes, and I hug him tightly. "I would be honored to have your name."

"What are you two in here crying about?"

Brady and Connor are both standing at the side of the bed, looking at us like we've lost our minds.

Kelly wipes the tears from my cheeks. "Zach is going to try and legally change his name."

Brady's eyes find mine, understanding in them. "I think that's a great idea. You hate your name and cringe whenever someone uses it."

"What name are you changing it to?" Connor asks.

Kelly answers for me. "Zachary Kellan Phillips."

Brady nods. "I get the Zachary and Phillips part...using your middle name, but where did Kellan come from?"

"He's getting named after me," Kelly says, his tone daring Brady to argue. "My name is Kellan."

"I love it. I'll be named after someone I love, just like other people."

Brady comes around to sit on my other side. "I think it's perfect, too."

"Okay, my work here is done. I've renamed our baby and cuddled him." Kelly hugs me one last time and kisses my cheek before climbing off the bed to step into Connor's arms. "Take me to bed, daddy bear."

Connor's face flushes bright red, but he's grinning. "Let's go, brat."

Brady follows them to the door and locks it behind them. "Who knew that them having sex together would get them to leave early? Maybe we'll get lucky and they'll also sleep in."

"Do you really like the name?"

He starts to unbutton his shirt while gazing at me. "I do like it. I think shedding that last bit of your past will help you embrace who you are better. You're not defined by your name, but at least you could be proud to tell someone your full name."

Watching him unzip his jeans reminds me that if we are going to do this...I have to suck it up and prep for it. "Umm...so I'm going to need a little bit of time to get ready." My cheeks are burning hot with embarrassment just at the thought of him knowing what I'll be doing.

"You don't have to be embarrassed, Zach. I know what goes on, and it doesn't bother me. Just do your thing and take your time; I'll wait."

Me not being embarrassed is most likely impossible, but I love that he feels that way. I climb off the bed and get the box I need from my bag, hurrying to the bathroom. I hope we can actually have sex tonight, or all of this will be for nothing.

Since I knew this was going to happen, I did my research and know what to do and how many times to do it. I take the butt plug out and put it in a throwaway cup they have for drinking water. Brady was smart and bought antibacterial soap from the shop in the lobby, using it for his hands after fingering me. I pump some into the cup with hot water and leave it to soak while I get this done.

It's not pleasant, but I get through it. I clean the bulb and butt plug before getting into the shower to scrub myself from top to bottom. I read that most men say to douche a couple of hours before having sex, but that didn't happen, so this will have to do.

I wonder if women do this before they have anal sex or if they just wing it. That leads to me wondering if Brady ever had anal sex with any of the girls he dated. My stomach hurts just thinking about it, and I have to push the thoughts away.

Before going out, I find myself pacing and trying to convince myself that I won't cry over being so close to Brady.

I can do this.

Brady is sitting on the edge of the bed, wearing nothing but his boxer briefs. He looks nervous for a second but then smiles and is his normal, confident self. "Are you okay?"

I'm positive my face is red, but I nod. "Yeah, I'm okay."

"You still want to do this? I'll understand if you want to back out."

Moving to stand between his legs, I run my fingers through his hair, staring into his intense blue eyes. "I want to this with you, but are you sure that you still want to? I'll understand if you don't and if it's too much with you being straight and all."

His hands slip around my waist to my bare ass. "I want to do this with you."

"I'm so nervous, Brady," I whisper, wishing I could tell him that I'm not nervous about sex, but that instead, it's about not being able to come back from being so deeply intimate with him. It's knowing my heart will get hurt.

Brady wraps his arms around my back, bringing me closer so he can kiss just below my ear, sending shivers over my skin. "It's just you and me… There's no rush in this, baby."

I turn my head to catch his mouth, and then all nervousness fades away because kissing him is everything.

Brady's hands are everywhere, caressing across my stomach and back, down my ass and back up to my waist. His fingers lightly run over my chest until my skin tingles from his touch. He lifts me effortlessly as he stands, turning to lay me on the bed.

Seeing his naked body crawling up to hover over me is enough to about melt me into the bed. I don't think he even realizes how unbelievably hot he is to me. His strong shoulders and the muscles that ripple when he moves. Those deep blue eyes that never stop telling me he cares or his arms always holding me. I'm so completely in love with him.

Brady lowers his body, pinning me to the bed. His mouth finds mine and devours my very breath. We kiss and touch each other like we are starving for this moment.

Needing to pleasure him, I push my hands against his chest until he's on his back and I'm straddling him. I trail my tongue down his body, licking and kissing until his hard length is bumping my chin. My tongue darts out to lick up the precum glistening on the tip. He tastes like heaven, and I stop torturing us both by sliding his dick between my lips.

"Fuck...I love your mouth." Brady props himself up on his elbows to watch me with lust-filled eyes.

Wanting to please him, I practice taking him deep and holding it for as long as I can before pulling off a little to breathe.

"Baby," he moans, entwining his fingers in my hair, "you're going to make me come."

I lift my mouth and turn pleading eyes on him. "You control it... I want you to."

Brady's eyes flare and then he nods, molding his hand to the back of my head. I lower my mouth on him and let him push my head all the way down until my nose is touching his body. His shaft is in my throat, and my every instinct is to pull off, but his hold is firm.

"Fuck...oh my God, baby...that is so fucking hot," he growls, gripping my hair to pull me off enough so I can inhale.

He pushes my head down again, and I moan over how I'm giving him this. It's a heady feeling to be able to give him pleasure, one I want more of.

Brady lifts my head off again, giving me a few seconds to breathe before pushing me down to take more. "Fuck...I'm going to come," he groans, raising my head and letting me suck as he comes in my mouth.

I lick and suck until he's yanking me up and rolling over on top of me, easing down my body until he's pushing my legs up and out. Brady drags his tongue up my erection, taking me into his mouth to suck and lick. I'm so close to coming but try to hold on.

He licks down over my balls and to my rim, lapping in this way that makes me see stars. Panting, I clutch the sheets and hear moans coming from my mouth that don't sound like me. "Oh my God, Brady... I can't... Fuck, that feels so good."

Brady doesn't stop licking my hole until I'm a melted, begging mess of pleas. He moves back up to take my dick in his mouth again while pressing a finger to push in my asshole.

"More," I groan, "please more."

He slips his finger out and then presses two inside of me. All he has to do is graze the sweet spot and I'm coming, arching up and moaning out the ecstasy I am feeling.

After swallowing down my cum, he raises up to kiss me, wild and passionate. I start to feel like I can't catch my breath, and he slows things down, lying next to me to rub his hands over my chest in this loving way that instantly calms me.

Brady cups my cheek, running his thumb over my lips. "You're so beautiful."

My lips kiss his thumb, but I don't take my eyes from his. "You make me feel beautiful."

He leans over to kiss me gently and slowly this time, his hand moving down to rub my dick just as softly.

It becomes semi-hard the second his hand is on it, and it doesn't take long before it's fully hard for him. I have a feeling that he had us both come so we'll last longer when we finally have sex.

"Do you want to be on top so you can control how fast or slow you do this? Or do you want me on top?"

There's no question in my mind that I don't want to be in control this first time. "You."

He moves to kneel between my legs, pouring more lube on his fingers to use on me again. Feeling them move inside of me has my dick jerking against my stomach. Brady uses his other hand to rub himself until he's hard, his eyes watching his fingers go in and out of my ass as he does.

"Please, Brady, I'm ready. Please?" I need him inside of me. No matter how much prep he does, it's going to hurt at least a little the first time.

He's trying not to look nervous, but I can tell he is, or maybe he's scared of hurting me.

"Brady, I need you inside of me. Please...I need you."

His stubborn, determined look takes over, and he uses the lube to coat his dick, drizzling some over my hole, too.

Relax...relax, I repeat over and over in my head, but it's not working very well.

"Knees up more," he orders, waiting for me to obey before slipping a pillow under my ass to lift me up higher. His eyes meet mine and soften as they gaze at me. "I love you, Zach."

My heart feels like it's going to explode, and tears prick my eyes. "I love you, Brady."

Brady rubs my asshole with the head of his dick and then slowly presses in against the tight ring of muscles. "Breathe, baby. Rub yourself; it'll help."

I hadn't even realized I was holding my breath and inhale deeply, reaching down to wrap my fingers around my erection at the same time. It does help to rub my dick while he pushes in, the pleasure causing me to relax into it more.

"Oh my God...fuck, you're tight," Brady grits out, pushing in a little more.

That brings on the burn and pain of being stretched to fit around his girth. I remember what Kelly told me and bear down as he pushes in more. It helps him to sink in further a little easier. A part of me is screaming his dick needs out of my ass—right now—but the other part is begging for more.

This guttural noise comes from Brady as he bottoms out inside of me. He stays still, letting me adjust, even though his face is strained and his eyes are begging me to be okay.

I'm panting, trying to adjust and get through this burning. "Brady...I need you to move."

"Oh, thank fuck," he groans, pulling out and sliding back in.

The intensity of feeling down there takes over my mind and all ability to think. Pleasure, pain, fullness...all of it mixes together in this all-consuming need to come.

Brady covers my body with his own, kissing my lips as he rocks into me over and over. I wrap my arms around his back, this anchor that I need. This is Brady inside of me, owning me.

Loving me.

FIFTY-FOUR

BRADY

My cock is buried inside Zach's hot, tight ass, and it feels like heaven. I've never felt anything so perfect around my cock. Zach's hands feel so small on my back, his body just as small underneath mine. His green eyes are glazed over with pleasure, moans and whimpers escaping as we kiss.

I'm making love to my best friend, the most important person in my life. That's what this is, making love. All the emotions and love that I have for him are coming out in this beautiful, physical way that is everything I imagined and more.

I kiss him tenderly while thrusting gently, wanting to express to him how much this means to me. He's hard between us but hasn't let go of my back to touch himself. I know that I won't last long because he's too tight and warm around my cock.

"Brady," he moans, "I love you inside of me."

"I love you, baby," I whisper, angling my thrusts to find that spot that will send him to the moon. I know when I find it because his eyes flare and he starts begging to come.

"Please, Brady…right there…oh God…please please…I need to come."

His pleas go straight to my cock, and I can barely hold on to any self-control. My balls are aching for release, the intense pleasure so close to overtaking me. "Baby, you can come for me. Stroke yourself…

I'm not going to last… You feel so fucking good." Tingling starts at the base of my spine, and I know my control is lost. "Come, baby," I growl out, my entire body tensing as pleasure takes over.

Zach is staring up at my eyes, and then he's crying out with his own orgasm. His hole tightens around my cock even more as he comes, bringing me so much feeling I could almost black out from the pleasure of it all.

I collapse when it's over and only just remember to keep some weight off Zach. It isn't until I hear him sniffle that I find the strength to move. Easing from his ass, I roll to my side and gather him into my arms.

"Did I hurt you?"

"It was just so beautiful," he whispers, kissing my neck and wrapping a leg around my back.

It was beautiful. I never thought it could be like this. "It was perfect… You're perfect." I lean back a little, tilting his chin so his mouth is close to mine, and kiss him softly.

When our kiss breaks, he's quiet and clings to me like I'm going to disappear. I wrap him up tightly, trying to give him the reassurance that I'm right here.

I know that what we did is something I'll need to process, but right now, I just want to be in this moment with him.

The silence is broken by Zach getting hiccups, and it helps pull us from the thick emotion that was permeating the room.

"Let's get a shower and clean you up," I say, kissing his forehead and releasing my arms from around him.

He sits up, raking his fingers through his hair to get it out of his eyes. "Can you hand me my glasses?"

I reach over to the side table for them and open his frames so I can slip them on for him. "Better?"

He nods, looking down at the cum all over his stomach. "I definitely need a quick shower."

My cock wants to wake up at the thought of him coming hands-free during sex. It turns me on way too much.

Zach reaches for my hand, and I get the feeling he needs to be close to me right now. I tug him with me to the edge of the bed, and as soon as I stand, I turn around to scoop him up, carrying him to the bathroom. Zach is glued to me in the shower and doesn't say anything as I wash him and then myself.

We don't bother getting dressed after we dry off and brush our teeth. Zach winces when he crawls into bed, scooting over to make room for me. "Did I hurt you, Zach? Be honest."

He gives me his beautiful green eyes that I love. "I feel like you stuck your mammoth dick in my ass, so I'm guessing a little soreness is to be expected."

His smart-ass tone makes me smile. "I suppose you're right, although mammoth is a huge exaggeration."

"It's mammoth. I would know; it was in my ass."

"I'm not sure you've seen enough cocks to know what mammoth is," I point out, walking over to the mini-fridge and getting us some bottles of water. I get into bed next to him and open a bottle for him before opening my own. "Do you want to watch a movie? Or I could read to you?"

"Can we talk for a few minutes first?"

"You know we can always talk." I gulp down a little more of my water and set it aside.

He turns to face me, and I hook his hips to tug him between my legs so he's closer.

"Was it okay for you? Like…it didn't gross you out or anything knowing it was a guy, did it?" He looks so insecure and scared about it that I feel bad for not saying more afterward.

"I meant what I said about it being perfect, and I wasn't grossed out at all. It was you, Zach. Not some guy that I don't care about or love."

He wrinkles his nose like he's thinking about it. "Do you think you'll want to do it again?"

Is that what he's worrying about? That his firsts are over, and we are done? The thought of this being over makes my stomach hurt. I'm not ready for it to end. "Yes, I'll want to do it again. I don't think you're ready to turn loose on the dating world yet."

He ducks his head and concentrates on peeling the label off his water bottle.

"Hey…do you not want to do it again?" I feel sick asking that question.

"I still want to…"

I tilt his chin up with my finger, wanting to see his eyes. "Talk to me, baby."

He crawls into my lap instead, snuggling in close. "I want to be with you again. I'm not ready to try stuff with anyone else."

It's different, both of us naked while he's sitting on my lap, and yet it just feels like we are still us. Still best friends, too. I kiss his forehead, my relief over his words too much for me to dissect right now.

"I'm not ready to go home."

We only have one more day here, and then we fly home on New Year's Day. "I know. I'm not either." There's this unsettling feeling that once we go home, this plan of mine will be over, and we won't be as close anymore.

"Will you read to me, please?"

"Yes, baby," I murmur, kissing his forehead again.

We lie down with him splayed over my chest and me reading to him, running my fingers gently through his hair as I do.

A half an hour later, he's asleep with a peaceful look on his face. I set the book aside on the bed and just watch him sleep.

What am I going to do? I can't imagine going back to what we were after this. Can a gay person be happy with a straight person? Am I straight when having sex with Zach is like fireworks and love all put together? How can I be gay if I'm not attracted to any other men? How can I be straight when kissing a girl makes me feel like I want to run the other way?

So many questions and I don't have answers to any of them.

Zach wakes after an hour nap and seems his usual self. We end up watching Enchanted, one of Zach's favorites, while eating strawberries dipped in chocolate and mozzarella cheese sticks. Halfway through our second movie, Beauty and the Beast, he's asleep.

I end the movie and take his glasses off to set on the table, turning off the light, too. Zach slides his leg between mine, and I go to sleep, wishing we could have one more week here.

ZACH CRAWLING over me is my wake-up call. He's looking for his glasses and soon has them on his face. I glance at the clock, and I am shocked to see it's noon.

Zach sees it, too, and his eyes go wide. "Do you think something bad happened to Kelly and Connor?"

"I think something happened, but not something bad," I answer with a smirk.

He tilts his head to the side. "Ohhhhh…"

"I doubt we have much longer before they come knocking on our door. Connor going without food past noon is a crisis."

Zach and I get dressed and ready to go. Now that we've had sex, I find that we both seem to be a bit clingy with each other. Stealing kisses and lots of hugs between things. It feels natural to be this way with him, just us loving each other.

KELLY AND CONNOR are coming out of their room as we are coming out of ours to go get them. Kelly gives Zach a hug and loops their arms together to walk in front of us to the elevators. I look over at Connor, nudging him with my elbow to get his attention. "You two are up awful late."

"We were busy doing things."

"What kind of things?" I ask with a smirk.

"Shut it, Wellman."

Kelly looks over his shoulder, and Connor smiles this stupid, lovesick smile.

"You have it so bad. You were never like this with Tessa."

"I never felt like this with Tessa. With Kelly, everything seems brighter…like he brings color to everything in my life. I can't explain it, but sometimes you just know that you've found that one person that is it for you. You know that if you fuck it up, you'll never find it again."

He's so sure of himself and how he feels. I wish that I had that confidence and just knew what was meant to be.

The day goes by too quickly. We eat lunch and then swim for a while. Afterward, we lie on lounges and soak up the sun, knowing that we won't be feeling this warmth again for months. By the time we get back to our rooms, it's almost dark out.

We've all showered and are now trying to decide what we want to do for this evening. I should say Connor and I are trying to decide what to do. Zach and Kelly are cuddled up in the middle of our bed, watching a Hallmark movie.

"They are so cute together," he says, watching them through the glass windows of the balcony.

Kelly kisses Zach's cheek and Zach smiles.

"Yeah, they really are. I just worry about both of them being so small. They had us learn about sex trafficking at the academy, and it's made me more protective. Young, small guys like them are huge targets." The stats and videos they showed us still haunt me.

"I worry about them, too. You have no idea how much shopping I had to suffer through while you were gone, just to keep an eye on both of them."

"Thank you for watching over Zach and for keeping me from being an ass when I got back."

"You're welcome. Thanks for letting Kelly live with us. I hated knowing he was living in an apartment alone, in a not-so-nice neighborhood. He's not as tough as he likes to let on."

I stare at the two of them cuddled under the blankets, shaking my head. "Yeah, tough isn't exactly a word I would use to describe either of them."

"We'll get a place together eventually, but I like knowing that if I'm gone, Kelly more than likely won't be home alone or at the very least will have your parents next door."

"Why do you think I bought that house? I wanted Zach to have my parents next door if he needed them."

"We're a bit overprotective," Connor admits, giving me a grin.

"Yes, but I don't think it bothers Kelly or Zach, and I don't see us changing anytime soon."

FIFTY-FIVE

ZACH

"I'm no longer a virgin," I whisper to Kelly, now that we finally have time without Connor and Brady hovering.

"How was it? Was it good? Did Brady freak out over gay sex? Did it hurt?" All his questions are rushed out in a jumble.

"It was unreal and hot and felt like complete bliss." I try to think of his other questions. "It hurt a little, but more like a good hurt type of feeling, where I didn't know if I wanted him to stop or keep going."

Kelly nods like he totally understands that feeling. "Did he freak out at all?"

I can still see Brady's intense expression when he came inside of me. "No, he didn't freak out. He seemed to be really turned on and said he wants to do it again."

"He's so not straight. I don't care what the man thinks he is, but it's not straight. I'm not one to tell people what their sexual orientation is, but come on…straight men don't have sex with other men and want to do it again."

We both sneak a peek at the guys on the balcony, but they are busy talking. "I don't know if we can go back to just being friends. How can I feel all this and then suddenly have to lie next to him without ever doing it again? It'll be impossible."

Kelly squeezes me tightly in his embrace, kissing my forehead. "I don't know either. I highly doubt that Brady will be able to just walk away from this and pretend like he hasn't had his prick up your ass."

A giggle bubbles up at how Kelly talks. "Prick?"

He grins. "What? Prick is a good word to use."

"I don't think prick sounds like something anyone would want in their ass—or mouth, for that matter. It makes me think of prickly."

"You are still my sweet little baby virgin and all innocent. Always will be."

I kiss his cheek and lay my head closer to his, tucking it under his chin. "How long should I wait before doing it again?"

"Errr…it varies. Once your ass is used to it, then it's easier to handle it back-to-back. But if the guy is big and your ass is tight, you might need a few recovery days in between."

"Is it normal for us to have such…open conversations?"

"Who cares if it is or it isn't? I'd rather you ask me than hurt yourself or find out something different the wrong way. You have to forget about the past and realize if you want to talk about something sexual or dirty, then it's perfectly fine."

Maybe I am still letting my past whisper in my ear that I'm doing something wrong. I need to stop letting it have a voice in my head. "You're right and I like being able to talk about it with you. It helps me."

"See? There you go. Besides, you haven't even heard some of the pervy convos that the group has together. We all love sex and aren't ashamed to talk about it or share stories."

I'm sure I'll get to be a part of those fun conversations soon. "Thanks for being here for me, Kelly. I couldn't have done this without you."

"You never have to thank me, my little babykins."

His nickname makes me laugh, and then I remember what I wanted to tell him. "When we get home, you're getting a kitten."

"What?"

"A kitten. Brady and I are getting you a kitten for your own."

Kelly moves so he can see my face. "Like my own kitten at your house?"

"*Our* house," I correct him. "It's your home, too, Kelly. You're a part of our family and should be able to have a kitten."

Tears fill his eyes and spill over to run down his cheeks. "I've had friends, but you guys really have become my family. I needed that."

"Aww, don't cry," I murmur, drawing Kelly into my arms to hug him tightly. "You've brightened up our lives and make everything better just because you're with us."

"Oh God, you're going to make me cry even more," he says, sniffling as he hugs me back.

"Why is it that every time we leave you two alone in here, we come back to crying?"

Kelly turns at Connor's voice and wipes some tears from his cheeks. "Because we are saps and cry, and because I'm getting a kitten!"

Brady and I exchange grins over how happy Kelly is about his kitten.

Connor shakes his head, his eyes never leaving Kelly. "You're crying over a kitten?"

"Well, that and the fact that I have a family now."

I squeeze my arms around him, kissing his cheek. I know what that feeling is like when you realize that you have a family that wants you.

"I suppose I can let a kitten sleep with us," Connor says, coming over to sit on Kelly's other side. I let go so Kelly can move into Connor's arms instead of mine.

Brady comes over to sit on my other side, and I lean against him. He kisses the top of my head and asks, "Okay, what do we want to do tonight?"

"We could find a gay club in Orlando to bring in the new year?"

Brady is immediately shaking his head no at Kelly's suggestion. "No, I'm not taking you two into a club on the craziest night of the year. Not in this big of a city."

"I have to agree with Brady. The last place we need to be tonight is in a crowded club, in a city that none of us are familiar with. Especially with two twinks that every guy will want to get with."

"They are having a New Year's Eve party downstairs for everyone that's staying here," I suggest. "It's for families, too, so I'm sure it's safe for us twinks and the two protective guys we will be with."

Brady pokes me in the side for my smart-ass tone.

Everyone agrees we will go down to eat and try the party. If we don't enjoy it, we can always come back up to the room and play games.

Connor is starving, so we all hurry to change clothes for the party. Brady and I manage to sneak in some hot kisses before it's time to leave. I'd much rather be staying in with him all evening, just the two of us.

The party is half indoors, half outdoors with strands of white lights hanging everywhere, making it beautiful and a little romantic. A DJ is playing music, and there are already people on the dance floor.

It's fairly warm tonight, so Brady steers us to one of the round tables outside for us to eat dinner at. It almost feels like an outdoor wedding that you'd see in a romantic movie.

The food is delicious, and we spend a lot of the dinner with Kelly discussing potential names for his kitten. We also talk about my idea of starting an LGBTQ+ community in Rockville, and they all throw out ideas to help get it started.

It's during moments like these with my friends, when I feel so incredibly happy, that I reflect on how different my life is now. How precious having a real family is and all the love they provide. Family isn't about blood. It's about who shows up when you need them. It's about who you laugh with and cry with and who loves you for you, not who they think you should be. Brady has given me a family and love. He's selflessly shared his own with me and changed my life. I shudder to think of what my life would be right now if I'd never met him. Would I still be hiding being gay? Would Matthews have killed me when he found out? I remind myself that none of that matters now. I only hope that I can help kids like me, give them a second chance at experiencing what having family and love truly means.

The back of Brady's hand running down the side of my face brings me out of my thoughts. I give him a smile, but he seems to know I was all up in my head. "Dance with me," he says, standing and tugging me to my feet.

Connor and Kelly follow us onto the dance floor, where Brady pulls me into his arms. It's a slow song, and I have to crane my neck to look up at him.

"You're beautiful," he says, giving me one of his smiles that melts me.

Seeing his intense blue eyes reflecting how much he means those words brings emotion thick in my throat. I swallow hard and give him a smile of my own. "I love you, Brady."

"I love you, baby."

The song ends and the next one has a fast beat that gets us all dancing together. I've never seen Brady dance like this, and we have a blast. He's not afraid to dance close and often has his hands on me. As the evening goes on, the families with kids leave, and the crowd becomes mainly adults. We dance and laugh, eat more food, and then dance some more.

When it comes time for midnight, everyone stands, counting down together. I hear a lot of Happy New Years, but all I see is Brady leaning down to kiss me. It's not a long kiss, yet it's passionate and sweet, bringing in the new year perfectly.

"Happy New Year, baby," Brady says softly near my ear, pressing his lips just below and hugging me tightly.

We pull apart, and I'm grateful to see that Connor is too busy kissing Kelly to notice what we were doing a few seconds ago.

The music starts up again, and Brady brings me close to dance. We do get some disapproving looks from a few older couples once in a while, but otherwise, no one seems to care that four guys are dancing together. Two girls about our age—that are definitely together—join our little group, and we have a great time dancing for way too long.

By the time we leave for our rooms, I'm dead on my feet and can barely function. It's like as soon as my body knew we were done dancing, it just quit on me. Brady leads me into our room, and I flop onto the bed facedown, not caring if I have my shoes on or not.

"Okay, baby, let's get you ready for bed."

I feel Brady pulling my shoes off, one by one. He rolls me over and unzips my jeans, tugging them down my legs until they are off. I try to help unbutton my shirt, but my fingers won't work. He chuckles and does it for me, helping me to get that off, too.

"Come on, let's get you in the shower."

"I'm too tired to shower," I mumble, wanting to sink into the bed and never leave.

Brady doesn't give me a choice because he picks me up and carries me into the bathroom. He deposits me on the shower bench so he can get undressed and turn the water on.

"You know when you get this tired, you fall asleep standing up?" There's humor in Brady's voice, and I open my eyes to see that I'm holding on to him with my head on his chest while he soaps up my hair.

"I danced too much." My words sound slurry, and I lick my lips in the hope it'll help them move better.

"Stay awake with me while I rinse your hair," Brady orders, moving us under the water more.

I manage to stay awake until I towel dry off with his help, but I'm so tired that I doze off sitting on the counter while he brushes his teeth.

"I love you, baby." I hear Brady say, bringing me out of my haze enough to feel him pulling the blankets up over us. I try to form the words to say it back, but sleep takes over.

FIFTY-SIX

ZACH

Brady's fingers trailing a path gently over my forehead and down my cheek is my wake-up call. My eyes open to find his blue ones moving over my face with this loving look that melts me. His fingers trace over my lips, only to be replaced by his mouth as he presses it against mine.

Maybe it's because we are going home today, but we kiss slowly and reverently, memorizing each other's lips, sounds, and touch. He's telling me that he loves me with his tenderness, and I'm telling him I love him with my soul.

Eventually, we can't hold back from the fire that burns underneath every touch and need more. Brady pulls me on top of his body so he can wrap his hand around both our hard lengths as I rock against him.

Our kissing continues even after we've both come, neither of us wanting this moment to end. It isn't until Brady's alarm goes off that we break away, breathless.

This fear that things will change when we get home hangs over me, and I'm quiet as we shower. The silence continues while we pack up our suitcases and check the room to make sure we didn't forget anything. Our backpacks have everything important in them for the trip home.

Brady tugs me over for a kiss before we go down for lunch. "Hey, we will come back again. I promise."

Wrapping my arms around him, I nod into his chest. "I know. Thank you for this present. It's been the best week of my life."

"Mine, too," he whispers, hugging me back.

WE EAT lunch with Connor and Kelly, who both seem a little melancholy about going home, too. It could also be that we stayed up way too late and even though we slept in past noon, we are all still tired. Kelly and I buy a couple more things at the little shop while Brady and Connor get our suitcases from the room. Brady checks us out, and then we are on our way to the airport.

The airport is busier than I thought it would be on a holiday, and I feel claustrophobic with so many people around. It's a relief when we finally get to our gate to wait on the plane, and I sit under Brady's arm in the corner, away from everyone.

We both sleep most of the two hours home, and things seem a little brighter because of it. We get our luggage and walk out to find Dad. He's pulled up to the curb waiting for us, and I have to admit that I missed him way too much. I rush over to his waiting arms, hugging him tightly.

"I missed you guys," he says, kissing the top of my head before letting me go so I can step aside and let him hug the others. "Mom missed you, too, and is home cooking a meal that will rival Christmas dinner."

That makes us all smile, and I feel the veil of sadness lift from me.

We load up the luggage, and Connor sits in front with Dad, while I sit in the middle between Brady and Kelly in the back.

"So tell me about your trip? What was your favorite thing that you did?"

Brady and I exchange glances because I think we both know our favorite thing isn't something we can tell Dad about.

"My favorite theme park was the Magic Kingdom," I offer, hoping I'm not blushing from my thoughts. "It was everything I dreamed it would be."

Kelly speaks up next. "Mine was probably the swimming and lazy river at the hotel."

"My favorite was the food...all the food."

We all laugh at Connor's answer, and Kelly rolls his eyes. "You're beyond obsessed with food."

"What about you, Son?" Dad asks Brady.

Brady squeezes my hand. "Mine was getting to spend time with Zach and watching him see everything for the first time."

I meet his eyes and can see the sincerity in them. "Aww, thank you, Brady." I want to kiss him so much right now.

"I was thinking this summer we could take a trip with the whole family. I know the girls want to see Disney, and it's been forever since we took a vacation. Plus, Grandma and Grandpa would like us to come down and visit them." Dad looks in the rearview mirror at Kelly. "The whole family, which means Kelly and Connor included."

Kelly blinks back a few tears and leans into me. "Thanks, Dad."

I put my arm around him and kiss his cheek. "See, you have a family."

That leads to Kelly telling Dad about the kitten he's going to be getting. Connor and Kelly argue about names and whether they should get a male or a female. Their nonstop banter keeps us entertained for the entire trip home.

Dad pulls up to our front door, climbing out to help get the suitcases from the back. "Better hurry up and head over for supper, or your mom is going to be upset."

"We'll be over in a few minutes," Brady promises. "Thanks for picking us up, Dad."

Dad gives me another hug before leaving us to drive next door.

We hurry inside with our luggage and to change clothes. There's something about airplanes that make me feel dirty. It feels good to be home with all the familiar comforts that I love. I can still smell my favorite Christmas candle scent in the air, and it makes me smile.

Brady and I pause only long enough for one kiss because I'm anxious to see Honey, Mom, and the girls. We get the gifts for them out of our bags and are ready to go.

The second we walk in the patio door, Honey is crying and jumping on me. I hug all over her, grinning at how much she missed me. "I missed you, too."

Honey switches to whining all over Kelly, who baby talks to her like he always does. I see Mom hugging Brady, and then she's hugging me next, checking me over to make sure I'm in one piece.

"He's fine, Mom," Brady says from beside me.

"I know, I was just making sure."

The next hour is full of love and chaos like usual. They open their gifts, and we eat a huge meal as if it's Christmas all over again. The girls find out that Dad wants to take them this summer, and then it's all about everything they want to see.

Every second is beautiful to me, watching my family together. Brady has his hand on the back of my neck, and any time I glance at him, he gives me these intense looks that make my insides quiver. The problem is, I think Mom and Dad have noticed the way he's looking at me, too. They are the last people I want to know about our arrangement of him helping me with all my firsts.

Brady and I are stacking the dishwasher and putting food away when his phone rings. He looks down at it and then hurries to answer.

"Hey Stella, is everything okay with Ruger?"

So Stella is the one watching his dog. I don't know how to feel about that.

"Really? You're here?" He starts walking to the front door. "I'm at my parents' house next door, the one on the right."

Stella is here. My stomach is telling me I shouldn't have eaten supper. Kelly and Connor both give me a sympathetic look. As Brady disappears out the front door, Kelly gravitates to my side and holds my hand.

"Honey, come here." I don't know if he's bringing Ruger in or what, but if he is, I don't want her rushing up into his face. She's sitting next to me when Brady walks in the door holding the leash that is attached to a rather intense-looking German Shepherd. Stella comes in behind him, as beautiful as she was in the pictures and all smiles, too.

"Everyone, this is Ruger, my partner," Brady says, squatting down to rub his ears, very obviously in love with his dog.

"And I'm Stella. So easily forgotten when he's with his dog," she jokes next to him.

"Sorry, this is Stella." He stands up and motions to the patio door. "Why don't we take the dogs outside for their first meeting, and I'll make the introductions out there. He's been in a car for eight hours and needs to run."

I didn't bring a coat with me, but I feel too sick over Stella being here to care. "Come on, Honey."

We all step outside into the backyard, Mom and the girls last because they grabbed coats. Brady holds on to Ruger as he and Honey meet, but he seems fine with her. More than fine. Honey loves all dogs and just wags her tail, wanting to play. Brady lets Ruger off the leash, and the dog is gone, running the perimeter of the yard. I'm pretty sure he's sniffing and scoping out everything as if he's making sure his new home isn't some drug house with guns.

We all watch him for a few minutes before Brady turns to Stella. "Stella, this is my family; my Mom, Emily, and my Dad, Michael."

She shakes both of their hands and then turns to the girls. "And you must be Anna and Meg." She gives them both a smile. "I've heard so much about you both."

Meg and Anna don't say anything back.

"Which one of you is Connor?" Stella asks the three of us not introduced yet.

Connor steps forward to shake her hand. "That would be me."

"Brady talked about you so much that I should have recognized that you were the football player out of the three."

Brady looks uncomfortable as he introduces us. "This is Zach and Kelly."

She offers her hand to me. "It's nice to meet you. Brady didn't tell me about you two, but I'd love to get to know everyone."

My breath catches, like someone just stabbed a knife in my chest.

He didn't tell her about me.

He told her about everyone in the family but me. My eyes go to his, and there's an apology there, but I look away, refusing to accept it. *Was he ashamed of me?* Ashamed to tell her that I share a room with him or of how close we are?

"Excuse me." I leave them outside and go in to finish up the dishes. Kelly and Connor follow, quietly helping me. Kelly is sad and upset for me, but Connor's expression says he is pissed off. Mom comes in, giving me a hug before helping. Great, I'm sure everyone knows I've gotten my feelings hurt.

Am I overreacting by being upset over this?

The others come back in, including the dogs. Brady's eyes are following me, but I refuse to look his way.

"What happened to us meeting tomorrow halfway?" Brady asks.

Stella does this little laugh that grates on my nerves. "I missed my sleeping buddy and thought we could spend some time together."

Sleeping buddy?

My head whips up involuntarily to look at Brady. He shakes his head as if he knows that she just broke my heart. Brady slept with her while I was here dying inside. He replaced me so easily that I couldn't possibly mean to him what he does to me.

I back up, needing to get out of here. Away from her. Away from him.

"Zach," Brady says, pain in his voice.

Shaking my head, I turn to walk to the front door because to get to the patio door, I'd have to go past Brady.

"Zach, wait… Let me explain," Brady calls out behind me.

My insides are jittery, and I feel like I'm going to throw up. I whirl around, my hand shaking as I hold it up for him to stop. "No, I don't want to hear it. You didn't tell her about me, and you replaced me in your bed so easily. Maybe she can take over now, and you can kiss her! Make love to her!"

Mom's gasp reminds me that my entire family is standing here, and I just blurted that out in front of them. Brady's face hasn't left mine, total anguish there.

I'm hurting him because he hurt me, and that's not who I am. "I'm sorry," I whisper to only him before turning to walk away.

Kelly is a step behind me, taking my hand as I walk to our house. How did I go from being so happy this week to feeling like Brady stomped all over my trust and heart today? All I know is that I need some space to think about all this. I'm in love with Brady and he doesn't feel the same way.

FIFTY-SEVEN
BRADY

Zach disappears out of the kitchen with Kelly at his heels. As soon as he's out of my sight, my chest fills with panic that I might lose him. *What have I done?* I can't lose him.

I hand Stella Ruger's leash and run for the door to follow Zach.

He's halfway to our house and doesn't stop when I call his name. Chasing after him, I grab his shoulder so he'll stop and look at me. "I don't want to lose you because of this, please, Zach."

His green eyes are raw with pain and emotion as he steps toward me, his chest heaving. *"You're my home.* Don't you get that? *You* are my home. You've always been my home. Always will be. But right now, I need you to give me some space because you hurt me." He rubs his hand over his heart. "You really hurt me."

Zach pulls from my grip and keeps walking, but not before I see the tears spill from his eyes to run down his cheeks.

His words are like a knife cutting straight through my heart. I hurt him. Something I swore I would never do. I hurt the one person I love more than anyone or anything in this world.

I stand here frozen, scared to go after him because I don't know if I have the answers he'll need. Scared to walk away and be any further from him.

The choice is made for me when he backs out of the garage, avoiding looking at me, and drives away, Kelly with him.

Fuck fuck fuck fuck! I pull out my cell to call him, but it goes straight to voicemail. I try calling again and again, but he must have his cell turned off.

What did I do to us?

I know that I should go back to deal with Ruger and Stella right now, but instead, I walk the rest of the way to our house to be alone.

Sitting down on the edge of our bed, I pick up Eeyore and hug him to my chest. Tears stream down my cheeks as the pain becomes unbearable. This room, this house…none of it means anything without Zach. He fills up my life with his love, bringing happiness to every part of me. Without him, everything is just empty. Void.

Connor walks into my room, and I can tell he's furious with me. I don't even care right now. "Go ahead, hit me…punch me. I deserve it."

He sits down next to me instead. "Yeah, you do, but if I punch you, it'll make you feel better and you don't deserve to feel better."

"He's gone." My voice breaks.

"Are you really fucking him?"

I flinch over the word *fucking.* "I made love to him…yeah."

"Tell me that you made a commitment to him before doing that?"

"No, I didn't. He was worried about his first time, and I was scared someone would hurt him, so I convinced him to let me help him." It sounds really stupid when I tell someone else.

"What the fuck, Brady! Why would you do that to him? He deserved to have his first time to be with someone who wants a relationship with him."

"I want a relationship with him!" I shout, getting off the bed to pace in front of him. "He's mine! He's always been mine!"

Connor throws his arms up. "I don't understand you! For the last five years, I've watched you with Zach. You're right; he's always been yours. You love him more than a guy loves his best friend. I've watched you let him sit on your lap instead of your girlfriend. I've watched you get up to get him food instead of your girlfriend. You take him to the movies and hold his hand. You get an entire football team to watch over him. You sleep practically naked, entwined together. It's like you are two parts of a whole. Everyone sees that you're in love with him, but you. Why can't you see it?"

"Because I'm not gay! Don't you get that! I'm not gay. There has never been a time where I saw a guy in the locker room or on TV or anywhere and thought, 'Wow, I'd like to do him.' Zero sexual attraction! I'm not gay!" I run my hand over my face in agony. "I'm messed up, Connor. I'm not attracted to men or women. I hated kissing girls, and I tried so hard to find chemistry with one of them, but nothing. The sheer thought of kissing another one makes me sick to my stomach."

His eyes widen at my confession. "Wait, what about Stella?"

"I never kissed her. Besides, she's a lesbian. I couldn't sleep without Zach, and I was so tired I could barely function. Stella took pity on me and slept in my bed, where I'd close my eyes and pretend she was Zach so I could sleep."

"Why didn't you tell her about him?"

"Because talking about him hurt too much, and I was barely holding it together. I didn't want to share him with anyone either, not after what Carrie did. Zach is mine, only mine."

"Did you feel sick kissing him?"

I sigh, sinking back down on the bed next to him. "No, it was perfect. Kissing Zach is just an extension of all the love I feel for him. I don't understand why he turns me on."

"He turns you on and you love him...so why are you fighting it so much?"

"I'm not gay, Connor. What happens when I don't like kissing him anymore? When that feeling hits with him, too? I'm broken sexually and can't offer him more because I don't know what's wrong with me. He's gay, I'm not. I can't make him happy long-term."

"That's the dumbest shit I've ever heard you say. Did you ever think that maybe you should talk to him about it? That he'd rather be with you for a lifetime of love, even if that didn't include sex? He loves you, Brady. No matter what, he loves you."

Visions of being with Zach forever play through my mind. Our house, kids, dogs...love. For a moment, I let myself think about us as a couple and how I would feel about it. All it does is fill me up with hope and love. Could we be happy as a couple? He deserves so much more than I can give him. I want him to have it all, not just someone who may feel sick every time we kiss.

Connor gets off the bed to walk to my door. "You need to fix this because right now, Kelly and Zach are out there alone. I'll never forgive you if we lose them."

I'll never forgive myself if that happens.

My eyes land on Zach's backpack, and I break out in a cold sweat.

He didn't take his inhaler with him. What if he has an asthma attack being away from me and can't breathe? I try calling him again but only get his voicemail.

"Zach...baby, please call me. I'm sorry...so sorry. Please come home. You left your inhaler here, and I'm worried about you..." I pause, trying to get control over my shaky breathing. "I love you."

Ending the call, I try Kelly again. No answer. I leave him a message that Zach forgot his inhaler. I text them both, too.

The last thing I want to do right now is make small talk with Stella and my parents, but Ruger is my responsibility and not one that I take lightly. Zach consumes my thoughts as I walk back to my parents' house.

Mom and Dad have so much disappointment on their faces that I can hardly look at them.

"Where's Zach? Is he okay?"

I force myself to meet my Dad's gaze. "He drove off with Kelly and won't answer his phone."

"Have you tried calling Kelly?"

Nodding, I lean against the island for support. My body feels shaky from the thought of losing Zach. "He forgot his inhaler..."

Mom and Dad both look super worried now.

"Sorry if coming caused so much trouble," Stella says. "I didn't even know you were gay."

She sounds offended that I didn't tell her. "I'm sorry that I didn't tell you about Zach...and I'm not gay."

The three of them exchange glances, but right now, I don't really care what any of them think. "I'm going to look for them."

Stella gets off the stool she's sitting on. "Do you want me to come with you?"

Dad shakes his head. "I think it's best if you stay here. Emily can show you to our guest bedroom when you're tired. I'll go with Brady to look for Zach."

Dad refuses to let me drive, saying I'm in no shape to be behind the wheel. I get Zach's inhaler and then put Ruger in the back seat of Dad's SUV.

Connor comes out and offers to go along, but we decide it's best if someone is at the house in case they come home. When he finds out Zach forgot his inhaler, he looks as sick as I feel.

"Any idea where they would have gone?" Dad asks as we drive around town.

"No idea. A hotel, maybe?"

Dad drives by the only Inn in town, and Zach's Audi isn't there. Our only option is to drive to nearby towns or head to Pine Falls to check hotels.

"He has Kelly with him, Brady. He will make sure Zach is somewhere safe."

"I know he will, but they are both so small," I say quietly. *Please let them be okay.*

He starts the drive to Pine Falls to check hotels there, the highway stretching out in front of us, and it feels like each mile takes ten minutes. I look over my shoulder to see Ruger lying down on the seat to sleep.

"Brady, your mom and I have tried really hard to stay out of your and Zach's relationship. We know your sexuality is none of our business and that you'll figure it out for yourself when you are ready. But I wish you would talk to me because I can see how much you're struggling, and I don't even know why."

"I don't know, Dad. I don't know what my sexuality is, and I'm all messed up."

"If you're having sex with Zach, I don't see how it can be all messed up. When did this start between you?"

My dad is not the person I want to talk to about sex, but I know if anyone can fix this issue, he can with some of his wisdom.

"Right before our trip to Disney. He's been so worried about dating and finding someone who will be gentle. I couldn't stand the thought of someone hurting him and came up with this idea of helping him with all his firsts...so he knows what he's doing when he finally starts dating."

Instead of telling me I'm an idiot, Dad is quiet for a minute while he thinks about it.

"Now that you've helped him with his firsts, if he wants to date and find another guy, how are you going to feel about that?"

"It's not happening," I blurt out. Even the thought of another man touching him, touching him like I have, makes me insane.

"Why? If you only wanted firsts, why can't he move on?"

"Because he's mine!"

Dad gives me an understanding look with no judgment lining his

face. "He's always been yours, Brady. More than I think you even realize. Are you sure that you did this to help him with his firsts, or did you
do this because the thought of being with Zach in that way was something you wanted?"

Staring out the window, I try to think about his question and be
honest with myself. Would I have been okay with Zach being on a
dating app and having sex with guys if it wasn't his first time?

No, I would have been sick over it. As sick as I was when I thought
he was with Kelly.

But did I want to kiss and touch him?

I think back to how I always woke up with a hard-on, or how sometimes I'd wake up rocking into him, or about the time I woke up kissing
his neck. It dawns on me that I never woke up next to Stella with an
erection; it's only ever been Zach.

As for wanting him when we were talking about his firsts, I don't
know. My body was turned on at the thought, but maybe it was just me
loving him and wanting to give this to him. I was turned on when I saw
him on the dance floor at the club, and I was turned on when watching
porn, picturing him instead of the men on there.

I'm so confused. "I don't know, Dad."

"I think deep down you do. Ultimately, only you can know how you
feel and what you want or desire. But I will tell you that you light up
around Zach. When he's home, you want to be with him. When he's
gone, you wish he was home. You hold him like he's the most precious
gift to you. You talk to him like you would to the person you're going to
spend your life with. You gave him your heart as if he's the only one
who has claim to it.

"Watching you date was painful. Every time you left, you dreaded it
and didn't enjoy yourself. You didn't come home laughing or excited
about being with them. You came home and went to find Zach,
holding him with relief on your face that it was over and you were back
with the person you loved.

"Your mom and I love you. All we want is for you to be happy. We
will support you no matter who you love."

"But I'm not gay, Dad. I even tried to look at men when we were
swimming, and nothing. I feel nothing. I've never once wanted to have
sex with a guy…or a girl, for that matter. I can think someone is attractive, but I don't have any desire for any of them."

"Yes, you do…you have for Zach. He's a guy, and you desire him."

"So what does that make me? Gay, but only for one guy?"

"Why does it matter? If you love someone and want to be with them, who cares what your sexuality is? Love is love, Brady."

I've heard the "love is love" so many times, and I've even said it myself a few times, but I let it sink in that love is love could apply to us.

"I'm scared, Dad. I'm scared of hurting him. I'm scared of promising him the world and then finding out that I am not attracted to him anymore."

"Everyone is scared when they fall in love. I was terrified of being what your mom needed. She gave me those blue eyes of trust, and I was scared I couldn't live up to that. But you know what? She was just as scared that she couldn't give me everything either. We are human and do things that aren't perfect. The truth is that your mom was way stronger than I gave her credit for. She held me up as much as I did her. We gave to each other, sometimes one of us giving more than the other, but then the other would give more when needed. We still do that for each other and always will. I know Zach is far stronger than you think, and he'll walk through fire to take care of you if you need him to. He's probably just as scared as you are right now."

Zach's face outside our house flashes before me. He was so hurt, and now he's not with me. I know he's scared and is needing me.

You're my home.

He said those words with so much emotion and conviction. *You're my home.* It resonates with me in a way no other words ever have—even more than *I love you.* Zach is my home.

My heart.

"He told me that I'm his home," I whisper, staring out into the darkness and praying he's okay.

"He told me once when you were gone that he was homesick. He was homesick for you."

Tears well up in my eyes, and I don't even bother wiping them away. "I love him, Dad. I love him so much that it hurts. It's painful because what if something happens to him or he dies? It'll be like my heart dies."

Dad reaches across the seat to squeeze my shoulder. "That is what love is, Son. Sometimes we do lose the ones we love, but can you imagine life without him? All you can do is treasure each day you have with him. Being afraid to love him fully is only hurting both of you."

"What if I find out I'm not attracted to him later? It would crush him."

"You have a lot of 'what ifs' that may never happen. The chances of you being attracted to him now and having that go away are pretty slim. What if every time you're together, it's more powerful than the last time? What if you love each other so much that life is beautiful? What if you have a family and support each other in every way? What if Zach laughs and smiles at you every day for the rest of your life?"

Dad's *what ifs* fill me up with want and hope. What if we *can* live every day loving each other more than the day before? "You're right, Dad. I don't want to waste any more time worrying about what may or may not happen. I just want to love him."

Dad gives my shoulder one more gentle squeeze before moving it back to the steering wheel. "Now we just need to find him so you can tell him that."

FIFTY-EIGHT

BRADY

W e drive around for two hours and can't find Zach's SUV anywhere.

Connor calls while we are on our way home, and I put him on speaker phone.

"Did they come home?"

"No, but Kelly just called me."

Relief pours through me. "Where are they?"

"He wouldn't tell me. Said they are staying with someone he knows and that it's safe. He also said that he has the spare inhaler with him from when we were on vacation. He's already had Zach use it."

If he had to use it, it means Zach's asthma flared from stress. "Did he have a panic attack?"

"No, Kelly said that he cried so much it had made him wheezy, but that he's sleeping now."

Fuck, my chest feels tight and painful knowing Zach was crying. "Will he let me talk to him?"

"I doubt it. He didn't even talk long enough for me to explain about Stella. He didn't want to wake Zach by talking on the phone."

"That's it? That's all he said?"

"Yeah. I'm sorry, Brady. If I knew where they were staying, I'd take you there myself."

"I know, thanks, Connor. We'll be home in ten minutes."

"See you then."

Dad tries to point out the positives. "At least they are somewhere safe, and Kelly has his inhaler. He's taking care of him."

It doesn't make me feel any better, especially knowing Zach cried himself to sleep.

When we get back, Stella has already gone to bed. Mom comes over to give me a hug, and I cling to her longer than usual. "I'm sorry I messed up the evening, Mom."

She kisses my cheek. "All that matters right now is that you're all okay."

I'm definitely not okay right now. "I should get Ruger out to run and then feed him."

Dad gives me a hug before I go. "It'll all work out, Brady. That boy loves you more than anything in this world. He'll come home, and you'll get a chance to explain. He won't want to be away from you for long. Trust me."

I nod, but inside I'm screaming that even one night is too long.

Ruger runs around outside for a little while, and then I take him in to get him settled. Zach has bought him bowls that have been personalized with Officer Ruger Wellman printed on the sides. I find toys, a big blue dog bed, and a giant collapsible wire crate. Zach really did think of everything he would need. I had planned on getting it all before going to meet Stella, but it didn't quite work out that way.

My K-9 training officer recommended that we keep the dog in a crate at night, especially in the beginning. It'll help them feel more secure because that's what they are used to and will help us to remember they are working dogs.

Not sure how long that will last, but I set up the crate in our bedroom and get him all settled in. Honey is lying on Zach's spot with her head on his pillow, her brown eyes depressed. "I know, girl. I miss him, too."

Connor and I end up in the family room, neither of us able to sleep. I'm restless and have a hard time sitting still when all I can think about is Zach. Is he sleeping or having nightmares? Is he crying still or having issues with his asthma?

It is killing me to know that he is hurting right now. All because he thinks Stella and I had more of a relationship than we did.

"You're going to make yourself sick worrying and pacing."

I sink down on the couch next to Connor. "I'm already sick from worrying about Zach."

"It's best you don't see him until you figure out what you're going to do with your relationship. You can't keep having sex with him and not have it mean anything."

It pisses me off that he thinks he has any say over what I do with Zach. "I talked with Dad. I want to be with Zach. In every way. All the time. And no one is going to keep me away from him."

Instead of being pissed back, Connor grins. "About fucking time you realize that you're in love with Zach and nothing else matters."

"If I ever forget it, I'm asking you to punch some sense into me."

"Don't worry, I'll do you one worse. I'll send Kelly after you."

We both give a small laugh.

"I miss them being here," I say, staring around the room like it's empty and depressing.

Connor nods. "I miss them, too. They do bring life and laughter to this house."

"To us," I add.

We talk about all the silly things they both do and the things we love about them. Connor ends up falling asleep, but I barely doze off before jerking awake from not having Zach curled into me. I know there's no point in trying to sleep without him, and instead, I watch mindless TV shows while thinking of Zach and hoping he's okay.

BY SIX IN THE MORNING, I've showered, fed the dogs, and taken them outside to run around. I'm going to find Zach today. Even if I have to drive through every neighborhood in every surrounding town.

The need to stay busy continues, and I unpack all our clothes, put in laundry, and throw out all the outdated food in the fridge from us being gone for a week.

Ruger is getting antsy, and I take him back outside to run through some training with him. Stella comes out while I'm working him and stands next to me.

"Good morning, Brady."

"Morning."

"Did you find Zach?"

"No, but Kelly called last night to let us know they were okay."

"That is good news. Do you want to tell me why I never knew about Zach?"

"Because Zach is mine, and I didn't want to share him with anyone."

She crosses her arms over her chest. "You must really love him."

"I do. Being away from him at the academy was the hardest thing I've ever had to do, and I'll never do it again."

"So you're not gay, but you're having sex with a guy that you're in love with?"

It sounds stupid even to me, but it's really none of her business.

Stella sighs when I don't answer her. "Look, I was going to stay and visit, but I don't think now is the best time. I have a girl that I used to date that lives about an hour from here. I called her, and she invited me to stay for a few days before I drive home."

Relief that I have one less thing to worry about right now flows through me. "Thanks, Stella. I know all this was my fault, and I appreciate you bringing me Ruger."

"No worries. I'm getting laid out of it, so we are all good. Besides, it's my fault for showing up without an invitation and calling you my sleeping buddy in front of your family."

True. Who does that?

She says goodbye to Ruger and gives me a hug before heading back inside my parents' house to get her things and leave.

Connor leans out the door, waving me over. "Kelly called. He's going to come over this morning and pack up a few things for both of them."

"Did he say when?"

"No. He did say Zach is not handling being away from you very well."

"Fuck! I can't take this, Connor. It's all just a misunderstanding, and I just need five minutes with him to explain."

"Let me talk to Kelly when he gets here. I think it'll go better than you jumping him when he walks through the door."

My first instinct is to scream no because I want to talk to Kelly the second he pulls in the driveway. But Connor knows him better than I do, and I need this to go well. "Fine, but only if you promise that you won't let him leave until I talk to him."

He gives me a quick nod. "I promise."

Now that I know Kelly is coming here, I can't leave to go search for

Zach. I pace the house for a while until my edginess makes Ruger get all keyed up. Slipping on a coat, I take him outside and watch him run around. I sit shivering on a bench that Zach put out under the only big tree in our yard. It almost feels like our first snowstorm of the year is coming.

Leaning over to rest my arms on my legs, I think of Zach. How I miss him and those beautiful green eyes of his. I miss his smile and laughter. I miss kissing him and touching him. I miss his crop tops and pj bottoms. I miss his awkwardness and the million times he's almost face-planted. I miss giving him pleasure and seeing him all needy for me. I miss seeing the love on his face when he's on his knees for me. I miss being able to show him how much I love him.

The patio door opens and Kelly comes walking out, holding a blanket. My heart jumpstarts because he's finally here and I'll have a chance to plead my case.

Kelly sits down next to me, spreading the blanket over us and cuddling close. He reminds me of Zach in how he leeches to my side. I put my arm around him and fix the blanket.

"What is it with you and Zach doing all your heavy thinking outside? It's freezing out here."

"I don't know. We can go inside if you want?"

"Let's talk out here first because I think you'll tell me more if Connor isn't listening in, and he'll hover if we go inside."

I nod, knowing he's right. "How is Zach? Is he okay?"

"He needs you, even if he won't admit it." Kelly shifts a little so he can see my face. "Connor told me about Stella and why you did the things you did. He also thinks that you're in love with Zach and want more than just his firsts."

"I do want more. I should have told Zach that, but I was so messed up in my head over my sexuality that I didn't feel I could promise him more. Now I simply don't care what it is and just want to be with him."

Kelly brings his gloved finger to his lips, tapping it a few times before telling me, "I want to hear your whole story, and then I'll help you figure it out."

If I can't figure it out, I'm not sure how he can, but I need him to want to help me. "Where do you want me to start?"

"Start from the beginning with meeting Zach. I've heard his version; now I want to hear yours. I know it might feel embarrassing or like I'm intruding, but I want you to tell me anything sexual between you two that you can."

I can tell he's being sincere and really wants to help. Starting from the beginning, I tell him how I met Zach and about our relationship over the years. I tell him about how I felt when I dated girls and pretty much anything I can think of that pertains to me being messed up sexually.

When I'm done, he starts asking questions. "So you feel like you can't be gay because you don't get turned on looking at guys?"

"Yeah, but I don't get turned on looking at girls either."

"But you do with Zach, and he's a guy."

I nod. "I'm scared that since I'm not gay, I won't be able to give him what he needs. That I'll eventually get that sick feeling of not wanting to kiss or do anything, and it'll hurt him."

"Have you ever heard of demisexuality?"

"I've heard it mentioned in some YouTube videos, but I don't really know what it means. I looked up pansexual when I found out that is what Connor identifies as."

"Demisexual is where you don't feel sexual attraction until you have a deep emotional bond with someone. You can notice if someone is attractive, but you don't want to kiss them or have sex with them. When you connect with the person you love, then that sexual desire is there."

His description slams into me, and I almost feel like crying. "That feels like me. You're describing me."

He gets out his cell phone and types something before handing it to me. "Here are a few descriptions of demisexual."

I read through them, and everything it says resonates with me. It's such a relief to know that I'm not the only one like this. "But does this mean I'm bi and demisexual or gay and demisexual?"

"I'm not one that thinks everyone needs a label. Sexuality is a giant gray area. You can be whatever you are, and it's nobody's business but yours. I also recognize that labels can sometimes help you understand yourself better, and people want that. It's obvious you really want to define your sexuality, but please remember that it's a wide spectrum. What you may discover now could change later. Don't beat yourself up because you haven't figured everything out yet." He goes on, "But since it's important to you, let's figure it out best we can."

"Please…I have all these questions in my head and want to know as much as possible."

"You felt nothing when you kissed girls?"

"Honestly, I dreaded it and felt sick over it. I only let Carrie touch me once and couldn't even stay hard. The thought of dating another girl makes me feel nauseous. It's not that I don't like them; I can be friends with them, but going down on a girl again is never going to happen."

"Would you say you and Carrie were close otherwise?"

I think back to the conversations we had before I found out her true personality. "I thought we were close."

"It doesn't sound like a deep emotional connection, but I don't think you would feel sick over kissing if you were bisexual. I have a demisexual friend, and even though he doesn't have a sexual attraction to anyone but his girlfriend, he definitely doesn't feel sick at the thought of being with a woman. He has no appeal to be sexual with anyone else, but I don't think he'd throw up at the thought. Do you think if you fell in love with Carrie, you would want to do it?"

Why didn't I ever ask myself that question before? Because I instantly know the answer. "No, I don't think so." I'm not straight or bisexual. He doesn't even have to say it for me to know it's the truth. I don't ever want a sexual relationship with a woman.

Kelly smiles. "I can see things clicking in your head."

"I think I might be gay." It's a relief to say those words. "Gay demisexual."

"It would be my best guess, but even if you're not, I doubt you'll ever find out otherwise because I think Zach is it for you."

"He is mine and the only person I want."

"We could just define you as Zachsexual." Kelly leans up to kiss my cheek. "You need to stop worrying that you're suddenly going to lose your sexual attraction for him. You love him and want him in every way, and that's not going to change. Your love has only grown deeper since the day you met him and will continue to grow. You might find that you have kinks or you want to discover new things with him, but you're not going to suddenly never want him again. Stop worrying about being everything for him and *just love him.* Love him and never look back."

I don't even realize I have tears streaming down my face until Kelly wipes my cheeks. "You're pretty smart, you know."

He nods, a hint of sadness in his eyes. "It took me a lot of heartache to figure out who I am. I also discovered that love is everything. I was happy with myself and doing my own thing, but when your family and Zach *loved* me, *it was everything to me*. It gave me healing and a feeling of acceptance that I needed. I finally feel like I belong somewhere...that I'm loved."

"I can see why Zach loves you so much. He told me you were special, and he was right. You fit in this family and belong with us."

Kelly throws his arms around me. "Aww Brady, you loveeeeeerrrs me."

Laughing, I hug him back. "There's a certain guy that's about to come out here and beat me up if you don't stop hugging me."

"Ohhhh, is grumpy bear jealous?" Kelly looks toward the patio door where Connor is standing outside with his arms crossed, giving me the evil eye. "Ohh, he's gotten all posseeeessiiiiiiive. I love it!"

"Before you two go at it, would you please take me to Zach so I can fix this? Please?"

"No can do. I promised him that I wouldn't tell you where he's at. He thinks he needs more time to be miserable and sulk." Kelly gets up and takes the blanket with him. "I should get some things packed and get back to him."

I'm about to protest when he stares me down. "And don't follow me...because that would bring you straight to Zach." His tone is telling me to take a hint and follow him.

"Of course, I would never follow you," I say back in the same level tone.

Nodding, he starts to walk to the house. I call Ruger and hurry after him.

Kelly reaches Connor and stands on his tiptoes to kiss him. "It's okay, grumpy bear, you're the only one I want. I had to help Brady figure himself out. I'm like the fixer in this family. We now have two sons, Brady and babykins."

Connor rolls his eyes. "I'm not the daddy of this family, brat...so get that right out of your head."

"Mhmm...whatever you say, daddy bear." Kelly pokes his stomach with a grin.

"You really think poking the bear is the best idea? I seem to recall you wanting me to do something tonight?"

Kelly bites his lip. "Okay, so maybe it wasn't the best idea."

I make a gagging noise. "Can you two refrain from all this…whatever this is…and focus on getting me to Zach?"

"I thought you weren't allowed to tell him where Zach is?" Connor says to Kelly.

The little minx turns to me and waves his arms dramatically. "I can't tell you where Zach is Brady! Stop harassing me! I have to stay true to my friendship with Zach!" He grins and wheels back to pat Connor's chest. "Make sure you tell Zach that I said all that."

"What are you two up to?"

Before following Kelly inside, I pat Connor's chest, too. "Watch Ruger and Honey for me while I go get my boyfriend."

Kelly waits at the end of the driveway until I back the truck out. He's careful to drive slow enough that I don't lose him. It takes about fifteen minutes, and I end up in the town I think Zach said Kelly was from. He drives into a neighborhood with nice, older homes and parks in front of a two-story house. I wait for him to get out and go inside before following.

Nerves set in and I'm afraid that Zach won't want to talk to me or that he won't forgive me for messing things up. I just want to see him and hold him.

FIFTY-NINE

ZACH

Brady's face as I drove away keeps replaying in my mind over and over again. I should have waited and let him explain, but I was scared of what he would say. Scared he would end what we've only just begun to have together. I don't want to stop kissing and loving him—touching him.

I've cried way too much, and all I want is Brady. I know he loves me, but seeing him with Stella and knowing he not only slept with her but didn't even tell her about me... It makes my heart hurt more than I can bear right now.

Rolling over in bed, I hug the pillow to my chest and swallow back the urge to cry again. I have to be the only guy alive who cries this much. I can't even imagine what Bane thinks of me now after crying all night at his house.

I run my hand down the pillow, wishing it was Brady next to me. I knew that I couldn't stay there with Stella, but now I just want to go home and curl up in his arms. I want to see his smile and hear his laughter. I want to feel his lips on mine and the fire we create when we touch. I just need to be with Brady, my home.

Here come the tears again, and I try to swallow down the sobs, but it doesn't work.

"Zach, I'm back," Kelly calls out from the other room.

It's not long before he is opening the bedroom door, striding in like everything is great in this world. Grabbing a few tissues from the side table, he sits on the edge of the bed and hands them to me. "Honey, you have to stop crying. Now blow your nose and get out of bed."

I blow my nose but don't move. "Did you bring Eeyore?"

"Oh…umm no, I forgot."

Something as stupid as forgetting a stuffed animal shouldn't make me cry, but it does.

The doorbell sounds through the house and Kelly gets off the bed, disappearing from the room. I hear Bane say something, and then I hear Brady's voice.

Brady.

Stumbling from the bed, I rush out of the bedroom and see Brady by the front door. He spots me standing here, and I can see the love in his eyes.

"Baby, come here," he says softly.

I'm pretty sure I run to him, but all I know is that a second later, I'm in his arms, my legs hooked behind his back. He holds me tightly to him, as if any space between us is too much.

"Brady," I sob quietly into his neck, "I love you."

"I know, baby. I love you, too." His lips press to my cheek as I feel him carrying me somewhere.

When he sits down, I raise my head to see we are back in the bedroom with the door shut. "How did you find me?"

"I followed Kelly here." He brushes the tears from my cheeks with his thumbs. "He wouldn't tell me where you were."

"I needed you," I say, my voice breaking.

His eyes soften, reflecting the same need that I'm feeling. "I'm here."

My worries from before come back, reminding me that everything isn't perfect. "What about Stella?"

"She left to go stay with an old girlfriend she used to date."

"Girlfriend?"

He nods. "She's a lesbian and has zero interest in me or any other boy."

"But why did you sleep with her then? I was back here dying without you, and you just replaced me."

Sighing, he looks away from me. "There are some things I need to tell you."

"Okay?" I lay my hand on his cheek, bringing his gaze back to me.

"First of all, when I was at the academy, I was miserable. For the first month, I hardly slept and wasn't functioning well because of it. I told Stella I was used to sleeping with someone, so she offered to sleep next to me and see if it would help. We didn't sleep like you and I sleep together; we just spooned. I would close my eyes and pretend it was you breathing, that it was your warmth I felt."

"Why didn't you tell me?" Now I feel bad for running off and not letting him explain.

"Because you didn't act like you were having a rough time like I was and I didn't want to bring you down."

"I felt like I was dying without you," I say, the pain leaking out in my tone.

"I know, Connor told me that night at the club. He came out into the parking lot and talked to me. Told me off about a few things, but I deserved it."

How did I not know this? "Why didn't you tell Stella about me?"

"Because if I'd talked about you, I'd have fallen apart and come home. Being away from you is something I never want to do again." He brushes some hair back from my glasses. "You know when I was dating girls?"

My stomach clenches. "Yes?"

"Every time I kissed one, it didn't feel right. I dreaded it and couldn't get turned on by any of them. I thought something was wrong with me, that I was messed up. I wasn't attracted to men sexually and I wasn't attracted to women sexually either. And then I kissed you, and it was everything I always thought a kiss should be like. I felt lust, passion…love. I was so confused because I didn't think I was gay, and how could I give you what you needed if I wasn't?"

"Wait…you didn't like kissing girls? But I thought you were out having sex and all that."

Brady gives a small shake of his head. "No, the first person I ever had sex with was you. I wanted to tell you it was my first time, but I was ashamed that I was broken sexually…and I wanted you to think I knew what I was doing."

His first time was with me.

I blink back a few tears. "You could have told me, Brady. I would have loved you and wanted you no matter what."

Brady continues. "I talked to Dad last night, and he helped me work out that I don't care about how I feel with others, only about being with you. And then Kelly came today and helped me figure out my sexuality."

"He did? So you're not straight?"

"No, I think I'm gay and demisexual…or as Kelly put it, I'm Zach-sexual." He cups my cheek, staring into my eyes with his beautiful blue ones. "I love you, Zach. I want to be with you in every way. I want to be boyfriends and lovers. I want to plan a future with you. I want us to travel together, get married, and have kids. I want it all." His thumb runs over my lips. "It's always been you. I was just too stupid to realize that my body wanted you, also."

"Brady…" I choke up at his words.

"You're my heart," he says, his own eyes filling with tears. "You're my heart. Always have been and always will be."

I'm his heart. His words fill up every corner of my soul with love. He loves me the way I love him. "You're really mine? We can go on dates and be boyfriends?"

He grins. "Yes, we can go on dates and be boyfriends. I'll kiss you in front of everyone, and they will all just have to deal with it because you're mine."

I lean forward to kiss him, and he kisses me back with the same passion I give him. He breaks away before things get out of control and we end up having sex in Bane's house.

"You know what this means? You went to Disney and then you got your fairytale, just like you dreamed you would."

"Oh my God, you're right! Dreams really do come true."

There's a knock on the door, and then Kelly comes barging in before we even answer. He puts his hands on his hips, eyeing us both down. "Did you two finally figure out your shit so I can go home to grumpy bear? He's getting grumpier by the minute and needs food."

"Did you even bring anything from home?" I ask pointedly.

Kelly bites his lip before grinning big. "Nope."

"So you knew he was following you!"

"Maaaaaybeeeeee," he says in a high-pitched voice, not looking sorry at all.

"Thank you," I say. "I needed Brady, and I'm glad you brought him to me."

Kelly rushes over to hug me, squeezing between Brady and me since I'm still on Brady's lap. "I knew you needed him! Besides, I fixed him for you before I brought him over."

Brady rolls his eyes behind Kelly but grins. "I'm never going to hear the end of how you fixed me, am I?"

I get a kiss from Kelly before he turns to kiss Brady's cheek. "Nope! This will live on until we are super old and I smack you with my cane, saying, 'I fixed you seventy years ago and you owe me.'"

A burst of laughter erupts from Brady. "You're ridiculous."

Kelly's eyes come back to me. "So can we go home now?"

I nod, which sends Kelly off my lap and out the door.

Brady looks around the room and leans over to pick up my inhaler from the side table. "Is there anything else of yours that you need to get?"

"No, I was too upset and didn't even think about bringing anything with me. I just left."

He gives me a scowl. "We need to talk about you running off— not answering your cell. *Forgetting your inhaler.* You had all of us worried —especially me. Dad and I drove for hours last night looking for you."

Oops. "I'm sorry. I promise I won't do it again. Unless another girl or guy shows up and calls you their sleeping buddy."

"That's not happening again because we are *never* spending another night apart unless I'm on duty with work. And even then, the only partner I'll be cuddling up with will be Ruger."

Before we leave, I offer to strip the sheets for Bane, but he shoos us out with the promise that we will all get together on Saturday.

Kelly drives my SUV home, and I ride with Brady, sitting in the middle under his arm. Something I've done a million times before. "Do you think everyone knew that we would end up together? I mean…how many guys do you know that sit in the middle of the truck with their best friend like this?"

Brady leans over to kiss the top of my head. "Probably everybody knew but us. Now that I've figured it out, I feel kind of stupid that I didn't know a long time ago."

"Don't feel stupid. We are together now, and that's all that matters."

Connor meets us as soon as we walk in from the garage. "So…is this crisis finally over?"

Kelly flings himself at his boyfriend. "Yes, grumpy bear. I fixed our family, and I even ordered pizza when I left Bane's. It should be here in fifteen minutes."

"Thank God, I was starving. Brady went on a cleaning spree at six in the morning and dumped everything out of the fridge."

"It was all outdated, and you do know how to order pizza and go to the grocery store. Kelly and Zach have you way too spoiled."

Connor grins. "Shhhh, don't tell them that."

"As if we didn't already know," I say, walking by him to find the dogs.

We take them outside and then walk over to Mom and Dad's to let them know I'm okay. I feel bad that I worried everyone. In my defense, I was with Kelly, and he did call them to check in.

Dad and Mom take turns giving me big hugs before I step back into Brady's arms. Both of them eye us and Dad raises his eyebrow. "So, does this mean you two are finally together?"

"Yes, we are together," Brady answers. He clears his throat. "Mom, Dad, I'm gay."

Mom smiles and Dad says, "We know, Son. Glad you finally figured that out."

"How did you know I was gay? You didn't say you knew last night?"

"We know because you've been in love with Zach for years and you never looked at girls like you did him. As for last night, I didn't say anything because I'm not you, and no matter how I perceived your sexuality, it's not up to me."

"Does everyone know I'm gay?"

Meg pops her head around the corner from the living room. "Yes."

"Great, just great. Even my thirteen-year-old sister knew I'm gay before I did. Do Grandma and Grandpa know, too?"

Mom goes over to stir the food on the stove. "Do you really want the answer to that?"

Brady groans. "No, I don't. Forget I asked."

"They don't all know you're demisexual," I offer. "You can at least have one thing you knew before them."

"Demisexual?" Dad asks.

I can tell Brady is still upset over his family knowing already and take his hand to hold close to my chest while I explain to Dad. "It's where you need a deep emotional bond with someone before you're sexually attracted to them."

"Ahh, I see." Dad leans back against the kitchen island. "Makes sense, Brady, considering what we talked about last night."

"Yeah, when Kelly told me about it, I felt like it clicked with me."

"As long as you two are happy together, I'm happy," Mom says.

Brady tilts my chin up so he can give me a kiss. I'm pretty sure my cheeks are red when I look back at Mom and Dad. They are both smiling, and Mom does this little, excited clap that I think she picked up from Kelly. "Aww, you two together makes me so happy."

Brady clears his throat and tugs me toward the door. "Alright, we need to get the dogs and get back for the pizza."

"Love you both," Dad calls out and Mom reiterates.

"Love you," Brady and I say before walking out the door.

"How did they know I was gay?" Brady's obviously still bothered by it.

"I don't know. I didn't even know... I only hoped."

Snowflakes are starting to fall, and I shiver as the wind picks up. Brady hurries me inside before calling the dogs in.

As we sit in the family room eating pizza, I find myself happy that Brady and I can fully show our love in front of people. Brady moves his plate, and I know what he wants without him saying it. I scoot over into his lap and transfer my pizza to his plate so we can share one. My eyes can't seem to leave his face, his eyes, his lips. I want to soak up every moment with him and never take a single one for granted.

"Can you help me move the dresser in Kelly's old room into mine?" Connor asks when we are done eating.

"I tried to help but can't lift it," Kelly explains.

"Sure." Brady gives me a long kiss before letting me crawl off his lap so he can get up.

Kelly and I cuddle in the middle of the couch. "Thank you for everything, Kelly."

"Always, babykins."

We make small talk about what we should do Saturday night until Brady comes back in the room and sits down at the end of the couch.

"Kellan Scott McMichael!" Connor yells from upstairs.

Kelly's eyes go wide and then he grins. "Ruh roh, looks like daddy bear is super upset. Got to go."

He gives me a kiss before scrambling off the couch and running out of the room.

Brady moves over to his spot to cuddle with me. "Why do I think the brat did something on purpose to make *daddy bear*"—he shudders saying those two words—"roar?"

"Probably because he did. He loves to poke the bear."

Brady pokes me. "Did you have to use *that* word! Not what I want to think about when I think of Connor."

I laugh at the expression on Brady's face. "I highly doubt Kelly is the one doing the poking upstairs. They seem to have this whole Daddy-brat kink going on."

"Are you into kinks?"

His tone is serious, so I pause to think for a second. "I honestly don't know. I've only just kissed a guy for the first time in the past ten days. I think there's time to figure out if I have kinks later." I pin my gaze on his, trying to sound serious. "Why? Are you wanting me to poke you?"

Brady makes this gagging noise and then glares at me. "Don't ever say that again. Us switching positions is a whole lot of wrong."

"Some tops do bottom occasionally...or so I've heard."

He moves back an inch, really looking at me. "Is that something you really want?"

I know if I say that I do, he'll try it for me. "No, I don't. I would try if *you* wanted to, but I like being the bottom."

"Want to be the bottom right now?" His eyes are heated just asking me.

I don't even answer, just get up and run for the bedroom with him chasing me. We kiss breathlessly for a few minutes before I go into the bathroom to get ready and shower. When I come out, Brady has moved Ruger's crate out of our room and both dogs have been shut out. "Where are the dogs?"

"Ruger is in his crate just outside the door. I'll slide it back in here later. And Honey is on a dog bed next to him. They've become buddies."

I crawl across the bed to where he's lying, naked. "We are not moving them out every time we do anything. What if I want to wake you with sex?"

He rolls us so he's on top of me. "I'll take that into consideration. I moved him out because we make noise during sex, and I don't want him to think you're hurting me."

"Ohhh, okay." I forget about the dogs as he presses his erection against mine, and we both lose ourselves in showing our love to each other.

Brady is deep inside of me, his blue eyes looking down at me full of love. "I didn't know this is what it's supposed to feel like. Passion and magic and heat, all wrapped up in the gift called love. It's like my body is suddenly awake and never wants to sleep again. You do this to me, baby. *You.*" His thumb runs over my lips before he crashes his mouth into mine. Tears and love entwine in our passionate kiss, and I want it to go on forever.

"I love you, Brady," I whisper when he lifts his mouth from mine.

He tenderly presses his lips below my ear. "I love you, baby."

I've found my home in Brady, and I know that I'll always be his heart.

EPILOGUE

B rady lowers himself and pats his back like he has so many times before. I grin as I loop my arms around his neck and let him carry me up the hill behind our house.

We haven't been out to the tree house in the last two years, but maybe that's because we spend every waking moment in each other's arms. Sure, both of us have our jobs and I still cuddle with Kelly every day, but Brady are I are pretty inseparable. If I'm not touching him, I want to be touching him.

I lean up a little to press my lips to his cheek. "This brings back memories of when I was tiny."

He tilts his head so it's pressed against mine. "You're still tiny."

"Pfft…I'm like a foot taller now," I scoff in protest.

"Wow…a foot taller than the tiny four feet you were then."

"You be nice to me," I say, tickling his side until he about drops me.

The tree house up ahead quiets both of us, and I'm lost in all the memories it brings back. As we get closer, I notice the ladder looks new and some of the boards on the roof have been replaced. "Did you do this?"

Brady nods. "Dad and I replaced some of the wood yesterday. I wanted it to be safe for me to bring you out here again."

My heart flutters at the many little ways Brady constantly shows how much he cares. He motions for me to go up ahead of him and then follows me. I open the door to the tree house and look around in surprise. There are colorful flowers everywhere, with petals strewn all over the floor and on the sleeping area. Strands of white lights twinkle above us. The whole place looks like something out of a fairytale.

I turn to Brady, and he's watching me with intense love in his eyes. "Brady…"

He smiles and takes my hand to tug me over to the mat we used to spend so many hours on, reading and talking. We curl up together, and I can't take my eyes off him. Brady's tender gaze always expresses to me the love he feels, warming every part of my heart.

He runs a finger over my forehead and down my cheek before caressing his thumb over my lips. "Zach, do you remember the pact we made to each other?"

"Of course I do…and I'll never break it," I whisper softly.

"Will you make another pact with me?" His fingers trail down to the side of my neck and lower until they rest over my heart. "Will you marry me? Please, baby?"

Tears fill my eyes as I nod rapidly. "Yes! Yes, please, I want to be your husband."

Brady grins. "Husband…that does have a nice ring to it. Zach Wellman sounds perfect to me."

Wellman. I grin back. "I can't wait to take your name." I don't think there was ever any question which last name we would use. The Wellmans are my family and having the same last name will make me feel…complete.

Brady leans back from me and digs into his pocket, pulling out a ring. I offer him my hand, and he slides the white gold band onto my finger. It's not wide like a typical man's ring but not quite as dainty as most women's rings that I've seen. Diamonds glitter from the band, and I figure he's spent more on it than he should have.

"It's beautiful," I whisper, staring down at the symbol of our love.

Brady tilts my chin until my eyes meet his blue ones again. "I solemnly swear that I will protect you and cherish you forever. You are my heart and the one I love more than life itself."

I remember us saying "I solemnly swear" all those years ago, and it means so much to me that he remembers our vows to each other, too. Laying my hand on his cheek, I softly make my own vow, "I solemnly swear to take care of you and make your life beautiful. I also promise to be your sleeping buddy forever."

He gives me a smirk at that remark.

I continue, "You are the only one that I'll ever want to call home."

Brady leans in closer to press his lips against mine in a soft kiss of love.

We lie here in each other's arms, kissing and cuddling—neither of us needing to say more. Brady and I have our own way of showing love to each other—expressing with our bodies what we also say in words.

Brady sits up, tugging me with him, and reaches over to grab a container of chocolates. He holds one out for me to take a bite, his blue eyes never leaving mine. "Where do you want to get married?"

I finish savoring the sweetness in my mouth before answering. "Here? With just our family and friends?"

Brady nods. "I think you'll be more comfortable with less people."

The thought of a big wedding makes me shudder. "Do you think Dad would marry us?"

"I am sure he would. Let's ask him."

Once we are done at the tree house, Brady carries me on his back until we are at Mom and Dad's patio door. The second we walk inside, it's total chaos. Brady must have told everyone beforehand that he was going to propose because they are all super excited. Kelly is practically bouncing in Connor's arms and talking nonstop about planning the wedding. Mom and Dad keep hugging us, and the girls are begging to be bridesmaids or flower girls. Even Grandma and Grandpa are adding in their advice about honeymoon locations and where to go.

Brady just smiles, his eyes still focused on me. There's so much love in them; he takes my breath away. Over the last couple of years, we have changed and discovered more about ourselves, but that only seems to have brought us closer. I used to be scared of change, but now I embrace it. Change helps our love to grow deeper and deeper... more beautiful.

One thing is for certain, I'm incredibly proud of the man Brady has become. Life isn't always easy, but we navigate this journey together. A journey of love...

AFTERWORD

If you are struggling with acceptance from family and friends, please know that you are beautiful and perfect as you are. You don't need to change a single part of yourself. My heart breaks that anyone is made to feel ashamed or has to hide. It's not safe for many in this world to be free to love who they want, and that has to change. We all have to keep standing up for the ones who can't protect themselves. We have to keep getting our voices heard.

FROM THE AUTHOR

Dear Readers,

Now that you've read Zach and Brady's fairytale, I hope you love them as much as I do. This was an emotional story for me to write and very close to my heart.

You're My Home was never intended to be published or shared with others. I've been writing for years and have never shared my heart with the world.

This story all started with a dream. It was this beautiful scene of Zach and Brady after they had been together for years. Zach was showing Brady how much he loved him, and I could feel this intense love between them. I woke up crying and wrote the scene down so I could keep it forever.

About a week later, someone came to me and asked me to write them their own book. I'd never written a book for someone before, but I knew the dream was meant for their story. I didn't have a plan and just let my heart write.

Every so often, I would reread the dream because it helped me keep that emotion in my words. There were so many times when I sobbed while writing or when I had to stop so I could cry out the raw pain this book brought to me. I simply can't write without living in the book and being the characters.

I wrote Brady flawed—more like imperfectly perfect—because teenagers aren't wise little adults. They can make bad choices or say the wrong thing. They think they know themselves but then discover they don't. They have fears and insecurities that seem a million times bigger than they actually are.

As for the others, Zach is my heart. It's hard to share him because I want to protect him. I also adore Mr. Wellman and wish the Wellmans could adopt me. Kelly is one of my favorite characters I've ever written. He wasn't even supposed to be a big part of the book, but I knew the second he was on paper, he wasn't leaving. I truly love all of them and never want their story to end.

The special someone I wrote this story for read it. At the end, they were in tears and begged me to share it with others. "What if it helps someone who needs to read it," they said.

And so, this journey of publishing began. It's been scary and overwhelming. I have no clue what I'm doing half the time. Zach and Brady came from my heart, and what if a reader doesn't like them? What if they think Brady is stupid or think Zach needs to act older or they hate my writing? I wasn't sure my heart could take it. I'm still not sure my heart can take it. I'm trying to be confident about sharing a part of myself, but there's a lot of vulnerableness that comes with it.

Ironically, the scene from my dream never made it into the book. I was going to make it the epilogue but just couldn't force myself to do it. Maybe someday it'll be a part of a sequel, or maybe it'll stay mine forever.

Thank you for taking the time to read Zach and Brady's story. I would love to hear your thoughts or connect with my readers. You can find me on Facebook https://www.facebook.com/authorkatiemoore or you can email me at authorkatiemoore@gmail.com.

Also, if you could please leave a review on Amazon, Goodreads or any other review sites, I would be so grateful. I love reading comments and feedback from readers.

All the love,
    Katie

ACKNOWLEDGMENTS

There have been people along the way who have made a difference, and I want to thank them:

A heartfelt thank you to Karen Meeus, with Karen Meeus Editing, for editing my story. You are amazing! Your kindness helped make this process so much better. Thank you for never making me feel stupid for asking so many questions. Your advice and support mean more than I can express.

A big thank you to Nik for his never-ending support. For years he has read books I never finished and still kept encouraging me. He's suffered through a lot of conversations over this book. Hours of me trying to decide what my author name should be or if this is crazy and I should just give up. His gentle pushes to keep going have made all the difference.

Thank you to Traci for reading the book when no one else would. I'm not sure I would have continued if you hadn't become my number one fan.

I want to thank Lucy Lennox for being the one author who messaged me when I asked for advice in a book group. That meant so much to me. Thank you for finding me a beta reader and for sending me links to help. When someone does something selflessly like that, it truly does make an impact.

To Jess, who beta read this book for me—thank you. You took the time to read the book written by a nobody, and I'll be forever grateful. You pointed out things I didn't notice and gave feedback I needed.

I also want to thank Kelley, with Sleepy Fox Studio, for working with me on the cover. Your recommendation of Karen Meeus was a lifesaver, and I will be forever grateful. Thank you for the beautiful cover and everything you've done to make this better.

To Mark—thank you for helping to make this happen.

I want to thank the boys—they know who they are—for supporting me through this. I love you.

Most of all, I want to thank the readers who have fallen in love with this story. I'm truly humbled and honored that you would take the time to read Zach and Brady's story. Thank you <3

ABOUT THE AUTHOR

I've been writing in my head since before kindergarten. My parents were extremely religious, and we spent hours every week in church. I learned to live in my head and create stories to pass the time. We didn't have a tv, so I used my imagination to keep busy. My childhood best friend and I would spend hours taking turns telling stories that transported us to another world.

People say I live in my head too much because they will be talking to me and I'll be thinking of the story I'm currently living in. I forget they even exist and don't hear a word they are saying. If I'm not writing, I'm reading a book.

I'm my own worst critic and never feel that my writing is good enough. I think all artists feel that way.

As for knowing me personally...I am a compassionate person who cries when I see someone hurting. I cry when I even think of how not everyone can love who they want or be who they are. It breaks my heart that I can't help every single person who is silently suffering and alone.

I have four dogs, Bess, Skye, Violet, and Izzy. They are my cuddle buddies and give me so much love. I'm the director of a small non-profit dog rescue and feel very passionately about saving dogs.

Otherwise, I'm kind of boring and seriously introverted. I don't like to be the center of attention and prefer a quiet night at home versus socializing. I am very human and make mistakes or say the wrong thing. I try very hard never to hurt anyone and to be kind. Kindness is truly beautiful. When someone is kind to me, it warms my heart and means more than they could ever understand.

Printed in Great Britain
by Amazon